THE
CIVILIZATION

PRAISE FOR
THE CIVILIZATION

"An original blend of African-inspired mysticism and adventure."
— *Kirkus Reviews*

"The World Building is lush and robust... a riveting fantasy novel, *The Civilization* incorporates African mythology into its story of a whip-smart heroine who learns to claim her destiny and newfound ancestry with pride."
— *Foreword Reviews*

"*The Civilization* is an awesome Africa-based YA fantasy that I can't wait to recommend to everyone... With great character development and just a touch of romance, it's a thrilling read..."
— **Cassandra Orakpo**

"*The Civilization* is a great Africa-based YA Fantasy that I will happily recommend to all my friends, family, and the random person walking by on the sidewalk. I enjoyed that there was a little bit of romance in the book...The character development was great and I found myself rooting for our main characters and deeply despising the enemy."
— **Keeley Malone** - *Bookseller*

THE
CIVILIZATION

BY

K.M. MCKENZIE

ISK NCHI
African Perspectives

Published in 2024 by Iskanchi Press
info@iskanchi.com
https://iskanchi.com/

ISBN: 978-1-957810-12-6 (Paperback)
ISBN: 978-1-957810-22-5 (Hardback)

Cover design by Mike Johnson
Typesetting and design by AI's Fingers

Printed in the United States of America

About Iskanchi Press

Iskanchi Press is a US-based publishing house for African writing. We believe stories and ideas convey humanity to the future and that our progress to a better world is sooner achieved when all perspectives are heard and considered.

Our mission is to promote authentic African perspectives through a variety of books, including fiction, non-fiction, and children's literature written in, or translated into, English. We aim to redress the negative presumptions about Africa, satisfy the reader's interest in diverse expressions, and serve the needs of African immigrants and People of Color interested in seeing a more nuanced representation of their experiences.

Whether you're an avid reader, a bookstore owner, or a library representative, your engagement helps fulfill our mission. Thank you for being a part of our community and helping us promote diversity and inclusivity in literature.

To learn more about Iskanchi Press, discover upcoming releases, and stay updated on author events, please visit our website at www.iskanchipress.com and follow us on social media:

 @IskanchiPress    @IskanchiPress   IskanchiPress

Browse our catalog from Edelweiss

Browse our catalog from our website

ISK◉NCHI
African Perspectives

For my mom, Janet

CONTENTS

PROLOGUE

King Remu rose to his feet when the commotion reached the public courtyard. Another day, another problem. He glanced at Queen Oluchi, noticing the way her beautiful face creased and lined with worry. From the shade of the veranda of Paraa Hutat, he narrowed his eyes on the royal guards, Jiro Sion foremost, as they marched forward on the backs of sturdy abadas.

A handful of Nkuba warriors handed a young girl to Master Sion, who dragged her toward the royal house, her feet barely touching the pavement.

The guards were too harsh with her, he worried, before asking himself, why? Was she the root of the commotion that had put the palace on edge in the past couple of days? Judging by her oddly cut fabrics and trousers, he quickly realized she was a foreigner. The revelation made him pause. No foreigner had come to these lands in *ages*. What did this all mean?

Queen Oluchi chained her arms to his, saying not a word. He hadn't heard her approach.

"Divine King," said Jiro Sion, bowing when he reached the terrace, "Permission to speak."

The two Nkuba warriors behind him bowed as well, a knee to the ground, and a fisted hand to the heart.

"Speak, Master Sion."

"This is the stranger," said Sion, before lifting the lightweight young woman and planting her onto the veranda.

"Ouch!" She twisted, trying to free herself from his grip. The guards barricaded her with hands on their weapons; a bit over the top but understandable, King Remu thought.

King Remu glanced to the small crowd in the public courtyard, swarming under the twinning suns that formed glares above their heads. The Nkuba warriors kept the spectators at bay, but more were arriving, craning their necks to see about the fuss.

Why hadn't Sion taken a private route? "So there's nothing or no one else out there," he said to Sion, whose handsome face smeared with confusion, before settling with understanding.

"No, Divine King," he answered, "She was alone."

King Remu took a deep but subtle breath. When he'd sent the guards out to investigate the disturbances so many had claimed to witness, he hadn't known what, if anything, they would find. He supposed this girl was better than nothing; but what did this mean exactly? This young woman was barely taller than his eight-year-old son. And by the looks of her, she wasn't much older than the young prince either ... but she wasn't a child. She was a young woman, perhaps the same age as the Garden priestesses. That was a good thing; otherwise, her presence might have veered too far into mockery.

He swallowed and faced the young woman. "What is your name?"

She glanced to Jiro Sion but did not answer. "Does she have a name?"

"She does not understand our language, Divine King," Sion explained. "I've tried getting her to speak, but…," he trailed away and reached for the neckline of her strange attire. "She has this." He pulled the crude crystal dangling by a silver chain from her blouse.

Queen Oluchi gasped alongside the small gathering of warriors.

"Hey," the girl exclaimed and pulled the chain from his grip.

"I see." King Remu fixed his eyes on the courtyard again. The crowd grew. He couldn't handle this here, not now. "Take her to the confinement chambers."

"Right away, Divine King," replied Sion. He shoved the girl forward.

"Jiro Sion," called King Remu. The Nkuba warrior paused. "Be gentle with her."

"As you desire, Divine King." He marched the girl onward.

King Remu released his breath after they left. He took another glance at the crowd in the courtyard. They were murmuring. He would not address these people. Not until he found out more about this young stranger. He turned toward the palace. Queen Oluchi trailed him, returning with him to the sitting room. A servant placed a tray of fresh fruits on the table before them, bowed and excused herself.

Queen Oluchi eyed him after he'd settled into his seat. "My king, permission to speak," she said and curtsied before sitting down next to him. She didn't have to address him so, nor ask to speak, but she was raised a lady, and ladies did what was proper.

"What is it?"

"Do you think the girl is Abnr's gift?"

King Remu mulled over the question. He had imagined that if Abnr's gift was a person, it would be fashioned into the likeness of a hero such as Ndakr, the godsend first king of Marut. "She is not what I expected."

"What is your plan for her, my king?"

"She needs to be interrogated. If she came from the darkness, then we need to make sure she is not dangerous to us."

Queen Oluchi considered. "Why would Great Abnr send a girl?"

"Abnr has always been the most mysterious of gods," King Remu mused, and let the thought trail off.

"If she's not Abnr's gift," said Queen Oluchi, "then who is she ... who can she be?"

1

CAVE

The good news was that the cave no longer smelled like piss and camel dung. The bad news was that it went on forever. Grandpa Edoje dragged her deeper and deeper down into the pit, squeezing across thin dirt ledges and climbing over rocks.

Kadsa feared this was another dead end and could think of many other things she'd prefer to do than this, but she kept her mouth shut, letting Grandpa Edoje carry on with his latest plan. He wanted her to care about finding *their* homeland. She respected him too much to tell him she'd never considered it *her* homeland and increasingly doubted that it even existed. He was confident this time, but then again, he'd been confident all the previous times, too. Back in Kenya, they had at least two separate near-death experiences. In Tanzania, they were robbed, and back in Libya, they barely escaped the civil war.

Forty-plus minutes passed before they reached the bottom of the cavern. The room was spacious with large pointy rocks shooting up from the ground. She almost breathed her relief aloud in the stuffy, hot cavern, but a rumble—what sounded like crumbling rocks—shut her up.

This wasn't good, she thought, as the warlords in torn clothes, carrying knives and machetes hanging off their hips, walked out from behind high rocks. This couldn't be good at all. In no time, the thugs barricaded them in the cavern. All Kadsa could think was how they'd get out this time. Had their luck run out? What better place than deep inside a cave in the middle of the Tibesti Plateaus?

She was so tired of this and ready for something else. By the looks of these men, she didn't think she would get that chance. All the same, she reached slowly for the knife she had in the waist of her pants, hidden underneath her robe.

"Why are you in my cave?" barreled the deep-bass voice of one of the men in French.

Kadsa had picked up crude French during her time in Senegal and Morocco. She looked to Grandpa when the man spoke, trying to read his expression in the dark, stuffy cavern. He looked unmoved by the ambush, as if he expected it all along. Not surprising, considering that something always went wrong, one way or the next on these adventures.

The failsafe was that if one had to die, it should be him. That, of course, meant she was to run for it once the rumble started. Kadsa had to wait for the wink that he wasn't giving, hand nervously rubbing the hilt of the knife.

She wouldn't pull it out—hoped she didn't have to. She would just keep cool and make sure they never figured out she was a girl. For all the troubles she and Grandpa had gotten into over the years, he was pretty good at talking himself out of them, too. Maybe he could here. Get them not to get too close to her. Maybe.

"Are you looking for my treasure old man? Here to rob me, eh?" mocked the leader.

Grandpa did not reply.

"That's okay, old man, we only want to talk," the thug continued. "You came here for something? Tell me. What is it?"

Grandpa Edoje released a breath loudly. "I am merely touring the cave."

The thug chuckled, and it made Kadsa cringe. He spoke like someone who would be cracking jokes with you while cutting your fingers off, and he was brandishing one of the shiniest machetes she'd ever seen. Kadsa clamped her hand down on her own tiny knife. She wouldn't be able to escape without a whole lot of kicking and punching, and maybe even stabbing, but she was prepared to try.

The thug threw questions at them in his deep- throated French. Because she didn't answer even one, the thug asked if she could speak. Grandpa Edoje said she could not, a lie of course. She'd spent the past days pretending to be a mute boy. Try as she had in the past, her boy voice simply wasn't convincing. What's more? She wasn't good at small talk or being clever and witty. Years of living and communicating exclusively with an eccentric grandpa who spoke in riddles guaranteed that. "You won't tell me why you have come to my cave?" quizzed the main thug.

"I hear it has great wall art painted by the ancestors." That was a good answer, Kadsa thought. They almost never rehearsed what they would say if caught, though somehow the answer was always the same—sightseeing. But Chad wasn't exactly another place for them. Her father had died here. Grandpa had said, without saying, that he wanted little to do with the country. Now, Grandpa had reasons to return. They'd been here for a little over a week, waiting for some sign Grandpa was sure would reveal itself.

The thugs rolled off more questions—where are you from? How'd you find out about this cave, and what's the boy's name? Grandpa gave a pronunciation of her name that rolled off his tongue like gibberish. The thugs looked baffled, and she almost smiled. Grandpa had pronounced her name that way plenty of times before, insisting it was the proper way to say it, in his native tongue.

"Did you think this cave was empty?" asked the leader, dismissively.

"I only came to see the glowing rock," Grandpa said.

The thug's eyes narrowed. "Who told you about the rock?"

Grandpa did not reply—not right away.

Kadsa winced. Grandpa had been sure for days now that whatever he sought would be here. Had to be here. She'd never pushed him to say why he was so confident this time around.

Maybe she should've. They'd spent the better part of the decade trying to find the magic in this world. Dead-ends were minor setbacks, Grandpa Edoje would say each time she showed frustration. So, they would march on. Their search took them traveling all across Africa. And each time she asked for more specifics, his responses were the same. He would insist she'd know it when she saw it. She hadn't protested, though she had grown restless, anxious to move on to other things.

She'd wander away in the mornings on some days and not return until dusk. She'd go to markets and cafés with computers. She'd even seen her first movie in a proper theater. Once, he caught her hanging out with some teenagers who'd been amused that she'd never been to a real school. He'd wanted to know why she thought 'school' was such a good idea when she'd asked about enrolling. "Your education comes from living in the real world," he'd insisted.

"This isn't living. This is aimlessly searching," she'd snapped.

"What we seek will enrich you more than anything a school can offer you."

"Like friends? Living in the real world?" "Like family and purpose," he said coolly.

"And if we don't find it, I can't do it anymore." "We will find it. It's our birthright," he insisted.

What she'd figured out over the years was that Grandpa sought a key, and it had something to do with the stars. Grandpa was obsessed with the stars—the reason they were always sleeping under them. He'd told her the stars were aligning over the plateaus and that was why they had to come. What had this rock to do with a key?

The thug's laughter rang deeply through the cavern. "Ay, you were with the Yedina."

How would this warlord know that? Kadsa considered, suspicion setting off alarms in her head. Unless, she exhaled quietly, they'd been camping out among the tribesmen.

Kadsa did not like the Yedina shaman, not his heavy- set body, vulgar face and bulging eyes, which always seem to be on her, even when he spoke to someone else. She had spotted him a few times speaking to someone off in the woods in the night, though she couldn't say who. Now she considered if he hadn't set them up.

"Okay, I'll show you the rock. No harm. Then you can tell me what it does. You like that?"

Grandpa only shook his head. "Show me what you have."

The thugs pushed her and Grandpa through a narrow opening between rocks rising from the ground, into a space that could barely contain four people, that was mustier and dustier than where they were prior. A couple times, she coughed from the congestion.

They climbed over a narrow ledge, passed a deep, gushing stream that made her wonder if anyone else knew about this place. There were certainly always explorers and archaeologists hanging around the plateaus, and many tribespeople, too.

The little light that had been filtering through the pores in the rocks disappeared, and the heat rose up around them. The thugs pulled out more flashlights.

It was clear they'd been living deep down here. Not a bad place to live, mind you. The stream appeared to be fresh water; there was enough room to maneuver, and makeshift beds and tables littered the area, existing between the rocks that shot up from the ground.

Kadsa had to stop herself from dipping into the stream to cool down. She must have been staring too long around the area, because one of the thugs barked, "What are you looking at?"

She shook her head.

"You're just looking at it and telling me what it is," warned the thug to her grandpa.

The roving eye leader stared them down. The scar that ran over it let her know he'd seen his share of violence. He tugged his turban, and by instinct, she did the same with hers. They weren't supposed to know she was female, not while she wore a heavy robe and head wrap. The main thug watched her as if he knew the truth. Each time she moved, he moved as if to block her or lurch at her. Grandpa noticed this—he must have—and so he stepped forward. "Please show me the rock?"

The warlord shone his flashlight in Grandpa's face. "How much money do you have, old man?"

"Let me see the rock, first, and then we can negotiate, young man," Grandpa spoke up.

The heavy-chested man stepped forward to look Grandpa up and down, his machete brushing against his right leg in a way that made Kadsa nervous he might use it. He then pushed his hand out, fingers rubbing against each other, a gesture that translated to money in every culture.

Kadsa itched to speak but managed to hold her tongue— she could not make a bad situation worse. Instead, she shuffled, alerting one of the men, who stepped up to be closer, as if she might try something. To be safe, she gripped the hilt of her small knife. She had used it once—on a cab driver at the Kenyatta Airport who'd passed his place. She was prepared to use it again, but hoped she didn't have to. Grandpa had said that if anything happened to him, she must not look back and just run for it. She wanted to listen but wasn't prepared to abandon the only family she had.

"All of it," said the thug when Grandpa Edoje began sifting through his small pouch.

Grandpa handed over the whole leather bag.

The thug looked through it himself. He must have liked the amount—the pouch looked fat enough. Grandpa always traveled with a little money to pay for this and that.

The thug gave the go-ahead to reveal the rock and another of his companions yanked off the dirty sheet that covered a three-foot raised stone.

Grandpa gasped and stepped forward, almost on instinct, sparking a swift reaction from the thugs. They rushed to barricade him.

Kadsa took one step in his direction, hand on knife, but stopped herself, remembering what he'd told her— de-escalation. Grandpa was good at de-escalation.

"I need to be near that rock," he said, voice urgent, throwing up his hands. "Please, put away your weapons." "What is so special about this rock?" asked the main thug, eyes narrowing in the poorly lit cavern chamber. He was going to make this even more difficult. Still,

Kadsa had to keep her cool, watch and wait.

"Nothing about it is special," Grandpa said, but maybe too quickly to be believed. He'd already played his card. She didn't know what to make of his reaction. She'd seen him excited before—but all the other objects had been false leads. "I simply need to be close to admire its beauty."

The main thug cocked his head. "Okay, you can come closer," he said, voice casual and dangerous, almost sardonic. He was playing them.

Grandpa paused within inches of the rock. From where Kadsa stood, the rock looked both artificial and natural. What she saw was an overgrown rock, dull and typical for caves. It could've grown out of the earth that way or sculpted. Barely three feet high, as thick as the trunk of a typical baobab tree, the only thing curious about it was its colors. If anything, she'd call it a stalagmite, or a colored quartz.

It was nothing they hadn't seen before. But the way Grandpa caressed the empty air above the surface as if he could sense its energy, she wondered if it truly was something special. She'd seen him in these near- meditative trances before. He would always say he was searching for the magic in this world. She had her doubts, but also knew part of her did not want him to be right. If he were, it would make it harder for her not to care, harder to walk away and live her own life the way she wanted, to do the things she wanted to do.

"I heard about you, old man," said the main thug, chuckling. "They said you have magic. Is that true? Show us some magic?"

The other thugs laughed. Kadsa fought back unleashing all her rage against him. All through her seventeen years, she'd fought anyone who mocked Grandpa. In every school she'd ever enrolled in, she'd been teased about her witch-doctor grandpa—crazy Grandpa Edoje.

When she was little, she truly believed Grandpa had magic. She had believed all his stories—the stories about his home world.

As she got older, and the realities peeled away the fantasy, she was almost ashamed to admit that she no longer believed in his magic. She'd been meaning to tell him—maybe if they survived this—that she wanted to stop the pursuit. But she didn't want to break his heart or hurt him or let him think she shared the same opinions about him that these people did.

She stepped forward, ready to yell and throw punches, but Grandpa spoke up. "I have no magic. I am just an old man, wishing to see the place where my only son died."

Kadsa's whole body froze, hearing him mention her father. She looked around the tight, closed-off space more closely, seeing it for the first time. Was it true? Was this really where her father had died? She'd never heard the story of how or where he died—only that he'd been caught in the civil war a few years back.

Even the thugs looked confused by Grandpa's words. "Okay, old man, make your peace with the rock," pushed the main thug.

"I have done so. Thank you for letting me see it," Grandpa said and turned on his heels in Kadsa's direction. "Where are you going, old man?" shouted the main thug.

Grandpa said tonelessly, "You can keep the cash." That couldn't be it, Kadsa thought.

"Come on, boy," Grandpa commanded her.

She hesitated, but spotted the look in Grandpa's eyes that said, trust me. She expected the thugs to follow them and kept an eye over her shoulder. They didn't come. It couldn't be that simple—just couldn't. What was going on here?

Kadsa only released her breath after she and Grandpa emerged into the canyons, shaded by the sun dropping behind the sandstone plateaus. She considered what to ask, as they retraced their steps through the high rocks, marching toward the guelta, the pool of water formed between the canals of the rocks, as the blistering heat swelled them. Though well into his seventies, Grandpa Edoje walked well ahead of her, with strength and purpose in his steps. She needed to know what happened there.

"How much did you pay them?" she asked, rushing to catch up.

"It is unimportant." "It's a lot of money."

"What is there is more valuable than money," he fired off.

That made her really look at him. "You mean to tell me that's what you've been looking for all these years?"

"That is it," he confirmed.

Her gut twisted with conflicting emotions. "What exactly does this mean?"

"We've finally found the key that will get us home." "The rock?" Pardon her for being skeptical, she asked as she tugged on her robe, anxious to toss it off and dive into any pool of water.

He stopped walking. "It is far more than a rock, Kadsa. It is a star."

2

KEY

The cassava bread grated on Kadsa's throat. She coughed. Grandpa Edoje peeked at her from across the weak wood fire and guffawed. He might have thought she was mustering the courage to say something, as opposed to genuinely dealing with a potential choking hazard.

Kadsa reached for the wooden water bottle and took a long sip.

"Tell me what is on your mind, my dear Kadsa," he said at last.

She considered—should she start with everything that happened today or everything leading up to that? She decided she should speak up sooner than later. What happened in the cave, assuming he was right, would surely affect her. "Do you really think that's the key this time?"

Grandpa sat upright, easing his back against the tree. He glanced up to the night sky, seeking wisdom, as he was inclined to let her know. "I really do, though it's more of a lock than a key." He watched her from across the fire burning between them. "You have your doubts. I understand, my dear Kadsa. These years have not always been easy. Especially on you. You're a young girl, after all."

Young woman, she corrected in her mind, and then quickly chewed down another piece of the cassava dough. "What does being a key or lock mean?" She wasn't sure exactly what she was asking but hoped to piggyback small tidbits to the big conversation … about the decision she'd have to make.

"This is how we'll get home to Marut, the land of your ancestors."

That was the problem, she thought, jerking up right with discomfort before she could stop herself. Then again, the piece of log had been bruising her bony bum. Maybe if she had more cushion down there like the Tuareg women had mocked, when they'd tried putting her through Leblouh, fattening. "Are you sure?"

Grandpa fidgeted. "You are not convinced."

"I'd been thinking," she started, taking a deep breath, "I want to attend college. Maybe in America or Canada."

Grandpa didn't flinch.

"I know it seems weird for me." "Not at all, Kadsa," he cut her off.

She almost choked again on the dough.

He shuffled on the log. "I am fully aware that you're a young woman ready to live your life."

"I'm not abandoning you, but when we were in Kenya, I visited the university there."

His head dipped. What was he thinking? "What do you want to study?"

She perked up, surprised by the question. She glanced around the dark woods aimlessly for a second. Now that she was thinking about it, and Grandpa was watching, "Archaeology." It was a prompt yet fitting response. "Maybe I could find out what happened to Marut that way."

"We know what happened to Marut," he cut her off. "But there's no evidence here."

"We found it today."

Kadsa considered her next words with care. "Are you sure of this, Grandpa? Those people live in that cave— likely to rob tourists. They won't let us just go in and mess with the rock. And that was a rock. Not exactly a key of any sort."

Grandpa chuckled, good-heartedly, but it was enough for her to take a deep breath and reconsider her thoughts.

"You need not worry about those men. And it is very much a lock, Kadsa. I felt it when I was close to it." He reached into his leather satchel and pulled something out wrapped in paper and aluminum foil. He unfolded it slowly. "I have been meaning to give you this. I was always waiting for the right time—when it would be meaningful. Take it."

It was a dull crystal, the size of a large egg. It dangled from a silver chain. She reached for it with hesitant hands. Grandpa never gave gifts aside from cash to buy this and that. This murky rock might have been his version of chic jewelry, but it was ugly, and clearly handcrafted.

"What does it do?" She laughed at her own question.

She knew Grandpa Edoje too well. "It is the key."

Her eyes flew up to meet his, that word she'd heard all her life suddenly felt hard to swallow, like those rock cakes she hated back in Tanzania. "What does it open?"

"You asked the right question, my dear Kadsa," he smirked. Even in the dark, against the backdrop of the fire, Grandpa's eyes shone with intrigue. "This rock is not unlike the rock in the cave. I felt it come alive in my pocket when I stood near that rock earlier. That's how I know that rock is what I seek. That's how I know we are close to home."

"But how does it work?" she asked, and worried that she didn't really want to know the answer.

Grandpa considered. "I told you once that I started my profession as a stargazer. I studied the stars like my father before me. A long time ago, before your father was born, I wandered from my home, in search of a star. I found the rock, and with a little magic, it led me to this world."

"So, my father was born here?" She said this quickly, and regretted it a little, because it might not have been the point of his story. Still, it was confirmation, and a distraction.

"Your father was born here, as were you. You are a child of this world."

"And what about my mother?" she asked, ignoring the last statement.

"You are Maruti. It is in your blood."

All she had ever heard of was his homeland, a place not located on any maps she'd seen, though he swore it existed.

"You never say anything about my mother."

"Your mother is of no consequence," Grandpa said, sounding rather bitter about it. His response was in line with his usual response on the topic. But something else she'd come to realize; Grandpa had never once said that her mother was deceased.

An older Yedina midwife had said she had known her father since he was a baby and had hinted that her grandmother might have been Toubou, to be exact. Grandpa insisted they were all from Marut.

Before she could say another word, he continued, "That crystal is meant to guide you home, to your legacy. It will reveal who you really are."

"I just want to know the truth about my mother," she said, refusing to back down. This topic of her mother was a source of grievance to him, but now more than ever she wanted to know what was in Marut for her.

"Your mother was spiteful, a miserable woman," Grandpa Edoje snapped. His dark eyes narrowed on her.

"But she *is* alive?" Kadsa pushed.

"Not that I am aware," he said, tossing a bit of log into the fire.

This revelation got her thinking. All these years—her mother might be out there *somewhere*. Was she thinking of her or missing her? Had she moved on with her life? "Why did she abandon me?"

Grandpa considered, tossing another piece of twig into the fire. It blazed quickly and died down. "Marut has fire said to come from the gods themselves. They burn with great colors."

"Grandpa," she cut him off.

"Your mother didn't understand, refused to accept your natural talent, *gifts*. I feared she wouldn't help to develop them."

"I don't have any gifts, Grandpa," Kadsa admitted, and it wasn't just to her grandpa, but to herself. Grandpa Edoje had always gone around telling everyone they met that she was special. He told the Yedina shaman that, too. Ever since she began dominating him at akuto, the game of holes and strategies, he'd been convinced she was some sort of genius.

"You don't remember," he said, amused. "Not surprising. That's partly why I did what I did." His eyes dropped to the crystal. "I knew you had the gift of the godtalkers, when as a child, you held that same crystal in your hand and revealed to me what you saw in it."

Kadsa's shoulders dropped. The memory wasn't coming but there were so many more thoughts floating around in her head. Grandpa had a way of asking her to do things. He was always testing her. "Tell me what you see—what you think?" he'd say about this and that. He'd always say her instincts were right—that she'd make a good godtalker. Suddenly, watching him across the fire, she was a child in his arms, holding the crystal.

"There's a boy in there," she had said, "He's sleeping."

This whole memory felt like a dream now that she remembered it, and maybe that was why she'd almost blotted it out.

"You remember, don't you?" Grandpa said, his calm voice filling the space between the crackling flames of the campfire. "You can do it, again, but you need the light."

Before she could speak, he jumped ahead. "The crystal attracts light. But you need to hold it," he gestured to the burning logs before them, "Peer into it, you can tell me what you see."

"Why didn't you use this method to find that rock, if it works so well?"

"Many reasons, my dear skeptical girl, many reasons. The stars had to align. For a time, this crystal was lost to me. You might recall Libya. That was when we recovered it."

"I stole it from the seller. You said it was an egg." Kadsa shifted with her own words. She had no idea what she'd stolen at the time, only that Grandpa gave instructions to grab and run, and so she did.

"Now you know the truth," he said. "That rock in the cave is a cosmic lock. We have a little over a week's time to make the most of this moment, according to my estimate." Grandpa Edoje reached for his sleeping bag.

Kadsa didn't want to let Grandpa off the hook so lightly. Still, she fluffed her sleeping bag and prepared to settle in for the night. Sleep eluded her, not just because she kept peeking up at the stars but also because of everything he'd said, and thoughts of her mother. He'd all but admitted her mother was alive. She loved her Grandpa, but it was insensitive, if not a criminal thing to keep her from her mother, regardless of how he felt about her upbringing. And maybe her mother had her reasons for not wanting to let him exploit her *talents*.

She rarely got angry with Grandpa, but anger brewed inside her, eating her up, maybe because it made her think of all the lost possibilities. All these years, she could have been with her mother, could've maybe seen another side of life besides being a nomad. Now that he found his lock, she wasn't sure she wanted to take this trip, especially with her mother alive out there. All her life, she'd wanted a mother. Now she knew the truth she had always suspected. She couldn't just let it lie. She had to find the truth. She just had to.

Deep into the night, she quietly packed up her bag, detaching the bedding. She considered taking the kapok- fiber bedding because she'd made it herself when he'd temporarily abandoned her among a group of women in Ghana. In the end, it was unnecessary, so she left it behind. She was done sleeping next to trees and under stars. She carefully sidestepped Grandpa as she wandered into the unknown toward the desert village of Borkou. She could catch a caravan out toward N'Djamena, the capital city of Chad. From there, she'd have to find out what else was there, the truth.

Grandpa could take care of himself. He'd clearly been manipulating her and this whole situation all this time. Kadsa abandoned the camel to a handful of children on the outskirts of the city, subsequently hitching a ride with two Kanembu women in a wagon to N'Djamena.

She shut off her burner phone. By now, Grandpa knew she was gone.

3

CONSULATE

After four days, the caravan arrived in N'Djamena in the mid-afternoon. Kadsa said goodbye to the women and spent half an hour wandering the bustling and crowded city, before arriving at the cyber cafe in the city hub, where she purchased time on a computer. She sat aimlessly for a long time, considering what she was doing, and how she'd go about it. What did she know about herself? Her name: Kadsa Abasi.

No hits.

Grandpa's name got no hits, but then something jumped to life in her brain. He had more than one name. He'd used the name Barak before. And when she typed that name, she came across the story from years earlier:

Toronto Woman Accuses Father-in-law of Kidnapping Her Daughter.

She read the article and stared at the photos of the four-year-old child, certain she was looking at herself as a little girl. The photo showed a child with neat pigtails and twists, very different from Kadsa's shoulder length locs. The child's name wasn't

Kadsa, that strange name grandpa said meant *key to the stars*. The child's name was Skylar.

"Skylar." She mumbled the name under her breath a couple of times. She was Skylar. Did she look like a Skylar? What did it mean? She queried the meaning and felt a certain pride— Scholar. That was what she wanted—to go to school and study. It was perfect. Kadsa was a stargazer. She'd always been Kadsa. Could she be this person—Skylar?

Her mom's name was Lorraine Labelle, and she was from Toronto, where she worked as a radio station manager. Kadsa stared at her photo and tried to remember her. Tears came down her cheeks from the strain. This woman with her greying locs and stern face was a stranger. Grandpa took that familiarity from her. And what for? Some fantasy of another world.

"Are you all right?" asked the man two seats away from her.

She nodded and wiped the tears away. Grandpa was horrible for doing this. How could she have forgotten her mom? The story said her mother brought her to Kenya for her father's funeral, and that was when Grandpa took her away.

Kadsa scribbled down the information about her mother in the small notebook she carried. There was a phone number for anyone with information. She took that down. Strangely, she didn't know what to do with any of this. For the longest time, she just stared at what she wrote down, blanked brained. What would she say? "Hello, my name is Kadsa. I think I am your missing daughter, Skylar." That sounded reasonable in her head, but also weird.

Lorraine would think she was a scammer or a fraud. She was certain there was at least one warrant out for her and Grandpa in Kenya.

Kadsa stormed from the café. Later, she checked into a small home owned by a woman who was happy to have her only customer. In the night, she checked her phone to see that Grandpa had spammed her with commanding messages. "Kadsa, you must come back." She rolled her eyes. He was melodramatic like this. When she was younger, it was kind of endearing, because it was just the two of them, but she was somewhat resentful. He'd been lying to her this whole time, controlling her.

She wouldn't call him. Something she would do— visit the Canadian Consulate. She was a foreign child, not a Maruti child. One of the articles had said her father studied in Toronto, and met her mom there, but returned home to take part in Grandpa's adventures. That ended her parents' marriage. It also ended horribly for her father. That must have been the fate her mother wanted to save her from; a destiny that Grandpa insisted was her birthright.

Try as she did, lying in this small, sweltering room with a single small fan that barely made a difference, she couldn't hate Grandpa. She wasn't ready to see him again. She let her thoughts drift to her mother. Would she know her, or would she care? It had been over twelve years.

Kadsa had to try.

In the morning, she washed her hair. Grandpa had let her hair grow into locs because he hadn't a clue how to deal with it. Seeing those photos of herself in pigtails and twists, she imagined her mom combing through her thick, coarse hair, and parting it in the center to make her look nice.

She had always considered cutting her locs, but she was content with the shoulder-length hair. Thinly trimmed, it resembled the Hamar braids she briefly had back in Sudan. She had only to wash and put in the occasional oil that she purchased from markets to keep it from drying out. Clothes were simple, too. She hadn't many other options aside from trousers.

After showering, she put on jeans and a T-shirt. She was most comfortable with this look. She put on her only pair of sneakers that she got in Kenya a couple years ago. The rule was not to get many things, since they were always traveling. What they needed—nothing too valuable in case they had to split fast. That was what happened in Kenya. She salvaged the sneakers because she had been wearing them. Everything else had been abandoned. That was when she knew she couldn't do this forever.

Back on the streets of N'Djamena, she purchased a handful of berries and baked treats in the market, and then used a payphone to dial her mother's radio station. "Hello, is Lorraine Labelle available?" She'd been trying to affect a Canadian accent all morning, as if it would make her mother believe who she was more. She couldn't tell if she was doing a good or bad job. Her accent was indeterminate, as she never stayed in one place too long.

"May I ask who is calling?" asked a toneless voice, maybe a secretary.

Kadsa choked hard. "Um, is she available?" "I'm afraid she's busy. Can I take a message?"

"Um, no, it's okay," she said, and fumblingly hung up.

Kadsa blew breath loudly, frustrated. How could she choke like this? She needed to get out of these long robes and head wraps. When she traveled, she dressed for the culture and the convenience of not getting harassed. Chad was no exception. But there were women in Western clothing in the marketplace. She tugged and yanked on the headscarf but didn't pull it off. It shielded her eyes from the hot sun that bore down on her in the alley of the marketplace. She then set off to the Canadian Consulate. If she was a citizen of Canada, they could afford her a visa and passport to travel.

The Consulate staff stared her up and down as if they were assessing how truthful she was. Eventually, they gave her their time. They had her on record as Skylar Labelle Abasi. She couldn't prove she was that person. She had no identification. The few documents she carried had falsified information.

"We need stronger evidence—paper trails," said the middle-aged woman in front of her, when she explained to her about the information she found on the web.

They were really making this difficult. She wanted to ask them to contact Lorraine, but of course, she doubted her mother would recognize her. Then she realized, only one person would verify her for sure—Grandpa Edoje.

She wasn't ready to deal with him, but stepped outside of the Consulate and started up the burner phone.

"Kadsa, my dear stubborn star child, I have been worried sick," he said melodramatically.

She rolled her eyes but stopped short of questioning this sentiment. Was he truly worried about her or was he worried because the day for him to find home was coming up and he needed her talents? "I just need to know if you have any documents with my real name on it."

"Kadsa," he fumbled on the other end.

"My name is Skylar," she cut him off. Those words were angrier than she intended. "Yeah, I know the truth, Grandpa. I need to sort this out. If you can come down to the Canadian Consulate."

"I cannot do that," he snapped.

He might be worried about getting arrested. She didn't want to see that happen to him. She wasn't that angry with him, but she needed answers. "Do you have any identification for me?"

"My dear, the star alignment ends in a few days. I need you," he pleaded, ignoring her question.

"I don't think it's real, Grandpa," she dared herself to say it aloud.

"It is real. You know that." His tone was rich with conviction and authority.

"No, I don't know that!" she fired back. Her brain flooded with the stories he told her about growing up in Marut, riding the buzoa, some striped unicorn-horse called an abada, and some other stuff, like stories about the gods. She had very much wanted to believe—had believed in all of it her whole life. Part of her wanted to see this place, still hoped it was real. But she had to put her foot down. I am going to contact my mother," she told him flat out, hearing him sigh on the other end of the line. "I know she's in Toronto. I am going there."

"There's nothing for you there, Kadsa," he scolded. "That is not your home."

"What's there for me in Marut?"

"Your ancestors, your blood."

"Even if this place were real, I would be a stranger there. I would have no one," she fired off, feeling all her emotions rise to the surface.

"You will have me," he said in a quieter voice.

"Why do you want to go so badly?" She pushed, ignoring the car horns as she leaned into the phone in the shade of the Consulate. "This is your home. This is where dad was born, Grandma, too..."

"You don't understand," he cut her off. "I made a promise to the people; an oath to the gods."

She closed her eyes, took a deep breath, away from the phone to cool her temper. His tone sounded dire, but this could also be him trying to manipulate her again.

Grandpa Edoje breathed heavily on the other end of the phone. "Kadsa, listen to me," he said, "Marut is in trouble, the doing of a long-ago reveal I had while working in the temple of the stargazers. That was the reason for my journey here—to find answers. I don't know what went wrong but I do know I must return. The stars align to reveal the era of Ma'at, goddess of decisions, judgments, and catastrophe. Either the sun will set on Marut by the end of the current cycle, or it will rise into a new dawn. How it unfolds depends greatly on what we do—the reason we must get home."

She gritted her teeth, pushing out the weight of her conscience. "You can do this without me."

"I cannot," he said, voice pleading earnestly, the type of tone that made her heart sink.

"Why not?" she snapped, hating the way he made her feel. Expectations—years and years of it. All she ever wanted was to do simple things. She never thought she was special. That was what he said. She just wanted to go to school, make friends, and maybe settle down.

"I have no one else," came Grandpa Edoje's quiet response.

His words were daggers plunged into her soul. Kadsa stiffened. "I am not special. I can't help. This is on you. Not me." She resorted to another angle to counter rather than give in to guilt. "You shouldn't have taken me from my mother. It wasn't right."

She waited for him to say he was sorry, but nothing came out of his mouth. He was stubborn like this, set in his ways. Never had she known him to apologize for being wrong. And because of this, because he clearly couldn't say what he did was not right, she said, "I have to go, Grandpa. I have to go back to Toronto." She hung up before he could protest.

Back inside the Consulate, she stood in line again. Despite her trepidation, she asked the agent, "Can you contact Lorraine Labelle? She's my mother. She can identify me."

The woman squinted at the paper with Lorraine's information. "Alright. Give me a couple minutes."

Lorraine might reject her or give her a chance to prove herself. Chances were that she'd want to test if it could be true. Kadsa wanted a real life. Regardless of the result, she wouldn't go back to Grandpa Edoje.

Minutes went by while she sat in the lobby and tried not to cry or be angry. People walked by and glanced her way, some looked worried and others just curious. Nearly an hour. She paced. Grandpa called a few more times, but she didn't pick up. She had to do this for herself.

Kadsa jumped to her feet when the official came out to see her in the lobby. "We could not reach Ms. Labelle but have left a message."

Kadsa sulked.

"Go home and return tomorrow. Hopefully, we will have better news."

Kadsa wasn't sure she believed her, but she gave her the benefit of the doubt. She gave the woman her phone number, which she almost never gave to anyone, according to the wishes of her Grandpa. There were so many shady things. Signs that he'd been in the wrong. Not allowed to enroll in school unless she used a false name. Always on the move.

Back in the tiny, rented room, she paced, brain swelling with the many different scenarios of how this might turn out. What if Lorraine rejected her? She tried not to dwell on this. Instead, she forced happy and positive thoughts. She imagined Lorraine flying down, or maybe sending a plane ticket to Toronto. She'd been all over Africa but had never been on a plane before. Thinking about flying made her a little lightheaded. Their reunion might be weird. How might she appear with her locs and funny, hard-to-place accent? Would her mother be disappointed?

Kadsa took deep breaths, trying to push out the negativity. She drank too much malt, which only upset her stomach. When she and Grandpa hung out with the Masai, they drank a lot of blood-milk. She never got used to any milky products. How could she be so nervous?

In the morning, Kadsa jolted from sleep to answer the phone after the first ring. She sat up in the tiny bed, rubbing the sleep out of her burning eyes. She should've known it was him. "Grandpa, I told you already…"

"We have only a few days, Kadsa," he said, "I really need you."

So does my mother, she thought. "My mother should be contacting me soon." She hung up.

Waiting was a nightmare. She traveled to the market to get street food, eating sweet corn and roasted delicacies. She'd run out of money soon. To her relief, the Consulate official called to say they'd made contact with Lorraine Labelle, but that there had to be some stipulations. The first was a DNA test. Kadsa didn't trust needles, so she offered hair and saliva samples. That would take weeks. She didn't think she could wait that long.

"The good news," said the consulate official after she gave the samples. "She wants to speak to you."

Kadsa froze. All of a sudden, her throat was craggy and her palms sweaty. "Hello?"

"Skylar?" came the voice, strong, emotional and authoritative.

She blanked and took a while to realize that she was Skylar. Not until the woman on the other line said the name a few more times did she respond. "Yes. It's me," she said, and her voice broke. She was a stranger and yet that didn't stop the flow of emotions rushing out.

Kadsa began twisting a single strand of locs in her hand, without even realizing it. She closed her eyes and tried to picture Lorraine's face. Only the picture from the web came to mind. A soft-faced older woman with greying hair. Did she look like her?

"We're gonna get you home, okay," Lorraine assured her.

All sorts of thoughts rummaged her brain. Nothing felt real. "Do you want to make sure it's me first?" she asked, and then cringed because of how silly it all sounded.

"Yes, we're working on it," Lorraine said. Kadsa didn't know what else to say.

"Is that grandfather of yours still alive?" asked Lorraine, sounding angry.

"Yeah, he is," she said, wondering if she should say more—tell her how angry she was with Grandpa Edoje and or something.

"I'm getting you home and away from that man and his foolishness," Lorraine declared at last.

Kadsa kept saying, "Yeah, I want to come home." The Consulate officials took the phone from her. She stood nervous and confused. Something gnawed at her conscience while the consulate officials explained the next steps. She would miss Africa. She was born somewhere else, but she couldn't recall that place. Africa had always been home. Maybe that was the real reason she'd been hesitant about Marut. At least she had her mom in Toronto.

She was going home.

4

CRYSTAL

The boy wasn't a boy but maybe the same age as her. He wore a heavy brown robe with an oversized hood that covered his face entirely. He was scribbling on a brick wall. Symbols that looked odd with a golden glow. He was talking to someone or maybe himself, speaking a language she didn't understand. But which?

She spoke English, French, and Swahili, with general understandings of indigenous languages, like Yedina.

"What are you writing?"

The boy looked her way. Just as he was about to answer, the scene darkened—a shadow descended like an oversized vulture spreading its wings.

Kadsa jumped from her sleep.

She was still in the rented room. The crystal Grandpa dumped on her poked out from under the pillow. She had been messing with it last night, out of sheer nervousness. The hint of a glow quickly vanished. She hadn't meant to carry it with her but had discovered the thing in her backpack last night.

Shaking off the effects of the dream, Kadsa rolled out of bed in a good mood. She had connected with her mom and wanted to call and speak to her.

Kadsa stumbled backward with a yank of her knapsack. Some thief was trying to pull it off her back as she wandered through the market. She wouldn't let him, and they fought in a thug of war. She twisted the strap around her arm, so it was hard to pull away without ripping her hand off. People watched but no one came to help, which didn't surprise her. She didn't need help. This man wasn't very big, and though he barked for her to let go, she refused.

When he lurched at her with a small knife, she unleashed on him, kicking him in the groin, and then twisting his knifed hand the second he stumbled, effectively wrangling the knife out of his grip.

The knife fell to the ground. Kadsa hammered the man with another jab to the face before he collapsed; he slowly dragged himself back up and ran away as the spectators descended. Some people applauded.

Kadsa untangled her knapsack and was surprised to see the side pocket unzipped to reveal the sparkling crystal. She was sure she hadn't left it open. She stared after the would-be thief who was long gone and pondered if he hadn't been stalking her since perhaps the eatery, trying to steal it from her.

Taking a deep breath, she removed the crystal from the pocket, masking it fully with her fist before wandering off. Why was it glowing? Kadsa wandered into a less crowded part of the street and brought the egg-shaped crystal to her eyes under the hot sun. It had been a dull, murky rock when grandpa handed it over. Now, she could see hints of light inside of it, and wondered, truly wondered, if Grandpa was right about his claim that the crystal responded to light.

She quickly turned into a quiet corner on the street, where she could get some privacy. The effects of the crystal on her eyes were blinding at first, but her eyesight adjusted. White light spotted the center of the crystal, and another thing—a foreign land.

There were people—celebrating. She'd traversed enough of Africa to recognize traditional clothes and garments, but she'd never seen anything like what these people wore. Something about their garments screamed foreign.

If you peered long into the abyss, it would look back. Grandpa had taught her this phrase, and she'd thought it meant that if she looked long enough, she'd see what maybe she didn't want to see. A roaming cloud of darkness crawled across the land, smothering the people. Kadsa pulled back, gasping. She wasn't imagining this. Was this what Grandpa Edoje meant by her *gifts*? Maybe he planted those images there. No, that made little sense. How would he be able to do that? Kadsa suddenly didn't know how to feel. This couldn't be happening. Not now, not while she'd found her mom. She didn't want this to be real. Why was this happening now? She hurriedly stuffed the crystal into the deep of her jeans pocket, remembering where she was and what had just happened. Maybe it was nothing. Fingers crossed—it was nothing.

She spent the remainder of the day looking up things about Canada at the cafe. Her mom was from Toronto. The consulate had closed early today, and she didn't have her mom's phone number except for the radio station. She didn't want it to seem she was harassing her so she didn't call her place of work and chose to wait it out.

She got a little excited looking things up about Toronto. Would she fit back into the city she hadn't been in for so long? But home was where family was, just like her Grandpa would tell her. She would be seeing her mom. Nothing could cull that happiness inside of her. Lorraine wouldn't see her as a stranger.

Later that night, she jolted awake, sweatier than she should be, even as the small fan oscillated. Someone had sounded out her name—Kadsa. She didn't know, nor could she tell where the echo of her name came from—a fevered dream. Before she could return to sleep, she glimpsed a light at the head of the bed, coming from her backpack, stashed between the crease of the single bed and the nightstand.

Why was it glowing still?

The egg-sized rock warmed in her hands when she brought it to her eyes. The scene moved by so erratically, she wasn't sure what was happening. But she could hear and see Grandpa Edoje, struggling with a big man under a heavy robe, who resembled the Yedina shaman.

The thugs from the cave roughed up Grandpa. Did he return to the cave? Of course, he did, without her. Kadsa couldn't make sense of the scene or why she was seeing it, but she believed wholeheartedly that what played out in the crystal was really happening.

The cave wilted into a dark jungle, dense and frightening. The scene vanished.

"Grandpa?" she whispered into the crystal.

No response came. She reached for her phone and dialed his number. It rang but no one picked up. She hung up and dialed a couple more times, but there was no reply.

Kadsa paced the room, terrified about what could happen to him. That skeptical part of her brain tried to convince her this wasn't her plight anymore and that Grandpa Edoje had only himself to blame but she couldn't just let him get hurt.

She grabbed her bag and marched from the home, making sure she didn't disturb the landlady. She had no plan; she only knew she had to return to Tibesti.

———————

Two days into the journey, and countless phone calls to her Grandpa that died into the abyss, she could finally see the Tibesti plateaus with the twisting sand dunes and high rocks, back to where she and Grandpa had been a week ago. The van dusted past eroded sandstones and palm groves, one of the few signs of life in the Sahel. The small group of people in the van watched her closely for some reason. She bit down on her dry and brittle lips and smiled at the round-faced woman with the small child. She didn't want to be here, not now, not under these circumstances. She was tired, hopeless, and anxious. She had barely slept in the last few days, barely eaten anything, not while she was worried sick that something bad had happened to Grandpa Edoje. Part of her was angry, too, that maybe he was doing this to keep her with him. Why couldn't he just let her go? These thoughts weren't right. Deep inside her gut, she knew something had gone wrong.

"Are you going home?" asked the Toubou woman rocking her baby next to her in the back of the van.

"No," Kadsa said. Home—where was home? She was merely going to find out what happened to Grandpa. Around here, the authorities were hard to come by. The woman pulled her sleeping child closer under her bosom.

Kadsa considered her mother. Yesterday she had told the consulate during a phone call that she would be busy for at least three days. Lorraine had offered to provide a plane ticket for her. That should be at the consulate tomorrow, or today. It was early morning.

Kadsa just didn't think she could live with herself if Grandpa wasn't safe. There was a little guilt from telling him to do it without her. But he had to know this would happen—that he couldn't have just re-entered that cave. And how would she even save him? She had the little knife and gadgets for tricks, and this crystal. Maybe they'd take the crystal in exchange for his life.

On the onset of dawn, she arrived at the plateaus, blood-red against the horizon. The sandstone bulwarks resembled giants and great beasts against the pre-dawn skyline. The desert was cool. A soft, sandy breeze blew. A small group of people lingered along the wadis, while their camels fed from the guelta d'Archei water holes.

She wore only a scarf around her head and wished she'd bothered to wear the long, heavy robe to protect her from the dust and the sun.

Kadsa took a sip of water from the small bottle to quench her dry throat. Climbing was a skill she prided herself on, because her childhood had mainly been spent in the wilderness, but she barely remembered the entrance she and Grandpa had used the first time. She knew it was beyond Emi Koussi. Grandpa had said Grandma's people, the Toubou people, had named the plateaus' highest peak after her. Not true, but such was her grandfather's imagination. And he didn't get to go away without her having a say about it.

The dark cave was hollow. The sound of water droplets rippled from deep down. It smelled like wet dirt, and even a bit of camel feces and urine. Her little flashlight only worked to save her from ringing her ankles on edgy stones or stepping into anything gross.

Further down from the cave, the hollowness shifted, and the smell disappeared. The ledges were steep, the path worn down by feet. The deeper down she traveled, the more visible the art became on the walls—faded drawings of stick figure people and animals grazing. Grandpa said these were ancient and showed the landscape before it became a desert. She had seen them before. Now they made her think of her dream about that boy drawing on the walls.

Grandpa had said there was a difference between a dream and a vision. The latter was of things to come. He said many such things. Eclipses were signs of doorways and such. Maybe if he was here, she could pick his brain a bit more about what her dreams could mean.

Kadsa reached for the crystal in the side pocket of her rucksack. The faint light warmed her hand. Maybe it would show him to her again. She brought it to her eyes and thought long and hard about him. Nothing.

No light.

She continued walking until she reached the area where the thugs had been squatting. Their things weren't there anymore and that made her stop walking to question if she took a wrong turn. But everything looked the same. And because of that, she continued with caution.

The rock was there, uncovered, too.

An eerie nausea-like feeling washed over her. A pull. The crystal was getting hotter in her hands. She took a step forward but paused with the echoes of what sounded like voices.

"Grandpa!" she muttered, moving the flashlight around. Maybe they held him here. Kind of silly, but short of turning every corner in this very hot underground cavern, she was at a loss to find him.

Maybe it wasn't a vision she'd seen but some illusion. Or maybe it was a dream. She'd tried calling him en-route to the plateaus, but his phone was dead. There was no service in the desert or down here.

It was the fear of him getting hurt that drove her. While she wanted to keep her distance, she couldn't stand to think of him getting hurt, certainly not at the hands of that shaman.

Kadsa walked around looking for signs of him. The cavern went deeper. And though she started in one direction, she changed her mind. It looked like a dead end from here. She turned back to the clearing proper, returning to the rock. Her crystal practically leaped from her hand toward the rock's magnetic pull. She had to clamp down on it hard.

Grandpa was right about the rock and the agate.

Kadsa spun at the sound of dirt falling away from the earth, coupled with a swift movement of shuffling feet— like someone trying to sneak up on her. "Grandpa?"

The figure stepped from the shadows to her left.

Kadsa drew in breath. The Yedina shaman.

"So, you can speak, and you are not a boy, after all," he spoke, looking as menacing as she first remembered him.

No need to lie anymore. It wasn't as if she didn't think he knew the truth beforehand. He'd spent enough time prizing her up with his creepy eyes. "Where is my grandpa?"

The shaman's bony face was stern under the weak flashlight.

"Where is he?" She pressed on. She was half- expecting an ambush. So far, it was just him, standing still and watching her.

"Where is the crystal?" he asked, unmoved. "I need to see him first."

He chuckled, seemingly amused by her stance. When she was among his people, she had noticed the way he treated the women around him, even slapping one woman to the ground. He was a boar who didn't take women seriously.

"Your grandfather is in a place you cannot go," he said coldly.

His words deflated her hope like a pin to a balloon. But she needed to know for sure what he meant. "Where?"

"Is it not the place you have been seeking?"

Kadsa steadied herself, biting back against her anger, not wanting to believe what he was implying. "What did you do to him?"

He took his first step forward, but she didn't budge. There was no place behind her except for that long, deep cavern. The rock was two feet off to her right.

"You have something I want," he said.

She tightened her grip on the crystal, and slowly brought her hand behind her back.

"Give it to me—give it over," he commanded, hands stretched out in her direction.

"Where's my grandfather?" She pushed. "He has gone *home*."

She winced, that last word rushing over her face like a warm breeze.

"Did he not tell you the story of how he got here?" mused the shaman.

For some reason, she kept trying to remember this man's name. When she had arrived at Yedina land, he had spoken of her grandfather as if he'd known him forever. Did he know of Marut? Grandpa was wary of who he told. Not just because people laughed, but, as he told her, they might want to destroy it.

"Your grandfather has been on a long trip from home."

"How did he get home?" She surprised herself with the question.

The Yedina tribesman stared at her. "The other side opened up."

"I don't believe you!" she fired off.

He stepped closer and she backed up, toward the agate rock. He wasn't a small man. Wasn't young, either, no doubt he could overpower her. She'd have to do something drastic like knee him in the groin, or worse, use the knife.

"Very well," he said. "The rock was ignited a few days ago. It's slowly closing. It will close come sunrise."

That wasn't possible, she considered, glancing at the brightening agate. She couldn't say if he was lying. Then again, Grandpa did say he felt the power of the rock when they were here last. Was that what had happened— why he'd been so confident? The rock gave off heat. Did it open and swallow Grandpa? If so, then why had he called the crystal a key? Can locks open without keys?

"Only the crystal can keep it open or close it. But what matters here is that you hand me that crystal, girl."

Girl curled on his tongue in a very repulsive way. "I have nothing."

The shaman's eyes dropped to her right side. She kept her hand behind her back, but the crystal glowed— burning her hand. She wouldn't be able to hold it any longer.

"The sun rises on the horizon. If it disappears, this rock won't open again for a very long time. And your grandfather will die."

Kadsa stared him down, refusing to accept what he was telling her. She didn't know for sure that he hadn't already killed her grandfather.

"Don't you want to see your grandfather again?" "Why should I believe you? You betrayed us."

He sniggered; eyes sharply set on her. "He did say you were stubborn and skeptical. Your grandfather lied to me about who he was, and why he'd come among us. But believe me. He's not here anymore."

The thought of Grandpa being gone for good hurt. She had to know if it was true. She brought the burning crystal from behind her. The Yedina shaman gasped. She backtracked to the agate. "You're not getting this," she told him, glancing to the agate that grew brighter and hotter. It was almost translucent. "Not until you bring my grandfather back."

"There's no other way you're leaving this cave with it," warned the shaman.

"I'm not afraid of you."

He chuckled. It was frightening. He leaped toward her. It was fast, so fast she almost didn't get out of his way. She staggered and by the time she caught her balance, he was coming after her, again. Something wasn't right about his movements, not for a man his age and body size. But she hardly had time to make sense of him. He knocked into her, pushing her toward the glowing agate. She had expected him to bash her head against the rock, but he screamed out in pain and leaped backward so quickly she was left confused. She couldn't see him, not with the light of the agate flooding the cavern room, breaking down tangible boundaries.

He must have fled from the room or buried himself in the dark crevices.

Kadsa searched for him, narrowing and squinting her eyes here and there. Something growled; a terrifying, guttural sound. She stumbled back against the wall, feeling not hard rock, but nothing at all. The cave wall was gone. She bumped her heels against what felt like vines.

That couldn't be right.

The moment she blinked, the flood of white light twisted into a thick bolt of lightning and vanished a swift moment after, leaving her in darkness.

Only a bright blot of white light lingered ahead of her. The crystal. It lay on a tree stump that barely rose above ground. Kadsa's sense twisted when she realized the crystal had absorbed all the light and now glowed like a shooting star. How? *Magic,* came her grandfather's voice in her head.

Kadsa looked around. The cave was gone. Tibesti? Where was the Yedina shaman? Heck, where was anything? Darkness and wilderness surrounded her. Kadsa realized she was trembling.

What now?

5

JAKUBA

Kadsa had never witnessed anything like this, not even during the time she had spent trekking through ghost forests in Niger. A thick blanket of darkness had been pulled over the land, for a few minutes she believed she had gone blind. Rubbing her eyes was no longer effective, and she swallowed her sigh at the realization that she hadn't gone blind. The world had just gone completely black. How had she gotten here from the cave? It made no sense that she had been surrounded by stones and rock, and in a flash of light, she was outdoors in vast, never-ending blackness.

She was surrounded by jungle, high canopied trees, thick and unbreaking, endless. She didn't know where this was, except this was not the desert of Chad. Deep in the back of her mind, she believed she'd been transported *someplace* else. If this wasn't Chad, then where was she? She was afraid to find out the answer.

Kadsa stopped walking after realizing she had been doing so in circles, bumping into things, tripping over things. She wasn't afraid, not after years of running into and from wild animals, even the human variety. She just wanted to understand what happened and how to get out of this. Where was her grandpa? And that ghastly shaman?

Only the light of the crystal had any impact on the dense blackness. When she tripped over undergrowth for the umpteenth time, she encouraged herself to breathe and think. That was the only way to get out of this. Her mission was to make sure her grandpa was safe, and then she'd get to be with her mother and start her new life.

Kadsa took a deep breath. She just had to focus.

The light of the crystal dimmed. It wouldn't remain for much longer.

First, she had to create a torch. She dropped to her knees and began feeling for scraps of tree bark and leaves, pulling vines out from the dirt, mindful of the whispers of the trees and the bristling of the bushes, the chill that penetrated the woods. Even though it made little sense in the back of her mind, she was fairly certain this was not Chad.

But she didn't care where she was, so much as how she was going to get out.

The darkness emoted a warning that she belonged to it and whatever it sheltered. Everything was so awfully dark. The tops of the trees canopied the forest, creating the illusion that she was in a closed space. Nothing in the jungles of Tanzania could compare to this. At one point, she'd pulled out her phone. The digits showed the time was ten in the morning. An attempt to dial any number returned silence.

She managed to uproot a foot-long branch, pulling and tugging so hard that she nearly broke her hand. All the while, she pried over her shoulders, searching for signs of trouble—wild animals, hogs, boars, even monkeys. She was certain there had to be some. Hyenas. Those were the worst. Once, she and Grandpa had to be rescued from a pack of hyenas in Tanzania. This very cute boy had come out of nowhere to help them, chasing off the beasts, and practically wrestling one over a cliff. She didn't know what happened to the boy.

Because they were always sleeping in the bushes and under trees, they had to keep an eye out for everything. They'd been robbed and bitten. Somehow, they'd always survived.

Grandpa, where were you?

Kadsa hurried to tie the vines and leaves, wrapping them tightly around the branch.

Next step was lighting it. She knew how to work rocks together, but she carried a lighter in her backpack. A couple of tries before she got an almost wilting fire. The small droplet of flame was slow to catch but spread around the torch.

Breathing a sigh of relief, she stood. The torchlight illuminated a decent distance, she saw only trees. Kadsa stepped into the wilderness, hopeful she'd find her way out. She didn't know how long the torch would last so she moved fast, seeking some signs of civilization, a heavily treaded footpath, or some other hint.

Trees led to more trees. Doubts crept into her mind—maybe she should've involved the police, taken a chance that they'd make the effort to help an old man kidnapped by warlords. She couldn't have made a mistake. She would survive this.

"Come on, think," she willed herself under her breath.

She reached for the phone again, digging around her bag, pocket after pocket but it wasn't there. She must have dropped it.

There was no way she could recover it in this wilderness. Kadsa pulled the crystal from under her blouse. A small blot of dwindling white light filled its core. At that moment, she was grateful to have it and its light, and maybe, like her Grandpa said, it would guide her through this darkness.

The sound of snapping branches accompanied by growling caused Kadsa to seize up, eyes darting around the dark woodland, even if the torchlight could barely penetrate more than two feet at a time.

"Hello?" she called, and second-guessed why she did. Did she really want to attract unnecessary attention? She pulled her backpack to her chest, only then remembering her knife. She couldn't find it. Did she drop it in the forest?

The growling grew louder and closer. Despite her hatred of cowardice, she ran off.

Growls and tree whipping trailed her. It came from all around. Craning her neck this way and that, she tangled in the undergrowth and tripped, cussing on the way down.

Clumsily, she clawed her way upward, reaching for the fallen torch before it could set the brambles and bushes on fire, though now that she thought of it that might not be a bad idea. Nothing like fire to ward off danger.

Stay calm, she thought as the growling drew closer. The most atrocious sound broke through the darkness— the mad shriek of a tortured animal. Her nostrils clogged up with the strong stench of something very moldy that came on suddenly out of nowhere.

She scanned the wilderness, trying to pinpoint … what was she looking at? Nestled in the blackness were feral white eyes. *Those were not human.* A wild dog? Not with those bright eyes.

The wrong thing to do when facing a predator was to make a sudden move. The knife was slippery in her hand, and she tightened her grip, trying to make sure she was steady on her feet and in a position where defending herself would be easier.

The creature growled, the sound of its feet trampling the woods like a stampede on its way toward her. Still, she did not spot the creature, not until it was on her. She threw up her hands to shield herself from the attack, stumbling backward, and hitting her head hard against stone or a piece of log. Life was nearly knocked out of her, nothing else made sense. Somehow, she scrambled behind the nearest tree, dodging a second assault. She spied what had attacked her through hazy eyes. Her worst fear came true—she was cornered.

Four pairs of curious white eyes pierced the darkness. What were these creatures? The coterie broke into a cacophony of nonsensical sounds—what she could only think of as battle cries, something between barking and howling.

Kadsa dashed off, crying out a second later when the claws of one of the wild animals buried into her back, pressing her body against the floor of the forest. Kadsa had little time to think, breathe or move, as she lay face down, waiting for the end.

The creature with its foot on her back sniffed her, letting a droplet of stale saliva fall on her face. She would become food. Kadsa attempted to wiggle out of the foothold, but the creature's foot slammed down harder. It grabbed a tight chunk of her locs and pulled her up, so she faced its seven-foot-tall frame, dog-hyena face with the large fangs.

Kadsa cried out desperately, bracing for the pain of fangs and claws digging and cutting into her flesh. The beast holding her down shrieked, the most horrifying sound that crashed into squeals of pain and torture.

The creatures released Kadsa and rushed back into the bushes. Confused, Kadsa stared after them, and then glanced around to see if some even worse predator had shown up. But there was nothing, except ... her crystal was glowing, brighter than it had been before. That was the only difference. What was happening? The blot of white light she'd spotted in the pendant radiated outward. She'd glimpsed a spread of light when she was on the ground but had assumed it came from the now- extinguished torch.

The crystal created a flood of light that stretched deeper into the forest than the torch had and revealed with clarity everything in front of her.

Was this why the creatures ran? Was this what they were afraid of? Fire and light?

Then again, they lived in darkness. Well, she thought, deciding not to waste any time, she needed to take this opportunity to get out of here before her luck ran out. Kadsa reached for the snuffed-out torch, and squeezing the pendant, backed away from the sharp-eyed creatures.

A few problems revealed themselves during her trek through the forest. The bright-eyed creatures weren't leaving—they were trailing at a safe distance, their eyes bobbing in and out of bushes. Even worse—the crystal's light was fading. Its illuminating effect was not working. Kadsa fumbled inside her bag for the lighter.

Igniting the torch became a tougher challenge. It wasn't catching. She yanked at leaves and thin vines from the trees as she passed them, coiling them around the torch. The fire caught and then died, and with each attempt to ignite the torch, the crystal's light dimmed. More bright eyes joined the trail. There was something about their behavior. They seemed to be talking to one another. The howling, barking, and growling all seemed intentional somehow. Grandpa always told her not to underestimate the intelligence of animals.

Kadsa brought the lighter to the crystal, a desperate move, to see if she could boost the illuminance. It wasn't working.

A sharp growl pierced the deep night. Kadsa froze. Two aggressive creatures tumbled her way, clawing at each other. One of them grabbed her left foot and she kicked at it until it let go. She whacked another with the torch a couple of times and then threw the whole thing at him.

Kadsa ran while begging the pendant to work and wishing the horrible creatures would tear themselves apart and leave her alone.

Luck wasn't on her side. They kept on her trail.

The glow in the crystal dwindled to a barely visible swirl.

She had never run this hard in her life. Signs of civilization had to exist. But where?

The forest floor broke away from under her feet, sending Kadsa and her scream down a ravine. Needles and pegs on the jungle floor poked and scraped her body, as she crashed violently against a fallen giant tree near the bottom of the valley. She was in the worst, body numbing pain of her life as she crumpled against the tree, almost grateful for its support. She could've stayed there forever, just soaking up her pain but the creatures swarmed atop the ravine.

Were they this desperate for a meal? To her horror, one of the creatures leaned over the edge and peered down, looking *for her*. She stiffened, hoping with all her heart that they wouldn't spot her, but with those bright eyes, she doubted it.

More of them came to stand atop the hill. The horrendous, cringe-inducing growling started.

The rowdy creatures began their descent down the hill.

Kadsa backed up against the giant tree, trying to hoist herself over it, only for her hands to fall through the dry rotted bark. A desperate thought entered her head, and with no time even to run, she dove into the rotted interior, fighting her disgust as wet, rotted foliage swallowed her, some even getting into her clothes and mouth. Crawling over dead leaves and grime, she dug deep into the trunk, hating everything about this moment, but knowing she had to survive. She wouldn't just die here in nowhere land.

The creatures assaulted the tree, tearing and clawing at every angle. Parts of it collapsed, nearly burying her. Fire, she needed some fire to ward them off. Reaching for the lighter in her pocket, she pushed the flame to the dull crystal, willing it to flood with light under her breath.

Nothing was happening.

The creatures pounded against another weak spot in the bark. It caved.

Kadsa crawled deeper into the tree, stopping when she realized the bottom half had collapsed, blocking her path forward.

She reached for the lighter again, struggling to get it to even produce a tongue of fire. Frustrated, she made to throw it until a thought seeped into her brain. Desperate, sure, but a thump in the tree alerted her to the presence of the ghastly creatures breaching the space. She wasn't ready to be food, not yet.

Kadsa scuttled to her right and pushed the foliage toward the noisy creatures, whose moldy stench clogged up the already smelly bark. Satisfied with the distance, she fiddled with the lighter, willing it to work. "Don't fail me now," she said, holding her breath. A meager flame sparked, and she moved with as much care as she could muster in the given situation, setting the fire to the foliage. The rotted bark blazed. Crawling to the other side, she frantically brushed away the dead leaves and bark, stifling a scream when she spotted the silver white eyes of one of the creatures.

Kadsa had been holding on to the lighter's trigger for dear life, keeping the flame alive, and in a quick gesture, she pushed the lighter toward the foliage before the growling creature could leap her way. A strip of fire ran toward the creature. It leaped from the tree.

The sound of the screeching beasts, whatever they even were, was music to her ears. She eased back, taking a quick breath, only to inhale smoke.

The flames consumed the rotted tree at an alarming pace. Realizing she could burn, too, Kadsa banged her fists against the rotted bark above her head to break it open. It wouldn't budge, so she threw herself on her back and kicked at the bark until it broke away. She dove from the tree and began a quick roll about the ground to put out the fire on her clothes and bag.

When at last she wasn't ablaze, she looked up. The tree was a raging fire. The creatures retreated a good distance, their eyes focused on the fire.

The crystal glowed again.

Kadsa spotted the yellow flame of its core. Maybe the lighter was too small a source. She was so confused, as she again fixed her eyes on the burning log. The inferno could spread throughout the forest. She needed to get out of this place, wherever this was. More bright eyes descended on the scene. They were everywhere, though none came her way, too enthralled by the blaze. Alongside the crackling of the flame and the growls, the sounds of other creatures ricocheted throughout the woods, as if the forest was waking up.

Nothing existed but the forest, for miles, with a single exception. The reddish peaks of cliffs loomed a great distance to her right. *The Tibesti plateaus*, she thought excitedly. Maybe she wasn't that far away after all. Just a sleight of hand trick had propelled her here. She could find her way back.

Kadsa adjusted her partly burned backpack. It was salvageable. She had gotten it way back in Niger, made by tribespeople from natural indigo dye and not the fake factory-manufactured stuff they sold in stores. The color had faded some, but it was still in one piece. She had only a few things in it—some fruity chewable, a wooden water bottle that was all but depleted, a notebook that she hadn't written in in ages, and not much else.

Kadsa adjusted the bag. A few steps toward the direction of the cliffs, one of the Bright Eyes jumped out from among the group and into her path. She stumbled, gripping the crystal as if it were a weapon.

The animal paused outside of the glow's shrinking range.

"My name is Seth," said the animal in a hushed, calm voice.

Kadsa didn't panic, not as she thought she would've. This was as she suspected. These ghastly creatures had some intelligence. Well, this was more than intelligence. They could speak. Then why were they trying to gobble her down?

"Listen to me very carefully," said Seth with a mouth that moved unnaturally to form words, and white eyes focused on her. "Very soon, they won't be distracted.

Then they will come after you again. Please come with me. I will take you to safety."

"And why should I trust you?" she fired off.

"I have nothing else but my words. But I am telling you the truth."

"I think I'll take my chances on my own." "You are the only human here. It is foolhardy."

"Where were you when your friends were attacking me?" she fired off, somewhat angry. "Why didn't you say something then?"

"I was not with them. I am here now." "I'll still go it alone," she said walking off. He trailed her. "Please let me help you."

"Why?" she asked, and then considered. "How?" "I can bring you to your kind."

She stopped walking and faced him. "My kind?" "Humans."

"You just said I'm the only human here."

"Yes, I did. I only mean in the woods… these forests.

But, there is a place where humans are."

Kadsa glanced off toward the plateaus and bluffs. "Those look like the Tibesti Plateaus. That's where I'm going. Is that where you mean?"

Seth didn't look in the direction she stared. He took a careful step forward. "It is a region called Bourchul. There is no life there or anywhere in this forest," he said in a resigned tone.

"There has to be something—some other place." "Only Mehronur," he said, taking another step forward, still avoiding the light. "Listen to me." His white eyes pinned her. "You must come with me at this moment, before the witch's army shows up."

"There's a witch here?"

"I will explain on the way," he said, "Just walk beside me."

Kadsa studied him, feeling he was genuine. In her heart, she had suspected that the cliffs looked too good to be true, and then, seeing she had little choice, she said, "Lead the way, Seth."

"Thank you," Seth said and jumped ahead of her, leading her from the scene of the fire. She had many questions about him as she trailed him from the valley into the woods. As the light of the crystal faded, the distance between them dwindled. He nearly reached her chest, despite being on all fours. The sound of howls broke the woods, and Kadsa swallowed her fear that the creatures were ready to torment her again.

"What are they saying?" she asked, while Seth remained visible in the light before her.

"Many things—none of which is important," he answered dismissively.

"Can they all speak like you?"

"Yes, but not all of them are decent—blame the darkness."

"Why were they following me?" "You give off heat."

"What does that mean exactly?" She pushed.

"No one has seen a human in a very long time—not here," he said and exhaled loudly.

When they broke a corner, Kadsa glanced behind them to see if the rowdy creatures followed. No bright eyes were visible except for Seth's. The spread of the crystal's light had dwindled into the core, but she could still make out things in the dark. The crystal had enhanced her eyesight. How long the effect would last, she didn't know.

Some time into their walk, barking and growls erupted through the forest, echoing behind them in the distance. Seth paused.

"What is it?" she asked, knowing this couldn't be good.

"Please get on my back," he said.

"What? I don't think so. I'm perfectly capable of walking," she said, even as her feet burned from all the walking and running she had been doing so far and she could use a break.

"The journey to Mehronur will be faster if you get on my back."

Kadsa hesitated, feeling queasy about it.

"You almost died. This isn't the time for stubbornness."

Kadsa sighed and climbed onto his back. It wasn't comfortable. She pondered for a second if this was a buzoa, the creature Grandpa had told her about. The buzoa had horns. But he never said anything about it being able to speak.

The second she grabbed Seth's upturned horns, he raced off into the deep blackness.

6

STRANGER

Kadsa hissed in pain when a thorny vine grazed her arm as the creature pushed through a narrow bushy path. She couldn't ask him to slow down or not use paths with thorny vines and brambles. He'd already lectured her on using well-traversed paths--not safe.

Still, traveling on its back was rough on her. "Are you alright?" the creature called back.

"Yes," she said, refusing to complain about her discomfort. So far, he'd been answering all her questions. She'd been struggling to understand the context of what they had discussed. From what she gathered, this was Marut. Grandpa Edoje had spent his whole life trying to find this homeland. Okay. Why was it so dark? She pushed. A Dark Enchantment, he explained. Seth went on to extrapolate about a sorceress obsessed with power who had cast a destructive darkness over the land.

"The wilderness was not always like this. Once, there were people, towers and sunlight," he explained in a sad, woeful tone.

Kadsa was having a hard time accepting all of this, though considering all the stories her grandpa told her, it should be easy.

Once she was no longer a child obsessed with her grandpa's stories, she became a skeptic. She kept it all to herself because she didn't want to hurt her grandpa. Now she was here and having a hard time accepting it.

"How long until we get there?" she asked, changing the topic.

"Not much longer."

Kadsa had felt they'd been traveling forever. When he declared they were out of danger, she had requested to walk and he obliged. A few times, she had let down her guard with him only to panic when she remembered that she wasn't speaking with a person but a creature. This was especially true now that the light in the crystal had vanished and she relied exclusively on his voice and eyes to guide her.

"I will not harm you, girl," Seth had said during one of those moments when she had expressed horror at his sudden movements, "You are Abnr's gift. We have been waiting forever for you to come."

"Abnr's Gift?" She winced, hoping he wouldn't notice. Those bright eyes saw everything.

"Yes, the patron god of wisdom," he said.

Seth reminded Kadsa of Grandpa Edoje. She had a vague knowledge of the gods of Marut, though the one her grandpa cited and spoke of the most was Ataro, god of doorways—the most important.

"Don't take this the wrong way," she said as they marched on through the woods, pushing away brambles, bushes, and vines along the way, "But, how are you able to speak?"

His eyes squinted, as if the question was insulting. "Jakubas are *naturally* intelligent."

"Your species is called the Jakuba?" she asked, ignoring the way he emphasized natural, as if to imply something she was to consider.

"Around these parts, yes."

"Animals that talk. This is strangely wild and interesting."

"I am not an animal." He picked up his stride, harrying her along.

"Hey, I'm sorry. Slow down. Didn't mean to insult you," she said.

"That's alright," he said, obeying.

Why was he so offended by being considered a talking animal? The answer seemed somewhat invasive, and so she didn't question him further. She kept one hand on his upturned horn as he guided her through the forest toward some place he called The Divide.

After he'd sensed *something* in the woods, the Jakuba had started moving at increased speed again, desperate to reach the other side of the woods, convinced it was the witch and her minions. Her feet were starting to burn but, she wouldn't return to his back.

He insisted they were close to Mehronur each time she slowed. Kadsa fantasized about clean drinking water, since the pond they'd drank from had twigs.

"There is sunlight on the other side of the trees," he said, when she rubbed her arms and trembled. She wore only a T-shirt and wished she had stuffed the robe in her backpack.

"Why are you helping me?" she asked the question that had weighed on her for some time. "I mean, your friends were trying to eat me."

"They are not my friends," he said in a quick, dry tone, his bright eyes darting to her when he spoke. She liked his eyes now. More than their brightness was an innate intelligence. And his voice, too. He sounded wise, an older gentleman with what her grandfather had dubbed, *character*.

"I didn't mean to offend," she said.

"Perhaps not."

Kadsa wondered what his deal was. He seemed overly sensitive and clearly out of sync with his own kind. Why was he really helping her?

"You should know, I am helping you because I vowed to do so," he said quietly, moments later, as if he could read her thoughts. "It was my promise to Abnr, god of light, patron god of Mehronur. An oath on the kingdom's heart."

She had not a clue what any of this meant, but he sounded sincere. Kadsa scratched her throat. "You said I was Abnr's gift. What does that mean?"

His bright eyes found her again. "You are sent by the god, Abnr to banish the darkness and save the kingdom." Kadsa almost choked. Her throat was so dry and felt like she had twigs in it from that dirty water. "Darkness is part of nature. I cannot banish what is natural."

Seth stopped walking and faced her. "It has to be you. You are the first human to walk the dark forest in forty seasons."

"That's a long time, I guess?"

"A very long time—years, by your calendar. Time passes differently here."

Kadsa nodded along but only thought that this was right in line with Grandpa Edoje always claiming she was special. Aside from self-proclaiming herself the master of the board game Akuto, she didn't feel smart or special. That this Jakuba thought she could help his dark kingdom was scary. But she thought, maybe something went wrong. Grandpa Edoje had mentioned that he'd made a promise to the kingdom—that's why he had to return, that he needed to help it. They were expecting a savior and that was to be him. But where was he?

"I'm looking for my grandfather," she said. "I think he's here somewhere."

"You are the only human I have sensed in this forest of darkness."

"Is there a chance he could be in Mehronur?" "Perhaps. But, you are the only human in the forest." "My grandpa might be from around here," she said, uncomfortable with the hint of responsibility in his words. "He was trying to return. He believed he had to save his kingdom from some doom. Maybe you are confusing me for him. But if I can find him, maybe he can help you."

Seth looked away and by default disappeared from her view. Then his bright eyes found her again. "Do you speak Maruti?"

"Not really. When I was younger, I spoke a little. I lost the grasp of it. Why?"

Seth's white eyes narrowed on her. "You have the right acumen. I know Great Abnr sent you to help us. You are a godtalker."

She waited to speak until after they squeezed through a narrow pathway of shrubs. "My grandfather used that term. I don't really understand what it means."

He breathed loudly. "Only that you can understand the innate forces of the gods."

"Magic, you mean?" she asked.

"If you see it as such," he responded. She sniggered. "Can you read minds?"

"No. I cannot explain how I know your language. I just have a gift for knowing things."

"I came here because my grandfather went missing. I came to find him and make sure he is okay. Then I go home."

The Jakuba pondered. "I do suppose Ataro would re-open the doorway for you."

Kadsa stopped herself from raising her voice in protest. He refused to accept what she was saying. She wasn't here to save a kingdom, only to find her grandpa and head home.

Seth flinched and stopped walking.

"Is it the witch?" she asked, concerned. Even just saying that word, *witch*, made her cringe. People had thought her grandpa was a witch-doctor, and she had seen her share of Bruni practitioners in her seventeen years. Most were dishonest. The shaman of the Yedina had gotten her into this mess, maybe her grandfather, too. What did a witch of Marut mean?

"That, too, but more importantly, we are at The Divide," Seth explained.

All Kadsa saw was darkness and trees. Where was the majestic kingdom he'd been blabbing about?

"The Divide lies behind these trees," he explained, eyes darting toward the bushes ahead of him.

Kadsa again believed he could read thoughts, at least expressions. "Then we should do this," she said, taking a deep breath. She'd been in this bizarrely dark place long enough. It was cold and she trembled.

Seth parted the bushes, while Kadsa adjusted her knapsack. She took two deep breaths before pushing through the trees and deep into the clearing on the other side of the dark forest. The warmth was instant, as if she'd been deprived a lifetime of sunshine until this moment. The warmth of the sun was so refreshing that she closed her eyes and allowed it to work wonders underneath her skin.

Basking in the sun, keeping her eyes shut for so long, she almost forgot the Jakuba was behind her. Then he scuffled. She faced him, expecting him to be right beside her, only to find that he lingered in the bushes. It was a good thing she didn't cower easily, because all she saw when she stared back were a pair of feral silver-white eyes watching her amidst blackness.

"Why are you back there?" she asked, even if she knew the answer. The sunlight.

"I cannot leave the Dark Forest. If I cross over, I will combust."

"That's horrible."

"Yes," he agreed, and then his eyes dipped, as if he wanted to hide a painful memory or thought.

"This is where I leave you then?" She asked.

"We may meet again, if the ley of the land is rebalanced—if Abnr is redeemed." He seemingly considered more. "What matters is that you restore the light to its full glory with as much haste as you can. If you can do that, I will hope for a reunion."

Kadsa nodded, even when she wanted to reiterate that she was no savior. Retrieving her problematic grandpa was the only reason she was here. "I guess this is goodbye then?"

"Yes, this is goodbye … for now," Seth spoke in a softened tone.

Kadsa seized up a little bit. "Thank you for helping me."

"You're welcome," he said. "May Ataro guide you on this journey."

She pressed her lips into a smile, understanding the reference too well. Grandpa certainly prepared her for this trip, more than she had realized. She glanced to the sky, looking past the rainbow dome that bled into the blackness. There was a kingdom, and even the two suns that seemingly overlapped. There were no stars.

Whoever Ataro was, may he guide her indeed, *and her grandpa*. He was the most important. Then she narrowed her eyes on the walled kingdom buried at the belly of the meadow. *Grandpa, here I come*, she thought and stormed off.

———

Kadsa dropped to her knees within ten feet of the mudbrick wall. *Finally made it.* The distance from the forest to the wall had been longer than she'd anticipated. But, if what Seth said was true, on the other side of this imposing red mudbrick wall was civilization, maybe a bed to lie down on, and water to ease her thirst. She studied the wall—really examining its intricacies. Kadsa's shoulders slumped, and she groaned loudly. Hopelessness stifled her excitement. The wall stretched on both sides of the meadow with not even a hint of a gate or any other means to get through it.

The sun, along with its eclipsed twin, hung so very low in the sky, she believed she could reach up and tug them down—if only to snuff them out and end the unbearable heat scorching her skin. She had a flash of memory of Seth calling them, sasaan. They overlapped. Freaky physics. She'd never seen anything like this before. But she wasn't in her world anymore.

This was Marut.

When she looked at the darkness, she gasped. It loomed like a storm cloud. Another thing ... and she stopped breathing when she realized this ... the darkness looked *alive.* It stirred and seemingly crawled forward. Watching it, and heeding its threat, her whole body filled up with dread. She did not want to stay in this meadow any longer. Kadsa picked herself up with renewed motivation.

The mudbrick wall stood around twenty feet high. They clearly built it to separate whatever was on the interior from the forest. *More reason to get on the other side.* The perimeters of the wall stretched out of view and the sun was so blisteringly hot she didn't want to risk collapsing from heatstroke while circling it to find a gate. *No, not going to happen.* Nevertheless, she needed to get beyond it, and that meant her only option was to climb. Kadsa buckled the waist straps of her bag and stretched her arms and legs. Climbing had been a hobby when she was little. She had scaled trees and even the fence of a church once. *She could do this.*

The wall wasn't pristine. When she rubbed her hands over it, dirt rolled off. Kadsa kicked the structure to create holes and used them to anchor her feet while she lifted herself up. A second after hoisting herself up, she slid down the wall's surface, scraping the skin of her left arm in the process. This wasn't like scaling a fence at all.

She kicked the wall even harder, creating more holes in it. She nearly broke her toes doing it. Kadsa's fingers crimped and throbbed with searing pain when she buried them into the wall. Her weak muscles strained. Her scrawny arms trembled with the effort exerted to pull herself upward. *Don't look down, don't look down,* she repeated with each pull upward. Her muscles felt as if they'd pull apart, but she ignored the aches and limitations of her body.

Just push on, she told herself.

Kadsa clawed her way to the top of the wall and let out a loud cry of triumph when her whole body was on the surface. She took a few minutes just to collect her breath. While sprawled out atop the narrow ledge, her whole body pressing against the surface, she dared to look over to the other side. An unkempt garden filled with withered twigs, rotted vegetation, and bricks. Above the garden, small mudbrick houses dotted the landscape, and a long red dirt road slanted upward between the houses.

Signs of civilization.

Kadsa's heart skipped and then stopped abruptly with the realization that she'd have to climb to the bottom as she had climbed to the top. *Just no easy way to do this, is there?* She couldn't sit there forever, so she took a deep breath and balanced her upper body on her elbows while her lower half hung over the wall. Her feet sought to kick holes on the inside of the wall as she'd done before but her grip loosened, and her arms strained in a weak effort to hold up her weight.

Down with all this. Kadsa held her breath and then let go. She fell on her back into the patchy garden. Twigs and thorns slashed and poked her all over, but all her limbs were still working. Lying crippled on her back, she focused on the unnaturally colored yellow and orange glow of the sky. Twinkles of stars dotted here and there. *Strange. Beautiful. Alien.*

The sound of movements reeled her focus back to her present situation. When she twisted her head toward the top of the garden, she spotted two human faces peering down on her. Boys. Maybe about twelve. *Real people.*

"Hey?" she called out.

They watched her with curious eyes.

Kadsa sat upright amidst a rush of sharp aches in her lower back. "Hey, can you help me?"

The boys glanced at each other with wide eyes and then ran away.

"Hey, don't run!" She shouted after them, but they were gone. She got to her feet, plucked out the small pebbles that had lodged themselves into her skin, and dusted off her clothes. The scrapes that covered her arms stung, and the flesh of her back, but nothing was broken. She was on the other side of the wall. She made it!

Maybe these people—whoever they were—could help her.

There were no signs of the boys in the garden. Abandoned mudbrick houses sat on both sides of the dirt road, but that was all. Kadsa was worried something was wrong—maybe she'd come too late to help them. Her mind returned to the boys. They were people—she was certain of it. She just had to walk a little farther.

Minutes into her walk, the sights remained more of the same—houses clustered in large shared yards. Some were brightly painted with geometric designs, while others were basic clay or mudbrick homes with thatched roofs. Kadsa leaned over the fence of one of the yards. Only clay pots and dry weeds. No people.

She walked some more, tempering her mood about the lack of residents. More empty houses. *More reasons to worry.* She admired a pasture filled with emaciated cattle and a pen filled with equally half-starved fowls. Signs of life. One factor remained the same: no people. Where was everyone? Had it not been for the boys she first saw, she'd think it was an abandoned kingdom.

King Remu watched the gathering in the courtyard from the safety of the palace. Mothers, fathers, children, elderly people with slumped postures, and even laborers who otherwise should not be here. Not even the blistering heat deterred them. Somehow, the news had spread against his desire to control it. The gatherers chatted and paced, grumbling louder than the last time they'd filled the public courtyard.

King Remu had addressed them only a week ago. They had demanded answers about the sundial debacle in the great temple that had predicted an earlier-than- normal flooding season. The clumsy watchman in charge of the disk claimed it had chimed by accident. The citizens believed it to be by design. Its single stroke had moved within an inch of the flooding season and sent everyone into a frenzy. Crops were uprooted early. Farmers were angry about the impending devastation of yet-ripened crops.

Answers, answers, answers, they'd shouted.

King Remu knew what had brought the crowd out again so soon. He was even more anxious about facing them this time around. Two days ago, a washerwoman had brought word to the palace that she had seen light near the dark border of the kingdom. A vizier had accused her of lying. She'd spat angrily at his feet and the guards had arrested her. Yesterday, others had come forward to support the woman's claims. They too had seen *something* in the dark sky. King Remu had to release the washerwoman. Now a crowd gathered in Paraa Hutat's public courtyard, demanding to hear from their king about the rumors.

What would he tell them?

The kingdom's people had grown restless. Their frustrations were palpable. The nights had gotten darker. King Remu had pondered if the growing darkness could change a man's very soul. Had the nearing night agitated his people more than he'd realized? He sympathized with his subjects more than he could let them know. The warmth of the sun against their skin didn't change the fact that it waned. The dome had been safe all these years, but it kept them imprisoned. The comfort in these things they'd trusted was quickly fading.

What to tell the flocks of people noisily crowding the courtyard? Bokor should have answers. Where was his appointed advisor? He'd been waiting too long. Soon, he'd have to face the crowd.

King Remu paced up and down the veranda. He was mindful of the guards' curious eyes but could not stand in one place. He stilled only when the sound of soft footsteps reached his ears. Queen Oluchi walked from the interior of the palace. King Remu straightened up when she looked his way. He couldn't let her see him slump.

"My love," Queen Oluchi called, lowering her head in reverence. His wife's neck was so slender he worried it would snap off with the weight of her heavy bell- shaped headdress of cloth and gold spirals. "Bokor has arrived."

"Bring him here," King Remu said to the guard nearest the hall entrance. His eyes followed the guard until he disappeared.

Queen Oluchi faced the courtyard. The blistering heat created sun glares above the crowd. "I have not seen them like this before."

"They are convinced this time." "I hope they're right."

"All the other times they weren't right."

Queen Oluchi's soft face creased with lines of worry. He expected her to argue against his pessimism. She only watched him.

Heavy footsteps accompanied by clacks against the marble floor alerted them to the arrival of company. The guard he'd sent out returned with Bokor trailing at a comfortable distance. Though leaning on a staff and standing taller and fatter than any man in the city, Bokor walked with smooth agility.

King Remu tried to decipher the man's expression when he stopped in front of him. Aside from the arrogance and pride that were his natural disposition, the medicine man showed little emotion underneath his white face paint, caked on so heavily it had become a mask.

"You're late," said King Remu, facing his advisor.

"I was looking into the evidence as per your request, Divine King," said Bokor dryly.

"Well, what have you concluded?"

"The people who delivered this news may not be correct."

King Remu's shoulders softened.

"How have you determined this?" Queen Oluchi asked.

"Nothing has aligned in our favor," said Bokor dismissively. "The disturbance must have been a mockery of the witch."

"And you know this for certain?" King Remu asked, settling into his chair.

"What the ancestors tell me has yet to turn out untrue," said Bokor.

"What do you suppose I tell my subjects?" King Remu motioned to the crowd. The restless gatherers shouted in the palace courtyard.

"You tell them that what they saw was not real, your majesty."

Queen Oluchi scowled, and though she faced King Remu, she said nothing.

"I don't like letting my subjects down," King Remu muttered.

"What good is lying to them, Divine King?" Bokor's blackened lips pushed together in a hiss of mockery. "Perhaps, you know better than I do about how the godtalker gift works." His bushy white brows lifted in scrutiny. "Have you received a new insight?"

King Remu pondered the witch-doctor's sharp words. "I have not had any visions."

King Remu had the gift of divine visions once. After the initial insight of Abnr's Gift, he had failed to receive others and had assumed that either the light was dying or he was.

"I do not think this sign is false, my king," Queen Oluchi said defiantly.

Bokor shifted his weight uncomfortably on the staff so he could face the young queen. "I don't need to remind you, *high queen*," he started, "I have access to the world of the Akonadi and the Orisas. It is unwise to doubt my knowledge."

Queen Oluchi did not flinch when she faced King Remu. "My king," she started with a soft voice, "we must not be so quick to dismiss the beliefs of your people as fraudulent. If so many people believe in the sign in the sky they claimed to have seen, then maybe we should trust them. At the very least, we should wait to see if the sign will come again."

Bokor scoffed but did not respond.

"I will express my doubt and my caution to them," King Remu said after considering. He stood and wobbled, causing Queen Oluchi to step forward. He waved her off. "I'm all right."

The royal guards flanked him at his command, following him at a measured distance as he made his way toward the courtyard.

Queen Oluchi trailed them. Bokor hesitated but stepped in line behind Queen Oluchi and the royal guards.

The crowd cheered when King Remu appeared on the courtyard platform. He raised his hand and they fell into silence.

"My people." His emotions were restrained. "I suppose you all know why I am here." His eyes roamed over the gatherers. Hundreds of people packed the public courtyard. "Many of you have reportedly seen a sign. A flaming sign, you say; red like the fires of Amut. I do not dispute your observations."

The crowd shuffled and whispered among themselves.

"Many of you believe the sign you saw came from Abnr. I do not deny you this belief. I want to believe it. However," he lifted his hand to quiet the bickering crowd. "We must exercise caution. We must be patient. We must not rush to make judgments about this sign. I do not deny your faith, but I ask that you remain vigilant until stronger evidence comes. That is all I ask of you, as your king."

"And as our divine king," said an old man standing near the front of the courtyard, "Will you also grant us the pleasure of seeing the heir to the throne?"

The people nearest the man clapped.

King Remu stayed cool. He was familiar with this mouthy old man. His name was Asau. He once worked as a cook in the kitchen of Paraa Hutat. Before that, he had been a storyteller.

"My son," said King Remu, glancing to his wife, "he is working on his lessons at this hour."

"We mean your *first* born!" Asau called out. "You don't let us see that one. You hide him in the dungeons. The cursed child the son of night."

King Remu wilted, holding his breath. This old man was a troublemaker. Who had put him up to this line of interrogation?

"What you speak is blasphemous, storyteller…" "You lie to us, King!" shouted Asau, brazen.

People clapped and cheered. A scuffle broke out and two guards grabbed the old man and another man. The crowd booed and jeered at the guards who stood between them and King Remu.

King Remu dismissed the guards. They reluctantly released Asau, eyeing the king as if he was mad—after all, this was a great disrespect. King Remu knew it. He was never the king of executions, and in his old age, he'd rather not become that king. But the guards expected him to at least imprison this brazen old man. "Release the old man," he said, surprising all around him, including the old man himself.

King Remu took a deep breath. "You want answers, I know," he spoke more forcefully. "As your king, I want answers, too. Mehronur is most loved by us, loved by the gods. We must not resort to savagery and cruelty. We must not fight amongst ourselves. We must not falsely spread blame.

"Now is the time for us to stand tall, proud, and united. This is a test. Our humanity, our reason, our existence—it's all being tested. Night may be all around, but we are not its children. We are still Abnr's people, all of us." His eyes roamed over the crowd, catching the scowling, Asau. "It seems strange that I should tell you to be patient. But I am asking you to stay calm. You say you saw a sign. Well, we'll wait and see what becomes of it."

"Wait, wait, wait," Asau blurted out. "All we ever do is wait. Time is running out. How much longer can we wait? You don't even know how much time we have left, do you, King?"

The crowd grumbled in agreement. "Show us Amunu!" Asau chanted.

Others soon joined in on the chant and it spread throughout the courtyard.

Amunu – night's son. The insolence of referring to his child as *night's son.* King Remu bit back against his anger. The memory of the baby lying on the mortuary bed filled his mind. That child's life had been a mystery to him as the gods themselves were. How dare these people?

"The child is gone… taken in death," he said quietly, almost to himself.

Only Asau seemed to have heard. "No, he isn't. I've seen him myself."

"If you say another lie, I will arrest you for treason." "Bring us Amunu!" Asau shouted. The old cook looked seemingly pleased with his disobedience, and the disrespect infuriated King Remu. Arresting him would cause even more problems. The crowd was clearly on his side. King Remu needed to get them on his side. "Silence!" King Remu yelled.

"Bring us Amunu!" "I said, silence!"

A wave of quiet washed over the public courtyard. The projected strength of his voice astounded King Remu. It had waned in potency in the last decade. On some days, he could barely utter a word beyond a whisper, a testament to his declining health.

"You want us to wait for our deaths!" Asau yelled. "We are not waiting for our deaths!" King Remu clutched his chest and gritted his teeth when he felt a small pinch in his heart. "We are waiting for the sign you said you saw. That's why we're here. That's what you came for—not silly superstitions," he said in a strong voice. Fever grew inside of him, but he willed himself to stay on his feet with raised shoulders.

"Now, if you will excuse me, I'll return to the palace to plan for the arrival of the hero Abnr has sent us. Good day to you all."

The crowd grumbled unhappily, but he turned his back on them, still clutching his chest. Queen Oluchi rushed to be at his side, falling in step with him. Bokor trailed. His painted face showed what King Remu could only describe as smugness.

———

Kadsa broke a corner of the kingdom to the unmistakable sound of hooves trampling down the dirt road. Four men rode in her direction. Her eyes darted between the riders and the animals they mounted. The horse that wasn't a horse, more like a zebra, but stockier with yellow stripes that covered its face and ran down its stomach before ending at its lower back. Abadas were real. Grandpa spoke about them, along with buzoas. For years, she'd wanted an abada. Too young to have known better, she'd believed him, and when she began sketching, all she drew were striped unicorns. And everyone thought she had this great imagination when really it was Grandpa who'd planted the thoughts there. He was right.

Nervous and excited, she waited. All the absent people she couldn't find before suddenly crawled out of nowhere. Within no time, a small crowd descended on her.

The riders were regally dressed in red and brown leather tunics overlaid with mahogany red scarves that masked their heads and their faces. Only their eyes and brown leather headbands were visible underneath their scarves.

The riders dismounted the abadas. She smiled at the sight of the animals, but soon peered up on the serious face of one of the warriors.

He must be the leader. "Hi?" Her eyes dropped to his hands hovering near the weapons in his thick waist belt. The hilts of his four knives dazzled in the goldenness of day. All four men had knives in their waist belts, and their fingers all touched the hilts as they swarmed her.

Kadsa straightened her shoulders and relaxed her face with a smile, so as not to look scared or threatening. *This might be a matter of life and death.*

The leader's dark eyes inspected hers with suspicion.

"*A-na Jiro Sion. Lati a-re.*"

She shook her head—"I don't understand."

His dark eyes narrowed under thick eyelashes and brows and all she could focus on was his intense look. He didn't exactly look friendly.

"*Fi a-ru da?*"

Kadsa shook her head. "I don't understand."

The words flew out of his mouth rapidly and all she could do was shake her head and make faces.

An older woman pushed through the crowd and grabbed her hand, dropping to her knees. *"Ja' Abnr"* were the only words from the woman's lips that Kadsa somewhat understood.

"Ja' Abnr," said Kadsa, pointing to herself. She believed the words meant "Abnr's Gift." Seth had used those words in the forest. Looking back, maybe she should've asked more questions about this kingdom when she had the chance. For some reason, she'd assumed these people would understand her. Seth had.

One of the armed men pulled the woman away. The leader narrowed his eyes on Kadsa. *"Fi a-ru da?"* *"Ja' Abnr,"* she answered. The words weren't smooth on her tongue. She wanted to ask for shelter, food, and water. It frustrated her that she couldn't find words to say what she really wanted. Grandpa had spoken to her in Maruti when she was younger, but somewhere along the way, she'd lost interest in the language and he didn't force the issue.

More people crowded them to watch the spectacle. A few people touched her, tugging on the sleeves of her T-shirt, while others gossiped and murmured. The armed men circled her, barring people from coming near. She struggled to keep her composure.

"Shiru!" Two of the guards shouted at the crowd.

"A-ru wa," said the leader of the armed men. When she failed to reply, he grabbed her by the arm with a firm grip.

"Hey! This is not necessary." Kadsa fastened her eyes on his metal cuffs, imprinted with the insignia of a circlet with a sword running through it. *These are officials. Maybe they wouldn't hurt her.*

Seth gave her the impression these people would welcome her. His grip was tight, not welcoming at all. She tried wiggling from him to no avail.

"I'll come with you, okay? Just ease up a little."

The leader shoved her into the arms of two of the men behind him, and Kadsa glared at him angrily. He uttered a quick command and the warrior lifted her off the ground.

"Hey! Come on!" She struggled against their grips but they dragged her to the yellow-striped zebra.

"Fine then." She flashed his hand away.

The leader climbed on behind her and barked at the crowd before riding off.

The animal trampled down the dirt road toward wherever. Kadsa held her breath. During the short but bumpy ride, her eyes flashed over everything within her view. The houses got more clustered. More people and more stares. The noise level increased. Kadsa started to relax a little. Everything looked civilized, albeit ancient, like buildings she'd seen in Egypt and Timbuktu.

When they arrived at what she assumed to be a public courtyard, she spotted a palatial compound, partially carved out of natural rocks—maybe limestone or some other glittery rock. Towers with cone-shaped roofs made out of similar rocks spread out on all sides of the courtyard. Stunning—all of it. This must be where the important people lived.

The warriors steered their mounted animals toward the palace grounds. Kadsa held her breath, partly hoping she'd get to step inside this majestic wonder. A small gathering of about six people stood on the terrace. A worried-looking middle-aged man dressed in an indigo blue robe and wearing a small gold diadem on his head stood with his hands clasped in front of him. *A king, perhaps?* Standing beside him was a slender woman, beautifully dressed in similar blue garments and matching headdress. The woman looked to be in her early thirties. She could've been the man's daughter, but Kadsa suspected she was his wife because of how close to him she stood.

Flanking the two people were several men with broad-blade knives or curved swords tucked into their waist belts. They wore the same reddish-brown tunics as the warriors manhandling her right about now, and they looked downright serious.

Kadsa's emotions see-sawed between relief and fear as the men pulled her off the abada and began dragging her toward the terrace.

"I can walk!" she yelled, but they didn't care. Nearing the palace, taking in the very different looks of its inhabitants, Kadsa thought to herself, *Whatever happens, stay cool.*

7

ASAMANDO

Familiar barks ruffled the stillness of the forest. A horde of aggressive Jakuba jumped from the bushes and crashed into Seth.

"Hello, old friend." Taroq spoke in a hostile tone. "Friend? You're no friend of mine."

Taroq's minions—Khoum, Auks, and Edu circled him. How intimidating, Seth thought, and proceeded to ignore them. He was used to this from them and it didn't matter anymore.

"I hear you've been busy, moving back and forth through this forest," Taroq spoke accusingly. "Do you know something we don't?"

"I know many things you don't." Seth shrugged dismissively and pressed on.

Taroq stomped a foot down in front of him to halt him.

"We suspect you have a new companion."

"My only companion is that scarecrow you brought to keep my company," Seth admitted, knowing that Taroq would easily remember the human-shaped stick figure he and his posse had set up a while back to torment him into thinking a human roamed the forest.

"Don't anger me!" Taroq barked. "How does it feel to be a traitor?"

Taroq tossed Seth to the ground and stood over him, his forelegs on either sides of his face. He growled. "You've been busy, haven't you, old boy?"

"No more than usual," Seth admitted.

Taroq released a small, flat, square-shaped object on Seth's chest. "Where's the owner of this device?"

"I have never seen that before," Seth declared. It was true, he had not. But he was confident it belonged to the girl. "Is that some new torture device from the witch's well?"

Auks kicked him.

He groaned, twisting with the pain. "Where is the stranger?" Taroq insisted. "Oh yes. I have no idea."

Taroq growled and gritted his teeth. "What are you doing so close to the shield?"

"Once in a while, I like to enjoy the view."

"You do, don't you? Well, we should take you back." Taroq said coldly. "Grab him."

———

The swampland was nothing Seth had seen before and everything he had dreadfully imagined it to be: cold and dead. It was darker than the rest of the forest, and he was sure of this. Towers of stone and wood bled into one another with nothing to distinguish nature's work from that of the witch's minions. Lean and ghoulish fortresses swayed with unnatural stirrings, and thick, intertwined vines formed cocoons that seemingly trapped animals on the inside.

A dark pool sat in the center of the swamps. Howling caves circled the ground and even they looked spun from magical darkness. He had never bothered to step foot in Asamando in all his years in the forest, and he had vowed never to do so. Even before the enchantment, Seth had known Asamando was the final resting place of anyone who dared to find it. When the darkness upended his life, he decided right away to resist Akwanshi and protest the takeover by avoiding the place.

Now, they forcibly brought him into the swampland, bound by a rope of vine. Taroq and his minions dropped his bruised body at the bottom of a cold stone platform. The stone seat near the cave informed him this was the witch's dark temple. It was a long time before he heard the bristling of the witch's movement.

The woman walked from the entrance of a high- mouth cave. His first thought was that she was a woman of tremendous height. If she hadn't moved, he would have mistaken her for one of the ghoulish towers. She shared the same coloring as the trees, wearing the pale green as if camouflaged.

The creatures, including oversized crows, jackals, hogs, and slimy serpentines, howled, barked and chittered until Akwanshi silenced them. It made him angry to hear Jakuba crying out alongside these real animals. It was a reminder of how they were losing their true essence.

Akwanshi settled down on the stone throne. "And what is this?" she asked.

Taroq kissed her hand and bowed at her feet, an act that disgusted Seth.

"My queen," Taroq spoke softly. "This is the traitor I told you about. Seth. He lives in the open forest."

"Traitor?" said the regal woman, glaring at him through pool-black eyes.

"Yes, my queen. He is a traitor to the Dark Goddess." "And how so? Have you committed a crime against Nenet, the goddess who serves you?"

"I have committed no more crimes against your deity than she has committed against me."

Akwanshi's expression was unmoved. "Tell me, *creature*." She pinned Seth with her dark beady eyes. "What crime has Nenet committed against *you*?"

"She destroyed my land. My home. She separated me from my family, my child. She has brought cold and dark to the land so most loved by all the gods. Nothing good comes from your reign. I spit on it."

Taroq kicked Seth and he groaned. He was about to kick him again, but Akwanshi lifted her hand. "So you think Nenet is a curse?"

"Marut has always been the land of Abnr. We are the *children of the light*."

Akwanshi stayed stern in the face. She kept her eyes on the Jakuba bound at her feet. "You have such naïve convictions about what is good and what is bad. It's almost charming."

The witch stood. "You are, in fact, a supporter of a dead deity. How sad. If you watch your tongue, you could live to see what a true god looks like and can really do."

"I will never become a servant of your god. I'd rather die first."

"What is this Jakuba's name?"

"It is Seth," answered Taroq acerbically. "He was once a chieftain of Elon. A Divine Warrior of Marut. He once led a rebellion against you during the first years of your reign, my queen." Taroq laughed coldly. "He still thinks he's a warrior, a high-ranked noble warrior at that. He's a joke who refuses to accept reality."

The spectators growled, howled, and barked their approval.

"How does it feel, knowing you're a turncoat?" Seth mocked Taroq.

Taroq gnawed at him angrily. The spectators barked in excitement.

"Silence!" Akwanshi's discordant voice washed over them.

Every creature fell silent. Even the trees stilled. Seth knew then that the rumors were true. He had heard the witch called herself Akwanshi because she hosted many spirits. The voice she used didn't belong to a single woman. It sounded like many voices woven together.

"Bring him closer," Akwanshi commanded. Auks and Edu dragged Seth to Akwanshi's feet.

"Servant of Abnr, I like your loyalty. I will make you an offer."

"I want none of your accursed promises, witch." Seth's words dripped in disgust.

"Lucky for you, I am in a good mood. The new age is soon upon us, after all."

"And it's about time," Taroq shouted. The creatures roared.

Akwanshi raised her hand and silenced them. "When the new age arrives, I want you to witness it. I want you to see me take the throne of Mehronur, become the immortal ruler. When I am—"

"It will never happen," Seth cut her off. "As we speak, Abnr's Gift is in Mehronur. She will stop it all from happening."

"Abnr's Gift, you say?" She replied, cocking her ear to him.

"My queen, I meant to tell you." Taroq stepped forward. "We arrested this scoundrel because we feared he allowed the stranger to pass through the land and cross The Divide. There was nothing we could do."

Akwanshi's angry eyes fixed on Seth. "A human stranger—is this true?"

"It is certainly true," Seth spoke happily. "On the heart of Abnr, I swear it. She is here. She came to restore the light."

"Did you say the stranger is a female?"

"I did and she will undo this curse you've brought upon us." He stared her down, believing wholeheartedly this was true. He had to believe.

A smile formed on the witch's lips. "We'll have to see, won't we? There are other ways to make sure night falls on Mehronur uninterrupted. Imprison him."

"Mistress, I think we should kill him now," Taroq interrupted. "He's been defiant since the beginning. There's no point in keeping him alive."

"Why did you not kill him before the stranger arrived?"

"We thought he was a fool. We had no idea what he was planning."

The witch mused over his words. "Keep him alive for now," said Akwanshi, getting to her feet. "He has information about the stranger that may prove useful to us. Torture him. Try to get it out of him."

Akwanshi turned away and disappeared into the opening of the cave.

"You see how much of a forgiving Queen Akwanshi is? You have one more chance," Taroq said before Edu and Auks dragged Seth down the stone platform and through the woods toward a dugout, surrounded by bones. The rotting corpses of the dead littered the boneyard, as did altars and stakes of sacrifice, torture chambers. Jackals and hyenas feasted on the remains of the dead.

The Jakuba kicked and beat Seth and demanded answers about the flat rectangular box, but he said nothing. They tossed him into a hovel in the cold ground, leaving him imprisoned in the underworld.

Seth lay wounded in the prison pit of Asamando, listening to the cries of other captured or tortured creatures. The thin dirt that served as barriers could barely shut out the moans and groans of the dying creatures. With his wounds, he'd die in this place. That was the reason for keeping creatures locked up in hell— to have them die painful, long-drawn-out deaths. He was in pain, broken even to reposition his body.

Kadsa, Seth thought. *Please try*. Soon it would be over—all of it.

Akwanshi quickly made her way to the conjuring room in the cave. There she stood over a wide-rimmed pot buried deep inside the ground. Hot black fluid boiled in the pot. She reached for a wooden bowl from the nearby stone table and poured a red powder into the cauldron.

She uttered the words of release that turned her black eyes deep red, channeling the magic of the herbs she'd ingested. She had been patiently allowing the days to wither away, waiting for judgment, and was certain no human stranger could pass through the land that served as a doorway between the mortal and underworld without first coming to her notice.

The land of night swept over the surface of the black fluid. Her eyes moved through the forest, searching for a bright light but finding none. Then her red eyes reached The Divide and then went black again. She mumbled the name below her breath: "Servant of Nenet."

He did not answer.

She poured more red powder into the bowl and her eyes burned again when she called to him, again, massaging the surface above the pot and creating air bubbles in the liquid. The pockets grew larger.

The kingdom of Mehronur came into her view, shrouded by a white cloud. She strained her eyes to make out the varied sights and sounds. More massaging made the bubbles grow larger, but she was careful not to stretch them too much, or else they'd pop and she'd lose the vision. A crowd gathered outside the main courtyard of Paraa Hutat, the royal house. The glimpses of daily life in the kingdom jumped. She pushed, trying to get inside to hear, but the visuals faltered and the bubbles in the pot simmered out.

Akwanshi gave up in frustration. The swampland had adopted her when she'd first fled from persecution in the medicine house as a young priestess many years ago. The old hags had thought she wasn't good enough a practitioner to outclass them in potions and healing. Now she had exacted her revenge against them and reduced them to nothing.

Within the darkness of the forest, she'd found great powers, enriched beyond her mortality. She, in turn, nurtured, fed, and cared for the darkness, becoming its queen, growing powerful under the auspice of the dark goddess's magic, something only she knew how to manipulate. But it wasn't enough. Each day, her body reminded her just how human she was, despite her long life. But she was working on the right formula to make sure she never got tired or halted by useless boundaries like the one that kept her from Mehronur. When the new age came, her powers would grow and she would sit on the mortal throne, ruling this land and perhaps the next. The people of Mehronur wouldn't truly know her until they were worshipping her, no longer the parvenu with a strange name, but their immortal goddess.

She watched the pot, again, fisting one hand. She was so very close to her grandest ambition of becoming the immortal earthly vessel of the Dark Goddess. She'd known since she arrived in this land of gods that she had more to offer than simply being a healer. The doyennes at the medicine house had hated her all the same, but had they not chased her from the house, she might not have realized her true ambition. Once she ascended to the throne, the Mpundulu that had been breathing down her back could keep her precious dead world. It wouldn't matter. Akwanshi would be a living goddess with worlds at her fingertips. The past years had been grueling, just waiting for the protection shield that held Mehronur to break apart.

Only days stood before her and its collapse. She couldn't allow herself to be overwhelmed with excitement. The hour hadn't arrived yet, and here was potential trouble. This strange girl had appeared, presumably from the mortal world, the second such intrusion in the past days. If the doorway was opening, then it must mean trouble. Waiting would not be enough. If only the prince had come to her voluntarily as she desired him to, the collapse of the light kingdom would have happened already, and she'd be sitting on the throne at this very moment. The boy was more strong- willed than she imagined, resisting every torment and lure she placed before him. Of course, it didn't help that that servant of hers was so incompetent and fickle. He'd wasted precious time, much of it buttering up the dying king and eating.

After everything she had done to give him his power. Why wasn't he answering? Why couldn't she break through this sight shield? *Oh, Abnr, god of dying light, let this be your last fight,* she mused, watching the pot slowly begin to bubble. Akwanshi paced, thinking what she could do about the Dark Prince, anything to ensure that nothing fell out of place in these final days. The young man who held the ultimate key to her immortality remained distant and defiant.

She'd have to wait for the day to become night before she could rope the darkness and use it to strengthen the psychic bond between them. She could now get into his head, even if not long enough or deep enough to sway him. She'd have to be patient. Time was of the essence, and it moved in her favor.

8

ROYALS

Jiro Sion marched through the dark hallways of Paraa Hutat, trailed by two younger Nkuba guards. When he reached the dungeons, he stood back while one of his accompanying guards flung open the doors that led to a holding cell. The stranger slept coiled on the hard ground but jumped awake when they entered the room. The *girl* smiled, her dark brown eyes burning with fear or fascination. Those two emotions were always so hard to decipher for him.

When the guards stepped forward, she threw her hands up, showing her palms, and speaking very slowly in a hoarse foreign language that made no sense.

Sion faced the two guards by his side. "Take her— but do not rough handle her."

The girl clutched her belongings and spoke in her harsh tongue as the guards led her from the cell. Sion had never heard such a coarse language before. He was curious about her homeland for the same reason everyone else was. She was a foreigner, the only one they had seen since before he was born. The girl hadn't been in the palace for a day and already there was commotion. He had difficulty believing she was Abnr's star. Aside from her harsh-sounding language and oddly cut clothes, she didn't seem very different from any other young female that lived in the kingdom.

At least one of his companions had suggested she was a local impostor, and yet another had mentioned that the Great Ndakr had been described as such when he first set foot in Marut. He just didn't know what to believe. What he did know was that she'd been summoned by His Majesty, and as head of the palace guards, he'd been trusted to pick her up and deliver her to the king.

Sion and the guards pushed their way through the isolated corridors into the main halls of the royal house, where servants gathered in the hallways to peek at the small girl.

Sion knocked on the door of the main sitting chamber. "Divine King, Jiro Sion has arrived."

The king's soft voice penetrated the hardwood door and Sion entered the sitting room, tailed by the guards holding the girl. He bowed before the royal party—king, queen, and the medicine man, Bokor, who looked as arrogant as usual with his painted white face, harsh frown and raised shoulders. They stood near a long table.

"Bring her here," demanded Bokor, tone harsh intentionally or not.

King Remu stayed silent, prompting Sion to obey Bokor. He released the girl before the medicine man.

"Is there anything else, your Divine Highness?" Sion asked, facing the slumped shouldered king by the side of the room, his face scrawny and withdrawn.

"No, that is all," said the king in a voice weakened by age and illness. "Please keep guard at the door."

"Yes, Divine King," Sion said and left.

King Remu noted the girl was sharp-eyed and nervous. She glanced about and folded her lips inside of her mouth. When she caught his eyes on her, she smiled with discomfort. Bokor moved, circling his large body around her. She squinted with suspicion. King Remu wished the big man wouldn't do this. He was very intimidating to everyone, and perhaps that was the point. Bokor liked knowing he was feared, equating the emotion with respect.

"Guards, remove this package," Bokor commanded, pointing to the girl's bag.

The girl objected to being stripped of her belonging and a tug of war ensued when one of the guards stepped in to remove it. She pleaded, grabbing for the bag.

Bokor used his snakehead staff to slap her on the wrist. She cried out.

King Remu cringed and stepped forward, but stalled. That was an unacceptable act, but rather than chide the man, he stayed silent. Bokor had insisted on taking charge of this situation. *It wasn't safe*, he'd said.

The girl rubbed her wrist, spitting angry words. It was both amusing and worrying.

King Remu wanted to ask the guard to return the item to the girl, but Bokor was in charge here.

The medicine man glared at the young woman with hostility. "You are on the grounds of Paraa Hutat, and all properties brought here belong to the palace." Bokor faced one of the guards. "You, open it, let us see what this parvenu carries."

King Remu watched with curious eyes as the guard struggled to open the unusual bag.

The girl moved forward and Bokor used his staff to block her.

King Remu grew impatient with the medicine man's behavior but waited. The guard dumped its content on the table. Nothing among her scant belongings was familiar. Bokor used his staff to touch the items. The girl shouted, yelled, barked in her harsh tongue.

Bokor barked for silence. He lifted a bound leaflet, shook it and dropped it carelessly. He pushed around other items with his staff.

"Is there something you can tell us?" King Remu asked, losing his patience.

"I do not recognize any of these things." "I can see that. But what do they mean?"

"I cannot say," he responded. "If she is a sorceress, then she's disguising herself well."

King Remu rolled his eyes. "Could she be Abnr's gift?"

Bokor looked insulted. He lifted his head, staring King Remu down from the top of his nose. "I would not be so trusting of this girl, not before we find out more about her origins."

"All of this could've waited until after breakfast. And since you insisted on dragging her here at this hour, we should extend the invitation to have her eat with us."

"To invite her to the table…" "It is courtesy."

"She came from the darkness. We will be foolish to trust her so blindingly."

"Bokor, please make the necessary arrangements for our safety later. For now, we shall eat."

"Very well, Divine King," said Bokor, looking slighted. "In the afternoon, I shall return with more *thorough* information about this *girl*."

"Please do," King Remu responded before facing the guards. "Tell the kitchen staff to bring breakfast."

The girl looked confused, if not a little angry. She eyed her things as the guards led her from the room. When they entered the breakfast room and he encouraged her to sit, she smiled with a look of relief and uttered something harsh sounding in her foreign tongue.

King Remu watched her closely during breakfast. Nothing about this *child* seemed sinister. Despite Bokor's hostility, he believed, wanted to believe, wholeheartedly, that she was authentic.

"We should make arrangements for her clothes," said Queen Oluchi across the table from him. "She will also have to learn to speak Maruti."

"We have to show great caution with this girl. And we must be mindful of Bokor."

"Bokor is tedious. He behaved like a complete boar," Queen Oluchi said dismissively.

"He means well," replied King Remu. *Sometimes.* He had accepted Bokor's aggressive and off-putting ways, not because he cared for them, but because the man was highly skilled and knowledgeable in matters of medicine and *Reveals*, the latter of which was a fascination for him, the son of a prophetess.

Queen Oluchi's eyes and expression showed disagreement in his assessment of Bokor, but she was mindful of the girl's presence, and rather than argue about the medicine man, she sipped her porridge.

"We must not dismiss his concerns." King Remu spoke again. "We don't know what this girl is capable of. It is important to let his investigation run its course."

"I just hope it is something that can help us.

Otherwise, we have nothing else."

He reached for Queen Oluchi's slender hand. "Do not worry too much, my queen. You are too young to waste such energy. Let me deal with everything. It is my duty as king."

Queen Oluchi smiled, but her smile did not reach her eyes. She would worry. That was all anyone did in Mehronur–worry.

After breakfast ended, and the servants were removing the dishes and plates, King Remu wiped his mouth and stood shakily, barely balancing himself on his feet. Nausea grew inside of him again. Always after he'd taken his medicine. Soon, his body would start to quake, but first, he had to speak to the young woman. When he smiled, she smiled back. So far, he did not know what to make of her. Bokor had been unceasingly harsh.

"Thank you for coming," he said.

The girl's roaming eyes met his. He stepped forward and placed a hand on his chest. "I am grateful that you are here." Just saying the words caused some of the burden he'd carried for all these years to lift. "I am Remu, first of my name, and son of Jbar."

Her dark eyes narrowed in empty focus. "Reh-mu." He pointed to himself.

"Reh-moo," she repeated with a smile.

Why had the gods sent such a young person who did not understand the language?

Queen Oluchi stood, following his lead. "I am Oluchi of Faro," she said and nudged her head slightly in Kadsa's direction.

"O-loo-chee," the girl repeated. Queen Oluchi nodded excitedly.

The girl's face lit up and she exhaled, speaking slowly. "And what is it you are called in your language?"

King Remu asked.

Her eyes widened and so did her mouth, an almost comical response. What was her age, he wondered. When he had first laid eyes on her being dragged across the courtyard, he'd assumed she was no older than his son, Sahu. Looking at her now, even taking note of the way her brows wrinkled, and her expression crunched, she was clearly a young woman, an adult, closer to Queen Oluchi's age, but younger, more similar to… he dropped the thought quickly, but not before concluding, *they could meet.*

"Kahd-zsa." She pointed to herself, copying their gestures.

King Remu laughed. Some gestures were universal. Queen Oluchi repeated the name twice, and he once, with elation. The girl looked happy with the breakthrough. Kadsa wasn't a foreign name. It had meaning in Maruti, the lady of the sky. Maybe it was coincidence. Maybe it was not. This was a good sign. A good sign, after all.

"A-nuwo Sahu." Queen Oluchi gestured to their son.

The girl's face twisted, and she opened her mouth but promptly closed it.

"Saah-yuu," Queen Oluchi spoke slowly. "Sahu," she repeated.

Everyone smiled. The introductions over, King Remu pointed to her necklace. "I have dreamed of the day when we'd receive a sign and am glad to see it."

Kadsa reached for the crystal from under her blouse and pushed it toward him. King Remu realized she mistook his words for a request to give it to him, and he waved it away.

Queen Oluchi gasped. The necklace glowed.

Prince Sahu looked up, squinted, and returned his attention to his meal.

King Remu smiled and stepped before her. "Give me your hand." She obeyed. He erased the space between them and gripped her shoulders gently. "This is important." Their eyes met briefly before she dropped hers to the floor. He lifted her chin. "Kadsa, I'm glad you are here." He reached over to kiss both of her cheeks.

A hint of confusion, before she pressed her dry lips into a safe smile.

He almost laughed. A whiff of nausea rippled through his body and gripped his head. He staggered, unable to stay on his feet. The room spun. The girl's face turned cold with horror. She backed up. Queen Oluchi screamed. The last he saw was his dear, sweet wife rushing to his side, shouting at the guards standing near the door.

9

UNSEEN

Kadsa paced the small sitting room, halted, and then exhaled, folding her arms at her chest. *I hope they don't think I did something to him,* she worried, and then, with even more alarm, *what will they do to me?* A king fainting in her presence wasn't good, not at all. They'd locked her inside of the small room with just a sitting stool and some cushions, slightly more welcoming than the cell she had slept in, but still a confined space.

Shuffling outside of the wooden door stilled her heartbeat. The lock clicked. A guard stepped inside, bowed, and spoke coolly. She hesitated to move, and caught his dark, narrowing eyes. *Yeah, I get it, come with me,* she thought, walking toward him.

The guard led her to the same dining hall. Queen Oluchi greeted her with a tight smile, her expression muddling with concern. Kadsa held her breath. The queen didn't look exactly angry with her. Did that mean the king was alright and they didn't blame her? "Hello."

The young queen did not respond with words and gestured for her to sit.

Queen Oluchi said nothing to her during a feast of fried cassava chunks, meat slices and bitter malt. Kadsa grew wary, rolling her shoulders. A handful of times, the door squeaked open, bringing into the room fast- moving servants who whispered into the queen's ear before exiting as quickly as they had entered.

Kadsa slumped in the soft cushioned chair. What were they saying? It was tiring trying to figure out what was going on. More and more she suspected *something* was happening, but she couldn't tell if it was good or bad. Queen Oluchi always smiled when their eyes met, even while the servants whispered in her ear. After the umpteenth servant shuffled out, Kadsa leaned forward, "The King ....," she started when a commotion broke out on the other side of the room.

Prince Sahu had been wandering around the room with the wooden water bottle she had given him from her bag, and a servant woman now struggled to pull it from his scrawny grip.

Queen Oluchi muttered beneath her breath and stood, holding a hand up in ceasefire. Both the servant and the young prince froze.

Queen Oluchi uttered a soft phrase with a smile, and the servant released the bottle. Prince Sahu grinned, but then Queen Oluchi spoke to him in a sharp, almost scolding tone. His shoulders slumped, and then the servant woman escorted him from the room.

The queen faced Kadsa and smiled, exhaling before sitting again. She uttered something that might have been an apology since she also gestured toward the door. "Don't worry about it." Kadsa nearly rolled her eyes.

A second later, another fast-moving servant entered the room. By now, Kadsa had lost count of how many had walked in overall, and whether it was the same servant each time. The female servant muttered into Queen Oluchi's ear and then left.

Kadsa's eyes followed the woman out of the room. What was going on? Her mind again settled on the king, and discomfort fluttered inside of her stomach. Queen Oluchi's face contorted with a mixture of worry and calm, not too much like someone whose husband was dead. Kadsa didn't believe the king had died, hoped not, but the way he'd collapsed had been terrifying.

The double doors flew open, and two guards, one of whom she recognized as the guard who had arrested her, wandered into the room. Queen Oluchi stood abruptly.

Kadsa's heart nearly leaped from her chest. Was this it? The guards bowed, and her arresting guard exchanged cool words with the young queen.

Queen Oluchi wandered from her seat and extended her hand. Kadsa's eyes dropped suspiciously to the woman's skinny fingers, perfectly polished nails, surprised by the gesture. The queen's lips smeared with a smile, a relaxing, *trust me* sort of gesture, but Kadsa's heart fluttered all the same. She took a deep breath and placed her hand in the queen's soft palm. Queen Oluchi led her from the room, flanked by the guards. Kadsa smiled at the guards, as if a smile could change any horrible fate they planned for her.

They led Kadsa through a beautifully decorated foyer and then toward a terrace in another part of the palace with open walls and high-reaching marble columns. Kadsa had noticed that the only enclosed areas in the maze-like building were the private wings, where the dining room and the bedchambers were located. Servants wandered the halls freely. Young women in white, off-shoulder robes with their hair in braids, and men dressed in leather and red tunics—those were the warrior guards. Who were these people?

Dearest Queen Oluchi kept up her smile throughout the long trek. Kadsa's mind filled with imagined nightmare scenarios of hanging as they wandered into a vast outdoor courtyard. Torches and lamps lit the courtyard, and the heat of the night roasted her skin.

A hundred, maybe closer to two hundred people crammed into the courtyard. Musicians moved their fingers over freestanding lyres and lamellophone-type instruments like what grandpa used to have back in the day before he pawned it for cash in Mauritania.

Kadsa settled down a little. This didn't look like an execution, but then again, they were leading her to the raised platform, on top of which she noted a stone block, like something they'd position a person's head on for chopping.

"Queen Oluchi?" she called nervously, but the queen wasn't paying attention. She was already waving to the crowd, lost in the excitement of the musicians, singers, and dancers who shuffled around them.

Queen Oluchi traded words with the guards at the stone platform before facing Kadsa, murmuring soft words with a straight face.

Kadsa stepped forward on the queen's nudging, relying on the queen's facial expressions and tone and her own general observation to make sense of what was happening. When she marched onto the platform, the crowd roared.

Kadsa was so taken back by this that she broke into nervous laughter. *Maybe they won't kill me.* She scanned the courtyard, noticing the way people tilted their heads to get a better look at her, or pointed in her direction. Whispering. Clapping. Some yelling.

It dawned on her that this was a positive celebration— these people looked not like people who came to witness an execution. Her gut sank when she mulled over this point.

Queen Oluchi stepped forward. "*Ka-sa ume d'Abnr, saa u-re,*" said Queen Oluchi.

The crowd grumbled.

What is she saying? Kadsa tried reading the queen's thin lips, but all she took from her was "star and Abnr." Where was Seth right about now to translate? Grandpa Edoje spoke this language. People always asked about his accent wherever they went. When he would speak in the language, it sounded fluid and musical. Queen Oluchi spoke in a slow deliberate tone.

Kadsa sighed, wishing she'd kept up her lessons with her grandpa. Maybe remembering the language would be like riding a bicycle, or however that analogy went, since she'd only ever ridden or attempted to ride a bicycle back when she lived in Kenya. She'd sprained her wrist. Weirdly enough, there were some words she understood.

The word, *nu'at* jumped out. It had been spoken more than once, by Seth in the forest, and Bokor, the king's medicine man. *Nu'at, night, darkness.* Kadsa's eyes settled on the dark cloud that clustered at the kingdom's border, forming its skyline. It was a darkness apart, intense and menacing, even when compared to the night currently engulfing the kingdom.

"Kadsa?" Queen Oluchi faced her.

She pursed her lips into a nervous but polite smile and followed the queen to the stone chairs near the back of the raised platform. Throne seats. One for the missing king. Where was the king? She'd feel a little better if she knew for certain he was all right.

The chairs were hard on her body, but she sat without complaint, keeping an eye on the darkness on the horizon. The other eye was on the movements or gestures that yanked her attention among the partiers.

Someone yelled from the crowd. They erupted into cheers.

A group of dancers settled before the platform and began gyrating their hips, circling a fire. The dancers wore skirts of reed, necklaces of teeth and bones, and painted masks, reminding her of that stupid big man who had assaulted her and took her bag earlier.

Queen Oluchi glanced to her a few times, still happy. Every time Kadsa convinced herself to relax, something or other jolted her. During one of the many performances that stretched into the night, a seemingly dead man rose from his grave. She could have jumped from her seat if the queen hadn't touched her to keep her steady.

Queen Oluchi's voice was calm, as if to say *this was all normal*. Kadsa wasn't so certain. The Buried Man walked from the fiery grave, turning with deliberateness toward the platform. She darted her eyes to the guards, about eight of whom flanked the platform. They stood with spears and knives, confident and poised, enough to put her at ease. She almost relaxed, but then the Buried Man walked by the guards, and not one of them moved. Kadsa's brain drifted between panic and calm.

Maybe this is normal. But I don't like this. The Buried Man stumbled forward and walked towards her. She fidgeted, stumbling upward from her seat with the intent to get away from him. Queen Oluchi held her hand, pinning it to the chair's armrest. Their eyes met. Kadsa sought comfort in her soft warm eyes and found it.

This is likely nothing to worry about.

The Buried Man paused, eyeing her without a readable expression. The crowd quieted, tilting their heads, and adjusting their positions to get a look at the impending spectacle. *This is a magician's trick.* The Buried Man's face was covered in striping white paint, and red dye was dabbed around his eyes, forming circles. The outline of ribs was painted over his naked torso, and a thick blotch of dark fluid stained his left breast.

I don't like this.

Queen Oluchi stiffened, her grip on Kadsa tightening with tension. Kadsa's gut dropped. She turned when the queen did, facing the guards to their right, in particular the one who'd arrested her. He reached into his belt, yanking out a short, curved sword with a broad blade that glistened under the yellow light of the torches that burned around the platform.

The world dissolved, stifling the laughter, cheers, and music of the courtyard crowd. The moment dulled into a series of slow-moving events. The Buried Man grabbed Kadsa by the neck, shutting off her airways; his rough hands were fire-hot rods scorching her skin. He lifted her off the ground. They locked eyes. Those eyes. Black. No trace of white anywhere. His mouth opened, revealing a swarm of insects wiggling on his tongue. Kadsa wriggled, screamed, but nothing came out. Hissing echoed from deep inside of his throat. Black fluid leaked from his mouth.

No! No! No!

Kadsa grew lightheaded, and her vision blurred. She kicked at him, digging her fingers into his arms in a weak attempt to free herself from his grip. The guard who'd arrested her popped up behind her attacker. His hands lifted high, and fell down swiftly, burying his knife into the Buried Man's back. Her attacker jolted, losing a step. More guards descended on him, their weapons dipping in and out of his body that stubbornly refused to drop or release her.

Each stab brought loud gurgling and hissing, but he wouldn't release her. She was losing consciousness, was nearly gone when her body thudded to the ground, with the hacked-off limb of the Buried Man still wrapped around her neck. He had come to kill her, and even in pieces he intended to carry out his mission. One of the guards dropped next to her and used his knife to slice off each finger of the hand.

Kadsa heaved, taking in a desperate gulp of air, and then more huge gasps. Queen Oluchi grabbed her arm, pulled her to her feet and dragged her from the platform. Trailed by two guards, they dashed toward the palace. Kadsa glanced over her shoulders and spotted the Buried Man tumbling to the ground, overwhelmed by the guards who stabbed and hacked at him with their weapons. *What now?*

The Dark Prince crawled from the corner block into the rotund hall. He pushed the stone back in place before climbing to his feet. This was his second time sneaking into the top level of Djehut. It was not any easier this time around, either.

The top level was the domain of the high priests. Its only staircase led to a mechanized lift at the bottom that had a lock, for which only a small group of people had keys, the High Priest and his assistant, mainly. Ultimately, it didn't matter, of course. The Dark Prince had long discovered that a handful of the cornerstones built into each level of the Great Library were secret passages.

Once through the opening, he used the chain ladders and wooden bridges built into the crevices of the interior wall to reach each level of the Great Library. It took time and all his stamina to climb to the top. He took breaks, balancing himself on the crypt-like boxes that protruded on the inside of the walls. He believed wholeheartedly that these were the coffins of interred priests. The death factor should've stopped his quest, but he'd grown ambitious over the last few months and was determined to uncover the mysteries of the priesthood.

Once on the top level, he slid against the back walls, hiding behind columns until he was near the library room of the scribes, where the priests kept the temple writings in neat quadrants on shelves. He was nearing the library room when voices rang out from its direction. He quickly pressed himself behind the nearest pillar and held his breath.

"We simply don't have an answer," said the voice of the High Priest of Seshat, the stargazer temple that twinned the library.

"And the Oracles?" asked the responding voice, the Chief Librarian-Priest of Djehut.

The Dark Prince's body tingled with excitement. Rarely were these two men together. This must be a matter of some importance.

"They've been summoned," answered the High Priest of Seshat.

"So what else is there for us to do, then? What happened during the courtyard celebration is not our specialty."

The Dark Prince expected the men to shuffle down the stairs, but they remained on the steps, just outside the library room.

"Have you ever seen an animated corpse, Hju- Garo?" asked the Seshat Priest.

"Once again, it is not the concern of Djehut."

"It is all our concerns. His Majesty will expect us to be present."

"His Majesty listens only to his witch-doctor these days."

The Dark Prince, breath caught in his chest, pondered their words. *Animated corpse? In the courtyard?* Well, tonight had been interesting in more ways than he had realized. He'd briefly stopped to watch the courtyard celebration but must have missed the part with the animated corpse. The celebration was unexpected. The only event in the kingdom that hadn't yet succumbed to disinterest was Jua, and the season for the festival of light had passed. Had he snuck around the courtyard a little longer, he might have seen this animated corpse affair.

The High Priests were badmouthing Bokor. Nothing they said of the king's witch-doctor was inaccurate, and sadly, he'd known all too well how powerful Bokor's influence on the king was. He'd dealt with all the consequences of it.

You cannot be seen, you know why, Bokor had scolded him.

The High Priests descended the steps, leaving him free to pursue the reason for his visit to the Great Library. After slipping inside the main library room through another cornerstone lining the base, he returned the scrolls he had borrowed two nights earlier. Thanks to these scrolls, he had taught himself how to read the stars, predict the seasons, tell time, and so forth. Based on all he'd learned, he now believed he had what it took to become a priest of knowledge himself.

That's what he planned on informing Bokor next. He'd found a purpose, something to do besides waiting around for the king, or Bokor, who increasingly spoke for him, to decide his future, if not his fate. Bokor already looked bored with babysitting him, and maybe he'd be happy to let him go. And if the priests were correct about the *animated corpse* in the courtyard, Bokor would have plenty to occupy his time, as the so-called link to the spirit world.

After replacing the scrolls, the Dark Prince slipped into an adjacent room hidden behind a walled shelf. He was careful in his steps. The room was small, densely packed, with squeaky floor, a fact that surprised him, but then again, it served as a good alarm against thieves.

He sniggered a little at this thought. He didn't consider himself a thief, but a student of knowledge. And besides, he always returned what he borrowed.

The shelves of the sacred room were neatly stacked and stretched high into the ceiling. He knew the so- called Kalec scrolls were here, they had to be. The special collection of sacred scrolls had been mentioned in a few of the writings, and he'd done his own mapping of their potential location. They were said to have come from the original seven priests of knowledge, and Ndakr, the first king of Marut. The so-called Jlecu were said to speak directly from the gods, and the knowledge in the scrolls could give one the powers of a god, or so the legend said. He had to see these scrolls for himself to accept such a rumor.

He took a deep breath, knowing he had to beat the clock, he began going through the scrolls, lifting, unfolding, and then returning them neatly to their place, so as not to alert anyone of his intrusion.

After a short search, he discovered a small grouping of scrolls stuffed in the back of a square slot that it shared with a thicker pile of parchment. His heart jabbed.

Grabbing them, he moved toward the nearby small table, spreading them out. If he was correct, this might be the very thing to help save the kingdom, *and maybe himself*. He pondered on this *hope*, letting it settle inside of him. Saving himself? *You cannot be seen, you know why*.

The Dark Prince shoved the thought out of his mind, focusing on the scrolls. Normally, he waited until he was back in his chamber to read the scrolls, but curiosity got the better of him.

He placed them down on the nearby corner table and was about to unroll them when...

Rumblings. He jolted. No time to solve the mystery of the scrolls. He tucked himself between two of the back shelves, priding himself on the smooth speed of his movement. The footsteps outside the room drew closer. Voices strained out from behind the wooden door.

"Are you certain?" the older man asked. The Chief Librarian-Priest had returned.

"Unfortunately, I cannot find them anywhere," said Rafq, the High Priest's assistant.

The Dark Prince worried they spoke of the scrolls he'd stolen two nights ago. The priests rarely noticed when a scroll went missing, and he was often careful with his timing.

"High Priest, what must I do?"

"Calm down, Rafq," said the High Priest. "It is likely you misplaced them—that's all."

The priests pushed aside the door and entered the room. The Dark Prince kept his eyes on them as they moved to the far side, and with each step, he backed toward the door.

"This is carelessness on my part, Hju-Garo." "Explain to me your exact steps."

"I cleaned the shelves like you told me to and brought all the scrolls back to their shelves, including the Kalec scrolls. I am certain of it."

"The Kalec Scrolls? You touched those?" "I returned them. They should be safe." The Dark Prince shut his eyes, freezing.

Rafq stormed toward his direction, pausing with only a high shelf between them. The young priest shuffled through the shelf from which The Dark Prince had taken the sacred scrolls.

"They're gone," he said. The High Priest grumbled. Rafq began apologizing.

The Dark Prince dared not move.

"I promise, I'll find them," Rafq said in a strong voice.

"Whatever you do, hurry, and don't let any word of this get out. There are already enough new problems as it is. Just find them."

The High Priest stormed from the room, leaving Rafq behind. The young priest stared at the shelf, puzzled. "They were right here," he said to himself.

The Dark Prince tiptoed from behind the high shelf, using the wall to guide him along. When Rafq shuffled, he halted. The young priest walked toward the end of the room, slinking behind another shelf, and the Dark Prince took the opportunity to exit.

His heart burned to know what the writing of the Great King Ndakr looked like. When he was outside of the main library, he leaned against one of the high columns, from which an oil lamp hung. He loosened the pile of seven parchment sheets and lifted the first to the lamp. The wavy gilded lines of the writing shimmered in and out of focus. He lifted another, shocked to see it was much of the same. This was it? This was the sacred writing of Ndakr and his sages?

The Dark Prince stared at the parchment papers. The gilded script slowly filled up the pages, Growing in visibility. He shifted away from the light, and the writing became even more legible.

His brows knitted with intrigue. The wavy lines of the writing were impossibly beautiful. But another issue puzzled him. What did the writing mean? He understood enough High Maruti to know this was not it. Considered the script of the priests, High Maruti was an art form taught in the Great Library, and Seshat. It was a script of interlocking cursive lines and loops. This exotic script had raised tails, thin curved strokes, and symbols that were indecipherable.

But he was certain these were the right scrolls. He'd tried in the past to borrow them but hadn't been successful. But these looked about right.

He slumped, rolling his shoulders. He had read about the seven priests of knowledge; they were equally important to the kingdom's founding as the Great Ndakr. These scrolls were the only link to the kingdom's past, and maybe its future. Now that he had them in his hands, he had another mystery to unravel, a new language to learn. Not that he didn't love a challenge.

The sound of footsteps alerted him to the library room. The High Priest returned to the room, and soon his voice clashed with Rafq's on the inside. "Did you find them?" he asked.

"I'm sorry, High Priest." Rafq's tone sounded defeated.

The Dark Prince paused, feeling some guilt about his actions. It was not his intent to get the young priest in any sort of trouble. He folded the scrolls, listening as the voices of the High Priest and Rafq descended deeper into the library. Minutes elapsed before the High Priest bolted from the room again, allowing the Dark Prince to tiptoe back inside.

Rafq was not in the main area, but in the back room with the sacred scrolls. The Dark Prince hopped to the nearest table, covered in loose leaves and parchment paper. This was a good spot to leave the sacred scrolls, bury them under the pile.

"Lati a-re!" rang the young priest's voice, as he emerged from the back room.

The Dark Prince jolted upright. He would certainly not *show himself* as Rafq demanded. He dropped the scrolls on the table and dashed for the door.

Rafq scrambled after him.

The young priest was fast, catching the neck of the Dark Prince's robe, and ripping the hood from his head, halting them both. The young priest froze in his tracks, his brows furrowing. The Dark Prince flipped his hood over his head and hurried toward the exit. Rafq's face. It creased with the same ugly and confused expression that marred the face of everyone who had seen him.

You cannot be seen; you know why, Bokor's voice echoed in his head.

10

DREAMS

K adsa couldn't sleep. Every time she closed her eyes, the sight of that Buried Man... dead man... crawled into her brain, squeezing her neck. Her throat burned. Queen Oluchi had the servants apply a soothing salve, but it still hurt each time she swallowed, each time she took a deep breath.

Kadsa tried massaging the drumming and music out from her head. The shaky memories from the affair. She should've followed her instinct and not stayed seated. Queen Oluchi made her stay, and for that, she was somewhat peeved with the queen. There wasn't much to do about it because she was still a guest of the royal family, so she had to hold back her temper.

I'm not in my world anymore. She turned on the hard bed. It was made of brick with beddings of weaved straws and wool blankets wrapped around it to soften it. Kadsa tossed and turned and sweated under the fleece blanket.

The face of the dead man wouldn't go away. He stood before her with blood leaking from his mouth and insect sounds chittering.

Kadsa stood in an artificially green meadow with sunflowers reaching to her chest. A cartoonish yellow sun shimmered above her. She petted the flowers absent-mindedly, passive to the surreal nature of her environment. Something was very strange about it.

A veil of dread crawled upon the dream world. She was one and then she was two. The first version of her petted the flowers, and the second, muted and absent in body but very much present, called out that something was wrong. No sound came from her mouth. Only chittering insects.

A shadow crawled over the sky, blotting out the sun and sending a flood of darkness over the flowerbed, engulfing her. Kadsa spun to find herself face to face with the darkness, sculpted into human form. The tar-black entity was perfectly shaped like a man. It had no defined facial features—nose, lips, eyes or anything that made up a face. It lifted its right hand and reached for her, choking her. She screamed.

Kadsa jolted upright. Her bedroom door closed creakily and her pendant glowed.

Someone had just left the room. Her heart stopped. She sprung to her feet, glancing about before rushing to the door, determined to find out who had been there. She waited amidst the dimness of the dying torches that lined the walls. Silence engulfed the halls. Nothing could be heard above her shallow breathing. No human sounds, footsteps, fumbling, anything that hinted at the intruder's movements.

Kadsa returned to the room. The wind had slammed the door. It couldn't be anything else. These halls were safe, *as safe as the courtyard,* she grimaced. Kadsa's eyes burned, so did her brain, starved of sleep, and even her neck had begun to hurt again.

She plopped down on the hard bed and looked around. Someone had been inside this room watching her sleep. She had gone to sleep with the heavy wooden door fastened shut. Kadsa shook her head. *At least I'm still alive. For now.*

11

INSIGHTS

Deep night did not set over the kingdom, except around the border towns that were near shrouded in the darkness. Instead, a phenomenon she could only compare to an eclipse occurred. One sun darkened, moving to conceal the other, creating a halo effect. Daylight happened when the hidden sun danced to the front, and the dark sun brightened. This was instant. There was no dawn or any grace period. Back in the forest, Seth had called the suns' behavior a dance and embrace. These were near-perfect descriptions of the way these suns moved around each other, sometimes seemingly pulling light from each other.

Graceful and strange.

Kadsa was slipping into the frumpy dress Queen Oluchi had sent her when someone began banging against her door. Queen Oluchi's dress actually fit. She didn't mind that the queen had done this, though she knew it was all because of guilt. She nearly got her killed.

When she opened the door, the face of the stern- looking royal guard popped up. Kadsa noticed the guard's thick lashes that masked his dark, intense eyes. There was something very soulful about them. Grandpa Edoje always encouraged her to meet people's eyes because that's how she would learn the truth about people. His eyes told her he could be trusted. And he'd saved her life, throwing himself on the Buried Man. She liked him better already.

The guard winced and spoke without pulling his heavily lashed eyes from hers. *"Ba'ra-a,"* he said.

"Good morning." She recognized that phrase.

She didn't understand the rest, but it didn't matter because she'd have to follow him anyway. Kadsa wished she could thank him with meaningful words. Instead, she trailed him in silence. Two steps in front, he led her out of the room and through the corridors, turning once or twice, before entering the dining room in which she had dinner the previous night.

Queen Oluchi rose from her chair, and Kadsa noticed she wore a small, amethyst blue diadem with a wide gold band stitched around it. It fit her better than the heavy bell-shaped burden she had on her head yesterday. *"Ba'ra-a,* Kadsa." Queen Oluchi kissed both her cheeks.

"Ba'ra-," she spoke stiffly. No one had ever been this happy to see her.

Queen Oluchi's eyes searched her face. The queen's expression marred with worry. Her next words were soft, serious. An apology? Words of sympathy? The queen touched her shoulders and gestured for her to sit.

They ate breakfast in silence before the door opened and King Remu entered.

Kadsa's heart nearly leaped from her chest. *He was alive ... he didn't look well.* He limped into the room and walked toward them, toward the head of the table. Queen Oluchi stood, and Kadsa followed.

Queen Oluchi helped him take a seat.

Kadsa didn't sit down until both were seated.

The king's weak eyes narrowed on her. His words were soft, a murmur that evoked a response from his young queen. They both studied Kadsa. She could only guess they were debating what to do about her presence, or how the Buried Man nearly killed her last night.

Kadsa smiled tritely and continued to eat, wishing she could understand what they were saying.

After breakfast, Queen Oluchi took Kadsa's arm and led her on a tour of the royal house. Kadsa told her to her face that she hoped not to get killed this time, but of course she delivered her message with a smile and the queen had returned the gesture.

Even so, Kadsa was mighty grateful that the heavy- lashed guard who'd saved her life walked a short distance behind them. The palace was bigger than she'd assumed, and it broke into quarters, the public, open areas, the private, and servants' quarters and such. Each had its own courtyard or terrace. The kitchen was a spacey, half- enclosed, half-opened area with fire pits serving as ovens that rose from the ground. Big pots steamed with fussy women standing over them or beating vegetables and chopping fruits to the side.

The private rooms impressed her the most and she lingered there the longest. Its courtyard was enclosed, and it had a private garden. The whole place felt like a dream.

Lastly, Queen Oluchi led her to the public bath. An underground aquifer fed it water. She had never seen anything like it. The queen swerved through the bedchambers, passing her own and leading her down a long foyer, stopping short of a dark, shadowy corridor with a narrow walkway that led to the nearly isolated back regions of the palace.

Queen Oluchi's brows furrowed.

Kadsa held her breath, keeping her fingers crossed that this wouldn't turn into another Buried Man episode.

She could still feel his huge, hot, rough hands around her neck sometimes. She glanced behind her to the guard, noticing how closely he watched them. The hilt of his knife dazzled in the sunlight. *I can trust him.*

Queen Oluchi muttered something—words of assurance and turned back on her clapping heels. When they had walked two-thirds of the way, Kadsa glanced at the guard again.

"What is your name?" He did not reply.

"Kadsa." She pointed to herself. "You?" she gestured to him.

The queen intervened. "Jiro Sion," Queen Oluchi said.

"Jiro Sion," Kadsa repeated.

The queen gestured to him. "Jiro Sion Oranyan." "That's a good name."

"*Mu'a-na jaro,*" the queen told her in a whisper, as if she didn't want Sion to know they were discussing him so openly.

Kadsa nodded.

The queen gestured discreetly to Sion's uniform. "Mu'a-na Nkek jaro ."

Jiro Sion reminded her somewhat of the Maasai and Taureg men she'd met during her lifetime. She winced when she remembered how one of them had proposed marriage back in Mauritania and her grandfather had to put his foot down.

That was the first time any boy had ever shown interest in her in that way, and that was when her grandpa had insisted she wore heavy trousers and robes. She hadn't minded at all.

Sion winced a little and then looked away. Kadsa smiled. He might be too old for her. And besides, she was here to find her grandpa and head back home to her long, lost mother, who she was trying really hard not to think about out of fear she might have lost her again. What if Lorraine was trying to contact her? Would she break her heart again? She wished she could reach out somehow and let her know she didn't mean to. But she was here, and she had made good. The first thing was learning the language.

The tour consisted of Kadsa repeating the word for each item the queen touched. She pointed; Queen Oluchi explained.

Jiro Sion led them on a rather long ride through the streets of the kingdom. He rode before them, eyes scanning the streets and people they passed with caution. Four guards rode briskly behind them. People bowed and gifted them fruits, which the queen took before passing them on to the guards. The kingdom was larger than she had imagined. There were many villages.

The ride drifted into the evening and the kingdom grew denser. The courtyards and temples surrounding the palace were massive, shiny, and nicely designed. Most had cone-shaped roofs.

Smaller and more densely stacked one-story buildings populated the far villages. People stopped their various labors to stare at them. Soon they had ridden into an arbor with few paved roads. Kadsa had never seen anything like this kingdom. It was trapped in time, but in a good way, except for the darkness on the horizon.

Jiro Sion muttered something calmly to the queen, who did not respond. They rode through a back village filled with sparsely strewn temples, smaller and less lavish than those near the palace, a handful of homesteads sandwiched the temples, more farms than homes. Few trees were in the kingdom, and those that existed were spaced widely apart. It was like leaving the tourist section for the badlands. Kind of depressing. In the back of her mind, she knew something was off, and kept glimpsing the darkness that the queen was clearly pretending didn't exist.

Jiro Sion slowed his abada when they neared a hill. He muttered something the queen did not respond to. In the near distance, a large temple stood teetering too near the edge of the forest. Only a small patch of land and the kingdom's redbrick wall separated the temple from the darkness. Kadsa shuddered. How could anyone ignore that threatening, unnatural darkness?

How did they live with it?

Seth's words drummed into her brain. This was a kingdom on borrowed time. Many of the homes they had passed had been vacated. The vegetation in these back villages had withered. *She refused to stay here longer than necessary.*

Jiro Sion glanced at her, his dark eyes strong and intimidating. *She trusted him!* He adjusted his headscarf and spoke, facing the young queen. At the same moment, a young servant girl exited the temple and advanced on them. The woman bowed curtly to the queen and greeted the rest of them with soft words. Kadsa tried to read the tone of the young servant to figure out if it was urgent or frightful but couldn't decipher.

The queen nodded and gestured politely to Jiro Sion.

Queen Oluchi said her name and uttered something, a declaration, maybe. Jiro Sion traded cool words with the young servant and turned his abada around. Queen Oluchi followed, so did Kadsa and the guards.

Kadsa frustratedly wondered what that had been about, and whether it was good or bad. She concluded that it was bad, smiled at Sion, and uttered, knowing he wouldn't understand, *you will keep me alive.* A different view of the palace greeted her on their ride. The clock in the courtyard was the most unusual structure in the entire kingdom and the temples took on a faded, misty glow the further one was from them. Rings of gold formed on many of the monuments that stood atop the temples.

The route back to the palace was not the same as the one they had taken at first. This was a backroad, an isolated dirt road, complete with broken-down stone monuments. She even noticed a trail that led to nowhere, dying shrubs and bushland, partly swallowed up by the darkness.

Explosive noise burst from the dark boundaries and caught their attention. The biggest bird she'd ever seen took flight from the lone fortress standing buried deep into the palace yards, a good one thousand yards from the palace's farmland. The bird flew through the shield and into the Dark Forest.

"I thought nothing in Mehronur could go out there." Seth had claimed that nothing could cross over the divide.

Queen Oluchi's forehead creased. A look of fear danced in her eyes, and Kadsa became alarmed. *What aren't these people telling me?* She glanced back to the darkness, spotting nothing of the bird, if that was what it really had been. It was simply too large.

Queen Oluchi smiled at Kadsa before turning to speak to Sion.

They rode on the wide side of the stone forest. The grim-looking structures didn't belong to the palace proper. Its stones were darkened, likely by time and erosion. It loomed creepily. She imagined this was where they sent prisoners. Solitary confinement.

Sion tugged on the reins of the abada, using the animal to block Kadsa's path, when her abada seemingly veered toward the tower. She pressed her lips into a smile the guard did not return, though some amusement simmered underneath his dark skin.

"We can go back," she said to Queen Oluchi.

———

It was almost nightfall when they returned to the palace. Queen Oluchi released Kadsa long enough for her to tidy herself up and return to the dining hall, where they were just beginning to serve dinner. King Remu waited for her, and she was happy that he was there, but when the other man at his side stepped out in the clear, she scowled.

Queen Oluchi repeatedly referred to this arrogant man, who ate greedily beside them, as Bokor, so she identified this as his name or proper title. Bokor handed medicinal vials to the king, who coughed throughout dinner.

The big man with his puffed chest stared her down in a threatening manner during dinner. Next day, it was much of the same. During breakfast, Bokor ate greedily, darting his eyes to her with suspicion. When he finished eating, he stood, pushing his chest out, reminding her of a blowfish. He spoke to the king in a low, controlled tone, but his voice resonated harshly. He exchanged words with Queen Oluchi and then faced Kadsa.

They all stared at Kadsa.

The queen's eyes opened wide, making Kadsa think Bokor accused her of something shocking.

Bokor faced the royal family, the words firing from his lips. He made dramatic hand gestures and the harshness of his tone told her it wasn't good.

Kadsa had many questions she wanted to ask, but her ignorance of Maruti limited her. She had been wracking her brain about the ease of learning the language. She'd already picked up a few words, but nothing this man was saying formed any meaning in her head. Where was her godtalker gift to help her?

"A-ru gyban o'da?" Queen Oluchi asked Bokor.

The medicine man darted angry and condescending eyes toward the queen, speaking from between clenched teeth.

Kadsa hated him, everything about him seemed like bad news. In many ways he reminded her of the Yedina shaman, the same size and look. She lingered on this thought a bit. They could even be the same person, only this man's face was covered in paint and costume.

Queen Oluchi stiffened.

Bokor continued to scold Queen Oluchi. The queen eyed her a few times. They were speaking about her, Kadsa knew, and only hoped Queen Oluchi had her back. There were some words Bokor annunciated very slowly, while giving Kadsa the evil eyes.

"Abiku," he had muttered, and then, "Akonadi."

Queen Oluchi let out a disappointed sigh but composed herself gracefully enough.

King Remu's expression muddled with grief, as if he'd received bad news. He did not speak.

Queen Oluchi shuffled, turning her attention back to Bokor.

She spoke in soft clear terms, words that were pronounced cleanly, and still Kadsa was lost to the meaning, relying on the queen's expressions and tone to interpret them. "*K'Abnr*" again jumped out from the queen's words.

Bokor's face twisted with arrogance and irritation. His fist hammered down heavily on the table, drawing a flinch from the queen, and a slight stir of the body from the king who spoke calmly to Queen Oluchi.

Queen Oluchi slumped, falling quiet. Her eyes fell on King Remu. Bokor eyed him, and so did Kadsa, bathing in nervous energy.

The king coughed, started speaking, and then coughed again. He spoke with a hoarse voice, slow, and arduous. He faced Bokor, speaking his words very softly.

Bokor responded in a harsh tone. Queen Oluchi slumped a little bit more.

Kadsa didn't understand. Why were they deferring to him? How did he have so much power over them?

The king sipped from the mug of herbal tea Bokor had served him. Seconds later, he faced Kadsa, using his hands to usher her to her feet. He gave a command, and desperately, she looked to Queen Oluchi, expecting a translation.

Queen Oluchi pressed her lips into a smile, gestured to Bokor. Kadsa nodded, facing the big man who pushed forward his chest, tossed his one-sided shawl across his shoulders, lifted his head and then bolted for the door.

Kadsa drifted behind him. What would he make her do?

No one else followed him but her. As soon as she was at the door, the sound of shuffling feet drew her attention to Queen Oluchi rushing toward them. The queen said something to Bokor, and he stiffened with a look of insult, but he did not respond.

Kadsa relaxed a little when Queen Oluchi took her hand. They navigated through the palace, from the bustling parts to the isolated, past the bedchambers, and into a darker, colder corridor.

When they exited the back of the palace, they mounted the abadas for a long ride.

The back road they took from behind the palace led them past olive groves and large frond palm trees. Kadsa distracted herself with the sights they passed. Her gut didn't like what was happening, but Queen Oluchi was by her side, and despite what had happened with the Buried Man, she felt the queen was an ally.

Bokor brought Kadsa into the large stone temple isolated from human settlements. It sat across a hill on which stood a baobab tree. Kadsa especially admired the human-idols that formed the doorframes and archway of the temple. These looked exactly like the makeshift gateway she'd seen back at the stone monument in Ghana, the one Grandpa had thought could've been the doorway. Kadsa was so deep into this journey that she wondered if she'd ever get out. The wooden idols were stacked one atop the other in perfect standing structures that not only formed a blueprint of a doorway outside of the temple, but also served as freestanding structures themselves. Bokor shoved her forward while Queen Oluchi and a guard stood by.

The big man spoke confidently to the queen, lifting his chin.

Kadsa studied Bokor, making sure he noted the annoyed expression on her face. She had no clue what he said but knew by the way he glowered at her, and by the concerned look on Queen Oluchi's face that he must have had something cruel planned.

What was he going to make me do?

Queen Oluchi spoke softly but firmly to Bokor and then bowed politely before stepping away.

Did the queen give him permission to do something to her? "What do I do here?" Kadsa asked, studying Bokor, whose face was set in a frown. How she hated his arrogant face.

Bokor entered the archway, bowed three times, and knocked.

Seconds later, a young woman opened the wooden door. Upon seeing Bokor, she bowed and the two exchanged words. When she gestured, Queen Oluchi and the guard who tailed her entered the temple. Kadsa and Bokor followed.

The vast interior of the temple had lily-white walls. It was simply decorated and almost empty, except for two altars, one that stood before a long drape, sitting atop four broad steps and another that stood in the center of the room. Many doors existed in the temple, each decorated with idols and symbols she didn't understand.

The young girl who let them inside moved to the front altar that had a bowl. Bokor followed her. He inquired about the bowl. He soon returned to where she stood with Queen Oluchi and spoke calmly.

The queen nudged her head in agreement.

The young girl poured liquid from the altar bowl into a wooden dish that sat on the head of one of the idols. Afterward, she disappeared behind a door. When she returned, another girl who looked younger than she was, about fourteen, trailed behind. Kadsa had figured out by now that they were priestesses of some sort. A third young woman joined the procession. Each of them carried a large gourd which they balanced in two hands, never taking their eyes off the gourds.

The dark liquid in the bowl looked and smelled like blood. And the square cut stone altar at the center looked oddly like a chopping block. Kadsa swallowed her fear, holding her breath.

The three young women placed the bowls on each level of the altar. They turned to look at the four people who stood to watch them in the dark room.

Bokor grabbed Kadsa's arm harshly, pulling her to them. Kadsa wanted to protest, but she stayed calm for reasons she didn't know. Her heart raced.

These girls seemed friendly enough. But…

Bokor stepped back until he was again standing next to Queen Oluchi and the guard. Kadsa kept glancing back at him until something wet swiped her forearm. The girls wiped dark fluid on her strategically—two on her arms, one in the cavity of her throat, on her face and so on.

The smell of raw blood saturated her nostrils.

Witchcraft! Sacrifice!

She tried to pull away. They held her firmly. Soon, they forced a bitter liquid down her throat. It burned her throat with an acidic taste.

Bokor's mouth spewed rapid and harsh commands.

What was she allowing these people do to her?

After they finished, the young women led her away from the altar that sat atop the four steps. Kadsa kept craning her neck to look at Queen Oluchi, searching for a hint of trouble, and yet, the fine-boned queen stood only to watch. The young women took her behind the drapes where a steaming herbal bath waited. Kadsa protested, but their grips were firm. They tugged at her clothes, removing them piece by piece until she was naked. She tried to cover up, but it was useless, they brought her into the bath. Weeds slobbered her skin and entangled her. What was the purpose of this bath?

Ritualistic cleansing? That wouldn't be so bad.

When Kadsa tried to bring her head above the smelly water, the girls, who had joined her in the bath, pushed her deeper down in the water. Kadsa wrestled against them. They were trying to drown her. She screamed and gasped for air, struggling until she couldn't anymore. Then she felt nothing.

She opened her eyes to darkness.

She was back in the Dark Forest … *No!* She was lying on a dirt surface with her face pressed against the floor. Her skin stung and itched. Goosebumps formed on her skin.

She remembered drowning in the herbal bath, drinking the bitter, burning liquid.

The unmistakable whisper of hissing forced her to sit up. Glancing around wildly, she discovered snakes all around her. *That man dumped her in a snake pit!*

Thinking under pressure, she reached for a scrawny piece of stick lying some feet away from her. She poked the snakes toward the wall. One latched on to the stick, coiling itself around it. She shook the stick to get it to fall off, but it didn't budge. When it encircled the stick, she dropped it, kicking it away from her.

"Let me out of here!"

No one answered. She could not see an exit anywhere in sight. Another problem plagued the room: darkness. Not even a crack of sunlight to indicate an exit. He imprisoned her in a snake-infested dungeon. But why? The Jakuba said they would welcome her here. Queen Oluchi, who smiled at her so sweetly, stood back and allowed *that man* to imprison her.

The hisses of the snakes grew louder around her, causing her chest to pound harder. How many were in the room?

She had to take a leap in the darkness if she was going to get out. She stepped forward, kicking something hard. She picked up what she kicked—an idol. Idols were everywhere. Idols tumbled down from the walls, having been piled atop and aside each other.

There were too many to count. A hundred, more? Kadsa moved through the idols, feeling along the walls for anything remotely close to a lock. Snakes slid from behind the idols, moving toward her, hissing. One grazed her leg. She screamed, kicked at it. She hated snakes and never foresaw the day when she'd have to be near them. She banged against the walls.

"Let me out!"

The snakes crept toward her, for some reason she was certain this had to do with Bokor.

The wall cracked and something snapped forward, scraping her head and causing quick pain. She felt a small trickle of blood. Kadsa reached for the idol, but found it was stuck in the wall. Another feel of the idol indicated it came from an indented space in the wall. Desperate, she felt inside the cavity, gripping a handle or a lever.

She took a deep breath before she pulled on it. The wall gave away. A snake touched her feet. She flicked it off and looked up again. A narrow walkway stood before her, and she rushed through it, not wanting to spend a second longer with the snakes.

The walkway was so narrow she could not fully stretch her arms out on both sides without hitting the walls. She kicked up dirt from the floor. She felt her way through the chilled hallway, scared of where it might lead. The passage led to a thick concrete. On both sides of her were hallways, equally dark, cold, and narrow. Kadsa listened for some time, waiting for sounds, like the sound of snakes hissing or some other creature entirely. She rubbed her hands over the wall, seeing engraved symbols on it. It was a maze. She'd give Bokor a piece of her mind when she saw him next if she ever got out of here.

Kadsa was barely brushing the wall when it gave way, shifting to the side just barely to allow her to slip through; she did so, suspiciously careful. She found herself in a tiny and window-less room, slightly warmer than where she had been.

In the far end of the room, a woman stood with her back to her, fingering something on a slender altar. Kadsa could not see what, even while she craned her neck.

"Hello Kadsa," said the woman without looking at her. Kadsa swallowed hard. It wasn't that the voice was so startling, but that the woman knew her name.

"You know me?"

"Everyone knows who you are," said the woman, turning around.

The woman, old-aged and dressed in the robes of the priestesses, sat on a stool beside a round table on which she placed a bowl. She reached for the small pestle in the bowl and crushed the ingredients in careful stabs.

She spoke after some time. "I have been expecting you. Please, come closer."

"Where am I?" Kadsa asked, walking to the woman. "You're in the temple of the Akonadi."

"Wait." Kadsa's eyes narrowed on the woman's line creased face. "I can understand you."

"For now, yes."

"How?" Kadsa wondered aloud.

"I'll tell you if you sit down." The woman gestured to the table.

Kadsa didn't want to but sat down on the low stool. "How come you can understand me?"

"I am communicating with you at the most psychic level. The language of the soul has no barriers to overcome."

The woman smiled and used the pestle as a brush. She was painting the table with ink from the white fluid in the bowl. Kadsa watched her paint a leaf inside of a star.

"Who are you?"

"I am the High Priestess of the oracle." "Oracle, as in a psychic?"

"If you think of it that way."

Kadsa rolled her shoulders back. There wasn't any other way to think of it. Rather than dwell on the matter, she faced the woman. "Why am I here?"

The woman reached out her hands, and recognizing the gesture, Kadsa placed both of her hands in hers. The woman began painting her palms. The white liquid tingled her skin, burning and itching. She slapped Kadsa's palms down in the two symbols painted on the table, and then closed her eyes and mumbled what sounded like gibberish. Kadsa's palms were getting very hot.

The woman's eyes opened, revealing milky-white cataracts. Kadsa gasped and yanked her hands back, but the woman's grip was firm. She twisted her arms and rested a finger on a vein just above her palm. Kadsa's pulse throbbed.

The woman's white eyes rolled forward and were black pools again. "You have a lot of energy." The woman smiled and pulled her hands away. She pushed the chair back, walked over to the altar, picked up another bowl and returned to the table.

"What did you do?" Kadsa pressed her.

"I was communicating with the ancestors."

"What do you mean by the ancestors—dead people?" "More or less." She shrugged.

The woman watched Kadsa while cracking nuts she removed from the bowl.

"You know I don't believe in any of this?"

"No," she answered, almost with sarcasm. She analyzed the two pieces of the nuts for a time but did not speak. The priestess's silence frustrated her.

"What is all this about?" Kadsa asked, breaking the silence.

"It's for me to discuss with Bokor. He sent you." "Why?"

"He wants to know if you are who you are—the gift that came from Abnr."

"And?"

The woman grinned slyly. "It depends." "On?"

"On what you do. Your actions."

"My actions? I am only here to find my grandfather." She had a sudden epiphany. "Can you help me find him?" "I knew you'd ask that," said the oracle with a laugh.

"Well, can you?"

"No." Her voice was cool.

And you're a psychic, Kadsa thought snarkily, not amused. "I want to leave."

"You can return back through the room." She glanced behind her. "It has snakes."

"Those snakes, the ancestors of our people, did not harm you. The ancestors were just sniffing you out. That's all. You made it out alright."

Kadsa winced, puzzled, but no sooner than she had thought about the woman's words, she had given up on it. She hissed her teeth and stormed to her feet in frustration.

"Kadsa," said the woman when she was at the door. "Give this to Bokor."

She dropped one-half of the nut in her palm. Before Kadsa could speak, she blew white powder in her face, blinding her. Kadsa couldn't breathe or scream, and the last thing she saw was the fading and smiling face of the old woman. Then, the room spun.

———

Kadsa opened her eyes, finding she was back in the bath, the one in which she had almost drowned. She rolled on her side. The large bath was free of the herbal liquid that had filled it. What happened? She was holding something in her right hand—a piece of nut.

Kadsa's stiff back tightened as she climbed from the bath. After tossing on her clothes, she moved toward the door. It flew wide open. A young girl, wrapped comfortably in a white robe with her hair in large plaits, stared at her. The girl's smile was shy, forcing Kadsa to smile back, though she had been hesitant, if not peeved. Kadsa moved toward the door. She paused, about to say something to the girl, when she remembered she did not understand the language.

The girl led her out of the room. She took a few steps away from the platform before the door opened and Bokor's face greeted her. Queen Oluchi beamed happily beside him.

Bokor walked toward where she stood at the center altar. Kadsa fought back the urge to slap the smug look from his face, glaring down into her eyes, and speaking with cool, slow words.

But, of course, she didn't understand what he said, and didn't waste much time trying to figure it out. Instead, she tossed the nut at him, which he caught at his belly. She gave him the dirtiest look she could muster, since the intent was to show she was angry. He studied the nut with care and distance, before he turned to the queen, who watched him with eager curiosity.

The queen's soulful eyes fell on Bokor, and she spoke coolly.

Bokor's response was the same as she'd gotten used to—stern, scolding and dismissive.

He sounded almost bitter.

Kadsa tried to read the queen's expression to interpret the tone, but the woman's very pretty face gave little away. In fact, she smiled, lips pursed.

Bokor again spoke, his dark, bloodshot eyes narrowing like daggers on her. Again, she compared him to the Yedina Shaman. Her suspicions of the shaman had been right, which meant she had to be careful of this man who looked as if he could've been his twin. Surely, if they were the same man he'd have recognized her, since last they had contact, he had been trying to attack her.

Bokor spoke again, tone low and deadly, chin lifting and eyes narrowing down.

She put on the same bluster, chin lifting and returning his glare. "I don't like you, either."

Bokor's eyes squinted as if he understood. He raised his heavy chest and slammed his snake-headed staff against the floor, turning his back coldly on her.

Soon after, they were returning to the palace of Hutat.

12

SONG

B okor stayed on Kadsa's mind all night. Not just the snake room incident, but the stuff about the Yedina shaman. From the get-go she hated the Yedina shaman, his arrogance and stares, and that memory of him talking to someone off into the darkness. Was there a way to know for sure what the witch-doctor's deal was? If he was indeed the shaman, then that might mean he knew exactly what happened to her grandfather. She wracked her brain just thinking about it. Back in the cave, he had said her grandfather lied to him. What did he mean?

When she fell asleep, she dreamed of the sun, red- hot and smoldering like volcanic lava. She could not escape its presence, melting under its heat. It hissed her name in hushed, sibilant voices.

When she woke in a sweat, pendant glowing, there was a figure dashing from her room, slithering out the door, like a shadow crawling against the wall. It left a lingering chill and cold draft behind.

Kadsa jumped out of bed and raced after it, arriving at her door in time to see the figure lingering at the hall's bend.

"Wait," she called after it, but the figure disappeared swiftly into a dark corridor around the bend.

She ran after it but could not find it. She walked back to the room disappointedly, only to find Jiro Sion standing at her door, waiting. He looked slightly stunned to see her walking back.

"I missed him," she declared.

Jiro Sion shook his head. "*A-ru buya ru'a kame.*"

His eyes dropped to her bare feet. Kadsa became aware of how she appeared to him—out of place. She turned on her heels and walked off.

Sion trailed.

"*Ba'nu* ," he said with a smile when she entered the room.

"*Ba'nu.*" *Goodnight.*

———————

Over the next days, Kadsa saw little of the royal family. Since the trip to the temple with Bokor, Queen Oluchi had been behaving very formally with her, no hand holding anymore. She missed Queen Oluchi's company. She worried they'd grown tired of her. King Remu's health had deteriorated. He was holed up in his bedchamber.

Where was her grandpa?

Kadsa ate alone, and when she took strolls through the palace and its courtyards, Jiro Sion or another guard pestered her.

One morning, after breakfast, a guard escorted her to a private room where a man in a white robe with gold hemlines waited. He nudged his head upward and his eyes roved over her. His expression showed little in the way of interest. *Well, excuse you*, *too*, Kadsa thought.

Kadsa had begun wearing her new clothes, courtesy of Queen Oluchi, which included pleated dresses and a lovely indigo-hued chiffon headscarf. She loved it all, though she struggled with the exposure of skin and felt out of place.

The way this man eyed her made her feel awkward. He stepped closer and dropped his eyes to the table between them. When she saw the scrolls, she knew why she was there. He was some sort of instructor.

He scratched his throat. "*Alaan, ka-su.*" He nudged his head in a slight bow.

"*Alaan, ka-su .*" His face curled.

"*Ndiya, n'do.*" He gestured to the polished wooden stool.

Kadsa didn't move, and he repeated the command. She pulled the chair and sat, hands folded in her lap. She had a long day ahead of her.

The instructor sat on a squeaky wooden chair and unrolled a foot-long scroll. The cursive rolling symbols that made up the written language looked exactly like the writing of the letters her grandpa had shown her a few years ago, after they'd moved from Kenya. He had said she should only read the letters if he was no longer alive. He had put them in a safe box and buried them.

The Itzat unfolded another scroll of similar length to reveal hieroglyphs, complete with drawings. He showed it to Kadsa. She felt better about looking at the images with the inscriptions than the rolling, hooped cursive script. The man revealed a third scroll and spread it flat on the table, next to the others.

"*Ndya guka.*" He forced her to stand. He poked Kadsa until she walked to the far end of the table.

What's with these old men and walking sticks?

"*Ndya iga,*" he said when she reached the end of the table. He repeatedly loudly, "*Ima!*"

She believed she had the meaning, but to be sure, she walked off.

He yelled again, "*Ima!*" "Stop."

The lesson consisted of the instructor barking commands. He used his foot-long staff to point to the objects on the scroll. A chair—*Sihla*. Her task was to repeat after him, and if her pronunciation was off, he'd slap his staff to the table. "*Si'ahla,*" he repeated, and so forth. By the end of the first lesson, she knew the names for chair, table, boat, and many more household objects. Language lessons grew into a daily routine, usually starting after Queen Oluchi took her for morning walks in the gardens and courtyards of the palace. Once the walk ended, Kadsa headed to the lessons, which took up the rest of her afternoons.

By the end of seven days, she could point to things and name them—most things anyway. Her tutor called himself Itzat, or maybe that was his title. She couldn't say. When she tried to ask him his name, there might have been some confusion.

He kept saying "*ooh-o, itzat.*" while shaking his head in protest. Nonetheless, she felt her lessons were coming along, even though her tutor often looked annoyed if she struggled to remember the previous day's lesson.

By the end of the first two weeks, she graduated into writing. She didn't have to draw the hieroglyphs, but she was expected to mimic the rolling cursive symbols.

Kadsa struggled with the writing. Each time she screwed up, the Itzat would grab the parchment, flip it, and force her to start again. The writing looked rather artistic, putting her poor penmanship to shame. She hated it, and she worried she was ruining the parchment that someone took a great deal of time to create. Each time she screwed up, she slouched, and the Itzat would give her the evil eye or the wagging index finger. She was supposed to be a quick learner, like when she played akuto with Grandpa, and he'd been amazed at how fast she'd mastered the strategy. Unless he'd just been buttering her up because he wanted her to think she was special.

The scribe liked dictating with his hand folded behind his back as he paced. It was distracting. Many times, he was rambling. She wanted to tell him to slow down but didn't know the words. Whenever he'd slow down, it was to scold her. Kadsa tried cheating—flipping the scroll to see what he'd written and copying it. Once, he caught her and slapped his staff down on the table, wagging his finger.

"*A-sjeru iji.*" He pointed up to the ceiling. She'd assumed he referred to the cartouches but changed her mind. "*O'o kere sjeru.*"

"*Seeru.*" She hoped he'd clarify.

"*Che-jeeh-ru,*" he said. His grasp of the word was crisper and more musical.

After lessons, Kadsa wrote in simple letter form on parchment paper to her grandfather, mimicking the letters he'd written for her in the past. She hadn't forgotten why she was here. She tolerated the tyranny of the Itzat so that she could learn the language and ask questions that might point her to her grandfather. The more she learned about Marut the more she missed him and wished he'd continued to speak the language to her. Everything would've been easier.

"*Sjeru.*" He pointed to an image on the picture scroll—a drawing of a man wearing traditional Maruti clothing of tall, colorful caftans, with a shimmering sun disk hovering above his head, and a fiery and flaming bird in one hand.

"*Keer Abnr* ," said Itzat. "*Keeer,*" she repeated.

"Ba," he barked, pointing to another image of a woman, dressed in a single-strapped dress, with plants and trees and water hovering above her head in a crown. "*Kaamma.*" His staff swept across the images "*Sjeru.*"

"Gods," she said with some understanding.

"*O'o kere sjeru,*" he said again, smiling and shaking his head.

"Don't do something to the gods."

His brow arched, but he turned away, returning to the lesson.

The Itzat wasn't as angry as she'd presumed. He had a sense of humor and liked acting out words. He pretended to walk— "*igaa,*" she'd yell out. He pretended to run—*igba*, to eat—*a-dla*. Slowly the lesson was coming along, but Kadsa still felt far from full comprehension.

She'd walk down the hall and struggle to understand what people were saying. The speech of the Maruti was fluid, fast on the tongue. She tried exchanging niceties, but people stared at her with expressions of confusion.

On her morning walk with Queen Oluchi, she tried to exchange greetings with a group of young priestesses tending the garden, and the girls giggled. It was frustrating. She could manage little more than, "Ba'ra-a" and "Ba'nu."

When King Remu decided to sit in on a lesson, the Itzat returned to his uptight professorial attitude. Kadsa tried her best to impress the king. She even wrote the king a short note about his improved health that read: "*Ba-ju- ra, a-kjr. A-na fadhi tat dar enhle.*" (Good afternoon, my king. I am glad you are here and well).

King Remu laughed happily but the Itzat's face tightened, looking unimpressed.

After the king left, he took the note.

"*O'o dai'a*"— this is not correct. "*Fadhi o'o dai'a.*"

She interpreted this to mean the word *fadhi* was not correct.

"*A-na fata'at dar enhle.*" When he said the word *fata*, he feigned a happy face with a mock laugh. *Fata* meant happy/pleased. For the word *fadhi*, he showed her a picture of a god, not Abnr, putting his hand on the heart of a king. She believed *fadhi* might mean faith/trust or vow—maybe respect. Not as if her word usage was completely off, but, oh well.

Kadsa very much wanted to impress the royals and her teacher, and a month into her lessons, she felt good about her progress, even if her pronunciation faltered in comparison to the musical intonation of the natives. Her written Maruti was coming together well.

The stylistic symbols used for the written language were hard to decipher at first. The language was not phonetic. It was written and read from top to bottom, not left to right. The stylistic symbol for *happy*, for example, looked like a knot with eyes, and nearly identical to the symbol for laughter, which had a slightly extended tail. The script required that words were linked in hoops and had to be the same height and length. Tenses and gerunds were formed with apostrophes and dashes. The Itzat's favorite word—"no" was formed with two squashed O-like symbols connected with a thin and delicate squiggly line running across both letters.

One night, as she wrote out some Maruti phrases in her notebook, her bedroom door creaked. About two and a half weeks into her lesson, she'd noticed that whoever had briefly spied on her had disappeared, perhaps due to a guard forever stationed at her bedroom door. In the last few days, however, the guards had stopped patrolling her door, and her admirer had returned to lurk around her room.

The bedroom door squeaked slightly ajar. "Hello?" she called.

The door slammed shut. When she got to it, and looked down the hall, there was no one.

The next night, she prepared for her intruder by setting a large footstool by the door, so he'd stumble over it. The secret admirer did not come. Instead, Sion stood sentinel by her door the whole night. She wasn't off the suspicion radar yet, despite the brief absence of guards.

The next night, Kadsa ate dinner with Prince Sahu before she retired to bed under the keen eyes of Sion. She wondered if he rested at all. Maybe he didn't need rest.

Four nights into her plan to catch the spy, Sion buckled, well into the wee hours of night.

After he left, she climbed out of her bedchamber, intent on exploring the corridor toward the far back of the palace, wherein her admirer had disappeared through the walls. Kadsa dragged her hands gently along the sidewalls, guiding her way forward, since the torches hoisted up on the wall were almost burned out.

The sound of a wind instrument compelled her to stop. She pressed her ear against the wall. It sounded as if it was coming from the inside of the wall. She didn't know specifics about musical instruments but thought it sounded like the lamellophone her grandpa used to play. That gave her hope—what if this *entity* was her grandfather trying to reach her? What if he was locked away somewhere around here? She considered that she was far off in believing this could be her grandfather giving her a sign, that this could be a trap.

The attack by the Buried Man wasn't that long ago. It still gave her chills. Yet she wanted to get to the bottom of this night mystery. Tracing the wall led her to the back lands where she and Queen Oluchi had ended up after their tour of the kingdom. Her brain played sleuth. She was certain the figure came from here and had run toward this direction. Nevertheless, no doorways were visible. How did the figure magically disappear into the walls? Nothing was on the other side of this wall, except for the farmyard at the end of which stood the fortress.

Kadsa believed the figure might have come from that fortress, the isolated brick building that occupied the small chunk of the palace back lands. She initially thought it might have been a farmstead, but none of the farmhands cared to venture anywhere near it. It stood at an unsafe proximity to the Dark Forest. Even when compared to the deep darkness of the forest, the small stone fortress looked spooky.

Staring at it, even in daytime, a shadow, more defined in form than the overall darkness, hovered around it. She couldn't think of a purpose for it. Were they hiding something in there? Her mind flooded with all sorts of horrors that might be inside of the fortress—deformed hunchbacks, snakes. It was too far away from the palace, sitting almost outside of the kingdom.

Crackling echoed from the direction of the fortress. Kadsa ambled toward it, paused with common sense, and then began backtracking. She squinted, trying to get a closer look at the area of the darkness where the sound resonated from. A behemoth-sized bird wandered into view, and Kadsa backed up toward the kitchen enclosure before pausing. It was a size and a half bigger than an ostrich. It stomped toward the farmland, and every instinct told her to run, but she remained flatfooted.

"Do not be afraid." Its voice washed across the lawn. "Wait a minute," she said with a jolt of excitement,

"You're speaking my language." "Yes, it's a nice language."

The peculiar-looking bird wandered within feet of her. It was every bit as odd as the Jakuba from the forest. Feathered patches of gold and red covered its large body. It had crimson wings and a red beak. Two crimson feathers sat at the crest of its head, and its tail feathers were regal red and gold. Its deep, round eyes watched her, waiting for her assessment of it to finish.

"How do you know my language? No one knows I speak that language except for the Jakuba."

"Would you prefer I speak Maruti to you?" "That's not what I was thinking. Who are you?" "My name is Bennu. I live in the forest."

"In the darkness," she said. "If that's the case, then how can you cross over?"

"I am old. I come from a time before the gods were fighting." The bird moved closer, and though she flinched, she kept her feet planted where she stood. She was interested in what it had to say.

"It was very common for me to travel between worlds before the separation and the darkness. I took no sides."

"Your name, Bennu, means seed of night, doesn't it?"

"More or less. You do know a little Maruti."

"I'm taking lessons," she said. "How do you speak my language, again?"

"I was born from the flames of Abnr. I am not mortal in the true sense of the term—I understand many things."

"You're a godtalker."

Bennu chuckled. "Not quite, but close enough." "But seriously, this is getting more confusing."

He laughed. "I can clear up anything you need me to, young lady."

Kadsa considered long and hard. She had a myriad of questions in her mind. "What is Nenet exactly? Is that another name for the witch?"

"Nenet is eternal—it refers to the celestial darkness, the motherly sea of existence that is the basis of the universe. Nenet is not the witch, though the witch has manipulated aspects of it for her cause."

"It's not evil?"

"Nenet is not evil. It will always exist in your world and this one. She won't be as strong as she is here, but she will still exist."

"You said the witch manipulates aspects of it. Did she cause the darkness?"

"I am not certain of the witch's true powers. Many believe she did cause the Dark Enchantment. How? It's not clear."

"Do you know how to undo any of it? If it spreads, that's not good for Mehronur."

"What you should do is restore balance. Right now, all the light has been concentrated in Mehronur. The dark is all around. There was a time, just before the cosmic shift, when it was not like this at all. Now, you can see night, permanently over the sky. You must restore it so neither is so heavily concentrated and both share equal power over the land—such as is the case in your world."

"How am I going to do that?" she asked, weighed down with worries.

"I advise you to visit the Akonadi in the temple of the Horned Lady. Everything after that should make sense." "I don't want to go back to the oracle lady, if that's what you mean by Ak— whatever." she dismissed, remembering all too well her bizarre experience with the snakes and the strange old woman. "Where else is a good place to start?"

"It's all I can tell you."

"I went already. They didn't help me."

"Did you ask for help? The Horned Goddess is the patron goddess of ritual blessings. The shrine is not well known, but it's a place many from the priesthood have visited to seek spiritual cleansing and truth."

"That's another thing." Kadsa exhaled. "These gods—they're not real, are they?" Kadsa still had trouble making sense of her new reality. The Itzat made many references to the gods, in particular Abnr, and a great scribe, but Kadsa just didn't get it. She accepted it, but didn't believe any of it.

"For the Maruti, their gods are real." "But they're not really real?"

"Kadsa, they're very much real to the Maruti. Here, the priests serve as mediums between the gods and men. Here, kings are descended from godmen."

Kadsa wasn't satisfied with the answer. She'd yet to see any real evidence that the gods of Oluran were living beings. Anyhow, she didn't want to waste her precious time with Bennu, so she considered more questions to ask. "Is Bokor a priest?"

Bennu considered. "I have heard of him. He's the head priest of the Order of Medicine."

"The Order of Medicine? Is that like a medical doctor?"

"In a way, yes, they tend to people's health." "So Bokor is…"

"A high-ranked priest of medicine. He is head of the medicinal temples."

"He is powerful. That explains his arrogance. Honestly, I don't like that man," she declared. "Between me and you, I don't trust him. The first day I met him, he poured powder on me. He left me in the temple with snakes, and I don't even know why."

"He might be testing you."

"Still don't like him." She faced her strange new friend. "Can you tell me anything else about Mehronur, or Marut? I'm failing miserably to understand how anything works."

"The society is very much like yours. You have your different sectors. Laborers, priests, officials, and so forth."

Bennu took a step back when her pendant began to glow.

"Why are you backing away?"

"I can feel the burning power of your crystal." "Really?" Kadsa eyed the pendant. "It bothers you?" "It has a dizzying effect."

Kadsa raised her brows. "I'm not even sure why it's glowing now since there's no fire around."

His laughter rung out in deep baritone richness. "Your crystal stores and traps natural light."

"Okay, that I get, but it glows at odd times. And ever since I got here, it's been one strange dream after the next and I know it's the pendant."

"When you say strange dreams, what do you mean?" "I mean exactly that," she said. "When I dream, darkness is always everywhere. I'm being watched by someone, and then out of nowhere, everything turns char black, like a big shadow blankets the sky and paints everything that color. Then there's just darkness. I don't know what it means, and I can't ask because my Maruti is terrible. But I am pretty sure it's the necklace that's causing these dreams."

"Your dream is about Mehronur," Bennu said. "The darkness surrounds the kingdom. The sudden rush of darkness is what will happen if the cosmic age comes and you do not restore the balance of light and dark. All that is here will disappear and come to resemble the forest, cold and black."

She shuddered. "But why's it showing me these things?"

"I suspect it's feeding off your own thoughts and melding all the energies and your consciousness to it, the reason why you see these visions."

"You know, I kind of suspected that. Still strange, though. You know a lot about a lot of things."

Bennu laughed. "As Abnr's gift, you soon will learn plenty of things, too."

Talks of her being Abnr's Gift made her nervous. She couldn't shake the stomach-twisted feeling that she would fail them somehow. "It's my grandfather, you know."

Bennu's beak jutted out.

"I mean. They think it's me who's Abnr's gift, but it's him. This crystal is his, and he speaks the language. That's why I must find him. I'm an imposter." Kadsa bit down on her lips, cringing that she just admitted this to him.

"Where has he gone?"

She shrugged. "I don't know. The crystal can't show him to me, but I feel he's here somewhere." She exhaled. "If I knew the language, or anything crucial, I could find him. It's frustrating."

"I am sure you will figure it out." He shook his feathers. "Kadsa, I must go, if it's all right with you." His voice was soft.

"Why?"

"I am tired."

"Oh. You mean bored of my rambling."

"No, you are very entertaining. I mean, I must go. I am tired."

"Hey, will I see you again? Will you come back, I mean?"

"I come by the same time every night."

"Why do you?" she asked, and then quickly added, "I'm sorry. That's nosy."

Bennu laughed. "It's all right." Silence again. "The food here is better than what exists in the forest."

"Okay," she said. Seth had given her a rundown of the food, or lack thereof, in the forest. She understood perfectly. They were near the kitchen, and there were plenty of food scraps everywhere, along with pens and cages for livestock.

"Is there anything else you need for now?"

"No, I can't think of anything. I should probably get back inside before the guards wake up and discover I'm not there."

"Have a good day, Kadsa." Bennu backed away.

Kadsa watched him take flight into the dark sky. She waited for him to disappear through the trees before she walked back to the palace. Inside the confines of the corridors, she listened for the sound of the instrument. Nothing. She'd try again another night.

13

MISTY

When King Remu next joined his family for breakfast, he looked thinner than Kadsa remembered seeing him. He coughed throughout breakfast. At one point, Queen Oluchi leaned over to ask him about his medicine, but he was dismissive. He offered to take Kadsa on a tour of the palace. Queen Oluchi instructed him that she had already done that, but he was persistent.

Kadsa walked beside him, while Queen Oluchi and Prince Sahu followed close behind. He took her hand in his many times, spoke his words with meticulous diction and stared her in the eyes.

In the afternoon, they left her alone, as was usually the case. The king tended to his duties, the queen to hers, and Prince Sahu to his. Kadsa decided to do as Bennu had told her, but not before first trying to find her grandpa through the crystal again. When she grabbed the pendant and asked it to reveal him, there was only a dark blot, and then it misted up again.

Frustrated, she changed her query. "Show me the way to the Temple of the Horned Lady?" She asked. Horned Lady was such a bizarre name for a temple. But the thought of there really being a lady with horns intrigued her. She truly believed it was a very real possibility.

The crystal revealed nothing. Kadsa let her shoulders slump before she straightened up again and brought the crystal to the window, where she lifted it up to the flood of sunlight. The pendant sparkled, its core filled up with white light. When she brought it to her eyes, instant hypnosis overcame her. The dirt road filled her mind, curving through the kingdom, cutting through a palm grove, leading all the way to a small ziggurat sitting a short distance from a baobab tree.

Kadsa jumped from her hypnosis with the same quickness she had fallen into it. She glanced around, bewildered, pondering about what just happened to her. She felt warmth filling her inside. That had never happened before. She studied the crystal. Maybe it could do more than simply trap light.

The images of the temple and tree remained fresh in her head, even after the silver-white light disappeared.

Kadsa got out of bed with the intention to leave the palace. On the terrace, she ran into her silent sentinel friend, Sion.

"I have to leave," she told him. "I'm going to the Temple of the Horned Lady."

Sion looked understanding, but when she began walking, he followed her. He might have thought she was asking him to accompany her, or perhaps, they instructed him to keep an eye on her. She took one of the abadas, intending to ride around the kingdom.

The sun was hot in the sky and reflected blindingly on the marble and granite objects that filled the kingdom. Sion trailed some feet behind her, not saying a word. The images of the temple and road in her head were now fading into a memory. She tried hard to prevent this. When it disappeared before she found the temple, she let out a groan.

"Sejat. Kasa. Horned Lady. Do you know d'at sejat?" she asked in broken Maruti.

Sion seemingly understood and pointed ahead before racing off. She followed him, worried he would lead her to some place she did not mean to go, but when they passed the palm grove, she spotted the large baobab tree in the distance and smiled. She had been here that night with Bokor.

Kadsa's mind burned with wariness. The last time Bokor brought her here, she had woken up in a room crawling with snakes and idols. Memories of the snakes made her tremble with disgust. And she had yet to make sense of what happened with that old woman in the room.

"Sion, you're a genius, a smart man," she told him before climbing off the abada and moving toward the tree on the hill. A small round temple sat in the valley, just under the hill, standing too close to the darkness.

"Why is that down there?" she asked, pointing. Sion looked but frowned.

Kadsa traced her hand over the giant tree while Sion began speaking rapidly about something. She faced him. He wagged his index finger at her, looking worried and superstitious. He pointed somewhat warily to the temple at the bottom of the hill. Perhaps he wanted her to consult the priestesses first.

Kadsa tried to heed his warning, yet she wouldn't have seen the vision of the baobab tree if it didn't have something to do with her quest for knowledge. She nodded to let him know she understood, and then she brought her attention back to the tree.

The tree had carvings of strange symbols on it. Some symbols looked like windings, others like vertical strings, and others were of animals. The carving of a female figure, adorned with white rays around her and a horned crown on her head, stood out.

The Horned Lady.

"I have no choice now. I want to go home," she explained. "Mehronur, Nenet, Star. I must do this in peace."

He stared at her but stopped speaking.

A young priestess moved toward them from the temple. Kadsa stepped back from the tree and waited for her to reach them.

The young girl smiled. "How may I help you?"

Kadsa blurted out. "*Fi'o a-smu ekwaa* (What are you saying)?"

Jiro Sion spoke slowly with deliberate words. She understood one word—temple. The muscles in Sion's jaws clenched visibly. Was he upset?

Kadsa leaned backward and stepped on the outgrowth root of the baobab tree. The tree released a crunching sound. The dirt around the trunk carved in and swallowed up Kadsa down into the earth. She screamed, tumbling downward.

While Sion circled the tree, trying to figure out how to open it, Kadsa was hanging upside down, dangling in vines and falling debris and panting, feeling as if life had just been stuffed back into her. When she was certain she wouldn't fall farther, she dared to glance around. The ropes that held her did so weakly, and she reached for the necklace dangling from her neck with slow and careful hands. It almost fell off. She brought it to her eyes. A little flicker remained in the crystal. It enhanced her eyesight to the full length of the hovel.

The room brought her dilemma into focus. Not only was she dangling above ground, but the distance from the top to the floor was staggering. She'd break a bone or two if she fell.

A dirt wall surrounded her. The room looked like it was in the early stages of construction. Perhaps an underground chamber. From the looks of it, the builders had abandoned it. She did not ponder the reasons why but wondered instead if it led back to the temple. The baobab tree wasn't too far from the temple, after all.

Kadsa tugged the necklace under the heavy fabrics she wore as clothing before taking a deep breath. She'd have to try to turn herself upright and swing herself upward, trying to grab the scrawny vines. They tore away from the wall, bringing down dirt on her head and dropping her about two inches. She yelped, and realizing she hadn't hit the ground, took a deep breath.

Kadsa took a moment before swinging herself upright a second time. The tree rope loosened from her grip and tore away, and she hustled to grab another to avoid slipping. Kadsa's breathing clogged her throat. She was upright, but still dangled about fifty dangerous feet off the ground. Now she had to figure out how to get to the floor.

Kadsa took a moment to breathe. Carefully tugging, she attempted to loosen the vines and lower herself inch by inch. The stupid ropes were so rotted, they peeled completely away from the dirt wall.

"No!" she screamed, breath seeping out of her, as she spiraled downward. She stopped dramatically, heart pounding. She hadn't hit the bottom, so not dead yet. Instead, she hung about seven feet off the ground. Kadsa breathed a huge sigh of relief, only to hear the slow tear away of the ropes. Oh no! Think. Kadsa held her breath and jumped. She landed on her feet with a slight stumble, and a pile of dirt came down on her head.

She rushed out of the way. The dirt slide stopped soon enough, and she was left soiled, spitting grains of dirt, but she'd made it!

Kadsa adjusted her clothes and looked around the dirt room. It was an unfinished construction site. The opening was a mole hole that ran through the side of the dirt wall. Instinctively, she moved toward it, determined that she was big enough to fit inside.

Kadsa weighed her options, thinking of the pros and cons of climbing through the hole. She didn't know what, if anything, was inside, or if it led to anywhere or was just a dead end.

"Ka- Kadsa!" called Sion from above.

Kadsa screamed his name back a few times. It went back and forth but didn't make a difference. Sion was saying something, but she didn't know what. Kadsa wouldn't stay down in the dirt dungeon waiting for Sion to rescue her—and it sounded as if he was trying, though he'd gone silent now.

She buried her hands in the dirt, pulling out a thin weed buildup that blocked the entrance. Dust flooded out and she coughed. Nothing but dirt existed in the tunnel. She crawled with care and caution, mindful that it might collapse. She was glad to be barely bigger than a child. If she was physically larger, she'd never fit through the small opening or worse, she'd get stuck in it.

Kadsa's fingernails caked with dirt as she made her way through the tunnel. Despite her shallow breathing, increased claustrophobia, and nervous thoughts, she refused to turn back. The tunnel felt like a vacuum. Hollow roars echoed through in different directions. Rather than turn back, she held her breath, telling herself the howling likely led to an opening or air pocket. She reached another passageway that curved to the right and hesitated. Her mind filled with all the horrors of what she might find through it. After hesitating, Kadsa took a deep breath and broke the corner. She was in too deep now, so she followed it.

The howling became guttural. She couldn't ignore it and she struggled to place it. To boost her confidence, she began checking off all the nightmarish situations she had faced already. The most frightening was back in the forest. That seemed so long ago. She put herself in these situations. She was used to this.

The Jakuba had terrified her, but she survived. She could survive this. Her skin smoldered. It was too hot and clammy down here.

The new passageway was shorter than the first one, and when she came to the end of it, a shiny fleck revealed itself. An opening. She hesitated, taking deep breaths. She sweated through her clothes. What were her chances of survival? She jolted with the deep howl that rung out behind her. Small mole rat creatures rushed toward her. Kadsa jumped and threw herself backward, losing her balance. She tumbled down the opening.

Kadsa screamed, biting back the pain of her body slamming into the hard wall. She rolled to a stop and laid there for a while, her mind numb as the pain worked its way through her body. When she gained control of her mind and body again, she was lying in a shallow pool of water. She pulled herself up, noticing the faint, blue glow reflecting in the water. Its illumination made it look like a pool with fluorescent bulbs.

Kadsa held her breath at the sight of the glare. Realization formed slowly in her mind. The light radiating in the pool came from her—not her necklace but her own body. She was radiating.

Breathe! She looked up to the passageway inside the wall from where she fell.

Her mind filled with cut and paste memories of what had happened at Tibesti cave. The crystal had broken her fall then. She studied herself again. Bennu had said the crystal drew from her own energy. Now the light emanated from her body. Maybe this was a side effect of putting the crystal to her eyes, but then again, it didn't just enhance her vision, but entered and permeated through her whole body as well. Kadsa fisted her hands and felt a sting of electricity run through her upper body. It felt strangely good. When she reached for the crystal, she noticed a dot of light in its core. What a strange object. Now more than ever, she wondered where her grandfather might have gotten it.

The howling caught her attention. For the first time, she studied the space in which she found herself. It was another underground sanctuary.

The stone mouth of what appeared to be a shallow well sat in the center of the small dirt hovel. She moved toward it, taking note that the halo around her wasn't going away. Other than a zap of electricity in her body, she felt completely normal.

Kadsa stared at the stone well, pretty certain the howling came from it. It stood barely four feet off the ground. She leaned over it, dipped her hand inside and gripped a small chunk of wood, pulling it out. A loud howl echoed from deep inside, and she staggered backward, dropping the object on the ground.

After catching her breath, she reached for the object and dashed it back into the hovel. But her mistake was made. The pit threw the idol back up. One then another. Chunks of wooden blocks rained out of its mouth. When it stopped, about twenty pieces were lying on the ground. She picked up one of them to analyze it. The wooden block was rectangular with crooked hands and bent knees. It had a grotesque face, wide-open mouth and bulging eyes. Each block was more of the same. The faces were ugly, distorted and exaggerated in their features. They looked identical, and the longer she studied them, the creepier and more sinister they appeared.

She should probably get out of here, wherever *here* was. A pinch of curiosity dragged her eyes to the stone well. Bennu said the Horned Lady was a goddess. Her curiosity quickly turned to anxiety. She might be desecrating the temple. Sacrilege. She needed to get out fast. Kadsa turned to leave but paused when she remembered why she came—to see an oracle. She didn't think she was in the right place, but something lived in this hovel.

At the very least, she picked up two of the fetishes and tossed them back inside. She waited for something to happen, and when it didn't, she began picking up the others and tossing them back inside. She was nearly done when she noticed that the bottom of the well had given way. She felt around the mouth but couldn't feel the idols. She hadn't realized it was that deep. The earth around her trembled like a sleeping giant stirred awake below it.

Oh, crap!

The pit yawned and groaned.

Kadsa steadily backed away from it, intent on running.

"Don't be foolish, child," spoke a masculine voice from the pit.

She paused. "I didn't mean to bother you. I was just leaving."

Another voice spoke in a foreign language she didn't understand. There was more than one of them in there. What they were she couldn't say.

"I'm sorry. I don't speak that language." Crackling. A howling belch.

Kadsa ran the moment a white mist burst from the bottom of the pit. The fast-moving mist twisted out and blocked her path. Kadsa raced from it but could not escape it. She fell to the ground and noticed she no longer radiated.

The mist wasn't really a mist. It was some entity of blue light with specs of glitter. It twisted into a human- like figure—a creature of mist and light.

"I came here to see the oracle," she declared. "Are you the oracle of knowledge—The Horned Lady?"

A crack of pressure sizzled out of the misty entity. Was it trying to speak? All she made out was hissing, whispering that grew and then a sharp scream that forced her to cover her ears.

"Kadsa," said a female voice.

Kadsa pulled her hands from her ears and watched it. "I'm sorry for disturbing you."

The mist twisted and a horizontal slit crept across its makeshift face, forming a mouth.

"You don't know what I am and yet you've come." "I came for knowledge from the Horned Lady."

"I am not the Horned Lady, but I am the knowledge you seek. Speak, stranger." It was yet another voice, this time gender ambiguous.

"I came to ask for your help. I want to understand Maruti."

The voice grumbled in a foreign language. "Please, I don't understand."

"I am the tongues of the world."

"I came here to see the oracle, or the ancestors or something. Is that you?"

"I am the only entity here. I speak for the ancestors and the oracles. I am their voices. What do you want?"

"I just want to speak Maruti well."

"Who sent you here? How did you find me?" "No one. I came by myself. I need help." "Abnr. I see Abnr in your eyes, I see. Are you?"

"I am Abnr's Gift," Kadsa said, cringing. She hated saying that phrase but hoped it would spare her. "I have no genuine understanding of what that means."

"It means you're a thief. You stole knowledge from me. Knowledge you had no business stealing." The thing swarmed her, wrapping tendrils around her throat, as if a rope.

"Please." Kadsa fought through the chokehold. "You're killing me."

"I'm taking back the knowledge you stole from me." "Please," Kadsa begged, "I didn't steal from you. I swear."

The Mist wouldn't let up while it suffocated the life out of her body.

"You're here to steal more knowledge, is that your reason for coming?"

Kadsa fell to her knees and coughed, gasping for air. "I am looking for the oracle of Akonadi. Please, stop!" Kadsa yelled this last sentence out with all her strength, and for her effort, the mist pulled away from her, leaving her fighting to breathe. Kadsa didn't understand why it had pulled away, but she could see its shape forming into a gel-like image of blue and white.

"You have one last chance to make your purpose clear."

Kadsa swallowed, wetting her throat. "I only came to learn how to speak Maruti, so I can understand these people. I want to understand their language. That's all. I swear it."

"Do you lie to me, girl?"

"No, I swear it. They said you'd help me."

"They?" hissed the mist. "Who's they—who sent you here?"

"Bennu, I mean," she stammered, swallowing the lump in her throat and getting to her feet. "He said this is where to find you."

"Bennu," said the mist, "the ancient one?"

Kadsa nodded and watched the shimmering thing before her eyes, waiting for it to decide.

"You're a fallen star. You've traveled from far. You've come to understand the ways of this land." It mimicked Bennu's voice.

"Yes," Kadsa said nodding. "Yes, I did. I want to help the people here. But I need to understand them, first."

"To help. How can you help them, girl?" "To fight the darkness."

"The Enchantment of Night," declared the Mist's symphonic voices. "The Night is long, forever and eternal. It cannot be defeated."

"Yes, I know," said Kadsa, remembering Bennu's words. "I meant the witch in the forest. Help me understand Maruti, so I can help the people. Please!"

"The witch called Akwanshi?"

"Yes, that's her." Kadsa blinked with uncertainty. She didn't know her name.

The creature shrieked disturbingly. It was cacophonous and painful to listen to. Kadsa covered her ears. The Mist spun violently, taking on a human form before her eyes. Soon it had molded itself into an image of a woman made of mist and light; she floated in slow motion above the open space. Kadsa stared in awe. How was this possible? Its blazing eyes studied her.

"You are impressed by this, child?" "What are you?"

"I am an old being that existed very long ago and no more."

"The gods made you?"

"I am the collected wisdom and spirit of worlds," she explained. "I am ancient. No one made me. I was here before your people."

"The wisdom of worlds?" "Yes—worlds." it answered. "What worlds?"

"Never you mind that," it said. "All you need to know is that I know everything. So, don't you think you can fool me. They fooled me once and once only. And that's why I am down here, trapped."

"I am not here to fool you. I want nothing to do with that." When the oracle didn't respond, she continued. "You can't leave this place?"

"It's best that I am here. It means I won't be disturbed. My knowledge is protected. I have been here for thousands of years. What I know is protected and safe. I don't move, but my knowledge grows still. That's all that matters."

"But you're stuck here." Kadsa watched the mist- figure. "You can't leave."

"I am to be released when the end is the beginning, and the beginning is the end."

"What does that mean—the end of what—the world or Mehronur?"

"When the end is the beginning again." Its words were dreamy. "The ones who trapped me will undo what they've done. For now, I am a slave to those words they uttered."

"The gods trapped you here with their words?" "The priests of mystery did it," snapped Misty. "I never understood the words they uttered. It was what confused me the most and led to my capture. Their ancient chants ensnared me where I roamed the skies, collecting my wisdom. They spoke a language I couldn't understand, even while I am the keeper of all mortal knowledge."

Kadsa watched this creature with confusion and some pity. How did this story fit into the greater mystery of Marut? Did it even? "Are you lonely here?"

"Kadsa, I am not human. Loneliness is a human sensibility."

"But you seem to hate the witch. Hate is a human sensibility."

"The witch," said the female voice. "I do not hate her for me. The witch is cruel. I hear her many voices— the ones she has trapped in her web of power. They cry and shriek all the time. They are in pain. It is endless torment."

"You can't shut out her voices? That sounds like a nightmare."

"It is the way it is for me. I hear everything, even cruelty."

"Is the witch human? Why does she trap spirits?" "She once was human, a very long time ago. She is not as old as I am, but she knows many things. She understands nature, nearly as much as I do. But while I am a part of it, she steals from it, and she uses it to do unjust things. This is why mortals cannot be trusted with knowledge. This is why I am safer here. But you found me."

"I'm really not trying to steal. I just need help with the language." Kadsa studied the mist-figure, recognizing her moment to sell herself. "There are so many things I don't know and understand about this place. But everyone expects me to help them. I can't figure it out alone, especially if I can't understand what they're telling me. That's why I came to you."

Misty didn't speak.

"Can you please help me learn the language, figure out what I am doing? How do I find the heart of the darkness? Where is it?"

"Bennu told you of me." Kadsa nodded.

"I trust him. He's as old as I am."

The mist moved closer and Kadsa stilled. "You've come to save the kingdom of light. When the time is right and the night is bright, you will find those things that are in your mind."

Misty brushed against her cheeks, sending a cold, thin thread of mist to her mouth. A tingling icy sensation ran down Kadsa's throat, filling her head, making her a little dizzy. Her breathing shortened and grew shallow. Her eyes misted up, making it impossible to see.

"I can't see. What did you do?" Kadsa cried in panic. She got angry and she squinted, trying to push against the cloud formed over her eyes. The Mist twirled away from her. Kadsa grabbed for it. From what she could make out and hear, it crawled back toward the mouth of the pit.

"Wait! Please!" Kadsa called. No answer.

Kadsa stumbled around part blind, angry, and scared. She blinked twice and slowly, the cloud Misty had pulled over her eyes clawed back, and her sight was restored to normal. She exhaled. She was alone in the hovel. A faint dull echo emanated from the pit, but there was no sign of Misty. Certain the gel-like creature wouldn't return, Kadsa tossed the miniature statues back into the pit, watching them fill it up. Misty didn't kill her, but she wasn't sure what it had done to her. Aside from her burning eyes, she felt alright.

Kadsa returned to the cavity in the side of the dirt wall and retraced her previous journey. She moved straight ahead rather than turn back toward the room where she had first fallen. A very narrow passageway brought her to the end of a tunnel. Kadsa sat upright, dangling her feet over the dark mouth of the tunnel.

"Can't keep doing this." she muttered, taking a deep breath and pushing herself down the slide.

———

A wooden window or miniature door existed at the end of the tunnel. This was a good fixture in the otherwise enclosed tunnel. Kadsa crawled to the door and paused. A woman's voice echoed from behind the window and she leaned in closer to peep. Through the creases, Kadsa spotted a young woman dressed in a crimson red robe. The color was astonishing with dreamlike shimmer.

"Priestess," said Bokor, his imposing figure moving toward the slender woman, "Once again, do you understand what I am asking you to do?"

Kadsa caught her breath in her throat when she nearly burst into laughter. She understood everything he had said. Whatever magic Misty blew into her had worked. She focused on the big man again, leaning closer to eavesdrop on what he was saying.

"I told you all I know of these prophecies," spoke the woman in red.

The priestesses Kadsa had met wore white. This woman looked very different. She had a clean-shaved head except for those parts that were carved into crop circle designs. Her lips blackened with lipstick, and her robe fitted her with a comfort that made Kadsa want to wear a dress, and she never wanted to wear dresses. Queen Oluchi had looked aghast when Kadsa began tying her dresses to resemble trousers.

"She has proven herself to be very suspicious." "My readings—"

"—Can be off," he spoke coldly. Bokor squashed whatever he had in his palm.

"High Priest," said the mysterious woman, "Isaan is never wrong."

"Your goddess was wrong about the girl."

"Why did you come here?" She circled him. "Why do you favor sabotage?"

Bokor stepped forward and grabbed her by the shoulders. "Remember Priestess of Isaan, this is your fate, too."

She pulled away from him. "We do not fear the darkness."

"You are directly under my command." "Isaan has no master—no god."

"Your temple will be the first to bow if you choose not to worship."

"There's nothing Isaan cannot see. In this great darkness, you do not exist," she said.

Bokor heaved, lifting his chest higher. Silence fell over the room.

"Bokor, your time at the temple is up," said the woman coldly.

Bokor looked ready to protest. He edged closer to the unflinching woman. "Think very wisely about your fate," he said and stormed out of the room.

The priestess stared after him and then exited the room soon after.

After they were gone, Kadsa fiddled with the door, eventually kicking it open. She crawled out of the dusty space, which was nothing but a low-built window in the room. No one would suspect it was anything more than a tiny, useless window. The room was small. It had one large table, wooden barrels, and wooden shelves. It was some sort of storage room. Kadsa skipped toward the exit that Bokor and the shaved-headed woman had used. She pressed her ears against the door. She could hear nothing, so she twisted the lock gently and pushed the door ajar.

The hallway was mostly empty, drenched in darkness. Kadsa wandered through the dungeon-like interior, finding herself in a spacious rotund room with burning red candles.

"Are you looking for the exit?"

"Yes," said Kadsa, facing the woman warily.

The mystery speaker, wearing a billowing red robe, stood. She looked identical to the woman from the room with Bokor, even down to the multi-tiered rings around her long neck. Kadsa didn't know if the women were the same.

"The temple has one exit. It is also an entrance. You were never invited inside."

Kadsa was a little nervous. Something about this woman intimidated and intrigued her—brilliant crimson red robes, the dark lipstick, ringed neck, and the shaved head.

"I got lost."

"In a house you were never invited into."

"If you show me the exit, I will gladly leave." The woman in brilliant red didn't answer.

"Okay, then," said Kadsa, intending to bypass her. "You are she of the Mystery's Reveals," said the woman.

"If you mean Abnr's Gift, then yes, everyone knows that." Kadsa didn't mean to give attitude, but she started it. Anyhow, she stared the woman down, noticing the way her eyes cut into her. She was reading her.

"But not everyone knows if you fail or succeed."

Kadsa swallowed. Did this woman really know what would happen?

"If I fail or succeed is up to me." "Maybe, maybe not," she said.

Kadsa stiffened, facing her. "Is there something you want to tell me?"

"Nothing I should."

Snarky. Annoying. "Who are you? Where is this?" "You broke into this temple."

"Technically, I did not break into the temple. I fell inside."

She had a snigger on her dark lips. "And where is this place, anyway?

"You are in the temple of the One-faced goddess. I am Isaan, priestess of the temple."

So very cool she was. "How do I get out?" "To your right."

"Thank you." "Kadsa," Isaan called.

Kadsa faced the woman's back.

"Find the Dark Prince. That's how you will save Marut." She blew breath ever so gently, and the flames of all the red candles in the room died.

Nothing was visible in the darkness. Not even the brilliant red robe. Overcome by an eerie chill, she raced from the room. The priestess said to turn right.

Kadsa arrived at a long staircase, but instead, she ran toward a tall and narrow red door to the right of it. The door opened to let her out and then slammed behind her with a force that hinted at something supernatural.

Kadsa raced into the waning light of day and found herself deep into a valley. Behind her was the darkness, no more than a few yards away from the temple. Why would these women stay so close to the darkness?

The giant baobab tree she'd fallen into cast a large shadow on the hill. Sion was waiting. Two young temple girls and an older woman were speaking to him. Down the other side of the hill from them was the temple of the Horned Lady—the temple she believed she'd been inside just now. The Isaan Temple, on the other side of the hill, wasn't visible at all. The steep hill hid it.

Kadsa rushed toward them, hearing Sion plead for help to find her.

"Did you miss me?" Kadsa asked, sneaking up on them.

The women's eyes widened with confusion.

Sion stared Kadsa up and down. "How did you get out?"

"It's a long story. I can tell you on the way back."

Sion's eyebrows arched almost comically while his face distorted with confusion.

"Your Maruti is perfect now."

Kadsa laughed. "I got it worked out."

Sion stopped himself from smiling, a bit of a win, really.

"Kadsa, I am Neith, the High Priestess of the Temple.
Master Sion informed me you were in some trouble." "I am
okay."

Kadsa wondered if she should bring up the Isaan. The High
Priestess spoke to the two young girls; they nodded obediently
and then bowed and walked away.

"Master Sion was upset. I'm glad you're alright," said Neith.

"Thank you."

"Master Sion told me you are here looking for something—
the Akonadi." Her expression looked strained.

"I am not looking anymore," she confessed, not wanting to
give too much information. "I just wanted to see the temple. I
heard about it."

Neith nodded with understanding. "Well, I am sure the
Horned Lady would welcome you with open arms," said Neith.
"She's our patron goddess of Ritual blessings and cleansing."

Something clicked in Kadsa's brain then, and she pondered if
she should ask about Bokor. She quickly changed her mind, since
she'd been eavesdropping and might not be able to explain her
suspicions about him.

Sion studied her. "We must go back. It's getting late." "Yes,
okay," she agreed.

She turned to Neith. "We have to go." "Kadsa," called the
High Priestess, "Be safe." Kadsa smiled and nodded. "Goodbye."

After she and Sion climbed onto the abadas, she took the opportunity to inquire, now that she could, if the abada was related to the zebra. Sion wasn't certain. "King Auta, King Remu's father, was a great explorer," Sion told her when she inquired about the equine. "He traveled to all the lands. One day, he returned with the abada after an expedition into the southern lands. They have been here ever since. He also brought with him a wife, Ramla, the prophetess, daughter of the king of a southern kingdom."

"By the way, Sion, why do you flirt with me?" she teased while they rode toward Hutat.

"I do not flirt. I don't even know what you mean by that."

She chuckled. "You know, Sion, I think this is the beginning of a beautiful friendship."

"If you don't mind me asking, where did you disappear to?"

"An underground world," she admitted. "What did you see?"

"I saw the Akonadi." Kadsa wasn't certain it was the Akonadi but she didn't know what she had seen. The Akonadi seemed an easy answer.

"The goddess?" Sion appeared to be thinking about her words.

"I believe so." She considered. "Come to think of it, I don't know if that's what she was. I assumed. Anyway, it doesn't matter. I can now speak to you."

Sion didn't say anything. They marched on without passing words between them.

At the palace, a sudden rush of excitement came over Kadsa. She made a breakthrough. Now she could start plotting how to get home again. First, she needed to find Grandpa Edoje, and that would start with asking the right questions.

14

AMUNU

Kadsa climbed down from the abada, thrusting it to one of the stable boys, before stopping to apologize for being pushy. She didn't get far into the palace grounds before realizing some celebration was happening in the public courtyard.

King Remu was giving a speech. One of the guards quickly escorted Kadsa into the event to stand next to Queen Oluchi on the veranda.

Queen Oluchi smiled at her and squeezed her hand. "What's happening?" she asked curiously, not sure if she should be excited or what.

Queen Oluchi did not answer.

Despite this, Kadsa pushed, far more excited than she should be, "I'm speaking Maruti."

The distracted Queen Oluchi smiled, but quickly brought her attention back to the king.

This speech must be serious, Kadsa thought and steadied her attention on King Remu.

"My loyal subjects," he said with a hoarse voice. "I know you've waited for this moment a long time. It is with great pleasure that I have served you. And I know you are weary." He paused. "The time has come for me to end my reign. No time is better than now," he started again. "The dawn of a new age is upon us. With a new age, you need a new ruler."

Bokor had a smug and knowing look, seeming pleased with something, that made Kadsa snigger, wanting to give him a humbled mask. Her grandpa also said smugness was a sign of evil. So what was this horrible man up to?

Bokor gave her a nasty look as if she was an insect. Now that she could speak the language fluently, she'd demand answers about everything, the Tibesti cave and her grandfather's whereabouts. One way or the other, she'd get him to confess he had something to do with it. When she gestured to the queen again, Oluchi brushed her off. "His majesty is naming his successor."

"Oh," was all Kadsa said, and thought, wasn't it obvious Sahu was his successor? Why did he have to give a speech about it? But she didn't ask this, and instead shut up and listened.

"What I will say may stun some of you, but it must be said." King Remu paused for a moment. "You can see me, and you can see that I am not well. I am an ill man."

The crowd grumbled and whispered among themselves.

"It is with great pain that I resign as your king. It is with great pain that I step down. I had hoped to see you into the new age, but I cannot. And so I think it's only right that I pass rulership to someone I believe is fit to see you into your new hour. It is with great consideration that I made this decision, and it is with great hope that I announce the name of my successor. The name of your new king." The king coughed—a mucus-heavy sound.

Bokor adjusted his robe and pushed his chest forward, not moving an inch to aid the king.

"But before I do that, I must get something off my conscience." The king started again. "I must admit the truth that many of you already know, the one indiscretion I made as king. This is my confession to correct it."

Queen Oluchi cringed. She had been holding her breath and upright posture for a long time. Kadsa wondered if the regal young queen knew what her husband's indiscretion was. Queen Oluchi brushed her robe and lifted her head with dignity, despite the heavy bell-shaped headdress that weighed her down.

"During the period before the endless darkness started," King Remu said. "I had a first wife. Not the beautiful and loyal one I have now, but another wife whom I loved. As many of you may have remembered, she was with child in the hours before the darkness."

Queen Oluchi lowered her head again, and Kadsa wondered where the king's speech headed. What was he saying?

"She had that child, a boy."

The crowd looked at one another in confusion.

An older man came through the crowd to the front then. "So you admit it, king," yelled the old man. "You had a son that came with the darkness."

"I do have a son—Yes, Asau, you are correct," King Remu spoke, defeated.

"Then you're admitting you lied to us about the cursed boy, your son."

The crowd erupted in uproar.

Kadsa did not understand what was going on. She turned to look at Bokor and saw a smile on his face. When he saw her looking at him, the smile disappeared, replaced by a frown.

"Please," the king begged, trying to quiet the crowd. "I must continue," he said. "I must say this."

It took the crowd a while to quiet down, and they did so when Asau yelled, "Speak, king."

"Thank you." King Remu gripped his chest. "My son, I told you he died with his mother during childbirth, but that was not entirely true."

The crowd murmured, but he quieted them with a hand. All the time, Queen Oluchi stared ahead, unmoved and serious, while Kadsa tried to make sense of the king's rambling words.

"I believe you know the circumstances of his birth. You know about Abnr and about Nenet and about his special burden," said the king in some pain.

"He's cursed! That's why you hide him," Asau yelled.

"No," King Remu said with temerity. "I hide him because I worry about him. I worry what you may do to him. He doesn't deserve to be hurt. I hid him because I could not live with myself if I killed him. What sort of honorable man kills his own son, his child, his flesh and blood? His firstborn?"

"You should've killed him as a king for his people. We all know the boy is cursed. He is the living Nu'at!"

"No." King Remu shook his head defiantly when the crowd roared in agreement with Asau. "He is not cursed!"

Everyone stirred in awe, shocked to hear his voice, so strong and powerful and so harsh.

"He is not cursed. The gods blessed him. He is my son. My firstborn. My heir."

Kadsa watched the king and wondered why he felt the need to reveal what he was revealing, but she soon understood why. He was a dying man who needed to get a burden off his chest. He was guilt-ridden.

King Remu brought his head up. "My son." His eyes roamed over the crowd. "He is to become your new king."

The crowd fell into stunned silence. Bokor moved forward. He was shocked. The queen was shocked. Bokor stood by the king's side.

"Please," he pleaded with the crowd. "Forgive him. He did not mean it. He is ill. He means to say his successor will be Prince Sahu."

"You are not the king, I am," said King Remu between clenched teeth. "I made no mistake."

"But Divine King, we agreed," said Bokor, eyes pinning him lividly.

"This is my choice. This is the best choice." He straightened up. "My people, your rightful heir is my firstborn son. He is to be your true divine king."

The crowd grumbled.

"You bring a curse upon us," cried the old chef. "You may have upset the ancestors. Bring the wrath of Nenet." "When I am gone, he will take my place." King Remu's voice was soft again. "Because it is right. I know this now."

"The only son whose ascension I can oversee is that of Prince Sahu, my king."

"You will do as I command you. My firstborn will take the throne in the days to come, as per my instruction." He faced the crowd. "That's my stance and it's final. Goodnight." He scurried away toward his queen, who smiled uncomfortably and placed her hands inside of his.

"I will support your choice, if you think it is best," she said.

Kadsa followed them, feeling caught in a hyena trap—this felt personal—family drama.

The crowd outside the palace dispersed, but not without grumble.

During the night, Kadsa eavesdropped on two servants gossiping about people gathering to call on their ancestors or to make offerings to the prince she had yet to meet.

Bokor looked angry for the rest of the night.

After dinner, she must have been thinking too hard, because when she looked up, Bokor was staring her down. He quizzed her about her whereabouts and wondered aloud if she had anything to do with the king's decision. She made it clear that she had nothing to do with it. He was still mistrustful of her even after she survived his snake pit. When she informed him she had visited the temple of the Horned Lady he looked in disbelief.

"You lie," he spat.

"Then how do I speak Maruti so well?"

"It's an easy language to learn. You've been taking lessons. The ancestors would never trust you. You barely survived the snakes."

"Abnr chose me."

"And you've yet to prove you are worthy."

"I survived the snake pit," she said defensively.

"You have been useless to the kingdom so far, foreigner."

Kadsa was quiet for a second until a thought flashed into her head. "Where's the Dark Prince?"

"The what?"

"The Dark Prince. I must free the prisoner."

"I don't know of whom you speak," he dismissed. "You're the wise man, Bokor. You should know." His painted expression curled before he scoffed, tossed his cape over his shoulder and marched off.

A dirty word she had learned among the Tuareg jumped into her thoughts, and for a quick second she worried she'd shouted it after him, but no one was looking at her, and Bokor didn't look back, so she breathed easily. This man tested her patience.

Fine, she'd just have to find the Dark Prince herself. That might be a good way to stay out of the royal family drama.

———

By the next night, King Remu had fallen deep into his illness, which shocked Kadsa. A royal guard brought her to his chamber. Bokor greeted her with dangerous looks before exiting. In his feverish state, King Remu joked about her newly acquired language skills. He was impressed that she spoke the language so well after struggling for weeks. He joked that the spirits of the ancestors must like her.

Kadsa tried not to look frightened, worried, or show any emotions that expressed her true horror about the king's rapid decline.

"They often hate to be disturbed," he said of the ancestors and laughed. His face turned serious. "I don't doubt for a second you are from Abnr's heart."

She forged a smile.

"You will guide my son when he sits upon the divine throne."

She nodded. "Do you really have another son?" "Yes," he said. "I have not treated him well. For that, I am sorry."

It was messed up that King Remu had another son that he hid. It made her think about how her grandpa had lied to her about her mother being alive. Somehow, she felt more pity for the king than her grandpa, though listening to him talk about his son made her think his son wouldn't be so forgiving. Why do these adults do shady things?

"Where is your other son?"

"Bokor knows," he said and coughed … and coughed some more. "I had a vision—the first in a long time. I am the son of a prophetess, you know. My visions are rare, but always come at important times. I haven't had one in twenty years. In my vision, the time had come to name my successor. It showed him to me when I lifted Marut's crown over Sahu's head. A radiant light shone, and I fixed my eyes upon it and there he stood with the most glorious crowns over his head—Abnr's and NKzum's. I know it is right."

King Remu coughed again. Kadsa brought the wooden cup with the hot herbal mix to him. He took a sip but rejected the cup afterward.

"I hate the medicine," he told her. "It's too late now anyway. Bokor…" He took a long pause between words. "He's been my personal advisor and doctor for the past three years. His medicines haven't helped at all—just filled my body with bitter tastes and drowsiness."

King Remu coughed again. Kadsa held his hand.

"We've been waiting a very long time for your arrival Kadsa Abasi," he started. "There were days when I thought you weren't coming, that I thought the gods had forsaken us. I thought they cursed and doomed us. I hated to think such thoughts, but hope is frail, a very fickle thing to cling to, if I dare say so. I never admitted this to anyone, not even my most beloved wife."

King Remu's cough was guttural, mucus heavy on his chest.

In a way, King Remu reminded her of Grandpa Edoje. He had the same twinkle of deep knowledge in his eyes. She wished there was something she could do to help him, to save him.

"I must tell you," King Remu started again. "It's important that you should know."

She exhausted her patience but waited.

"Abnr's chosen must restore light by the next season. We shall be ushered into the flooding season in a week and a half, my child. The world will be in chaos."

Kadsa's eyes widened. "A week and a half! That's not long. That's not far away at all. I thought there was more time."

"No, my child, there isn't." "Are you sure about this?"

He smiled weakly. "Yes, I am sure. The sundial is accurate. We had lied to the people about its chimes, to spare them. The stargazers are rarely inaccurate—the new season is upon us."

Kadsa mulled over his words, feeling the absolute worst. She pressed her lips into a cool smile, hoping to mask her fear, even if she was terrified. What if she could not do this?

The king seemingly knew what she was thinking, because he continued, "I am confident you will put it together. I am confident you know what to do. If Abnr sent you, if the oracle spoke to you, then you are divine reason in mortal flesh. My son, he is smart, too. He will help you when he becomes king."

The threads of doubt weaved the picture of failure with her stomach muscles. And for a brief second, she imagined how if she hadn't chosen to find her grandpa, she might be cozy with her mom in Toronto right now. Then she wilted. She was here and had to do this. It was the only way she might be able to see her mother again. "You will find the heart of the darkness. You will find the soul of Abnr." He spoke the words as if they were a rehearsed mantra and then shut his eyes, and for a second, she worried he was gone, but then he coughed as if he was choking. "My king."

He opened his eyes. "What is it, child?"

She took a deep breath. "I went to see the Akonadi." She edged closer when he frowned. "I asked her what to do, she said to find the Dark Prince and free the prisoner. When I asked Bokor, he claimed not to know who that was, but I don't believe him. Do you know anything about this person?"

"A prisoner—the Dark Prince ..." His voice broke and he coughed laboriously—too gut-wrenching. Too hoarsely.

"A-nuwo Khansu. A-nuwo," he murmured. "Happy you came. Tell my son I am sorry. Tell him that I love him, regardless."

King Remu fell back into deep silence. His eyes closed. Kadsa called his name for clarity, but he did not respond this time. She called his name a second time. No response. Then the door buckled open and Bokor emerged arrogantly. He gave her one long snooping stare before rushing to the king's bedside.

"King Remu?" he said. The king did not respond.

He picked up the king's mug. "Did you give him any of this?"

"A little, but he didn't want it," she trailed off. Bokor's glare was condemning. Seconds later, Queen

Oluchi rushed inside. Bokor continued to glare at Kadsa while the queen rushed to the side of her husband.

"My king." Queen Oluchi shook the king's shoulders.

No response.

Bokor stared at the cup accusingly. When Queen Oluchi gave up and the guards were at the door, Bokor took a deep breath and thrust his heavy chest forward.

"The king was poisoned!" he shouted. Everyone stared at him in shock.

"This medicine has been tampered with."

"What? By whom?" Queen Oluchi's soft voice reached a crescendo.

"By this girl"—He pointed to Kadsa—"who calls herself Abnr's Gift, the trick of Nu'at."

Kadsa's mouth gaped in shock. "It's absolutely not true," she yelled. "You liar!"

"You were alone with him. This isn't coincidental that he should die when you were alone with him. I warned you, this creature is from Nenet, not Abnr. She is an impostor, an abiku sent to steal the soul of the king." "That's a lie!" she spat back, fisting her hands to stop herself from lurching at him. "If anyone poisoned the king, it is you—O-ma-nu, servant of night." Kadsa pronounced each syllable of his full title. The look on his face revealed a man who knew she was onto him.

Bokor glared at her.

"I know it was *you* who sent that dead man to kill me at the welcoming ceremony. It was you—some version of you that attacked me in that cave. You know the truth. You knew what my grandfather was planning and you got rid of him. You don't want us to succeed. You work for the witch! That's how you could send your abiku to the cave."

Bokor's heavy chest pushed upward. He faced the guards at the door before his eyes dropped to King Remu's lifeless body. "My queen," he spoke calmly, facing Queen Oluchi. "With your permission, may I have the impostor arrested?"

Kadsa found Queen Oluchi's face, straining with conflicting emotions.

"Don't believe him," Kadsa pushed. "He's a liar."

The queen straightened herself up regally. "This matter will have to be investigated before any such thing is done." She studied Kadsa. "There is real chaos ahead and we cannot have in-fighting now." Queen Oluchi's voice trembled. She sniffled and sobbed but gathered herself.

"My husband is dead. We must make burial arrangements and then whatever issues exist, we will deal with it, but *after* the burial, and after he's been brought to his final resting place in the mastaba." She turned to Bokor. "You will see to it that the body is prepared."

"Of course, my queen." He nudged his head stiffly down. "As is appropriate."

Queen Oluchi faced Kadsa. "You can return to your room. You will have Sion as your personal guard until the matter is dealt with. Good night."

"You are the servant of the witch," Kadsa mouthed to Bokor and stormed from the room.

When no one else was in the room but him, Bokor faced the king's body and began humming a pleasing tune, while he removed rings from the king's fingers. He tossed them into the king's medicine mug. He removed King Remu's headpiece and admired it.

"The old king is dead. Long live the king." He fitted the diadem on his own head. It barely settled. He sniggered. He'd melt this down and get a bigger one made just for him.

15

WITCH

Akwanshi perched at the mount of the hill, separated from the fortress only by a thin stretch of land. Now she had come to see about the offering that was her Dark Prince. For a long time, he had been fighting against her presence. With each day counted off, she had been able to step a little further to his fortress and his mind. He was stronger than she had realized, but rather than be thwarted by this, she had accepted it wholeheartedly. It was simply a demonstration of the power she would have during her apotheosis. The stronger the soul, the stronger her powers.

She laughed. That old fool, King Aren, the scorpion. He had been nothing but an insect. The fool of a king had thought he would become immortal. For a second, she almost fooled herself, too. She was convinced it was his son, Kano—a weak boy, though much more stable- minded than Aren had been. How many kings had come and gone since those times? How long she had waited for the right king, testing the strength of the darkness, calling to its powers, listening to its whispers. And at last, the right soul had come.

The young man paused on the steps of the fortress. His struggle to keep from stepping over the threshold amused her. She had waited ages for this long-prophesied king, and never had she been closer to him and the tremendous power he held within him. Power not even he knew he had. She'd spent a good amount of time and effort that almost killed her, creating the abiku that possessed him. King's blood went into it—necessary to hold the soul of a so-called divine king. People believed abiku were simple evil spirits. They didn't know the half of it. Blood and death went into creating an effective soul-leech.

Akwanshi bared her teeth in a charmed smile when he stalled on the doorstep. The dark goddess would reward her for her hard work in a handful of days.

Come to me, she willed him. The boy placed one foot over the threshold. It was progress. Normally, he'd stop exactly at the threshold. This time, against his will, he crossed it. Her power was growing, and soon he'd be unable to resist the psychic pull between them.

"The time is almost here, my prince." She beguiled him, eagerness strong in her voice, echoing from the hill. Only he could hear her.

Even when her lips weren't moving, he could hear her.

"I….," he started and then hesitated. "No."

"You are drawn to me. We are the same. Soon you'll see there's no need to fight me. We belong to the deep mystery of Nenet. Don't fight it."

"I…," he said in protest but fell into silence.

"The stranger is an impostor. Have you not heard, Dark Prince?"

The young man cast his eyes to the wilting great house across the yard. It was deep night, and its torches were burning down, mimicking the dwindling light in the dying kingdom.

"Your Divine Highness, do one last thing before we are united," she muttered.

He projected his mood toward her: half-saddened, half-defiant.

"Destroy her for me—that fraud and joke."

"If she's an impostor, she's of no use to you. You should let her go."

Akwanshi laughed, not expecting this response at all. She understood completely why the buffoon called Bokor had such a hard time with this young man. He was of a brilliant mind. He was the chosen one. The sacrifice promised.

"Why do you want her so badly?"

"I have something she seeks. Something that we can negotiate about."

"What is it?" he pushed. His defiance was quite strong.

"Nothing to concern yourself with, my dark prince.

Just steer her to me."

When he didn't respond, struggling against her pull on him, she continued. "Do promise me you'll bring her to me." *Bring her to me. Bring her to me.* She drilled her voice into his head, repeating the same command: *bring her to me.* The boy shook his head, trying to get her out of it, but he was cracking. He looked up, his face twisted in agony, defeat. "I cannot make her come to you. I don't know how.

"Of course, you do," she purred. "I trust that you have means."

He looked surprised, confused. Slowly, his defiance fell away. "All right. I will try."

"Thank you, Dark Prince. Remember, soon we'll be united."

There was no need to stay any longer. She dove into the darkness, allowing it to transform her into a lovely night owl. How merciful the darkness had been to her.

The Dark Prince was miserable and frustrated by the time he retreated to his chamber. He sat on his bed and stared at the wall, summoning his willpower to push the witch's voice out of his head. He knew this witch's history well. He had read the account of her role in the disaster that was King Aren's reign. That was generations ago, before the darkness.

According to the official account, King Aren, nicknamed "The Scorpion", tried to kill his own son to extend his reign—an eternal reign. A sorceress promised him immortality. The sorceress was identified in great details as the witch of the Dark Forest, Akwanshi, formerly called Huna.

Whatever happened to King Aren would happen to him if he didn't find a way to resist her. Still, he did not quite know what she wanted with him—only that she'd been coming to haunt him for quite some time. She *believed* he could help her somehow and this upset him. Because of her power over him, he couldn't even trust his mind anymore.

He threw himself down on the hard bed and considered the girl, Kadsa. He wasn't certain of what the witch implied when she called her an impostor, but he would not be so quick to dismiss her. The final hours were vanishing into the final moment. He had no one else to rely on, and neither did the Maruti. The scrolls he found in the library, for all their promise, were almost impossible to decipher, mad priests had written them in a language no one could translate.

Kadsa was his only hope. But now that he knew the witch could get into his head, he didn't know how he would help the girl without also hurting her or helping the witch. Frustrated, he vowed to stay far away from the girl. It would not be easy.

———————

King Remu's funeral took three days to plan and three more days to carry out—days that included the mourning period. During this time, Kadsa couldn't leave the bedchamber. If she had to leave, Sion and his band of super serious guards escorted her and stood like sentinels by her side. Sion felt bad about it, or so he claimed, but his sense of duty tugged at him more strongly than whatever feelings of sympathy he might have had for her.

She'd spent the week fighting with her own thoughts about whether to mount an escape—she and Grandpa Edoje had staged these before. Part of her wanted to stay and prove her innocence.

"We will decide your fate tomorrow," said the somber queen, when she met with her a week after the funeral. "You will be presented before the council of Mehronur, and you will have your say."

"A trial in a court room?" "Yes," Queen Oluchi said. "What if I'm found guilty?"

Queen Oluchi shrugged. "You will be executed." Kadsa couldn't sleep. Bokor's accusations still stung.

How could they believe him over her? She had no reason whatsoever to poison the king. Would that arrogant oaf testify against her? She bet he would. What were her chances of being found innocent?

She wasn't a murderer—even when she could've gotten away with it all the times she had been in tough situations because of her grandpa. She found ways around it. Grandpa Edoje told her once that spilling blood was sacred—there was no going back. It did something to your soul. She had asked if he had ever killed anyone, and he hadn't responded. She didn't think he had, but knew he blamed himself for the death of her father.

Murdering a king, regicide, would translate to treason in any world, regardless of the civility that existed. She didn't want to think about how they'd try her. What would be the evidence? She sighed. If only she hadn't come in search of her grandpa, then she wouldn't be in this mess. Kadsa bit her lips as the bitter fear of dying gutted her. She hadn't lived yet. She hadn't reunited with her mother.

She wasn't staying in this place. She didn't like the darkness, but she survived it once before. Every time she made a move to leave the bedchamber, Sion or some other guard popped up.

How dare Bokor? Such an off-putting man with his crude, painted face. From the moment she met him and that Yedina witch-doctor, she knew she couldn't trust him. Looking back, Kadsa had never taken well to these *magic* men— she never found them credible, decent, or anything other than suspicious. Maybe that was why she got into so many fights when other kids would call her grandpa a witch-doctor, and cringe whenever he mentioned magic. Deep inside, she just never cared for these types—never believed or trusted them, and she didn't want to think he could be like them.

He wasn't like them, no more than she was a murderer. Bokor's treatment of the priestess in the Isaan Temple hijacked her memory. All those red flags. She believed he'd done something to her grandfather, though she feared *what*. What was in it for the witch- doctor? The answer was easy to come by—a seat on the throne, but that could never happen.

The Maruti swore by the divine kingship. While waiting for Queen Oluchi to figure out what to do with her, she had begged them to visit the Great Library, Djehut, to find something to read. What she found were scrolls of papyrus and parchment loaded with sacred writings.

Reading Marut's history and myths, she learned the kingship was hereditary. The kings descended from an unbroken line tracing back to a god-king named Ndakr.

If Bokor were to ascend the throne, it would be a gross violation of the practice of divine kingship.

What's more, King Remu had already named his successor, so Bokor could not become king. But she had yet to meet this son, and now that she considered it, she wondered if he could become an ally. The king had muttered that he was smart. But either this son or Sahu would be king. So how could Bokor possibly think the throne could be his? Then it hit her: he might be trying to kill the entire family. He'd annihilate the bloodline and he'd be the next best thing. Blaming the king's death on her absolved suspicion that would otherwise fall on him. It should be easy to turn the people against her. She hadn't done a thing to help them. He'd say she was a phony. Then he'd have her executed.

Kadsa swallowed hard, willing herself to think, but her mind conjured thoughts of King Remu. He had said something to her on his deathbed—something that had disappeared in the madness that had taken over the palace in the past few days.

The Dark Prince. What did he say about the Dark Prince? The puzzle led nowhere. She gave up, perplexed. But she had plenty on her mind. *That man* ordered her arrest for a crime she would never commit in a million years. He tried to convince them she was a servant of Nenet, the Dark Goddess, who, according to the cosmogony story, cast the spell of darkness against the kingdom because she wanted to hurt the light god who loved humans. She didn't even want to get into whether the Dark Goddess was a real entity or not, because two things alone dominated her mind— getting out of Marut and anger toward Bokor. She fussed about them both until her eyelids fluttered shut.

Halfway into sleep, she had a dream about her grandpa. Not a dream but a vision. Grandpa Edoje faced the sunset, a strange crystalline sun disk hovering over a vast red desert, a place that resembled the Tibesti Plateaus of Chad with the same high pillars and sandy rocks. Except she was sure she had never been here before. Grandpa's eyes dropped to her neckline. Only then did she realize she wore her crystal. Instead of swirling in light, its core swirled with dark mist.

"You said it draws only light," she considered, frustrated by a stray thought. Then why was there darkness in it? Where did the darkness come from?

Her grandpa began walking towards the dropping sun.

Why was he walking away?

Kadsa rushed after him. The sudden drop of sunlight jolted her attention to the sundisk on the horizon. It swirled to black. Darkness stormed the sky.

"Grandpa! Don't walk to it! We have to get out of here!"

He stopped momentarily to stare back at her; his features darkened. His mouth opened, as if he wanted to say something but was unable to speak.

"Grandpa?" Kadsa watched in horror as his form misted into darkness, not even a shadow but dark smoke. "Grandpa!"

The desert transformed into a dark jungle. Vines were everywhere, extending from the darkness that suddenly engulfed their environment. Thick vines pushed through the darkened sun disk like tentacles and cut into his skin, leashing and cocooning him. She screamed for her grandpa as the darkness swallowed him.

Kadsa's surrounding wilted and fragmented, becoming the halls of the palace. She believed that's where she had been transported to—just outside her sleeping quarters. A shadow brushed quickly and indifferently by her as it moved toward a side wall. The shadow pulled a torch that disappeared into the solid brick wall.

"Grandpa!" Kadsa jumped from her bed, shaking and sweating from the horrors of that nightmare—the darkness got her grandpa. She had no time to focus on her dream—or vision. Something moved. No, *someone* moved but not fast enough to avoid her eyes. For a long, confusing moment, the two stared at each other in the darkness of the room.

"Who are you?" she asked, struggling to make out the figure, though she was certain this was not her grandpa.

Kadsa grabbed her glowing pendant in the same second the figure walked out of her room. He was not running, but walking.

"Wait," she called to him. He didn't stop. She rolled out of bed, wearing her jeans and shoes. She'd been so upset by her treatment that she'd stopped wearing the traditional clothes of the kingdom. She was done with everything to do with this place. She quickly stuffed her feet into her sneakers and bolted after the figure. Sion's body lay unconscious against the wall outside her room. The figure stood in the corridor. Was it waiting for her? As she approached, it turned off into the recess.

"Wait, please!" she called out. She wasn't certain why, but she followed him into the dark alcove at the back of the sleeping quarters, into a narrowly enclosed rectangular lobby with strange-looking torches aligning the walls like sentries. The large statues held torches in their hands, some of which had already burned out.

Where did the shadowy figure go? She was certain she pursued him to this enclosed area. There was no place else for him to turn into unless—she recalled the vision—the walls. A crevice in the wall somewhere served as a secret entrance. But where? She quizzed her brain, determined.

In her vision, the figure had pulled something from the wall. Kadsa studied the statues with an eagle eye. All of them were human, with the same distorted heads as the statuettes at the temple of the Akonadi. The oddity among them was a figure of two animals, a bird and a feline, facing opposing directions with a round dial with spiked edges in the foreground between them. The bird was painted white and the feline black. A lamp sat on a round metal plate on their heads.

"Light and dark," Kadsa murmured, studying the figure. The disk in the foreground between the animals was someone's representation of the sun; the dark half was eclipsed. Grandpa Edoje's words flooded her mind. *An eclipse means a doorway is opening to another world.* She tugged the round dial. The thin metal dial spun squeakily. She tugged again, pushing it side to side, and then backward and forward. The thin metal flapped to one side, hanging loosely.

Kadsa jumped when a vivid royal blue scarab beetle with flapping wings sprung into the space the thin metal disk had been covering. The beetle's thin wings buzzed. She rubbed a finger over the smooth surface of the ornament. Its shell was hard, polished marble. Someone had put the disk in front of it to hide it. The sundial statue was too perfectly out of place compared to the other statue-torch figures in the room, so she knew it had to be the key she was looking for.

Kadsa pushed against the beetle and watched it retreat backward into the space, disappearing. The wall behind the statue slid to the side, revealing a rectangular opening, narrow enough for one person to squeeze through. Kadsa swallowed hard, took a deep breath, and then jumped through as the wall sealed her inside the dark pit.

The faint and hollow sound of a musical instrument echoed in the depths of the pit. The instrument filled up the dark space with a slow and sad melody. The story of the pied piper playing his flute flashed into her head. Kadsa reached for the pendant, bringing it to her eyes, allowing the light to burn into her eyes. Then, her eyes burned through the darkness like flames eating through paper. Steep steps descended into a dark pit. Kadsa took the first step, paused, and then continued her trek downward.

Chills consumed her in the dungeon. She felt like she had stepped into a different world. For a second, she worried that the path would only lead her to the land of Nenet. But she couldn't turn back. Not to face whatever fate Bokor had for her. When she got to the long underpass, Kadsa considered if it might lead to the distant fortress in the far back of the palace grounds. She had a nagging feeling that the shadowy figure lived there. Who was it? Why was it in her room? It could've killed her while she slept, but it hadn't.

The wall of the underpass stretched about two hundred feet ahead of her. It's length didn't impress her, not so much as what was on it. Gilded inscriptions and drawings— depictions of people, places, and things similar to depictions on the scrolls from her lessons with the Itzat. Some symbols looked more familiar than others, the boats and stars and animals. Similar engravings and depictions covered sitting stools and walls in many parts of the palace and the Great Library.

She recalled that dream she had in Chad, about the boy who wasn't a boy, scribbling on a wall.

The image of a fiery red bird flared into view when she stepped closer. With its striking red plumage, the image looked two-dimensional. In the Great Library, Kadsa had read that the sacred bird carried the mound that became the earth (Odua). She speculated if there was a clue written on this wall that could help her save Marut. A glyph acting as a stand-in for the heavens. The firebird in question was Abnr, the god who breathed fire—life.

The statues she'd passed on the way to this place had represented night and day, or dark and light. Abnr was the bird on the first side, and the black feline, the other half of the statue, was Nenet, the darkness. The beetle sat between them, representing life, and the sun disk represented time. Other objects of different geometrical shapes were drawn inside oval-shaped boxes, what the Itzat had dubbed a cartouche. Kadsa couldn't figure out what the images depicted or represented, though she deduced they must have been important names or ideas meant to be highlighted.

A shuffling sound, like feet dragging across sandy wood, drew her attention back to the dark pathway ahead of her. She'd lost focus of why she was there— following the shadowy figure from inside her room. "Who's there?"

"I am the unseen," called back a soft, male voice.

What did that mean? The musical instrument whistled through the air, coming from the direction of his voice. The notes were captivating, sad, and slow. She drifted toward the sound and him.

"Why are you hiding?"

"I'll tell you when you come."

Kadsa scoffed—that didn't sound smart. "I am a friend," he assured her.

"Is that so? Who are you?" "I am unseen."

Okay. "That means nothing to me. Maybe step out of the shadows."

"You're Abnr's Gift. I see you clearly from here." "That's beside the point. It's not okay to spy on me when I'm sleeping."

Silence. Shuffling. "I'm sorry for scaring you. It was not my intention. I simply...," he paused to consider his next words. "I don't know what to make of you. Bokor has said—"

"Bokor's a liar and a horrible man," she yelled, cutting him off, surprised by her anger.

The figure hushed.

"How do you know Bokor anyway?"

"Bokor is the only one who dares to look at me, to come close to me."

"Maybe you shouldn't hide in the darkness, if you want people to see you. Why are you hiding, anyway?" The answer was in the back of her mind, but she didn't want to jump ahead of herself, so she waited for his reply. When none came, she stepped forward.

"Do you want to know what the writing means?"

Distraction tactic. "Did you write all of this?" she asked, remembering her dream.

"The legends and stories of the kingdom. The language is in the simplified, dialect of the old kingdom. I will explain it to you," he said.

"Go ahead, but I'm not stepping closer." Kadsa glanced to the firebird symbol again. It blazed through the heavens; man took fire from the tree. She read over that part already. She moved toward the end of the wall, skimming over the other stories.

The black feline—too big to be a cat—represented darkness; it appeared in a cloud-like mist over the land. The feline loomed bigger than the firebird, where in the beginning, they were the same size. Another image showed a hippopotamus giving birth while a crocodile waited greedily to snatch the child from its mother. None of it made much sense to her. But maybe it made sense to him. In her dream, he was going to tell her.

"The story of our world," he said softly. She hadn't heard him move but he sounded very close, and it alarmed her enough to face him.

"Don't turn around!"

Kadsa froze in her step. "Why don't you want me to look at you?"

"You may not like what you see, Kadsa," he admitted. "I don't want to frighten you."

"I don't frighten easily." He did not respond.

"I'm gonna turn around now," she said when all she could hear was his breathing. *He breathed*—a sign of aliveness. But what was she dealing with here?

"Then you can turn around," he responded after consideration, "but don't scream."

Kadsa fought back her chuckle of defiance. Was that a sexist reference? Clearly *not a friend*, as he claimed. When had she ever screamed? *The noisy animal got speared* was a saying among the Yedina people. She never forgot that. Kadsa spun in a slow, careful manner, bracing for the sight of whatever it was that spoke to her. She anticipated some monstrosity.

Kadsa exhaled.

"You are frightened."

"No." *She was confused*.

The mysterious figure removed the hood covering his head to reveal his full face. Staring back at her, was the most empathetic face she had ever seen. The soft contours of his face made him look very young. And despite his exceptionally dark pupils, he looked more frightened than fearsome, fawn-like even.

"You're a real person."

He wasn't much of a boy—maybe late teens like her or early twenties. *The boy who wasn't a boy*, she considered, getting a jolt in her gut. All these dreams and visions were suddenly adding up and making sense.

He lifted his robed-covered hand and pointed to the wall. "I added to the wall over the years. This is the story of Marut."

She kept her eyes on him, but he never met them. "As above so below," he said. "The figure shows the split mortal manifestation of the gods—a double entity— two sides."

"What does that mean?"

"It symbolizes the two lands. It's the split jurisdiction between light and dark—Abnr's world and Nenet's world. The darkness came from magic spun from the depth of Asamando but it is held back by the light."

"How can the darkness disappear? That's my part— to remove the darkness. How do I do that?"

The magic that keeps the lands separated follows rules that allow for few exceptions," he explained. "What we have to do is find the clues in the story."

"How much of this is true? How is this real?"

He tried not to look at her but made a gesture of doubt, maybe.

"You have to understand—this seems very impossible. Here, everything is mixed up—the real with the surreal, the good with the bad. I feel lost."

"After a while, you learn to accept the contradictions and the madness that is Marut."

Kadsa exhaled loudly. "I don't know how I got myself mixed up in this. I came here to find my grandfather, and I am stuck."

"I'm sorry this happened to you." "I wasn't speaking Maruti."

"I can understand your language," he admitted. "How?"

His small, smooth face twisted with distress. "I can read the thoughts of others when I try to, and this allows me to know your language."

"You know what I'm thinking?" He didn't speak.

"You really *do* know what I'm thinking now?" She pushed, in awe of this revelation and the look on his face.

"Not without concentrating. No," he said after some time, his softly contoured face creasing with discomfort.

She didn't believe him but assumed he probably didn't want to admit to something so intrusive.

An awkward silence fell over them, and he reached into the sleeve of his robe and pulled out a small wooden instrument with holes. He lifted the flute to his mouth and began to play.

Kadsa listened, bewitched by it. The depressing song wooed her into a dreamlike daze, but she caught herself, snapping out of it, believing he was putting her to sleep. Was that what he did to Sion? "What is your name?"

"My name is not important. However, I will tell it to you. I was not to live in this life. My mother's rumored last words were 'He is air,' and so it is my name. It is Khansu."

"Khansu," she repeated. The truth exploded into her brain like fireworks. "The king said A-nuwo Khansu." She stared at the cloaked boy. "You're his son!"

He did not reply.

"You're the prince." She was suddenly so excited, she laughed. "The red priestess in the Isaan temple—"

"You spoke to the red priestess?" he asked, sounding and looking somewhat grieved.

She considered. "She was rather rude, but yes, she said to find the Dark Prince. When I asked the king about it, he said "my son, Khansu". I didn't pick up on it. You're him."

His face was expressionless.

"The king, he...," she trailed off. "I'm sorry about your father."

"We were never close. The Reveal said there would be a new king at the start of the new age."

Kadsa had questions, but only one bothered her enough to inquire about aloud. "Why are you called the *Dark Prince*, exactly?"

"My mother died giving birth to me."

"Queen Oluchi is not your mother." She knew that—the moment she spoke out loud. Queen Oluchi was far too young to have given birth to a twenty-year- old son.

"She's my father's second wife. He married her within the last decade."

Kadsa watched him with pity, remembering something King Remu had said on his deathbed. "Your father ordered you to live here—in a dungeon."

"My father is not a bad man."

"Then why are you here—locked away—because your mother died giving birth to you?"

"I was born at the beginning of the Dark Enchantment. I did not breathe when they pulled me from my mother's dead body." He touched his chest, dropping his hands a second after. "In this land, a child born under those circumstances is believed to be an ekok, a demon. And if such a child lives, he's believed to be cursed.

"Many believe my birth is the catalyst of the Dark Enchantment. They both happened in the same moment. Rumors circulate about me throughout this kingdom. They say I'm strange. They say I am the darkness. They say I am death." His shoulders dropped. "My father was torn between his role as king and his role as father to a child claimed by darkness. He said he did not have the heart to kill me as his people wished, so he ordered me to be locked away, for my safety."

"So you haven't seen your father since you were born?"

"I have seen him from time to time. I have heard from him. Sometimes he would come here and stop outside the door. He would just talk and apologize for everything. He was a man sickened by guilt. I never spoke to him, but sometimes, I'd look in on him."

"I'm sorry," she told him, and then she looked up cheerfully. "He declared you his successor to the throne. His last words to me on his deathbed were to tell you he was sorry and, also, to help you. He said you'd help me." "I believe you." He furrowed his brows. "But he's dead, so we have to move on."

"And you will be king. You'll stop whatever plan Bokor has up his scheming sleeves."

He shuffled with discomfort. "My father made a mistake. I cannot be king. I cannot wear the divine crown. The people do not want a king who is cursed."

"You don't look cursed."

"Looks can be deceiving," he said pointedly. Kadsa swallowed her silence and discomfort.

"Besides, they haven't heard the rest of the Reveal." "Which is …?"

He slumped. "Kadsa, I brought you here to warn you. That is all. Afterward, you must keep your distance from me."

"What makes you so bad?" An ominous feeling ran through her when she asked.

He sulked, dropping his eyes to the ground. The silence lingered. Kadsa wanted answers from him, but already felt bad, as if she had hurt his feelings.

"So," she said, choosing to change the topic, "the story about having to find the heart of the darkness and restore light. That's vague. Do you know what that means? That's the most important thing right now." She turned her attention to the wall. "Does it say anything about that on this wall?"

"I think the heart of the darkness may be a place." He perked up again, happy to drop the subject of himself. "I copied that from the priestly writings. I thought it was incorrect, but I have since re-checked the scrolls and my translation is correct. I have been thinking on it. You may have to travel to Asamando, in the forest—where the darkness originated. Perhaps kill Akwanshi."

"The witch?" Kadsa declared. "I can't do that. No, I have never killed anyone. I don't want to start now. Uh- uh. Plan B, please."

"You have your pendant. It is very powerful." Khansu pointed to the wall again. "That is the gift that Abnr gives." He directed her gaze to the oblong-shaped frame in which a figure stood with a spear in his hands. "Everyone thought it would be an object, but it's a person—it's you."

In scene two, the spear traveled through the air. In scene three, the spear connected to the heart of the leopard. The scene after that showed the leopard dead with the spear in its heart. In scene five, the person carried some sort of glowing box. In scene six, the person placed the box on some cylindrical platform and in the next scene, a rush of light pushed toward the sky and exploded over it. In the last scene, the chosen one stood beside a crowned human figure on a throne. Subjects of the kingdom genuflected before them. The story was fascinating, but she was concerned, for it made her more nervous about failure and disappointment. The expectation was heavy.

"King Remu said I had a little over a week to do this.

That was a week ago."

"According to my calculations…within the next three days." He watched her. "It's morning now."

"That's what I was worried about." She bit her lower lip. "Can you help me look for my grandfather?"

"Why?"

"He might know how to fix this." "Are you certain?"

She shrugged. "This crystal won't show him to me. But I know he's here. He's probably spent years figuring out how to fix your problem. That's why Bokor got rid of him. I think he figured it out."

"You see nothing in the crystal?" "Blackness."

"The forest?"

Kadsa wasn't sure. "I guess."

"Often when a person is lost to the darkness, they are believed dead."

"No, he's not dead," she barked, defied, denied. Khansu looked hesitant to speak. Then he said,

"Why don't you believe?"

Kadsa stiffened, before turning defiant. "What don't I believe?"

"In yourself, your mission, all of this?"

"Did you read my mind to come up with that theory?"

Her words came out sharper than intended, more defensive, and he sulked for a moment giving her a glib of joy that she'd won this showdown.

Khansu straightened up. "It is obvious since I have been watching you, been in your dreams. You believe this is a dream you'll wake up from."

She shrugged. "Magic doesn't exist in my world." "This isn't your world."

"And I just need to get back to mine. Let's find my grandfather. This is his domain."

"And if you don't find him?"

She swallowed, uncomfortable with this train of thought. Grandpa being dead just wasn't settling.

"He's alive. We all need him to be." She glanced at the wall, feeling overwhelmed by the burden spelled out on it. This was her grandfather's specialty. He'd know. "Do you have a plan?"

Kadsa took a deep breath before entering through the heavy brass door behind Khansu.

The small stone room boasted a hard bed, some wooden bowls and spoons sitting on a low-standing table that also held clay tablets, scrolls and an oil lamp. The most interesting thing in the rotund room was a shallow pit whose cemented mouth lifted about three feet off the ground.

The cold and dark room emanated strong gloom, creating a vibe like the Dark Forest. Kadsa rubbed her exposed arms under her T-shirt to warm herself up before facing Khansu.

"So, this is the fortress" "All of it, yes," he said.

Kadsa jumped at the sound of his voice. She hadn't realized he stood this close to her. The room wasn't exactly dark, not with the lamp burning, but, more than his closeness, was the matter of his presence. He was no longer a physical person as he was by the wall. He was a shadow under a cloak, standing as the manifestation of her vision—a figure molded from darkness. She struggled to make out his nose, eyes, mouth, or lips. His comment about being unseen suddenly made sense. All she could do was pretend not to feel threatened by him.

"You're a shadow," she said with a short laugh. "This is my natural state when I am in the room."

She tried not to look too distrustful, but he slid away from her self-consciously, passing judgment on her *akuto* face.

"Is this what you meant by the curse?"

"Once, I did not turn to a shadow in this place. It's a sign of Nenet's growing power. Soon, if you don't restore the balance, I won't be able to enter the kingdom of light at all … not that the kingdom will exist anyway, but you understand. The rest of the kingdom is under the illumination of Abnr. Here, the darkness is strong. It gets stronger by the day."

Kadsa was spooked. He was underneath the cloak but she couldn't make out his form. He might as well have been the night underneath that cloak. That was all she saw when she looked at him, nothing but the blackness of night. Khansu shifted and she remembered he could gauge her thoughts. When he put distance between them, the chill of the room went with him.

"I'm sorry," she said, feeling as if she should say something.

"It doesn't matter," he dismissed.

He was standing somewhere near the fire pit some feet away.

Khansu reminded Kadsa of the mist and the way it had taken on human form without looking very human at all. It wasn't the same, of course. He seemed human to her, not like Misty, an alien entity.

"If you go into the forest with me, what will happen to you? You're planning to go with me, aren't you?"

The cloaked figure nodded. "I may stay the same as I am now or become something else entirely. I do not know. I have never been to the forest."

Kadsa walked toward the pit and flares shot upward, forcing her to pull back. "What's down there?"

"It's a fire pit."

"If that is normal it shouldn't repel me."

"It clashes with the darkness around the fortress. It may stop flaring when the crystal's light dies down."

His words made her clutch the pendant harder and wished its light didn't fade. "Can you control the fire?"

"No!" he fired back, sounding as if she insulted him.

Control your stupid thoughts, she told herself. Kadsa opened her mouth to speak, but a male voice called for Khansu from somewhere behind the pit, or beyond the walls of the fortress.

"Who's calling your name?" "It's Bennu," he informed her. "You know Bennu?"

"He is my friend," he said moving to the other side of the room.

Kadsa tailed him towards a door she did not notice before on the other side of the room. Khansu passed through the door, as if it was a ghost barrier. Surprised by his move and believing that the door was indeed an illusion, Kadsa attempted to do the same but bumped head-first into the door, cursing herself. By the time she maneuvered the heavy brass door to create a narrow enough opening for her to slide through, he was standing beside the giant bird some thirty feet from the fortress.

Prince Khansu attempted to pat its beak, but his hands fell through. They both laughed. Kadsa fixed her eyes on the display of fruits, vegetables, and a sacrificed pig on the lawn. She knew worshippers had been outside the fortress—the rumors spread by the servants were correct. All the time the servants knew Khansu lived in this fortress.

Bennu helped himself to the food on the ground.

"I see you've found the prince," Bennu said when she reached him.

"I'm Abnr's Gift," she said. It was sarcasm, but there was relief, too, like getting it off her chest—warming up to it, trying to embrace it. Why did she feel like an impostor?

"Kadsa, it's nice to see you again."

"You never said you knew Khansu. It would've made it easier."

"True, but it was not my place to tell his secrets." "Of course." She rolled her eyes before facing

Khansu. The prince tried his hardest to lift a bowl from the ground. After trying and failing multiple times, he was able to grab the bowl and carry it to Bennu's feet.

"Thank you for the food, my good friend." Bennu dug his beak in the food.

"Don't thank me—thank the people who dumped the food here."

"You feed him." Kadsa faced Khansu, who'd removed the hood of his cloak after becoming tangible again.

"He comes here to eat, yes," he admitted.

"The cuisine of the forest is not up to your standard, is it?" she quizzed the large bird.

"If all you can feed on are the bacteria of the ground and twigs, then you are better than me. The bounteous forest has lost its taste. Besides, I have gotten used to cooked food."

"The Jakuba eat twigs in the forest and they're fine with it." Kadsa's face twisted when she pondered Seth.

"Do you know Seth? He's a Jakuba."

Bennu stopped eating his food. "I know him or of him. I heard from a credible source that your friend has been taken captive in Asamando—punishment for helping you come to Mehronur."

Kadsa slumped, grieved.

"Seth," spoke Prince Khansu, considering. "I have heard that name before. I cannot remember where, but it sounds familiar."

"He said he was a warrior for Marut, a Jorba or Jago," Kadsa explained.

"He was a great warrior and high general in the kingdom of Marut," Bennu chimed in. "He is also the ruler of Elon, which is why he's called Jorba. He stayed faithful to Abnr, unlike so many other subjects of the former kingdom."

"Jakuba and humans lived side by side here, before the darkness took over?" she asked, somewhat confused. "Jakuba are human beings, Kadsa," Bennu explained. "The people who are trapped in the darkness transform into Jakuba."

"Whoa!" was all she could say. She felt stupid for not knowing this tidbit of information.

"If the darkness reaches Mehronur in two days, then all the people here will become Jakuba. Over time, Jakuba lose their human instincts and can become animal-like, but they were once humans like you," Bennu explained. "That makes sense. Seth was offended when I called him an animal." She exhaled loudly. "Poor Seth, captured by the witch he hates. We must help him when we go into the forest. He would be an asset for us. He knows the forest."

"We may walk into Akwanshi's trap."

"We'll go into Asamando anyway. We can spare some minutes to help him."

"You plan to go to Asamando? What for?"

"The heart of the darkness is in Asamando. We think so anyway. That's where the witch is, right? And maybe she's keeping my grandfather hostage."

"Are you certain?" Bennu asked.

"I must do something. The wall mural showed the hero spearing the heart of the darkness. How else can that be interpreted?"

"The people believe that Abnr's soul was taken and is being held captive by Nenet. Destroying the witch may free the soul. That might be what is meant by restoring the light," Khansu spoke.

"And we have two days to do it," Kadsa chipped in.

Silence fell over them. The early morning suddenly felt colder as the realization sunk into her. There were so many questions. Abnr's soul—what could that be?

"Kadsa?" called Bennu. "I want to help you. Normally, I am neutral on these matters, but the forest is not what it used to be. The life force is almost non-existent, and the food source is empty. Even with my powers of regeneration, I am vulnerable. I want to help you restore the forest to its original state. If there is anything I can do for you, let me know."

"Most definitely."

"Now that I can see dawn breaking, I should be on my way. I wish you two well on your journey to Asamando. If you need me, just whisper my name into the crystal and I will hear."

"Even in the darkness, you will hear?"

"Yes," he assured her.

Bennu said he was old and neutral, but Kadsa still found it intriguing that the darkness didn't affect him. She could only see darkness when she tried to find her grandfather and wondered if her grandfather had become a Jakuba. So many things to figure out, she thought, when it came to the battle of light and dark.

"Thank you again for the food, most worthy prince." Bennu curtsied to Khansu.

It was very clumsy and awkward to Kadsa's eyes. But there was cuteness and lightness to it that she hadn't felt in a while now, not since she got here.

Kadsa and Khansu watched Bennu as his large body rushed across the lawn in preparation for flight. It hit her very quickly when she realized something.

"Wait!" Kadsa called out to him.

The bird stopped.

"Come on," she called to Khansu, running after Bennu.

She paused some feet from the bird.

"Can you drop us off in the forest, close to Asamando?"

"Kadsa, we're ill-prepared for this," Khansu started.

"We have two days," she told him. "That's not a long time. Besides, what reason do we have to stay here? Bokor's framing me for killing the king. The kingdom is going into chaos. I found you, as the Isaan priestess said. Everything is in place, so why wait?"

Khansu considered—"If you are certain, then I will accompany you."

She faced Bennu. "Can you drop us off near Asamando?"

"I am not a beast of burden."

"Oh, I'm sorry, I didn't mean...."

"It's okay," Bennu said. "Please hurry up."

Bennu knelt so she and Khansu could climb on. The bird took off shakily and Kadsa buried her hands into his soft plumage, trying not to grip too tightly, though she feared falling off. When they crossed The Divide, the temperature changed dramatically. Coldness replaced the heat that had warmed her skin.

Bennu's flight over the forest reminded Kadsa of how dark the forest was. It was a deep night, unnatural, electrified by chills and heavy with mood. She clutched her pendant, grateful some light remained inside of it, and brought it to her eyes. Her enhanced night vision kicked in.

16

NU'AT

After the funeral of the king, Bokor announced to the people gathered woefully in the courtyard that Abnr's Gift had been an impostor. "She killed your divine king!"

Chaos erupted. Those who feared Nenet and wanted her mercy worshipped at the footsteps of the fortress, others who remained loyal to Abnr prayed, visited the temples, and demanded that their ancestors advise them. Two groups of people clashed—those who thought the king's firstborn son should die in sacrifice and those who thought they should show him reverence. Queen Oluchi had never met this young man and could only worry that her own son would suffer the consequences of the kingdom's fears.

Queen Oluchi had confronted Bokor, who had all but taken control of the palace from the vizier, whom she could not find.

"I expelled him," Bokor had informed her arrogantly. "It is not your place."

"It is not yours, either."

"The council of Mehronur and the high priest—" "What about them, Lady Oluchi?" he'd said, reverting to her title prior to her marriage to the king. His insistence of using her former title, Lady, was proof he didn't respect her rank anymore. He wouldn't even use the proper title for the king's widow.

He would not bully her, she told herself. That he showed his ambition hours after her husband's funeral, and his disregard for traditions infuriated her.

"May I remind you, Lady," spoke Bokor in a chilled voice, "That we tread dangerous waters? These are trying times we're experiencing—nothing like what had happened before."

Oluchi tried to reason. It wasn't true. In the days immediately following the darkness, it was chaos. She was a child then. King Remu had been a new king and he had held the kingdom together. The fate of his people had been altered by a prophecy all but a few had known. He had put the stargazers and priests to work and discovered that all was not lost. Despite the initial madness of trying to defy their new boundaries, they had survived.

"We will survive this," she spoke strongly.

"No, Lady Oluchi, not this," Bokor had said in the most sinister voice.

"It was you who killed the king."

Bokor stared her down, his expression unmoving. Queen Oluchi remembered when he first came to the king. His superior, NrHonan, had just passed. Bokor had come with the full approval of Mehronur's chief medicine temple. Even then, she'd distrusted him, believing something was wrong about him. His inferiors at the house seemed to fear him. Now she knew why. What if he had killed his superior?

"This is for the best, Lady. It really is for the best."

Queen Oluchi saw then that he wore the king's gold band with the precious gemstones. His eyes dropped to his finger when he realized she stared. His white painted face lit up with a wry smile. "The king's gift to me."

Queen Oluchi held her temper and her tongue. He was a liar. Bokor had stepped forward and she had stepped back, feeling the physical threat from him.

"Lady Oluchi," he sounded gentler, "why don't you attend to your son? Spend these last hours with him while I handle the affairs of the kingdom. That is the wise choice."

Queen Oluchi had nodded, not because she agreed, but because this was a threat. She'd fled from his presence in search of Sahu and had run to Sion, the only person she believed she could trust. Sion had agreed to protect them. He'd looked guilt-ridden after admitting Kadsa had slipped under his notoriously sharp gaze. He couldn't recall what had happened, except he fell into a deep sleep and woke to find her gone.

Queen Oluchi didn't have time to worry about this.

She had to protect her son.

Kadsa and Khansu climbed off Bennu's back outside the deep jungle of Asamando, a region darker than any other place in the forest.

"Asamando is half a mile in that direction."

"Thank you, Bennu," she told him.

"You're welcome." He was staggering.

"What's wrong?" Kadsa asked concerned, overcome with guilt. Had carrying them on his back been too much for him? Afterall, he wasn't a beast of burden.

"It's time to regenerate myself," he uttered. "I can sense the new age coming."

"I thought you did that before."

"No, I have rested before," he said. "The flames burn at their strongest during the end of the cosmic cycle. That's when it's best for me to regenerate."

"The flames? You mean fire?"

"Yes, that is where I come from, the flames." "They regenerate you? How does that work?"

"My ancestors before me have used it to keep our species alive. It's primordial, ancient. Some say it's the source of life."

"That's good to know. Strange, but good to know." "Nothing's strange, Kadsa. We are the progeny of fire, all of us."

She nodded, not caring to argue this point to wherever it led.

"I must go now," Bennu said after the quiet. "I must be regenerated by the coming dawn. I hope to see you both then, friends. Until then, please take care."

Bennu flew into the sky, disappearing in its blanket blackness. The sound of his flapping wings echoed long after he was no longer visible.

Kadsa faced Prince Khansu. He was still a cloaked figure. "We must get going. Are you ready?"

"Yes," he said casually. She nodded and the two began walking.

"Any doubts?" she asked after some time had passed. "No," he replied flatly.

Tense silence clung to the night air, hugging them as they walked side by side. Kadsa glanced his way a few times, before eventually asking, "Did you know about regenerative powers of Bennu's flames or what he meant by the progeny of fire?"

"It's been rumored that there were flames here that could reproduce life. It's where the first child of the gods was born. It's called the Ankh. According to the Scrolls, Amma created Marut, helped by her son Abnr. She molded humans and he created the divine sparks of the ankh in which her creations came to know life. Ankh means, in the old tongue, 'belonging to his lord'."

"But does it actually exist?"

"It's never been found or confirmed."

"And could this be the fire Bennu is talking about?" "Bennu is one of the oldest species in Marut. Many believe Bennu was around in the beginning. No doubt, it could be the same flames."

"So what happened to the species?" "What do you mean?"

"Well, he seems to be the only one. Are there others?

"Khansu thought about it. Seeing her confusion, he said, "There has always been only one Bennu."

"But he said he's about five hundred years old. Marut is older than that, isn't it? The earth is older than that."

"But there has always been one Bennu. When they die and are reborn, their memories are downloaded into the newborn species while the new creature also develops a distinct consciousness. When they speak, they can speak of themself as being five hundred years old or they can speak of their ancestors for they are their ancestors as they are themself."

"That's rather interesting," she mused and then considered some more. "When my grandpa and I visited Egypt, we learned a myth about a bird that rose from the ashes after it incinerated itself in its own flames. It was called a phoenix."

"Yes, that would be it," Khansu confirmed.

Kadsa stole a glance at him and smiled. "It really is a small world, isn't it? All my life, my grandfather told these stories and was dismissed because they clearly couldn't exist, and now I learn they do."

The prince looked confused.

Kadsa let this new revelation settle into her brain. A moment later, she smiled. "What else is strange and fascinating about Marut?"

"I have been learning myself, of the many lures of this kingdom, in the great library," Khansu said. "We should visit Djehut one day."

She realized, maybe at the same time he did, that day might never come. Discomfort consumed them. They continued walking in hushed silence.

When Kadsa began speaking again, it was to inquire about the buzoa. "I know the abada is real, but have yet to see a buzoa," she told him.

"I have yet to see one myself," Khansu said. "They are common in the other districts, Bourchul and Elon, according to the writings. They are beasts no one thought were tamable. We might never see them." Sadness tainted his tone when he admitted that he didn't have much experience in touring the kingdom. He spent his entire life almost exclusively in the village of Hutat.

Kadsa didn't think talking about her own experiences touring Africa with her grandfather would help. She'd felt confined and trapped with him, wanting so desperately to do other things—what she considered normal things, like attend college; it hadn't occurred to her at the time that she'd gotten an abundance of experience that others might never get. She'd been to so many places, seen so many things, and learned so many truths, even when she hadn't thought of them as such at the time.

Khansu stopped walking abruptly when they got on the trail to Asamando. Before she could utter a word, he cried out.

Alarmed, she pulled back, watching him drop to his knees.

"I don't feel…." He cried out. "I feel …," he struggled to get out the words. "Something is happening to me. Get far away from me."

Kadsa froze, torn between heeding his advice and wanting to help him. Khansu cried out, thrusting himself backward. He puffed his chest out as if he needed to claw out something inside of him. He cried out one last time.

His hands shot upward, crimping and bending, and then extending. His fingers became thick black paws, claws protruding. Smooth black hair sprouted all over his body. Khansu's cloaked body collapsed to the ground, folding like a fetus. His face and body contorted in the most excruciating way.

"Khansu?"

He didn't move or respond, staying dead silent. She stepped vigilantly toward him, his body covered under the heavy cloak. When she was no more than two feet away from him, he threw off the cloak and sprung to his feet with feline agility, startling her into stillness. Kadsa stared at the prince, or what he had become, too stunned to even panic. He was no more a man or even a shadow but had transformed physically into a large black leopard with silver-white eyes.

"Prince Khansu?"

The leopard twisted its body and growled. It slithered toward her, displaying its agility. She backstepped until she stumbled against a large tree. She grabbed hold of her necklace and braced for an assault.

"I am all right, Kadsa," he said in the same voice. She stared at him, not so certain. "Are you?"

"Yes," he said lifting his claws to look at them. "This is just another stage in the transformation."

Kadsa watched him with sympathy, sensing the very human hurt in him, even as he looked like a giant predator.

"It's okay," she comforted him. "We'll fix this."

He did not respond.

"Look at the bright side," she said with a smile, "Your vision must be better than twenty-twenty now."

"Kadsa, there's something I must tell you." He said in a sober tone.

She waited for him to speak.

"I think if you stay with me, I may hurt you. I am meant to lead you to the witch."

"What do you mean? Why?"

"Her influence on me will only become stronger from here on," he confessed. "She came to me just before you did. I don't trust myself, especially not now. I think I should leave you."

"I trust you." She strode forward and paused inches from him, quite uncertain of her own opinion. "Please stay with me, please. I don't think I can do this alone. I need you."

His back was to her. "Kadsa, I do not want to hurt you."

"You won't," she assured him unconvincingly. "You're good. Your heart is—"

"Is corrupted," he cut off her sentence.

His words poisoned the mood with heartbreak, and Kadsa felt compelled to assure him, knowing she had to challenge the accusation he made against himself.

"I can't do this alone," she admitted. "The truth is that I don't know what I am doing."

The leopard growled, restless below its breath.

"I'm sorry." She was almost sobbing. "My grandfather got me into this, and I promised the Jakuba I would try to help. I didn't want to tell anyone that I thought they made a mistake about me, so I agreed to try. But, I can't do this alone."

He didn't reply.

"Come with me, please," she begged.

The leopard prince stared into the Dark Forest as if some unseen force or thing beckoned to him. "If we move with speed, then we can finish this before anything else happens."

Kadsa nodded.

"All right," he agreed with somberness. "I cannot deny you what you want. It's not in me."

His white eyes bore into hers like the eyes of the Jakuba in the forest, and she considered that this feature— white eyes—

distinguished them from real animals. *What kind of magic can do this to people?*

"Kadsa, promise me this." "I'm listening."

"Hold your necklace close, just in case I try to hurt you."

She was hesitant to comply, but she nodded all the same.

"Good," he replied. "I'll feel better if you kill me than the other way around. I cannot take Marut's chance of survival away."

Kadsa nodded, keeping her fingers crossed that it never came down to that.

17

MEHRONUR

Bokor wandered the palace grounds with a pleased smile on his face. How easily the stage was set for Akwanshi's ascension and his reign under her supremeness. The council and priests had backed off. They had reeked of cowardice. All the better—one less nuisance for him to deal with. He had informed the crowd the new appointed king would be Sahu. This was, of course, against the wish of the late King Remu.

The crowd looked confused, not certain why he'd addressed them, instead of a council member or the deceased vizier. Many were pleased with the news of Sahu's coronation, as it was not the cursed prince. What they didn't know and wouldn't know until they saw it with their eyes was that Bokor intended to sacrifice the boy to the witch, Akwanshi.

This part was a little bothersome. He felt bad about Sahu. He wasn't the intended lamb. However, the Dark Prince had vanished. Akwanshi wouldn't take the news well, but he figured one blood prince was as good as the other for sacrifice. Akwanshi wanted the divine bloodline, not the flesh, and the boys shared the same bloodline.

Bokor had no clue what happened to the Dark Prince. When he had gone to collect the boy, he was shocked to find out that he was nowhere in the fortress. He had spent the whole night dreaming up a convincing lie to bring him out of his comfort zone. He'd declare the girl a fraud, informing the young man of her role in the king's death. He'd agree to bless him, insisting it was his father's dying wish, and informing him that his ritualistic blessing would free him from his curse, when he'd just be preparing him for sacrifice.

The prince was gone when he arrived. He'd assumed he ran off to some back village, but his heart told him otherwise, that the girl was involved. He despised that girl from the moment he'd laid his eyes on her in the Yedina land.

Did she escape back to the forest? The guards could not find her anywhere in the kingdom. He had sent out guards to make it clear that anyone found harboring the fraud would be charged with treason. If she was in the forest, he was certain she would not survive. He should've killed her while she slept among the Yedina. Unfortunately, the sorceress' dark magic didn't create more than a weakly manifested golem barely resembling him, incapable of doing all but the basics of speaking and moving. When the witch had split him into two souls, it had been painful and terrifying, but she'd assured him that when the time came, he'd return to one person. She just needed spies in both worlds.

He worried a bit about what the witch might think now that he'd failed to kill the girl twice. But at least he'd delivered on her traitorous grandfather, he considered, trying to focus on the positive. That she and the boy were off somewhere shouldn't be too much of a concern. Soon, there would be no place for them to run or hide.

The dome was weakening. The Divide had shrunk overnight to a thin band in many parts of the kingdom. There was little heat felt throughout. Chill washed over an otherwise tropical kingdom. By the next day, there would be complete darkness. Some of the braver creatures from the land of Nenet were even trying to cross over, but the light was still strong enough to incinerate them.

Most citizens clustered near the only safety they knew: the Palace of Hutat. They crowded the public courtyards, desperately. The light hovered in a halo of concentration in this part of the kingdom. Bokor didn't know why this was, especially because the seven high temples that had been built to capture light from the sun were gradually losing their glimmer. Even so, he had faith that the fall of night would put an end to their shine. To be on the safe side, he encouraged the guards and common citizens to find Khansu, preaching against the one whom he now called 'the Dark Prince' for scheming convenience. He promised safety and reward for the person who located the lost heir. If he could locate the dark prince before Akwanshi's arrival, perhaps Sahu could be spared. He laughed. Most likely not.

The Maruti believed wholeheartedly in their divine bloodline. As long as the boy lived, he'd forever be the legitimate heir. He couldn't allow that.

Bokor had contacted the witch, asking her to send an army to secure the throne, fearing many of the guards and citizens were loyal to Abnr and looked ready to disobey. She inquired about the Dark Prince, and he lied. He had not told her about the Dark

Prince's disappearance, but instead told her he held the prince and the girl. This pleased the witch.

If he did not find the prince and the girl upon the witch's arrival, Bokor planned to lie and say that they escaped just moments before her arrival due to the treacherous nature of the guards whose job was to watch over them.

After the speech in the courtyard, he was exhausted. Kingship was indeed a sobering job, but he wouldn't want it any other way. When he addressed the courtyard, he felt like a god-like ruler, already cocky and over-confident.

Bokor threw himself down into the king's comfort chair, with the golden curved handles and soft cushioned seat, and threw his head back to drink from the king's golden chalice. He was pleased with how far he'd come. He excitedly anticipated his ascension to the throne of Mehronur alongside Akwanshi, the living vessel of the dark goddess.

The witch had first contacted him through dark magic while he tranced during a shamanistic ritual— some soul had wanted to curse an enemy or some other trivial affair. Those were the only reasons people came to him—curses and evil. He'd been impressed by the witch's reach, or rather, *breach* of the light, a sure sign that the light of the kingdom dimmed. She'd sent him to Hutat as her appointed representative in the light kingdom. He'd had doubts about the promises she made to him—that he'd reign alongside her—that she'd reign at all, but here they were. Everything was falling into place perfectly. All that needed to happen was for the witch's army to arrive and night to fall eternally.

18

LAIR

Seth stirred a little bit and hissed when a stabbing pain shot through him. His prison was nothing but a hovel in the cold ground covered by large pieces of lumber. How long had he been here? It felt like forever. He barely ate or moved in the deep pit. His captives often tormented him by withholding food, and when they did provide food, it was nothing more than leftover scraps that did nothing for him.

Such a long time had passed since he last saw the girl, and he was driving himself crazy just thinking of what might have happened to her. It took a lot of faith to avoid thinking the worst—that she might have failed. Yet the reality was that they were just a little more than a day from the new age and nothing had happened.

Howling and feet trampling sounds mixed above ground, disrupting his depressive thoughts. He tried to shut out the sounds at first, but they grew in magnitude. Barking. Running. Howling. Something was happening. The heavy pummeling of feet into the earth told him they were running hard and fast to somewhere away from the interior of the swamps. Seth gritted his teeth and stood on his weak legs. He craned his neck to the surface.

"What is happening?" he yelled out. "Someone answer!"

Trampling—it sounded as if the creatures of the dark swamp were in a hurry, trying to escape.

"What is happening?"

"Mehronur!" a voice yelled, drifting away from him. "What? Why?"

No answer came.

Seth had to do something. Against the limitations of his body, he jumped and clawed for the wooden lid that sealed him below ground. He repeated his actions, failing to get either his teeth or claws on the lid. He stopped to catch his breath and strength. His body ached, grumbled with hunger, and bled.

A crack of thunder rolled above his hovel, followed by a sudden rush of rain that fell in heavy thuds into the hovel. Seth stared at the droplets of water creating a pool at his feet. It was raining in Asamando, possibly the entire kingdom of Marut.

Rain hadn't fallen in Marut since before the darkness fell. This meant everything was now shifting out of order. It definitely explained why the Jakuba and the animals of Asamando were all leaving. They sensed something was happening. They were on their way to scavenge and salvage anything they could from the turn of events.

The rain pounded him in the hovel. The cell was not built to accommodate rain, or much of anything, except to provide discomfort and confinement to its dying occupants. To Seth's good fortune, the heavy rain, along with the mudslide it created, barreled down the lid above the hut, causing it to crash inward in the hole, leaving an opening to freedom.

The cold, wet dirt nearly buried him. He used the last bit of energy to climb from under the mud. He climbed atop the heap and wood and made a single leap to the surface. Seth walked only a few steps before collapsing against the cold, wet ground.

———————

Kadsa and Prince Khansu hid in a large tree with thick broad leaves. From there, they watched the procession of roaring, barking, and howling animals. They quickly discovered Akwanshi was passing through, sitting on a chair mounted on the back of a buzoa. Kadsa had imagined she and Khansu would get to see the buzoa for the first time under better circumstances. Instead, they clung to branches to watch the heavyset animal with the twisting horns wobble by.

Kadsa could not clearly make out Akwanshi's features, but the woman's presence generated a buzzy and stinging sensation that coursed through her whole body. Kadsa's heart raced. She hated this.

Akwanshi rode by and Kadsa hid in a tree, doing absolutely nothing about it. What now?

Akwanshi cast a long glance over the darkened forest, as if she sensed them, but she and her party didn't stop to search.

The black leopard shifted uncomfortably as Akwanshi passed through. When he could no longer sense their presence or see them, he told her to climb out of the tree. The prince shook himself, splashing water on Kadsa.

"Ah, do you need to do that?" Kadsa complained, shielding herself from the water.

"I'm sorry," he said with sincerity. "Excuse my lack of manners."

"It's okay," she told the soft-spoken, polite leopard.

They were soaked from the unexpected rainfall in the forest. It had come down so heavily that they could not get out of it in time to find shelter. It no doubt started when the witch left Asamando, Kadsa had thought, curious about the extent of the witch's powers.

What was she up against?

"Why didn't she sense me?" Kadsa asked when they continued their walk toward Asamando.

"Your life force is alien to hers. It exists outside of her reach."

"Because it's Abnr?" "Yes," he said.

"Why didn't she sense you?" "Your light shielded me."

Kadsa squeezed the warm pendant in her hand, stopping herself from saying something superficially hopeful like, "if the light shielded you that meant you'd be okay." Instead, she focused on something else. Maybe her grandfather was hidden by this witch's magic.

"Where do you think they were going?" she asked, changing the subject.

"Mehronur. They know the time is near. They're moving to secure the kingdom, put Akwanshi on the throne."

"This is very bankrupt." She shook her head in frustration. "There's no way we can get to her surrounded by all those wild creatures."

"Kadsa, we should find your grandfather first, and then we'll figure out what to do next."

Kadsa nodded, following the black leopard.

Thick vines created an archway around the entrance of the swamps called Asamando. When Kadsa and Khansu were close to it, the vines twisted and hissed. A bulky vine flung itself at Kadsa, knocking her on her backside. Khansu jumped in front of her as another vine slapped at her. The vine slapped him instead, knocking him away. Kadsa recovered in time to dodge another vine on her way toward the prince. He was already on his feet. When she caught up to him, he yelled for her to "Look out."

Kadsa spun to see one of the thick vines swinging her way. She threw up her hands and shut her eyes on instinct. When she opened her eyes, the vines slithering away cowardly. What happened?

Khansu moved from behind her. "You scared them off."

She touched the crystal. The spark inside of it retracted.

"It is very powerful."

"I guess." Kadsa was still unsure of what she did and how she had done it, but if it worked, she wasn't going to question it. She and the leopard prince marched toward the thick, twisted, haunted vines that formed a canopied gateway to the swamps of Asamando. The vines opened up without fuss and none came after her again. Kadsa paused to glance around the ghostly-looking swampland with suspicion.

"This place is creepy and uncomfortable." "I feel the unease too," he agreed.

Asamando was a scary place of desolate swamps, whose coldness was bone rattling. At its heart, giant trees twisted and spiked like primitive monsters, forming towers. Bones scattered all over the ground, with some rising from the ground where animals had perished and now rotted. Between the towers, the vast water body shimmered in eerie blackness. Howling echoed all around, and she figured it came from the ghoulish towers or creatures that occupied the dark district. Either way, it was a terrible sound.

Kadsa faced the large leopard at her side. "Do you sense any creatures nearby?"

"Some still linger. I'm guessing Jakuba. We must be careful," he warned. "Not of them, but of the other creatures, like the ekoks, the dwarf demon spirits. And Kondes, the two-headed boars, they are also present here."

Kadsa and Khansu moved through the dark kingdom with every careful step they could afford. He used his sense of heat to search for Jakuba, and she followed at a distance. If Grandpa Edoje was here anywhere, it would be nearly impossible to find him. Still, she searched for hints of him, convinced that the sorceress held him somewhere. Thick trees. Twisted stone monuments. Cave after cave turned up empty, and she was losing her patience.

"You don't think he was with the marchers, do you?" The leopard shook his head from side to side and they continued searching. There were many dead or dying creatures in the kingdom, many of them sacrificed to the goddess Nenet. Their remains were left where they died for vultures and other creatures to feed on. The sight of dead carcasses made Kadsa's stomach churn with uneasiness. She fought back regurgitation.

"Are you all right?" asked the leopard prince after she had vomited.

"Yeah," she answered. "The smell of rotted flesh is strong." She took a deep breath. "We'll just try to find him and get out as quickly as possible."

The leopard sniffed the dry air as they moved through the forest. The strange stench seemingly appealed to him. Kadsa didn't want to look at him, but asked, "What is it?"

"The unease you feel beside me. It's all right."

"It's not you." It was only a half-lie. She was vigilant around him, but the swamps scared her more than he did, and she was more concerned about what lurked in its vast darkness than the black leopard beside her.

"It is me," he argued. "I'm walking in the land of Nenet. If we fail before I transform, I will become fully Nenet. But I want you to know. I will die fighting to help you succeed."

She pondered his words. "You won't die. We won't fail," she assured him before they entered the narrow stretch of pathway behind them.

"Wait!" he told her. She paused.

"I sense something." "Jakuba?"

"I'm not sure," he said. "It's getting closer. Quick, behind this wall."

He pushed her back, well into a large crease inside a cave wall, to wait for whatever it was to surface from the corner.

Khansu bravely stood forward, ready to fight off the advancing creature. They were expecting something fierce, but when it turned the corner, she saw a wounded Jakuba, hopping and wheezing. Khansu tossed it to the ground on instinct, his claws planted squarely in its chest to keep it down. "Who are you," he demanded of the Jakuba.

"I am Seth," said the weak voice.

"Seth?" said Kadsa, stepping forward and rushing to the Jakuba's side. "It's Seth. He's on our side. Let him up."

The leopard did so with reluctance, falling back to watch her kneel beside Seth.

"Are you okay?" she inquired. The Jakuba slumped as if in pain.

"I never thought I'd see you again," Seth said, still on his back.

She hugged the Jakuba, despite his smelliness and wet coat. He groaned.

"Where does it hurt?" she asked, studying him.

"Everywhere," he answered with a stifled voice. "What happened? What did they do to you?"

"The usual evil things: beating and starvation. Now help me up. I'm better," Seth assured her.

It took Seth some time to stand on his own without her help. He barely put his right leg down. Kadsa tried not to cringe on his behalf. Now she had two things to worry about—a dangerous panther whose attention span waned, and who paused to do shady things like sniff the air and glare into the darkness. Then there was the broken Jakuba who could barely stand. The faster they could find the heart of the darkness, the better for everyone.

"Now." He faced her. "What are you doing back in the forest, especially in Asamando? What is happening?"

"We came to find my grandfather."

"I see nothing has happened then," Seth said, dully.

Kadsa winced at the disappointment in his words.

"Who is this strange creature?" Seth asked, changing topic.

"This is Prince Khansu, the ruler-apparent of Marut."

"I see," he said in a skeptical tone. "And where is the king?"

"My father passed away."

"He was poisoned by Bokor," Kadsa chipped in. "Bokor has issued a warrant for my arrest. I had to leave. Right now, Bokor rules Mehronur. Akwanshi's headed that way. We don't know how long we have until the apocalypse." Kadsa shook her head. "We came to stop her, but obviously we need a new plan."

"I see," he said complacently and faced the leopard prince. "I am Seth, loyal servant of Abnr. If you have the integrity of your father, it will be my pleasure to serve you like I served the previous kings." He dropped to his knees before the leopard. It hurt him to do so.

"Please, Seth, don't. I am not king yet and may never be if we don't do as is required to save the kingdom. Besides, I have heard many stories of your bravery. I am the one who should be honored to be in your presence."

"Spoken like a true prince," Seth mused.

As soon as the silence descended, the eeriness of their surroundings reached them.

"We must get going," Seth said. "We must find the soul of Abnr. It may be here. We don't have much time. I know a good place to look. We can start in the witch's chamber," he said, walking off.

Loud snorting ripped through the dark swamps. Kadsa spun to see a large two-headed creature galloping toward them at a speed that betrayed its full, chunky body. It ran toward her specifically, and she took one-step backward, before tripping on her own feet and staggering to the ground.

The leopard prince leaped between her and the creature, slamming the creature into a wall. Kadsa crawled to her feet while the leopard prince slammed the squealing creature, obsessively snapping its jagged teeth at him from both of its heads, positioned on opposite ends of its body. It was a scary creature and Kadsa was happy to see that the leopard was slightly bigger.

Seth slogged to her side, wanting to know if she was okay. She assured him she was, before bringing her eyes back to the squealing animal, losing a nasty fight. She could barely watch the leopard prince claw away the creature's flesh while it squealed. He slammed it against the cave wall repeatedly until it could no longer stand. When the panther was certain the creature was dead, he turned away to settle his temper.

"He's no longer a threat to you," said the panther, facing her.

"Is that the Kondes you mentioned earlier?"

"Yes," answered the leopard prince. "He sensed you.

We must leave this place. Others may come."

Kadsa wanted to inquire about the prince's state of being, but sensing he was uncomfortable, she simply nodded in agreement with him. Seth ushered them to follow him as he led them to the far back of the kingdom and up a stone platform, through a dark entrance, where bones and skulls of dead animals lingered along the walls. They trekked with caution to the back of the dwelling.

"This is very dark and scary," Kadsa noted, but it was the last cave and she put on her bravest face. When she'd last seen her grandfather's face in the crystal, he'd been leaning against something she'd believed to be a wall but couldn't be sure.

"You can see very well in the dark now," said Seth. She lifted her chin proudly, and then spoke in

Maruti, "I can speak your language, too."

"Over here," Khansu called from where he stood by a large natural well.

"It used to be an aquifer. She has turned it into witch brew."

"Why's this important?" asked Kadsa.

"This might be the source of the magic keeping the forest dark."

Kadsa placed her hands over it. No heat. It was empty. She related this to them and then added, "We need to find my grandfather."

"Why are you so sure he's here?" Seth asked.

She faced him, the answer deep inside her gut. "Besides the fact that this is the only place my crystal won't show me," she took a deep breath, "I had a vision— back at the palace, before I met Khansu. In the vision, my grandpa was there in the desert. Then suddenly, the darkness took him, and there were vines swirling out of the darkness. Where else has vines and darkness? I think the sorceress took him because he's the key, the one thing that can help Marut."

"Let us resume our search," Seth said.

Kadsa wasn't sure they believed her, but she didn't argue, not because she wasn't sure of what she believed but because time wasn't on their side. Nothing was in the large room except for the well, strange statues, some brass figurines, and a large stone chair and table.

Kadsa moved to the stone table where she spotted the flat-bodied object. "This is mine. How did it end up here?"

The burner phone shared a table with assorted objects, including hair, bones, cranium, mandibles, rocks, and herbs.

"What can that do?" Khansu inquired.

"Not much now. The battery's dead." She stuffed it into her jeans pocket.

"There's nothing and no one here," Seth declared.

Kadsa sighed, biting down on her lower lip. "I know he's alive. If not here, then wherever the witch is, that's where he is."

"We better leave Asamando. It's dangerous here. We can figure it out somewhere else."

Kadsa hesitated. "Kadsa?" called Seth. "I can't do this."

Seth breathed loudly, irritated. "Why do you think that?"

Kadsa swallowed, wracking her brain around his words. "I don't want to disappoint anyone."

"The day isn't over yet," Khansu spoke softly, nearly blending into the darkness of the cave. "Until you learn what happened to your grandfather, let us work together to tackle the darkness."

"You don't get it. He's the key. Not me." Kadsa's breathing was shallow, and her heartbeat pounded out her frustration. She was so hopeful Grandpa Edoje would be here.

"I know you don't believe it, but you have not disappointed us."

She let the thought settle. "But I haven't helped you.

I have just been here doing nothing."

"Kadsa," said Khansu, stepping forward. "You have given us hope."

Kadsa's emotions swelled her face, even with her best effort, she couldn't fight it. She turned her back to them to collect herself.

Silence drifted over them, bringing to life the eeriness of the forest again. A shuffle. Seth's voice broke through. "We should leave here. It is not safe."

Kadsa took a deep breath and then faced her companions. "Fine, let's go."

As they were walking back to the entrance of the cave, Kadsa glimpsed a shiny object to her right, leaning against the wall.

"Wait!"

It was a spear. As she looked closer, she saw an axe too, and other metal tools next to the wall.

"We better grab some of these," she said taking the spear and a small shovel.

Kadsa and her companions strolled quietly through the woods. Seth suggested that they return to his hut, and she and Khansu agreed. They were tired and needed to think and rest.

Queen Oluchi, fearful for her life, fled to the tiny sitting room adjacent to the king's private chamber. Bokor had convinced a great number of people in the kingdom to beg for the mercy of

Nenet, by welcoming the invading party of Akwanshi, which, to her understanding, were nearing the borderland.

Clutching Sahu under her arm, wallowing in her own stupidity, she sobbed. She should have protected Kadsa. It was clear that Bokor was the problem. The witch-doctor threatened Sahu's life. Despite his promise to the king, he now demanded the young prince as oblation to Nenet.

Queen Oluchi glanced to Sion. Unlike other palace guards, he hadn't abandoned them, either for the service of Nenet, or their own protection. He remained her sole protector.

Sion stood at the door with his weapon drawn; never once had he flinched, and this earned the admiration of both Queen Oluchi and her young son. He refused to sit, despite the urging of the young queen.

When the bombardment of the doors came, Queen Oluchi stood frightened, pushing Sahu behind her. Bokor's voice echoed outside the thick walls of the king's chamber.

"He knows we're here," she spoke softly to Sion.

Sion pulled his sword, waiting. "Is there a secret passage out of here? There must be."

Queen Oluchi was puzzled. She hadn't thought of it; a secret exit didn't register, and yet it seemed plausible. The two of them began feeling along the wall for an exit while Bokor and his rogue warriors barreled down the doors of the king's chambers.

"Lady Oluchi, I insist...," came Bokor's blusterous voice, at the same moment, the warriors flung the door open, finding them still in the room, stranded by desperation.

Bokor stepped forward, arrogantly. "Lady, why are you hiding here? Don't you know there's no point in hiding? The time has come."

"You're a traitor—you've committed treason," she spat angrily.

"You're a Garden Priestess." Ridicule stained his words. "We all have our flaws."

She fired back, "The King trusted you. Why did you betray him?"

He chuckled, his belly jiggling. "Don't you see we are fighting a losing battle? The true Dark Enchantment cannot be stopped. Putting faith in a dead deity and a little girl is silly."

"You will pay for your treason and regicide."

He chuckled and then became serious. "Take the boy. It's time for the coronation."

Bokor turned on his heels and left.

Queen Oluchi screamed for Sahu. He rushed into her arms. Sion's sword began swinging at the three guards who came after him. She did not have time to watch him as a fourth warrior came after her. Queen Oluchi pushed Sahu aside, searching around for any weapon she could find. She grabbed the nearest thing—a small sitting stool.

The guard manhandled Sahu. Queen Oluchi screamed, "Sahu!"

Sion turned from his battle long enough to connect a dagger to the guard's back.

The guard collapsed, but by the time Sion gave his attention to the other three guards, more guards had entered the room.

Two of them stormed towards Queen Oluchi and the boy, and the others joined the assault against Sion.

The big man, Bokor watched smugly, and Queen Oluchi wished she could wipe that smug look from his painted face.

As strong and as good a fighter as Sion had been, he was no match for five men, having to swing and kick from all sides simultaneously. Oluchi also did her best to pull her son away from the clutches of the two guards, one of whom grabbed her by the wrist and twisted it to restrain her.

As much agony as she felt, losing her son would be worse, and so she fought through the numbing pain, clawing and slapping. The guard didn't respond and continued twisting her hand; annoyed with her resistance, he slapped her so hard she fell to the ground.

Another guard lifted her kicking-and-biting son on his shoulders, dragging him toward the broken-down exit. Sion somehow managed to drop two of his attackers, injuring another. And seeing that the guard took the boy, the attackers leaped away from Sion.

When the guard carrying Queen Oluchi saw his fellow fighters fleeing and Sion storming toward him, he dropped Queen Oluchi and raced toward the exit. The guard barely reached the doorway when Sion's dagger connected with his shoulder blades. He cried out and staggered from the room.

The big man had long fled.

Sion shut the damaged door, facing Queen Oluchi as she rose to her feet.

"Are you hurt?" he asked, his eyes dropped to her bruised hand, which the guard had twisted; he looked mindful of touching her.

"I am fine. I will be all right." She studied him. Sion was covered in minor gashes and blood. "You're bleeding."

"I'll be fine." He turned away when she tried to touch him. "We have to leave this room now. They'll be back."

"They took my son. I cannot leave without him." "We'll think of something. First, we need to find shelter away from the palace."

Sion walked to the other side of the room and Oluchi watched him study the walls. Seconds later, she heard a bolt unlock and looked to see Sion standing in front of a long, rectangular entrance in the wall. "I found the opening."

"It's too late." She forced the tears into retreat.

"I promise I will try to rescue the boy," he said. "Please come."

"Where does it lead?" she asked, following him into a black entrance with a narrow stairway leading into the ground.

"It may be an exit," he told her, reaching for her hand. She put it in his, and he led her through the dark entrance to the steps, shutting the heavy door which camouflaged itself into the wall again. They descended with caution, Sion holding his sword out before him.

19

MYSTERIES

Kadsa dropped sluggishly at the tree stump in Seth's hut. *What now?*

Seth tossed tree branches into a shallow pit in the ground. He rubbed rocks together, and amethyst-hued fire blazed to life. It was the prettiest thing Kadsa had ever seen.

"How's fire here?" she asked.

Seth roasted hog meat he had dragged back to the hut.

"It's called an ayabba. It's an ancient light source that exists throughout the old kingdom. Rumored to have been one of the first places to receive divine fire in the kingdom," Seth explained.

Kadsa wondered if the fire was like Bennu's. It was strange how all these fires existed, but the forest was so very dark.

The leopard paced the room with growing agitation. He barely stayed still, just back and forth. Seth ignored him while he roasted the meat. Kadsa tried not to worry about him.

"Food is ready," Seth declared sometime later.

Kadsa ripped a piece of the hog meat and chewed into it. Her stomach thanked her with a growl. Everyone ate in silence, reducing the hog to bare bones in little time.

Seth tossed a bone to the flames. It flared.

Khansu jumped to his feet in agitation. "Why'd you do that?"

"This fire affects you?" asked Seth.

"It stirs something in me that I don't like. I am surrounded by Nenet here."

"And you are Mehronur's prince, ruler of Marut." "My father barely acknowledged me," Khansu spoke, agitation lessening. "The circumstances of my birth were too much. The people of Mehronur won't accept me. They may have no choice if darkness takes over. I will rule a kingdom of darkness."

The silence in the room dampened with tension and discomfort. Kadsa faced the amethyst flames that reminded her of Christmas lights. Christmas was one of the few times that she and Grandpa Edoje slowed down, and Grandpa Edoje never wanted to slow down.

He'd tell her that the light of Jua was much better.

"No magic in these artificial lights."

She sulked when she realized that not only might she never see Christmas lights again, if she couldn't get home, she'd never see anything familiar ever again.

"Jua—that's a real thing, right?" she asked softly.

The leopard stopped pacing and Seth's head rose from where his body had hunkered down across the fire.

"The festival of Abnr is very much real," Seth said, disappointment and longing in his voice. "I took my son there every chance I got to do so."

Kadsa wilted, learning this new information about Seth. He was human, and he had a son that he had lost.

"Mehronur still celebrates it, though not as happily as it once did. It is forced now desperate," Khansu chimed in. "Soon there will be no light to celebrate."

Kadsa swallowed her nerves. She should change the topic, but she would be delaying the inevitable. The leopard was already in the room. The tension wasn't breaking. The hut fell into uncomfortable silence. Defiance stirred inside of Kadsa. These people were relying on her, and she hated herself for disappointing them. There was also the fear that she'd never make it home, and if she died here, no one would know that this place ever existed. What was the point of connecting with her mother if that reunion would never happen? What was the point of all those years of traversing Africa with her grandpa only to finally find this place and lose it?

"Where is Marut?"

"What do you mean, Kadsa?" Seth asked.

"What's its location to other places in my world?" "I am not sure."

"When it was part of my world, where was it located?"

The Jakuba shrugged, and the leopard groaned with agitation.

"It was probably next to Egypt and Chad—exactly where we found the doorway," she reasoned, mainly with herself. "We circled and ended up right where we started. He'd thought the doorway shifted because the stars shifted, but it was a cycle."

"Kadsa, what are you saying?" Khansu asked. "Ancient civilizations fall. It's long gone with history, like Egypt."

"Your gods destroyed another civilization?" Seth's voice was sullen. He hissed every so often, still reeling from his sore body.

"The gods didn't destroy Egypt." Kadsa shrugged, rethinking her words. "It's time that destroyed it. And invasions, but mostly time. It's just *old*."

"Nkuzm controls time. Nkzum destroyed it, then."

When no one spoke, Seth continued. "I suppose we must accept our fate. Despite our divine origins, we will cease to exist."

Kadsa cringed at the same time a thought sprung to life in her head. It blossomed in many directions, branches extending and branching off on their own, but none was steady enough to grasp—threading and re-threading like reed rafts and baskets that she spent painful times trying to put together only to undo because some pattern was off. "Everything in Marut is divine. You believe that."

"This is the land of the gods, Kadsa. It's why we are fighting for it."

"Why don't you believe?" barked the leopard prince, his voice stirring her stomach.

"I need to see—"

"You've been seeing, just not accepting and believing. Not grasping."

Kadsa sat upright, her eyes dropping to the amethyst flames. She stood, knowing he was right. All her gut instincts had been right. She'd just been ignoring them because, despite her belief that she was brave, she had been afraid to be wrong.

"That fire is *divine*." She shuffled with restlessness, while ambitious ideas inundated her brain. "Seth, did you not say there was one of these ayabbas for each kingdom in Marut?"

"Yes," Seth answered after glancing to the ayabba.

"This is from Abnr. It's pure light," she proclaimed. "How many districts are there in Marut?"

"Five," Khansu chimed in, still agitated, "including Mehronur."

"Name them." It was a diversion. She needed time for her own bustling thoughts to develop into something she could grasp and express.

"Mehronur, Abzul, Faro, Elon, and Bourchul," replied Seth. "What are you getting at, Kadsa?"

Kadsa laughed while the ideas pieced themselves together in her brain like a puzzle. She wasn't crazy. She was working through mystery.

"Fascinating."

"What?"

"Never mind," she said, changing the topic. "Mehronur is the kingdom of the light, the center of Marut." She took a deep breath. "So what we need to do is to find a way to evenly spread the light from Mehronur to the rest of the forest. And this ayabba can do it. Think about it. It's the only light that can exist in the forest, mingling with the darkness." Kadsa laughed, barely able to contain her exhilaration.

"Kadsa, what are you saying?" Seth asked, voice laced with confusion.

"I'm finally figuring out this place—believing." She pumped her fist. "Don't you see? The heart of the darkness will be in Mehronur, not Asamando. You'll rule a kingdom of light *or* dark. It can't be both. Asamando is a fake heart. It will always be dark."

"Asamando has no heart!" Seth snapped.

"My exact point. The real heart is Mehronur. We must fight the war in Mehronur, because that's where the witch is now. This is the kingdom where the soul of the light, Abnr, is whole. The same kingdom is the *heart* of the world. The heart she wants to turn into the heart of darkness."

Kadsa was so nervous, she trembled. "It's the land of the gods. It's where the powers of the gods manifest, literally. Abnr manifests in Marut as pure light. That's his soul—the light that protects Mehronur, that pushes away the darkness." She blew her breath loudly. "Each ayabba represents a different chiefdom of Marut."

She laughed while the leopard and the Jakuba tried to make sense of everything she had said. "The ayabbas must be united and they must be united with the one in Mehronur. When they come together, they form a whole. A perfect soul."

"How will you unite them?" Seth asked.

"The pillar," she blurted out after a short time perusing her own mind. "The pillar on the wall...the one the hero places the box on. The box is the soul and she brings it to the pillar that's supposed to unleash it."

"Kadsa, how are you so sure of what you say?" Khansu asked.

She took a deep breath, cogitating, refusing to doubt herself anymore. "I'm good at figuring things out. That's my gift. Besides, there's no harm trying, is there? We must gather the ayabbas and get back to Mehronur. There is no use staying here," she said with some urgency.

"How will we gather them?"asked Khansu. "Rocks," Seth suggested. He was already gathering a piece of rock.

"I don't think that's gonna do." Kadsa shook her head.

"What do you mean?"

She grabbed the spear she had brought from Asamando. Kadsa moved to the flames and her crystal pendant lit up. "My crystal lights up when I'm near one of these things. It's like a magnetic attraction. They're cut from the same lodestone or something." She faced Seth. "I need the source of whatever is keeping this fire going." She stabbed the spear into the ayabba. Sparks flew in all directions, forcing them to duck for cover.

"Are you all right?" Khansu asked with concern. She nodded. "Yeah."

"You could've gotten hurt," Seth scolded her.

"Yes, but that confirms what I'm thinking. We need something that's at the bottom of the pit. We need to dig for it."

"Well, we can dig around it," Seth told her. "Grab the shovel," she instructed.

Seth pushed it to her. The two of them dug around the ayabba. Khansu stood some distance away to watch Kadsa dig and Seth scoop away the fire and the dirt.

Kadsa got on her knees. "Feel that. It's heat, raw energy." She faced the Jakuba.

"Careful."

Oddly, her pendant glowed brighter, almost jumping off her neck. An amethyst glow radiated below the dirt surface. Khansu and Seth drew closer. Kadsa hit the ayabba with the shovel and then scraped away the thin layer of dirt.

"That light is buried deep down into the earth. You cannot remove it," noted Khansu.

"I see that." Kadsa glanced to her companions, and then drew her breath in her throat and hit the ground hard, nearly breaking her hand. She cried out.

"Why have you done that?" asked an agitated Seth. "I don't know," she said, removing her crystal that was all but levitating off her neck. She did know—at the very least, she had an idea. She dangled the necklace above the hot bed of glowing rock. Whatever this ayabba was, she needed it. That crystal had *borrowed* the light from the torch when she'd first arrived in the forest. What if she captured all the ayabba lights in the crystal, what then? Kadsa watched the crystal fill up with a swirl of white with hints of purple.

"Help me up!" she called to her companions at the top, pushing the shovel toward them. The panther grabbed it, or tried to. It slipped. "Maybe tie it to a rope."

"There is no rope here," Seth explained. "I can wait for you to get some."

"There's no time," Khansu said, and leaped into the hovel, nearly knocking her down. She stared wide-eyed at him, shocked by the aggression. "Grab hold of me."

She obeyed, more out of fear than anything else, climbing on his back. The panther growled agitatedly, pulled back, and took two leaps to get to the surface, shaking her off his back within seconds, while he groaned.

Kadsa climbed to her feet, eyes on the panther. "You okay?"

"I'm fine," he snapped, and used his paws to swipe his face.

"Let's go find the other ones," she spoke softly. "Kadsa, what does this mean?" asked Seth.

She gripped the crystal around her neck. "It has the ayabba's light. We have to collect each ayabba in the crystal and then do something with it. I think it will show me what to do if they're united. But we have to hurry. The crystal doesn't hold the light for very long."

Khansu growled.

Kadsa nodded, more than a little worried about his behavior.

———

After they left the hut, Kadsa halted in the middle of the forest. "Which Kingdom is the closest to Mehronur?" she asked, realizing it might help to plan this beforehand.

"Faro, in the center of Marut," said Seth.

"We'll go there last, before Mehronur. It is easiest that way."

"But Kadsa, the witch's army will be expecting us to cross into Mehronur from Faro."

"Then what do you suggest? I'm trying to plot the easiest trip, and Mehronur must be the last stop."

"We can cross over to Mehronur from Abzul. There are hills and rock beds, but it's much safer at this point," Seth reasoned. "This border divide might not be as guarded."

"Then it's settled," she said. "Now, which district is the farthest from Mehronur?"

"From here, it's the stone kingdom of Bourchul in the west," Seth explained. "From there, we can go through Faro and then Abzul in the northeast, before landing in Mehronur."

"Then we'll go to Bourchul first," she said to Seth. "Can you lead us to Bourchul?"

A sudden burst of thunder in the sky startled them. The thunder cracked in quick back-to-back successions.

"We've messed with the gods," said Seth.

"The light is powerful. It's reacting to the dark," Prince Khansu insisted.

"It's covered." She clutched the cloak to her chest. "We have to get to Bourchul. Find the path to Bourchul," she murmured into the necklace, expecting it to show her the vision. Instead, it lit a pathway through the Dark Forest, visible at a great distance. The light died down in the necklace, but the path it carved through the forest stayed in her mind.

"Follow me. I can see the easiest path," she informed her companions.

Thunder cracked and parted the sky a few times. Once on the road to Bourchul, a crocodile from a shallow marsh jumped in their path, snapping its jaws at them. The lightning zapped it nearly to dust.

"Abnr is protecting you, Kadsa," said Seth.

Seth and Khansu walked alongside Kadsa but never jumped ahead of her. They needed to stay on the safer side.

20

DARKNESS

On the throne platform of the public courtyard, Bokor preached to a small group of gatherers, scolding them about how easily they had welcomed *Saa'o*, the False Star. Abnr was weak, dying; Abnr had failed to protect them; he had abandoned them. Many people were tired of listening, but many more agreed to listen and some even converted to servants of Nenet, chanting her name and offering their children.

This, Bokor knew he'd be rewarded for, and he was giddy just thinking about the coming night. And when he saw the lightning in the sky, after the rain had fallen, he and the witch, who had settled on the edge of The Divide at Faro, laughed, for they knew the time was now. The kingdom was falling.

When night fell over Mehronur, its residents believed they had experienced the last day. The night was darker than usual, colder than usual, and its mystery dramatized a supernatural danger. No stars were visible in the sky. The two suns remained eclipsed by shadows.

Abnr was dying.

Come morning, Mehronur would look like the thicket of Dark Forest. By the end of the day, the reign of Nenet would become official. What's more, they were under the attack of Akwanshi's Dead Horde. Creatures from the forest were already crossing over The Divide which had eaten away at the weaker parts. Many Jakuba and Asamando-dwelling wild animals got injured crossing over, but they did not die. They did not turn to dust, not like they used to, and so they braved the shield. A few people encountered some of these creatures, and few lived to tell their tales. Most of the residents stuck close to the public courtyards and temples of the palace, lingering around like refugees, lost and abandoned.

The path to Bourchul took Kadsa, Seth and Khansu through giant shrubs, snake-like trees that grabbed at them, and over a near-dried-up aqueduct centered in the village of Soek. Seth said the Jakuba of the forest had been feeding heavily on the water and the creatures at the bottom of it. Below them, amphibious critters jumped up and down in shallow water. Kadsa almost lost her balance once.

"Stare ahead and don't look down," Seth had warned. Some of the creatures crawling on land looked downright prehistoric. There were fishes with backbones and crocodiles ten feet long. Judging by the way they snapped their mandibles, she knew falling would turn her into fast food.

Bourchul was the kingdom of hard rocks, large caves, and cliffs. It was nicknamed the Stone Kingdom. Its people, Seth told her, were comprised of Dehu and Kuta tribes, desert peoples known as much for their navigation skills as their metallurgy. The kingdom on the rocks reached tremendous elevations.

They climbed to the top of a rocky plateau that gave them a view of the dark and canopied forest. She'd once sought these cliffs as her one chance of leaving the forest. It was a good thing Seth had talked her out of it. No life existed among the rocks. Bourchul was also known as the fire kingdom. Volcanoes had helped to carve the landscape of plateaus, craters, and cliffs to artistic and near-geometric accuracy.

"This landscape," spoke Seth, "is the handiwork of the gods."

"Who carved these statues?" Kadsa caressed a stone carving of a Jakuba.

"These are real Jakuba." Seth's voice softened in remorse. "The magic of Nenet turned them into monuments of warning to the disobedient."

Kadsa's stomach dropped. She turned away. That rock was once a living, breathing being. She again considered the power of the sorceress. She really didn't want to face a witch who had the power to do a thing like that.

It took a great deal of careful steps, but Kadsa, the agile panther, and stiff-moving Jakuba reached the zenith of a high plateau. Seth sensed heat there. To get to the top, they had to move through a cave's narrow tunnels which posed much danger by itself. The fragile pathway chipped away, and debris skidded off it now and then. It threatened to pull apart completely.

When they reached the top, Seth limped over to the ayabba.

Kadsa began to dig while the panther glanced off into the distance toward a desert landscape. Seth clawed around the heated area.

Digging through hard rock was an arduous task.

Kadsa worried about spraining her wrists.

"You should hurry. I sense we are not alone."

"I sense it, too." Khansu spoke with his back to them.

He kept a deliberate distance from her, and every time he growled, her heart sank.

"I'm working as hard as I can," she fired back, somewhat irritated by the harrying. She wasn't superhuman and they weren't exactly helping. A sprain- like discomfort pinched in her hands. She hit rock after rock, banging against it, and had to take breaks to massage her palms and wrists.

Eventually, the rock shattered, or rather, the red dirt around it gave way. Kadsa dug until the red fire emerged from under the dirt.

"And then there were two." She dangled the crystal over the rock, watching in awe as the red filtered in next to the swirl of purple. "White with a red glow."

Kadsa was returning for the shovel when the ground beneath her gave way and she and the cloak fell inside a cavity.

"Kadsa!" Seth and Khansu called after her when she screamed.

"Don't die, don't die, don't die," she muttered as she fell, squeezing her eyes shut. Then she stopped falling. No pain. She opened her eyes and looked down. A murky white light outlined her figure, like a halo. She stood above a rocky surface clutching the cloak in her arms.

Kadsa breathed and touched the shield that cushioned her. Her skin tingled. It was just like in the underground temple of the Akonadi, and it appeared to come directly from the crystal.

Kadsa gripped the pendant with relief. What now? She still hovered feet above a very rocky, unstable path. How would she get out of this safely? She looked around the cave.

A narrow stream curved through a winding passageway, whose end she could not see. Bennu had said the crystal tapped into her consciousness. If so, it meant she could will it to do as she commanded. "Show me the path outside," she mumbled and closed her eyes envisioning the outside of the cave. The pendant levitated almost to her mouth and shot out a bolt of light that carved a path. Fearing it might shut off too quickly since the pendant wasn't exactly reliable, she hurriedly kicked her feet out, mimicking the motion of walking. It worked. She was walking on air—light.

Kadsa walked toward the cave's opening and forced her feet down on the solid ground. She exhaled. That wasn't death-defying at all. The light shield remained around her. She had no idea how to dismiss it.

"Kadsa!"

Khansu and Seth rushed toward the cave entrance.

They both stopped.

"You're the living Abnr now," Seth told her.

Kadsa ambled toward Seth and Khansu and they took two steps back. "Oh right, you're allergic to this thing." She studied her pendant. "I don't know how to turn this thing off."

"Kadsa, wish it away," Seth instructed, "We must get going."

"Right." She squeezed her eyes shut. "Light, please go away."

Just like that, it disappeared, though not without an icy feeling running through her body. She felt silly for believing she had to do something special to put it out.

"Now we must find the path to the next kingdom," Khansu said when she moved closer.

"Right. To Abzul," she said, clutching her pendant, a bit disoriented and a little shaken.

"Faro, Kadsa," Seth yelled, but it was too late. The cave wobbled. Rocks and stalagmites fell from all around. "I'm sorry," she said, as she and her companions squeezed into the entrance of the cave, as it began to spin. Kadsa was not mistaken. She didn't think the crystal was this powerful. It wasn't just showing her the path to travel, it was taking her there.

The cave made a ninety-degree turn, and then the rocks pulled away from over them. The crawling fish spun about their heads alongside debris, dragged back with the cave by the tornado-like force unleashed. Now the cave was all but gone.

"Oh no," Kadsa said, unable to get out the path of the flood of water that rushed out of nowhere to garble them up.

Kadsa watched the Jakuba and the panther swim by her, carried off by the water.

She was a weak swimmer.

The water rose and dipped in waves, Kadsa sucked in as much air as she could, dipping under. When she raised her head above again, the water was dwindling. It was gone within seconds, except for the puddles.

"Seth? Khansu? Where are you?"

No one answered.

The area was dark and the mudslide that had washed them there had disappeared as if it never existed. The speedy travel zapped her energy. She took a moment to gather her strength. She was soaked but that was the least of her troubles. Kadsa spotted Seth, but Khansu was harder to find. When they found him, he shook with agitation.

"What is it now?" Kadsa inquired with worry.

"The light bothers me. I cannot travel by it again," he hissed.

Kadsa nodded and turned away from him. In fact, they both turned away from each other while they hunted down the rock crystals.

"Next time, perhaps you can manage an easier way of traveling," said Seth.

"We don't have time," Kadsa explained, and then looked around. "This really is Abzul?"

"It looks like Abzul, the easternmost district. And the water is clear evidence. We were to visit Faro."

"I screwed up. Jumped the trigger. But it's not a big deal, right?"

"It's not a big deal," said Seth coolly. "Nothing but hills and valleys exist between this kingdom and Faro."

"And where are we off to find the third rock?" she asked.

Khansu's eyes fixed on the forest itself. "Do you sense anything?"

"My sense of heat is fading," he told her dejectedly. "It must be after midnight in Mehronur. By the end of the day..." He allowed his voice to trail off.

No one said anything to him about the matter.

Seth stepped forward. "Follow me," he told them. The ground was so soggy, Kadsa had to drag her feet through the heavy mud.

Seth squealed ahead of them.

When they caught up with him, he was body-deep inside the sinking mud.

"Hold on," said Kadsa, pushing the spear toward him. Khansu helped her as much as he could without human hands. Together, they pulled Seth above ground, all collapsing securely against a tree.

"We must watch out for these," Seth spoke after catching his breath. "There may be many more around here. They serve as traps. I was locked in one in Asamando."

Khansu jumped to his feet and stiffened.

"What is it?" Kadsa watched him warily, fearing the dark transformation was complete.

The leopard stood still for a very long, disquieting moment.

"Khansu?" She called softly.

"Do you hear that?"

"What?" she asked, dumbfounded.

"The sound of the Mpundulu," he replied.

Kadsa held her breath. What did that mean? A large bird flew over them, moving so swiftly, she dove to the ground, thinking it might attack. Though it swooped in their direction, it circled, moving erratically around, as if scavenging for something or other. When it disappeared into the darkness, Kadsa studied the leopard prince, before turning to Seth.

"Was that the Mpundulu?" she asked. She'd never seen anything like that. It wasn't Bennu's size, but it wasn't tiny, either. Maybe the size of two vultures.

"The Mpundulu means death is upon us," Seth said, stepping forward. "It flies from Asamando to collect human souls. It hasn't flown since the last age because there were no humans in the forest."

"So, someone will die?"

"Someone will die, someone is dying, or someone is dead," Seth corrected.

Kadsa wished he hadn't spoken those words. Both he and Kadsa looked at Khansu. Neither said anything.

"Why don't we move on?" Seth suggested.

It took them a long time to reach the ayabba. They had spent most of the search stepping into mud holes and dodging landslides. They found the ayabba next to a shrub-covered rock that protruded from the ground. It reminded her of the rock she'd first clung to when she had first entered the kingdom, but she couldn't say if it was.

"Right here." She dropped to her knees to dig. The ayabba was underneath the rock. It had a bright blue glow. Kadsa was digging near the rock when she slid and fell inside a mud hole. She held her breath, her teeth chattering as the cold water soaked through her. The underground water body was deeper and wider than she had imagined.

She soon discovered she was inside of an underwater world, hidden under the shallow mud that melted away. She could swim for miles underneath it. Of course, she was a weak swimmer, and she would attempt no such thing. Who knew where it led. She had never seen anything like this before. How could so much water exist below the shallow surface of dirt and where did it all come from?

She forced herself out of distraction and pushed her crystal to the ayabba, skipping back to the surface where she was able to climb back to the top by gripping the spear that Seth and Khansu had stuck into the mud hole. Kadsa climbed to drier land.

"It's water—all water," she declared, nearly out of breath.

"Abzul is the water chiefdom, Kadsa," Seth told her.

"I know, but how can so much water exist under a surface that's so shallow? It's an entire world underground."

"Marut is a complicated kingdom. When it returns to its splendor, you'll see. Abzul stores the water of the kingdom in its underground city."

Kadsa nodded. "I'll take your word for it, but we better get going now."

"Faro," Kadsa spoke into the necklace, hoping it could take her to the last stop as speedily as it had brought her to Abzul, but without the spinning cave and flood effect. The pathway to Faro lit up. "Get me there by the speed of light."

Kadsa had heeded Khansu's warning about the light, but she sensed urgency. The leopard looked as if he would leap from the path of light, but the light had shot out faster than he could, resulting in the three of them getting consumed.

Within seconds they collapsed into a bush bed.

Neither Seth nor Khansu looked amused as they rolled around as if on fire, screeching and growling.

Kadsa watched them with some guilt. They'd have to understand.

Seth pulled himself together first and studied her. "Kadsa, that was not all right."

"I needed the faster less dramatic way. Either that or we had to walk. We don't have time, remember?" Seth exhaled grumpily. "It felt like my insides were on fire."

"Probably were," she admitted, feeling overheated, too.

They both looked to the agitated panther trying to calm himself. He growled.

Kadsa stepped back, worried.

The panther glared, baring his teeth, and in a second, turned around and leaped into the trees, disappearing.

"Khansu?" she called after him. No reply.

"Kadsa, let us hurry," Seth said.

Kadsa looked after the panther. "I didn't think he'd react that way."

"It's not the time to worry about him." Seth looked around. "I sense Jakuba everywhere. We are in the back of the kingdom, but the witch's army must be near the divide. We need to hurry up."

Kadsa sighed, worried about Khansu. She rubbed the pendant, feeling its warmth as its light faded. Another thing she felt was weak. She shook off the effects, still not believing the crystal teleported them there.

"Kadsa," called Seth, drawing her attention. "We have only hours."

Kadsa nodded and she and Seth went to work searching for the ayabba.

Some forty minutes or so into their search, the bushes bristled and Khansu poked his head out.

"Khansu," she called, wanting to run to him, but stopped herself. He still looked antagonistic.

"I have come to help," he said coolly. "Are you okay?"

He looked away and exhaled. "It's becoming harder to control myself."

"We'll hurry."

They again went to work sniffing out the ayabba. "What is it?" Kadsa let her words trail away, seeing what caused the leopard to stop walking. They were in the middle of an ambush. Jakuba began sneaking out of the forest from many angles. They came at them until they had backstepped into each other, rubbing against each other's bodies. Kadsa counted ten or more of the Jakuba, all with teeth exposed, all deadly looking and ready to charge at them.

"We mean you no harm," Seth spoke with a trepid, yet calm tone. "We are not enemies."

"Not enemies?" Spoke the female Jakuba in front of Kadsa.

"Anyone who isn't us is our enemy, and you're not us."

"You are Jakuba, and Jakuba are not enemies of themselves. We are from the same family."

"And which family is that?" A male Jakuba hissed from where he faced an aggrieved Khansu.

"The same family of humans who lived in the kingdom before the last age brought darkness and destruction. We are not animals who kill and slaughter ourselves," he scolded them.

The animals gnawed at the air. "Who do you think you are?" Hissed the female Jakuba. "We are not humans. Not anymore."

"I am Seth, and I know you never lose your humanity," he explained with calm. "Let us go. We were just here for the warmth."

"Seth," said the female Jakuba, cogitating on the name. "Yes, we know who you are now. You're the fool who dared to challenge the witch of the forest. We thought you were dead."

"I am alive. I mean well."

"How do you mean?" Asked the female Jakuba.

"I am trying to save Marut. Trying to restore the rule of Abnr."

The Jakuba went silent, shocked by the revelation. Then they burst into near harmonious laughter. It scared Kadsa. She wondered if all Jakuba laughed in such a downright scary way.

"Restore the rule of Abnr...," said the leader female. They laughed some more. "Have you not looked around?" asked the male Jakuba. "At this very moment Nenet is putting Akwanshi on the throne of Mehronur.

The state has fallen and by the end of this day, it will officially be gone."

"Believe me," said Seth, stepping forward. "If you let us go, we can stop the witch from ascending the throne." "And how will you do that?" A third Jakuba, a male, stepped forward.

"Because I am with Abnr's Gift," he said. The eruption of laughter, still echoing around them, stopped.

"Say that again?" asked the female leader.

"Abnr's Gift is here," he said. "The one prophesied to help us protect our kingdom from the witch. Do you not see her?"

All turned their attention to Kadsa.

"That is not an apparition?" Asked the female leader somberly, "That creature that radiates such strong energy, heat—that is not an apparition?"

"She is human, the living Abnr, the one sent to restore the light to the kingdom," he explained. They stared at Kadsa in horror.

"No human has walked the forest since the last cosmic age. No foreigner." Seth continued.

"You lie," accused the first male, stepping forward. "You see for yourself," Seth insisted.

Kadsa felt compelled to speak up.

"My name is Kadsa Abasi," she spoke in English, with a little more confidence. "I am who he says I am. I am trying to help you guys. Let me do that, or I'll never forgive myself."

They stared at her in silence. The female moved closer, forcing Kadsa to stand her ground, knowing she had to look confident in front of these creatures. The Jakuba only sniffed her out, sniffing and sniffing until she was satisfied.

"You speak a foreign tongue," said the female Jakuba. "Yes," she mused, "there was talk of an outsider in the land of Nenet." The Jakuba circled Kadsa like a predator toying with its prey.

"That is me," she spoke in Maruti. The female Jakuba paused.

"I am here with the King of Marut."

"The king?" asked the female Jakuba. The other Jakuba muttered and mumbled. "The king of Marut, you say?" she repeated, but did not wait for Kadsa to answer. "The king is dead. News of his death echoes through the land."

"Yes," she answered. "The old king, Remu, is dead. But this is Khansu, his named successor. The mortal son of Abnr."

The Jakuba looked to the quiet leopard. "You're the prince?" said the second male Jakuba. "We barely sense the heat in you. How can you be of Abnr when you look like Nenet? You're not even human."

"All you say is true. I am dying," he told them grievously. "If you do not allow us to do what is required to restore the kingdom, I will become the prince of darkness, instead of light. The one so greatly feared by all."

Khansu's words sent a chill down Kadsa's spine.

The Jakuba became quiet.

When no one spoke up, Kadsa said, peppering her tone with urgency, "He is with me. We must get to Faro, find the ayabba and return to Mehronur to restore the light before the day is done." Kadsa spoke with urgency. She remembered what Seth had mentioned about the divide, that the witch's army guarded it. "And we would like your help." She watched them through the darkness, and then she bravely stepped forward.

"Help you. Why would we? Akwanshi would praise us well if we were to deliver you to her," spoke the female Jakuba.

Seth stood beside her. "You do not want to do that," he warned. He could sense that this coterie of Jakuba were not followers of

Nenet or Akwanshi. They were vagabonds and outcasts who grouped together out of convenience and necessity.

"I know why you've come here to Abzul," he started again. "You came for the heat. You long for the heat. You don't worship at the temple of Akwanshi where it is cold and lifeless. You are like me. You are lost souls wandering the forest and longing for refuge—for the old world of heat and beauty, the world in which your humanity was valued."

The Jakuba listened intently. "The old world doesn't exist anymore. We'd be fools to believe it will return. It's a useless dream."

"It can exist again," Seth pleaded with them. "Here is Abnr's Gift and the prince who would be king. We just need one more rock, and with your help we can restore the light to the kingdom." He was face to face with the female leader. "What do you say— one last fight for the old kingdom?"

The female Jakuba looked to her clan and soon they were clustering and quarrelling amongst themselves. Kadsa, Khansu, and Seth could hear the words tossed back and forth: heat, light, Abnr, kingdom, foolish, no, believe, human, the star, the gift. It went on like this for some time before the female Jakuba faced them again.

"Alright, Seth Oranyan," she started, "You're the crazy one, but we don't blame you. We've seen enough of the darkness to hate it. This wilderness drives us all mad. And so, we will help you."

Kadsa let out a sigh of relief.

"Thank you," said Seth, stepping forward. "We don't have much time. We may need you at the Divide between Mehronur and Faro, to fight."

"To fight?"

"The witch's army controls the divide. We can't go through them alone."

"We can be brave enough to do that. We can gather more of us to take on the cause. First, we must know your plan."

"We plan to find the ayabba here and then head to Mehronur. When we are in the kingdom, we will restore the light," Kadsa explained. She didn't know the precise details of how she would do any of this and it prevented her from disclosing too much, which was not necessarily a bad thing. "We don't have a lot of time. Evening is here, and like you've said, Akwanshi is currently ascending the throne."

"I understand," said the female Jakuba. "I am Kana.

I am from Abzul. I worked as a healer."

"Kadsa Abasi and Prince Khansu," Seth introduced.

Kadsa said hello. Prince Khansu gritted his teeth and growled at the Jakuba. "Good to meet you."

"I know another entrance to Mehronur," said Kana. "You are heading in that direction. It's the cataract. It is tricky to cross, so you'll have to be careful. You must travel to your right, past the river and the stone temple of Auba. There in the valley, you will see the gorge."

"Thank you," Kadsa said.

"When we gather the others, we will carry on ahead to the Divide," said Kana. "We hope you are successful on your journey if not, we'll have to deal with the wrath of the witch. Though it will be a worthy fight if it's the last thing we do before losing our humanity."

The Jakuba returned to the darkness from where they had come.

"What's wrong?" asked Kadsa when Khansu began to pace. She knew what was wrong, but she needed to hear him speak to know that he was still with her.

"I'm changing. The darkness just intensified."

His speech was forced; he struggled to find the words. His eyes were losing the brightness in them. She knew what it meant. He'd become a true son of Nenet in just a few hours. She didn't dwell on it for both of their sakes.

"Can you still function?" Seth asked, stepping forward. "Or must we do something about you now?"

Kadsa's eyes widened, but she held her cool.

The leopard thought about it for a long moment and then he nodded.

"Let's move on, then," said Kadsa. "The shorter amount of time wasted the better."

Faro was the land of vegetative beauty. It was the last in the kingdom to fall during the takeover, according to Seth. During the walk, they came upon an array of elephants, gazelles, and giraffes. The district boasted a hanging garden, whatever this was. Seth said it was a wonder.

Lightning belched through the sky. Kadsa's heart almost leaped from her chest at the sight of the Mpundulu soaring across the dark sky. A gust of strong wind lashed them as they made their way to the tree by which the panther waited.

When she reached the panther, he merely gestured to the vine-engulfed monument and then walked off, keeping his distance.

It was already nearing dawn by the time they found the green prism buried near the vine-strangled tower— not the Jorba palace but the hanging garden.

"The garden was a gift from Nahrin, the land of Queen Aja," Seth explained. "It replicated the one that existed in her homeland."

Khansu did not know this about his mother, the foreign princess.

"I was among the royal warriors tasked with escorting the young queen to her new home for her wedding to King Remu," Seth said with a smile. "It was one of my first duties as a divine warrior."

Kadsa watched the green light mingle with the other colors happily, but worried that they might soon dwindle. The purple looked weak, as it was the first collected. Still, they were all there. She tightened Khansu's cloak around her body, and then faced her companions. "Now, we must get to Mehronur."

The panther raced ahead. She and Seth trailed at a safe distance.

Following Kana's instructions, Kadsa traveled through the gorge, with the rock-strewn riverbed and a cataract that gushed loudly, ensuring she could move without detection. The vast cataract gushed over the rocky terrain that served as natural blockade and divide between Mehronur, Faro, and Abzul.

The path through the gorge led to the east side of Mehronur. Akwanshi's Dead Horde was too busy helping themselves to the spoils of Mehronur to care to spread out this far. They probably thought the witch had already secured the kingdom.

Kadsa and her companions were careful as they navigated the rocky islets strewn with small boulders. Upon passing over the rapids, they paused in the back kingdom where the dome, faded and darkened, still formed a thin shield around the kingdom.

This was the abandoned part of the kingdom, but she was in Mehronur, where she needed to be. Only a tiny spec of the light shield remained. It hovered above the village of Hutat, visible yet darkend.

"That's where the ayabba probably is," Seth suggested of the speck of light above Hutat. "It's usually the strongest spot in the kingdom."

"I agree. And that looks like the fortress. Funny, it was always the darkest spot in the kingdom, and now it appears to be the brightest."

The only glimmer of hope lay in the fact that the kingdom didn't appear entirely dark; instead, a dark blue light, the color of soft night in Mehronur, settled over it. This meant she had some time to fix the problem and make sure the dawn came on cue instead of falling prey to the blackness.

"This is it." She watched Seth. "I have to get that rock."

"Kadsa, are you sure of what you mean to do?"

"I think so, I mean yes. Of course, yes." She took a deep breath. "I am certain, Seth."

"Good. We do not have much time—not at all. The light is almost nonexistent. Go, so we can see the morning again. Be safe."

Kadsa watched him with a mixture of emotions inside her heart. For the first time, she felt the urgency of the situation. Whatever doubt and sense of disbelief she had brought with her took second place to this immediate task. She had summoned enough belief to convince herself that Marut was worth saving. She had doubts about whether she was right in what she was planning to do, but she did not want to entertain these doubts. She wanted to appear brave and confident. She smiled at Seth Oranyan and then she turned to Khansu, again. Khansu looked like the living night. He was all eyes among the darkness. Kadsa empathized with the poor prince and tried hard not to show pity. He didn't want pity.

Noise boomed in the woodland, and each of them faced the bushes, where the new divide between the faded blue light of the kingdom and the blackness of the forest had formed.

"Akwanshi's army. They've come looking for us," Seth said. "Go! We must hold them off."

Kadsa practically leaped into the faded dome but paused with consideration. "You should come over, both of you."

"I'll stay here and fight," Seth said keeping an eye on the bushes.

Kadsa looked to Khansu. "I will fight," he told her.

She nodded with understanding, knowing that he was simply afraid of hurting her, and perhaps had decided fighting was the honorable thing to do.

"See you at the dawn of the new age." She forced herself to smile.

When the voices became louder and more aggressive, she rushed off, running toward Hutat, making sure she traveled on the hidden back paths. She ran hard and confident, never once looking back and barely slowing down. She took deep breaths as she paced toward the village of Hutat, never once letting up.

Seth and Khansu turned into the darkness.

"Where are our friends?" asked Khansu. The sound of the rustling bushes got closer and louder.

"I don't know," Seth admitted.

"You think they betrayed us or abandoned us, already?"

"Perhaps, but I don't know," Seth repeated. Then he looked at Khansu. "Are you prepared to battle?"

Khansu thought about it. "I am. What else is there for me?"

Seth nodded. "I knew your father, and he was a brave leader. We fought many battles together as young men."

The voice of Seth's nemesis, Taroq, heralded his presence from the bushes, where he had been hiding.

"Well, well, well, said Taroq, stepping out from hiding. "Look who escaped Asamando."

About forty Jakuba trailed behind him, moving out of the woodland like predators. No doubt the others were already in Mehronur, pillaging and bringing suffering.

Seth didn't respond to Taroq's words.

"Sneaking in through the back. We suspected you'd be foolish enough to try something. What is it, Seth? Are you blind? The Divide no longer exists. The reign of Abnr is officially over."

"We'll see," Seth said in defiance.

"Akwanshi is on the throne. As we speak, Bokor is preparing her for her ascension. Tonight, at the end of the age, we will dance and sing Akwanshi's praises."

"Not if we can help it."

"What does that mean?" Taroq asked. "Surely you don't think your absent hero has a chance?"

Seth did not answer.

"Where is your warrior, anyway," Taroq asked cockily, glancing about. "Did she run away?" He chuckled. I bet she ran away. Smart little human girl."

"Master Taroq, the human entered the city just now," said a Jakuba from behind him.

"Is that so?" he said in anger, but then he eased up. "Oh, well, the beasts in the city will have to tear her apart now. And while she's being torn apart, we'll have to do the same to you and your friend here."

A commotion started around them. Jakuba wandered out from the thicket of trees. Not only had Kana kept her word, but she had been able to get others to take up the cause. More nomads. They might have sensed the moment was here.

"Hello Seth," Kana greeted.

"What are you nomads doing here?" Taroq barked.

"We are here to fight for Abnr and Marut," Kana said with confidence.

"So you're with the crazy Jakuba?" Taroq scowled.

"You can say that," answered Siam, another Jakuba.

"You're all fools! Look around you. Mehronur has fallen," Taroq said with disgust. "The darkness is unstoppable."

"Mehronur is still standing. The night is not over yet. We are prepared to fight until the new dawn arrives."

"It will be a dawn of darkness and you won't live to see it." Taroq's voice was deadlier than ever.

"We're willing to die fighting."

"Very well, that is what will happen," Taroq assured them. "Charge!"

The Jakuba clashed in the battle with Seth, Khansu and Kana's army. Seth and Taroq did not meet. They fought other Jakuba. Khansu fought more ferociously than he knew he could. He had become stronger and more savage, clawing and biting away the Jakuba who charged after him.

While he clawed, the force of Nenet grew inside him, tingling in his blood and agitating him. He knew the violence was driving it deeper. It worried him, but it made him fiercer and so he fought on bravely.

In just a few hours, he'd join the witch in the darkness, either as her co-ruler or as sacrifice to Nenet. Until then, he'd give the fight everything he had. He'd become ruthless if it was required of him.

21

THRONE

Akwanshi shifted her weight on the stone throne. It was uncomfortable. The seat, she considered with distaste, wasn't worthy of a king, much less a goddess.

Mehronur.

Thinking of the kingdom made her smile.

Mehronur was a city of legend, rumored to be the birthplace of wisdom and men. It'd been a very long while since she'd been here, since a king promised her a seat by his side but failed to fulfill his promise. A lost cause swallowed by the darkness of time. She spied the deep darkness lurking on the horizon. Only a spot of light remained and she could hardly feel it. Bokor had taken great pride to organize the dance of ascension.

Akwanshi looked at the people swarming before her in the courtyard. They looked frightened and desperate. Some wept Some bowed incessantly. Others were offering sacrifice sacrifices in the form of animals and first-born sons in return for mercy.

She had waited for this moment a very long time. How many years had she been in Marut? A lifetime. The doyennes at the medicine house should see her now. The old hags would die of shock, if they had still been alive. Imagining their horrified expressions made her smile. She'd watched kings born and die. And King Aren, such a fickle yet important king. Had it not been for his obsession with immortality, she would not have been able to mix the brew that would make her apotheosis possible.

Bokor approached her with a sluggish walk.

"My queen," he said with a tilt of his head.

"What is it?"

"Will you need anything?" "Prepare the boy," she said. Bokor bowed.

He didn't know it, but after tonight, she'd have no use for him.

Back village gave way to more back villages with abandoned homes and withering vegetation. Kadsa couldn't make this journey on foot. Abadas were hard to come by. When she asked the crystal to take her to Hutat, it dumped her in a small oasis of palm trees and fronds and then the light in its core dwindled and dimmed.

The crystal didn't have enough to transport her to Hutat, she realized, and rather than mope about it, she set off through the oasis, walking until she arrived at a heavily bushed area with deteriorating stone towers. Fearing she'd returned to the forest, she again relied on the crystal. It provided a murky glow that was enough to pave a short path through the bushes.

Pushing herself on the dirt road brought her to the very back of Iunu, a village bordering Hutat. Only a handful of people lingered outside. Kadsa stole a meagre- looking donkey hanging out near a watering hole and rode it into Hutat. Careful to stay on the back roads, she arrived near the palace grounds, surprised to see that no guards defended it.

Many residents appeared to have locked themselves indoors or sought refuge someplace else. She had sneakily passed a group of Jakuba busily ravaging homes and raiding farms for food they had not tasted in forever.

While dismounting the donkey, a flash of lightning drew her attention to the Mpundulu that cawed and then perched on a tree just outside the fortress.

No! That annoying Tsetse.

The Mpundulu's red eyes scoured the kingdom below it.

Just leave already.

She didn't want to think about the souls it would scoop up and disappear with. Kadsa ignored the cawing bird and focused on prying open the heavy copper door of the fortress. Khansu had exited this door to meet Bennu.

It was nearly impossible to pull it open from the outside. She took a step back and eyed the farmlands. The closest entrance to the palace was through the kitchen, but she didn't want to enter the palace proper, not when Bokor likely had control of it

What now?

Kadsa banged her fists against the door in frustration and it opened very slowly.

"Sion?" she said in shock.

Sion stood in the doorway with his scimitar drawn.

Kadsa stepped over the threshold. He lifted the knife to her throat, halting her.

"What are you doing?" She took a deep gulp of air.

The knife pinched her throat.

He did not answer.

"That hurts," she said to him. "Sion, it's me."

The guard's face was stone-cold.

"I'm Kadsa, remember? I'm here to help you. I'm here to restore the light to the kingdom. Sion—stop!"

His angry expression twisted in conflict.

"Sion, come on, help me out here. I don't have time."

Queen Oluchi appeared in the doorway.

Kadsa smiled with relief and then lifted her chin higher when she felt the pinch of the knife. "Queen Oluchi, it's me. Tell him to back down."

Queen Oluchi tilted her head slightly back on her regal neck. She looked cold, serious, but even her stern expression was nothing more than a beautiful pout. She no longer wore her diadem and her loosely curled hair hung at her shoulders.

"You abandoned us when we needed you the most."

"No, I didn't," Kadsa fired back. Sion's scimitar pinched her skin. "I went to the forest to get the stupid ayabbas to restore the light. I had to, before Bokor could arrest me."

"What ayabbas?" the queen asked, stepping forward. Kadsa removed her crystal from underneath her

T-shirt. "This."

Queen Oluchi and Sion stumbled back.

Kadsa rubbed her neck, released from the scimitar's blade.

"It's Abnr's light. I'm trying to restore it. Let me inside before it's too late. Please."

The queen stared at her with distrust. It annoyed Kadsa, but she didn't have time to fuss, nor worry about why these two were cooped up in Khansu's dungeon. Queen Oluchi touched Sion's hand gently and he let down his guard and moved aside with reluctance.

"You're a hard one, Sion. I'll let it go. Because I get it."

Sion shut the door behind her. The room was dark, even as two candles burned dimly on the small table.

Khansu had started a fire from the mouth of the stone well to heat the room. Kadsa wandered to the stone piwhile Sion and Queen Oluchi trailed. Sion still held his scimitar.

"I would never abandon you like that," Kadsa proclaimed. "I would never do that now. Not after everything."

"You said you went to the forest—why?" Queen Oluchi asked.

"To find help," she answered. "I went to the old territories: Abzul, Bourchul, Faro and Elon. We went to get the ayabbas; myself and Khansu and Seth." Kadsa picked up the spear standing next to the pit.

"Seth Oranyan?" asked Sion, stepping forward. "Yes, that's his name." She poked deep into the shallow pit. "He was a Jorba before the darkness fell. Do you know him?"

"Seth is my father."

Kadsa stopped poking the pit to gape at the guard, trying to discern the truth in his expression, but Sion was never a man to lie, so she smiled with pleasant acceptance.

"I can see the resemblance—well, maybe not. He's a Jakuba. He's your father?"

"Seth was a great warrior-chief of Elon who fought for the kingdom. We thought he died in the last war."

"Oh, he's alive," Kadsa said. "He's still fighting for Abnr. He's been helping me."

Sion's brows furrowed, and his forehead crinkled.

He turned away for privacy.

Queen Oluchi faced Kadsa. "Is there a fight outside?" "Yes. Your stepson, Khansu, is fighting."

The queen's face stirred with emotions.

Then it occurred to her to ask. "Where is Prince Sahu?"

Queen Oluchi's face vexed and then settled into pain. The young queen gathered herself, as Sion now faced them again.

"Bokor took Prince Sahu. They will sacrifice him tonight at the festival for Akwanshi. We barely escaped to this dungeon." She looked at her hands, extending her fingers before looking up again. "Sion helped us after we were attacked. We've been here ever since."

"I'm sorry." Kadsa did not know what else to say. Thunder cackled outside the dungeon's walls. This grated on her more than usual— that Mpundulu bird or the ushering in of something worse. The rumble got louder, fueling her urgency, her refusal to fail. "Please, you must help me dig. Time is running out."

"What are you looking for?" asked Sion. "Underneath this pit, there is a stone, a crystal. I need it. We have to add it to the others to restore the light. Help me dig."

Sion grabbed the spear from her and took over the digging.

Queen Oluchi stared at her glowing crystal. "Will these ayabbas help us?"

"I hope so." She did not want to mislead her. She hadn't considered what she would do with the lights once she gathered them.

"There it is," she said when the white radiance permeated the dirt.

Sion pressed the spear against the stone, pushing it against the stones of the pit and pulling a portion of it to the surface. The stone fell to the brick floor of the dungeon and Kadsa knelt over it, dangling the crystal over it. All the white light seeped out from the stone, and into the crystal. That had not happened with the others. The stone charred on the ground, and Kadsa stood, her crystal glowing brighter than ever. "That's the last one."

"It's beautiful," Queen Oluchi said beside her. "What will you do now?"

"Now, they will be released at the pillar," Kadsa answered.

This was the hard part. The whereabouts of the pillar was a mystery. In her head, the pillar was a solid object; she imagined it as some sort of box, but where was it, and did she have time? The image from the dungeon wall resembled an altar. What else could it be? And it had to be in Mehronur, the heart of the kingdom. Kadsa took a deep breath. She didn't want to look clueless in front of Queen Oluchi and Sion, both of whom watched her. And then there was the dwindling light. It was clear, looking at the rocks, they ought to be inserted somewhere.

"Come with me." Kadsa marched ahead. Sion and Queen Oluchi trailed her to the wall outside the fortress.

"Do you know what this is?" She pointed to the pillar.

Sion shook his head.

"I'm sorry, Kadsa," said Queen Oluchi.

"I have to do something with this before it burns out—at that place, or rock, or whatever it is. It doesn't mean anything?"

Queen Oluchi and Sion shook their heads.

"That's what I thought." Her mission just got more complicated at the very wrong time.

What now?

22

AKET

Seth's eyes darted to the young Jakuba when his body pummeled against the ground. That was another one down. Nothing he could do. He and his rebels were losing against Taroq's more experienced army. Many of his men were hurt and limping. About a dozen had died already. Seth's body was failing him. He could barely stay on his feet, but the war wasn't over.

Taroq clawed through the rebel army on his way toward him. Seth ground his teeth, biting against the pain that ran through his body.

"You're a fool and you will die a fool," said Taroq when he reached him.

"You're a traitor to your own people," Seth fired back.

"I chose what was right for me."

"And we both know now that you chose the wrong side."

Taroq bared his teeth.

"It's not too late to stop this and redeem yourself."

Taroq screamed his rage and leaped at Seth, knocking him to the ground. As the angry Jakuba clawed at Seth, all Seth could do was prevent him from delivering a fatal blow.

Bennu had woken up from his rebirth just moments ago. It was earlier than he'd anticipated waking, and not under the right circumstance, but the blaze had been hard to sleep through. The girl's image burned in the flames. She bellowed his name. She was in trouble.

Bennu took a quick flight down toward Mehronur. He could see below him the battle between the Jakuba at the gate of the center kingdom. While the armies fought, every creature in the land had been on the move. Those in hiding crawled from caves and makeshift homes. It seemed to Bennu that everyone was moving toward Mehronur. He was somewhat disappointed. Kadsa and the Prince had yet to restore the light. Maybe he could play a role in helping to hurry this cause.

"Don't leave," said Queen Oluchi. Kadsa stalled at the brass door.

"We may get caught," said Queen Oluchi. "I have to do this."

Kadsa squeezed through the opening and wandered into the yard. Not much more than a twinkle of light existed in Mehronur. Kadsa had summoned Bennu through the crystal but didn't see him anywhere. Everything relied on him now.

While Kadsa had been pondering what to do next, Khansu's words about Bennu blew her mind wide open, and there it was before her on the wall. On the wall, a bird that looked identical to Bennu laid an egg on a pillar that was identical to the pillar used by Abnr's Gift.

The pillar was the Aket—the same Aket she and Khansu spoke about in the forest. The one Bennu knew. Bennu was an old creature. He was as old as Marut. As old as earth itself. The fire that gave him life, the ability to regenerate, came from the original place of creation: the Aket.

A loud cry alerted her to the sky. Bennu swooped downward, gliding across the lawn. Queen Oluchi and Sion, who had been standing behind her, gasped when the bird with the gold and fiery red plumage, identical to the bird on the wall, reached them.

"He's my friend," Kadsa said and then rushed to meet Bennu halfway.

"I received your message. You said it was urgent." "It is, and I'm glad you're here. I need your help."

"Of course. What is it?"

"I need you to take me to the Aket; your place of rebirth."

"Is there a reason?"

"Yes. I have the ayabba sources," she explained. "They need to be where you go to regenerate. We don't have much time."

"Are you sure?"

"Yes, please, we have to hurry." "Get on." He stooped.

Kadsa adjusted the cloak and climbed onto Bennu's back. "I'll see you soon. Be safe," Kadsa yelled at Sion and Queen Oluchi.

The bird leaped to the sky and was off into the forest. The palace's gleam dwindled by the second. People swarmed the public courtyard.

"My goodness," said Bennu, alerting her to the fighting in the Mehronur's meadow. "This is madness."

"Khansu and Seth are there," said Kadsa, desperate to know that her friends were alive. She had never had friends but had come to think of them as such. "Do you spot them anywhere?"

"Hard to tell Jakuba apart, but the prince ... I don't see a human."

"He's a panther," replied Kadsa. "Long story." "There!" Kadsa pointed when they swooped over the scores of fighters.

Prince Khansu ripped and clawed viciously through his opponents. Kadsa didn't need to speak to him to see that the transformation was complete. His movements were ferocious and savage. Her gut wobbled. It felt heavy. He batted off Jakuba after Jakuba. He leaped atop a Jakuba and ripped his face off.

"Kadsa, what do you need me to do?"

Kadsa was transfixed on Khansu. The panther leaped toward two Jakuba, one badly beating the other. He reached for a spear from the ground, clutching it between his paws before throwing it toward the fighting Jakuba. The dominant Jakuba, about to rip the other Jakuba's face off, grabbed the spear from the air with his clawed hand, spun in rapid speed and tossed it back in Khansu's direction.

The panther was under assault from other Jakuba when the spear hit him in the chest.

"Khansu!" Kadsa screamed.

It was too late. The Jakuba holding the panther dropped his limped body with the spear sticking out of his chest. The leopard groaned aloud and thudded backward to the ground.

The Jakuba barked at the sky.

"Kadsa," Bennu called, but she wasn't listening.

The spear-throwing Jakuba howled in victory only to find the feet of his victim—the Jakuba he'd been pounding—connecting to his chest. The spear-throwing Jakuba fell backward and within seconds, his revitalized victim—Seth—leaped atop him, giving him no chance to forge a defensive stance against the attack. Seth clawed at the face of the fallen Jakuba without mercy.

"Kadsa, we have to leave."

"Not without Khansu," she replied. "We can't leave him here."

"He's too heavy to carry…"

"There is something I can do. Please help me."

Bennu swooped into the clearing, and she climbed off his back while he ruffled his plumage. The Jakuba had moved toward where the spear-throwing Jakuba now lay. They didn't seem to care about fighting now.

Kadsa gripped her pendant and kneeled over the panther. There wasn't enough in the crystal. She willed it, but nothing came out. She sobbed.

"We have to leave the body." "Please," she begged.

"If we can get him on my back…"

Kadsa tugged at the panther's lifeless body. He was awfully heavy. Two Jakuba who'd been watching from nearby stepped up.

"Back off!" Kadsa yelled.

"We are with you, girl," said a female Jakuba. "Kana?"

"Yes, it's me," she said. "Let us help you lift him."

Kadsa said nothing as the two Jakuba lifted the panther and placed him on Bennu's back. Bennu slumped, but pulled himself upward, managing the weight. She felt horrible, but didn't want the Mpundulu to take poor Khansu's soul. Part of her believed if she could bring the light back, he'd come back to life, too. This wasn't even his original form.

"Kadsa, get on."

"I can walk. It's not far."

"Kadsa, I can manage. These bones are old and strong."

Kadsa climbed on behind the dead leopard. The bird took a moment to adjust to the weight. Bennu flapped his wings and lifted himself into the sky.

"Good luck, girl," Kana called behind them

———

Seth stared down Taroq, who struggled to breathe as blood seeped out of his mouth. From the corner of his eyes, he spotted the bird and the girl but couldn't disrupt this moment of subduing his enemy at last.

"It didn't have to be this way," he said. "You made all the wrong decisions."

"I made my choice. I can die with it." Taroq said. "You want to know why I chose the witch? It's because you disappointed me. Every noble thought you put in my head, making me believe in something that would never come true."

Seth said nothing.

Taroq coughed and then laughed. "It's too late now.

It's time to die."

Seth watched the life vanish from the Jakuba's eyes before they closed. Taroq looked at peace, and Seth couldn't help but breathe. He had been a promising warrior when he'd first come under his command. He'd treated him like a son and had hoped he'd return to the fold. Now that chance was gone, and he blamed himself somewhat for his change of heart. May the night guide his soul to Amut.

Bennu's flight was understandably slow, and he flew too close to the ground as if the weight might break him. Kadsa wished her crystal worked right about now. Thunder ripped through the darkened sky accompanied by lightning, flashing from all angles, clashing with rocks and trees. Bennu remained steady and steered clear of the sky's drama, but they barely missed a bolt that cut a tree in half and hit the crystal.

The bands of color in the crystal shot outward and began dancing around the forest, ricocheting off everything.

"What did you do?" Bennu asked, landing shakily into a clearing, and quickly dumping the leopard's dead body off his back.

Kadsa glanced around, watching the bands of light go mad in the darkness.

"Kadsa, what is your plan here?" "I don't know."

Kadsa didn't know what to focus on, the dancing light, or Khansu's body. She dropped to the side of the dead leopard. Tears clouded her eyes. She had failed him. He was the future king. She leaned over his lifeless body to brush his hair and smooth out the ruffles and twigs. Khansu was dead. It hurt. She hadn't known him that long, yet it hurt all the same. She liked him. She wanted more time with him.

"Kadsa," called Bennu softly. She glanced up at him.

"Something is happening. Look!"

Kadsa glanced in the direction of his nudging, watching in the moment as the lightning whitened the sky, and then hit the tip of the grey rock to the right of them, the same rock underneath which she'd found the Abzul ayabba.

This was the place of entrance. This same rock was present when she landed in the dark forest of the magical land of Marut. That night had been very black and frightening. She had sat at that very rock, clinging to it for dear life. Looking at it now, seeing it in the light, she noticed the immense gray beast looked out of place, even in a forest where nothing looked natural. The large rock emitted strong heat. Even from a good thirty feet away she felt its energy. This was Abnr's star, his gift.

"Where is this place?"

Bennu looked around. "I believe we're in the district of Abzul."

"We're east. This is where Seth found me." She knew so many more things now than when she had first arrived. What mattered, however, was what she did with this new knowledge.

The darkness grew more permanent, eating away at the blueness that dwindled over Mehronur. She needed confirmation.

"What is that?" she asked, pointing to the stone. "It's the place the tower of Abzul used to be," he answered. "All that remains are rocks and stones, I guess." "That's a tower?"

"The house of Abnr, so-called, yes. It once guided the fishermen and boats."

"This is what I came here for."

Bennu was studying it. "It's a rock. The tower is destroyed."

"No, it's not just a rock." She shook her head. "Look at it again. If you recall the creation story, it said Abnr sent a star to guide the humans to reason."

"Are you sure about this, Kadsa?"

"It's the fallen star, a cosmic rock." She pushed her drained crystal next to the bigger rock that simmered with white mist. The crystal energized and shot out a bolt of light. Kadsa let go of the crystal and it floated above the surface of the rock.

She smiled up at Bennu. Now, she understood this rock's connection to the portal that ripped open the cosmic doorway— the doorway Grandpa Edoje spent his entire life trying to open. This was the only object that had remained in the same position. This was where she came in when she'd been backed up into that cave. This was the agate from the cave, or its twin.

Trying to find the magic in this world, she heard Grandpa Edoje say.

Kadsa grabbed the energized pendant. The big rock trembled loudly, fizzing. Not the doing of the pendant, but the dancing bands that was firing up the forest all around them. It began pushing upward from the ground.

"The tower is rising."

The ayabba bands flew around them gravitated toward the ignited rock, and shot upward and outward, weaving together into a single strand that exploded above the dark sky. Kadsa watched the explosion of lights suck the dark from the land, eating it away like a vacuum.

"And then there was light," Kadsa declared. "We did it. Abnr is reborn."

———————

Seth marched toward Mehronur with the Jakuba from his ragtag army. Not many had survived the battle, but no one looked regretful, even if they were tired and torn. Above them, the Mpundulu flew back and forth, collecting the souls of the deceased. The girl had taken the panther's body before the Mpundulu could find it. Seth was indebted to the panther. If he had not thrown the spear, Taroq would've killed him. The panther's distraction gave him the moment he needed to destroy his rival. While he was prepared to die for Abnr, doing so at Taroq's hands would've been a cruel fate.

After Taroq's death, his army of Jakuba gave up fighting. They scrambled from the battlefield, wounded, and confused. Seth knew it wasn't over, but he did all he could. Now, it was up to the girl to do her part.

"Look!" someone yelled.

Crackling tumbled through the sky, distinguishing itself from the thunder that had been blaring around them. The Jakuba cast their eyes to the dark sky to see the rainbow coalition of colors exploding like sun flares. Some shot straight toward the interlocked suns, exploding. For a second, it looked like the eclipsed celestial bodies blazed.

"The light is back!" A Jakuba cried out.

In no time, all the Jakuba were cheering.

Seth could not laugh or show happiness, not because he did not feel hope, but because he did not know how to laugh and show happiness. He had been unhappy and bitter for so long that he worried his laughter sounded like cynicism and his cheers like mockery. Also, for all his faith, he had some doubt and wanted to wait to see the full effects.

———————

In the kingdom of Mehronur, the residents saw the light burst through the sky. Bokor stood by the witch who sat observantly on the throne. Both of their eyes froze on the explosion in the sky. The young prince, Sahu, lay tied to a sacrificial stone bed some feet away. He had stopped crying, to Akwanshi's good fortune.

The dancers in the courtyard stopped dancing the spellbound dance, and the singers stopped singing their haunted chants. Many removed their skull masks to stare in confusion. They wondered if what they were seeing was simply a cosmic display of trickery or something else entirely.

The witch gave Bokor a nasty look.

"I'm sure it's nothing, my queen," he said. "You fool! Does that look like nothing?" "I'll take care of it," he said hurriedly.

"It's too late. The dawn is here. Sacrifice the boy so I can have my feast," she commanded. She pulled a small vine from her hair and stabbed it into her forearm, mumbling an incantation into the dark crystal she wore as a pendant.

Akwanshi opened her mouth wide, echoing a sound that was a mixture of a cough and a choke. An endless succession of dark, bat-like shadows flew out of her mouth and settled over the courtyard. The shadows hovered above the crowd like clouds, squealing and bawling in a cacophony. The shocked crowd looked on in terror.

Akwanshi stood, taking a large gulp of air. The release of the shadows weakened her.

"Serve me, I am your new queen of the darkness," she declared. "The reign of Nenet has started. Those who are good servants will be rewarded with gold and riches."

People stared in horror. The shadows multiplied and some transformed into near-physical entities.

"Guard the gates and the courtyard. No one leaves or enters," she commanded, exiting the platform and entering the palace of vines.

Some of Asamando's thick vegetation traveled with her to Mehronur, and now covered the Paraa Hutat, choking, cracking and denting its marble and granite walls. It looked more like Asamando than the royal house—just the way she wanted it.

Akwanshi walked briskly to her magic room, the former sitting room, filled with all her herbs and magic potions. The release of spirits had weakened her. She had to make herself strong again. Invincibility was a budding taste on her tongue. She'd be damned to let it go. The darkness was gone. Some blue remained in the sky.

Dawn was mere hours away. She'd become stronger then. No need to depend on the vines of Asamando, but until then, she'd have to regenerate herself. It needed all her effort to hold the ghouls and the kingdom under her control.

As she mixed her potion, her mind strayed with vengeful thoughts. She'd put her fatal mark on Abnr's heart. Where was the Dark Prince? Bokor's incompetence failed her again. She had waited too long for the kingdom of Marut to succumb to her reign. Nothing could stop her from becoming the supreme living goddess.

Bokor walked to the boy lying strapped on the concrete platform. The boy stiffened when he reached him. Bokor stared into his blank eyes; he rubbed the blood on his chest and forehead and marked him with the white powder he prepared for the occasion. He checked the boy's heart and then reached for the knife, pulling it from a bowl of boiling black fluid nearby. As he uttered the oath to the dark goddess, Bokor lifted his hand and let out a loud and horrific gasp for breath. He looked down to his chest to see the ferrule of an iron spear protruding through his heart. He gasped for breath then turned around.

"You," he accused, staring into the face of Sion Oranyan, the royal guard. "You did this."

"Your reign is over," Sion spat, wringing the spear.

Bokor gasped. It was his last breath before he fell to the ground.

Sion pulled the spear from his chest and stepped over him to get to the boy. He cut the boy loose from the ropes that tied him.

Queen Oluchi stepped out from the dark of the palace and the boy ran into his mother's arms. The crowd looked around in confusion.

"We must fight for our lives," Sion told the crowd. "Fight!"

Akwanshi lifted her hand. The black fluid in her pendant bubbled.

"I call on you, children of the dark goddess," she began, tiredness threatening to weigh her down. "Come to me, your mother."

None came.

At first, she thought the Mpundulu was involved, but the Mpundulu was busy collecting the new spirits. The light penetrating the shallow earth trapped the vines. They were in pain. She channeled her strength to call on them to make her stronger.

Nothing!

She controlled the vines and spirits of Asamando for years and now they disobeyed her. She turned away for a moment to catch her breath. The one spirit she craved she could not find. His spirit was worth all these spirits combined and more. She starved for the soul of the young king, and he was not waiting for her as he should've been. Thanks to Bokor's incompetence, he escaped. She sent an army to find him, but they had yet to return. She feared now that they had not found him, and worse, that they were dead.

Akwanshi summoned the image of the Dark Prince. His image formed in her mind but faded into a black cloud. Still, she tried again. If the abiku still held him, it should've been enough to turn him towards her.

"Come to me," she called when his image formed in her mind.

It faded.

She closed her eyes and tried again. She detected something—a faint lifeline, but then it was gone, too weak to grasp.

Akwanshi's red eyes burned, and then turned black, like the swamp of Asamando. She screamed and called to the spirits again, using all her summoned strength. Spirits jumped into her body from the black cauldron, one after the other. When it finished, she staggered down, catching her breath and kneading the pain in her chest. They had attacked her body violently. The spirits did not like that she forced them to come into her. Her mortal body could not take this any longer, but until she had the Dark Prince, she had no choice. They fed her and kept her alive. She felt full.

Marut returned to something normal. The unnatural forest thinned along with the darkness. Kingdoms rose from the ground.

In Abzul, the aqueduct built to control the flow of the waterfall had been released from the tangle of trees and vines. The cosmic rock continued to spread light through the kingdom, although it was starting to fade, due to the rock's cooling.

The hanging garden of Faro was visible, as were the temples that decorated the chiefdom. The pyramids and towers of Elon reached toward the sky, as did the structures in Bourchul. All the artificial splendors of Marut made their return.

Daytime arrived in Bourchul, Abzul, Elon, Faro, and Mehronur, but the main courtyard of Mehronur remained captive under a strange dark cloud. The Jakuba did not transform to their original human form. Nothing organic had returned.

Seth was blocked at the entrance of Mehronur. They could not enter the inner kingdom. Spirits had taken over guardianship of the kingdom. Abnr's soul was restored, but the heart of the darkness was still alive and thriving. Many people feared for their loved ones. None could cross over.

While this occurred, inside the courtyard Sion instilled his people with hope outside of the inner kingdom. He told them of what Kadsa told him, of the light and what it meant. They seemed hopeful, despite the ghostly guards who kept them captive. It was dawn in Marut. Not the endless blackness they had feared. It looked like the real dawn of the morning.

———

"How did you know what to do?" Bennu's voice broke her concentration.

"Everything you guys told me, I put it together."

Kadsa rushed to Prince Khansu. She couldn't leave him there. The prince's leopard body twisted on the ground. Kadsa wondered if she had left him in that position, or if he had been touched. She felt excitement. Perhaps he moved himself. Perhaps he wasn't truly dead. The caw of a bird echoed above them. The Mpundulu. She panicked. The oversized Mpundulu swooped right down to sit on the leopard's body.

"Shoo." She warded it off.

Its red eyes just watched her. "Get off him. Leave him alone."

The Mpundulu plucked at his chest. Angry, Kadsa lifted her necklace.

"Get off him!" she shouted, zapping the bird with her crystal. The large bird cawed and toppled over on the ground but sprung back to its feet in no time to glare her down.

"His soul is not yours to take." The bird didn't leave.

"Kadsa," called Bennu. "I'm truly sorry for your loss, but his soul must be free now."

Kadsa glared at him. "He's the mortal Abnr, you know. If the celestial Abnr has been restored, so should the terrestrial Abnr," she spoke as much to herself as she spoke to him.

"Wait a minute," she said, realization dawning like the daylight around them.

"What is it?"

"That's it." She straightened up. "The Aket." "My cave?"

"Yes, I had it confused with the ankh. The rock is the ankh. Where you come from is the Aket. Similar names, different places. Help me get him back to your resurrection place."

"I won't question you. But I will say this; I cannot promise you it will work for him."

"We must try," she said. "I don't think the Abnr in him is completely dead. I don't believe that. We can't leave him here."

She and Bennu dragged the leopard through the forest, while the Mpundulu yipped in protest. Soon after, it flew off, conceding defeat.

"That damn bird!" she cussed, listening to its cawing above them.

Bennu dragged the body into the cave, through a complex group of steep tunnels. They must have moved through nine different levels in the cavern before they got to the very bottom, in a tiny space, about ten feet high, slightly taller than Bennu. No air entered the little area and it was mostly dark, except for the shimmer from the soil that covered the ground. It twinkled like stardust and illuminated the tiny space.

"This is it?" she asked. "This is where you were born?"

"This is where I rise from the ashes." He gestured to a dark spot in the room with silvery gold ash. He released the prince and told her to cover him with the ash.

"Where's the fire?"

"It's in the ground," Bennu said before he took a deep breath and blew on the silver-gold ashes. Gold and silver dust flew about, glimmering and then catching spark. A red and gold fire flared up around the prince.

"It's stardust. The first dirt. Stardust has natural heat that combusts with friction."

They stepped back to watch the flares set the leopard's body ablaze. Kadsa felt nervous, thinking that it might not work. Then, two separate slivers of smoke left the body, one white and the other black.

"He has two spirits? That's not natural, right?"

"We only have one—the one we are born with," Bennu answered. "The people of Mehronur believe that this prince is cursed, possessed by an abiku. An *Abiku* is a possession spirit. It can become like your real spirit. It's a parasite that may even be used to create a golem from your form. It aims to kill your natural spirit through corruption and domination. Often a newborn or unborn child is too weak to fight it off. It's rare that a child survives with such a leech on its soul. But this boy is stronger than most."

"There's no evidence that this prince is the true son of Abnr."

"No, there isn't."

"Why do people believe it?"

"The people believe the kings, going back to Ndakr the first, is the divine son of Abnr. It's called the Divinity of Kings. Kings are the mortal Abnr manifested. Despite his unusual birth, he is no exception. His natural spirit is therefore still considered a divine spirit."

"But it's not divine in the *real* sense. It's just called that."

"I cannot say."

Kadsa and Bennu watched the fire eat away at the leopard, consuming the spirits.

"What now?" she asked when the flames died down and all that remained were ashes.

"Now we wait till morning."

"And when he wakes, will he be the same?"

"I don't know what will happen from here," he admitted.

She looked at him from where they rested by a wall. "It's that uncertain?"

"Yes," Bennu answered. "This is the first time someone besides me has used this place for this purpose."

"At the worse he'll have a proper funeral." She didn't like the thought and wished she hadn't said it. She yawned, needing to change the subject. "Got anything to eat? I'm starving."

"We can travel to Mehronur, perhaps they'll have something."

"That's far." She exhaled loudly. "Maybe a nearby village. They may feed me."

Many of the manmade structures had risen from the ground.

"Where are all the residents?" she asked, a little confused. "The light has been restored."

"Something's not right, Kadsa," Bennu said when they approached an eatery—or what used to be one.

"I did what I was supposed to do, didn't I?"

"There is light in the kingdom, but…" He paused when two Jakuba approached in their direction. The Jakuba looked tired and weary, and one carried a fruit tied to a vine rope on its back. They paused when they saw Kadsa and Bennu. For a few seconds, the two duos eyed each other questioningly, trying to figure out if either's intention was antagonistic.

"Hello?" Kadsa stepped forward. "I'm Kadsa." Bennu remained behind her, unmoved.

"Can you tell me where everyone is and why…" She stared at the half-starved Jakuba. "How are you still Jakuba?"

"The curse hasn't been broken yet."

"But morning has risen over the kingdom. Look." She pointed to the lighthouse, dim under daylight that now covered the kingdom.

"You must be Abnr's Gift," said the male Jakuba stepping forward. "I am Lark. This is Petra. Thank you for all you've done for us, but it is not enough. The witch has imprisoned the kingdom of Mehronur. She holds it captive with ghouls and magic. No one can go in and none can come out."

"Until the witch dies, the enchantment will stay with us," Petra explained.

Kadsa looked to Bennu. "I must go back to the kingdom."

"Not before you get something to eat; you will need all your strength."

"We can provide food for you," said Petra stepping forward. "We once owned a bread shop in that hut there. We are on our way there now."

"Thank you," Kadsa said. "That's very nice of you." In the hut, Kadsa sat down and watched the Jakuba start a fire from a hole in the ground, where they roasted a breadfruit, the only food they could find. The shop had been raided, but Lark bragged that they wrestled the food from a group of Jakuba in Mehronur.

The gardens and vegetation beds had dried up during the enchantment and had yet to begin to grow again. It would take time. Many Jakuba had gone to Mehronur to search for food, and they had come from there.

"The breadfruit was all we could get from the kingdom before the witch enchanted the place with black magic."

Disappointment bubbled inside Kadsa about not doing a thorough job. She intended to return to Mehronur to complete the mission. For the time being, she was hungry and tired. The four ate the breadfruit in quietness. The Jakuba offered them a place to rest; they lived in an adjacent room in the hut. They took the offer.

23

MORNING

Each time Kadsa shut her eyes, her mind roamed and rumbled with frustration. How would she solve the Jakuba problem? How did the witch fit into the whole thing? She eventually slipped into an uncomfortable sleep. The witch was in her dream. Her face wasn't visible, only her figure, as she chanted over a cauldron.

Black tendrils slithered from it, crawling through the air like claws. The red robe of the priestess from the mysterious temple flared. The tower flooded the land with white light. It settled on the prince. What about the prince? Heartbeat. Whose heartbeat? The witch squeezed a human heart in her hand.

The witch's chant was loud, but Kadsa didn't understand what she was saying.

Akwanshi crushed the heart in her palm. Black fluid drained from between her bony fingers, what had become of the heart.

Screaming.

Kadsa jolted from her sleep. It was morning. Daylight. She knew what she needed to do. Bennu was still sleeping and the Jakuba were sleeping in their room. She left the hut without causing a stir, grabbing the short machete the couple used to cut the breadfruit. They had many more knives, but she liked that one the best. She fixed the machete to the side of her jeans with tight vines she pulled from trees..

She headed back into Bennu's cave, making her way down until she was at the very bottom, where she had left the leopard's body.

She stared in awe at the sight before her eyes. Lying on the ground was the body of a human male, curled up like a fetus. Stardust sparkled around him like a halo.

Kadsa grabbed the cloak hanging on the rock where she left it and ran to the curled-up figure. She knelt beside him, draping him in the cloak. She watched him for a time, not knowing how to feel. She tapped him on the cheeks.

"Wake up, Khansu, wake up," she urged.

It took some time before Khansu opened his honey- almond brown eyes. He stared at her sleepily, stirring emotions inside of her she struggled to control. Kadsa's nerves twisted.

"You okay?" she asked shyly.

He bobbed his head and looked around. "Where am I?"

His voice had kept the same softness. Even better, he still seemed like Khansu.

"You are in Bennu's cave. This place saved your life," she told him. "Come on, get up."

She pulled him to his feet, releasing him from her grip for about two seconds before his knees buckled like a young calf trying to walk; she grabbed hold of him fast and held him up.

"You okay now?" she asked, after holding him long enough for him to get used to his legs.

"I think so," he said.

She released him. He took two steps before stopping to stare at her.

"It's so confusing. What happened?"

"You almost died, Khansu," she told him honestly. "We almost lost the king who kicked the crap out of the bad guys for his kingdom."

"I remember it all," he said grabbing his head. "It's fresh in my mind, all of it. The battle, the transformation, you, my death." The last two words rolled off his lips in quiet shock. "My death," he said and paused. "I died."

"Only for a short time."

"Am I alive?" He studied himself. "You are alive and well."

"Are you sure?" "Would I lie to you?" He looked confused.

"Okay, don't answer that. Do you feel alive?"

He touched his heart. "I can feel my heartbeat. I can feel heat. I am no longer engulfed by the darkness."

"You're all human now." "I feel human."

"You are, but we can't stay here," she said. We must return to Mehronur and get rid of the witch. "Let's go!" "You mean the enchantment of Nenet has not lifted?" he asked, running behind her.

"It has, but the witch refuses to give up. She's holding the kingdom captive with ghosts. She's a sore loser it seems."

Khansu reacted to the brightness by covering his eyes, but Kadsa pulled his hands away.

"You're fine," she told him.

He watched the light, squinting a few times.

In the kingdom of Abzul, they stole, *borrowed,* Kadsa corrected, two donkeys that had been grazing the land. While they were riding, Kadsa heard her name and she looked to see Bennu. She stopped the donkey and got off. Khansu followed.

"You mean to leave without me?"

"I did not want to disturb you," she said. "Don't you sleep during the day?"

"I usually do, but I can make an exception."

"Hello again, my friend," Khansu said to Bennu. "It's good to see you," said Bennu. "I guess it does work for humans."

"I told you. Trust me. My instincts are good."

"I'll remember that." He chuckled and stooped. "Now where are we off to?"

"Mehronur," Kadsa admitted.

"I'll give you a ride; it'll be faster," Bennu suggested. She smiled and climbed on his back. The Prince followed. Soon, the bird was in the sky. Petra and Lark arrived in the hut of the doorway to wave goodbye to them.

Marut's daytime view was captivating, just as Seth Oranyan and Bennu told Kadsa it would be. The chiefdoms came to life in all their glories. The wide, long river of Abzul rushed with pure abandon, as it carved up the landscape from the northern tip of the kingdom to the southern tip of Elon.

"This river is amazing, but where does it get its water?"

"It once ran from the Nile all the way to Lake Chad."

Kadsa recalled a book on rivers and lakes she loved as a child. Lake Chad was landlocked. Its water came from underground aquifers. A strange lake that has since shrunk, Kadsa now pondered about the aquifers that fed it. Could Abzul's river still have some magical connection to the now-dying Lake Chad?

She fixed her eyes on the river again. Boats made of reed, some bigger than others, still lingered near the river. A few long abandoned, half-decayed Dak boats drifted into the newly flowing river. Others washed along the reed and rock shorelines.

Jakuba stormed the river in large numbers. Closer inspection revealed some of the boats lingering near the shore were actually homes. At the back of one district was an aqueduct scheme channeling water in various directions.

"Look at that!" Kadsa pointed when a glimmer high in the sky took her eyes away from the aqueduct.

A transparent crystal tower had grown out of the belly of the rock and now served as the tallest structure in the kingdom.

"What is that?"

"It's the tower of Abnr," Bennu said. "The true eye of Abnr. Kadsa, it never looked like this before. It was once a simple marble structure—a lighthouse."

"It must have grown from the ayabba rock crystals." The thick, dark forest had shrunk considerably in size, receding only to cover the districts of Faro and Elon.

"Is this all the forest land there's going to be?"

"Yes, Kadsa. The magic had magnified the forest tenfold." The rest of the kingdom was desert with large patches of grassland, savannahs and groves here and there. If Khansu was correct, Marut once existed just north of Sudan and south of Egypt and east of Chad, occupying a very fertile region of Africa.

The stone kingdom of Bourchul stood desolate on rocky terrains. The erect stone homes blended into the brown-red ground like camouflage. Some structures carved into the rock cliffs. Kadsa spotted only a few patches of green among the brown-red rocks. Below her, crocodiles splashed around in the shallow, dirty pool of water. Temples sat on high plateaus, and beyond the highest peaks, at the back of the kingdom, she spotted a desert, sandy red and isolated. Distant structures of erect gray stones were the only visible images in the desert.

The warrior district of Elon was as intimidating as Bourchul, except, unlike Bourchul's natural rock formations, Elon was almost all manmade. Gloomy stone towers, small pyramids, ziggurats, and other densely built fortresses clustered amidst a dense forestland. It reminded Kadsa of Maya and Aztec pyramids buried in the dense jungles of Central and South America. Elon had parted with some of the rainforest when Marut vanished.

Bennu pointed out the main fortress that stood at the edge of the kingdom. "The ruler of Elon, Seth Oranyan, lived in this residence."

Marching armies of Jakuba grazing the land was the sight that greeted Kadsa most frequently as she and Bennu flew over the kingdom. Most were in Faro, a district that was sad to see. Hardly anything had risen outside of the homesteads, temples and small pyramidal structures here and there. The Jakuba were looking for food but not much of anything was there: dried up groves, bare trees, and barren farmlands.

Bennu showed Kadsa the limestone fortress that was to have housed Aja's gardens. The weeds and vines had strangled it, and had since pulled away, leaving it bare of its flowers. Kadsa imagined how pretty the gardens would be once they were cultivated again.

"We are here," declared Khansu quietly behind her. He stayed very silent during the whole trip on Bennu's back.

After he spoke, Kadsa looked down. He meant they had reached Mehronur.

Large groups of Jakuba surrounded the kingdom, from all angles. Thousands more gathered inside the broken-down walls.

"Bring us to the back of the palace," Kadsa instructed Bennu.

A small, densely dark spot hovered above and around Hutat. The light of day pushed against the dark but did not penetrate it. A neutral area existed somewhere between the darkness and the daylight that triggered sparks of friction. Ghostly figures encircled Paraa Hutat, moving like swift black clouds.

Bennu flew to the back of the kingdom near Khansu's fortress. A large group of Jakuba gathered, but they were few in number.

Kadsa climbed off the bird's back and Khansu followed. She turned to the bird.

"Can you get through the darkness?"

"That shield of darkness is being protected by ghouls," he told her, studying the royal house from the yard.

Kadsa squinted. The darkness hovering about the palace was really a swarm of ghouls. They circled in a swift, mad manner. There must have been thousands of them just flying around. She looked to Prince Khansu.

"I am no longer helpful. I am free of my gifts."

She nodded with understanding. "I must confront the witch."

Kadsa moved closer to the darkness. "Who are you?" asked an older Jakuba.

"Are you the one who has come to help us?" asked another Jakuba when she moved through the crowd.

"I am Kadsa," she answered.

"But you're Abnr's star," the young Jakuba added.

Kadsa wrestled with her response as the Jakuba crowded her. They touched her, clawing at her and begged her to protect them and their children and loved ones. She was pleading with them to let her go through.

"I'm trying to help," she declared with frustration.

Someone whistled loudly, quieting the crowd.

Khansu broke through the Jakuba.

"Let her through. She must get through if she is to help you."

"Who are you?" asked a man, casting suspicious eyes over Khansu's human form.

"He is your king. King Khansu." The words felt strange on her lips, but it was the truth.

The Jakuba looked stunned. Khansu flinched.

"But it is you who brought the curse upon us," accused an old Jakuba.

"No, he did not. He fought for you. He helped you." "He is cursed, is he not?" A female Jakuba asked, studying them.

"No, he is a man. You can see that, can't you? He is the son of King Remu and Queen Aja. He is your king. You must listen to him if you want the witch gone."

The crowd was silent.

"I will not rule if you don't want me to, if you think me unworthy." Khansu stepped forward. "All I ask is that you let Abnr's Gift through and allow her to carry out her purpose. We can carry on from there."

The Jakuba looked at each other.

"I say that sounds fair," admitted the old Jakuba. The crowd agreed.

"Thank you." Kadsa moved toward the darkness.

Khansu, left alone with the crowd who watched him, looked uncomfortable.

"Are you truly him—the son of Aja?" asked an older female Jakuba.

"Aja was my mother's name. Yes, I am he."

"I worked for your mother when she was alive. I am a washer woman in the palace."

"What kind of ruler are you going to be?" asked a man stepping forward.

"I cannot promise you that I am perfect. I cannot promise you that I am wiser or purer than any other ruler before me; nor can I change the circumstances of my birth, but I can promise you this: I will do all in my power to reign similar to my forefathers to bring about a peaceful and beautiful Marut."

The Jakuba murmured their approval of his words. "By the light of Abnr, we want peace."

Khansu nodded.

Kadsa paused at the door to the palace, thinking of how she'd get through the coppice of darkness. She tested the smoky darkness by putting her hand near it. As soon as she did, a ghostly creature reached out its mouth and snapped its fangs at her, forcing her to pull back.

"Okay, I see what this is." She grabbed the necklace and brought it to her eyes. She could see all the swirls inside of it.

"I am an avatar of Abnr. I believe that," she mumbled under her breath, though it sounded silly.

The Jakuba gasped from where they stood feet away with Khansu.

Kadsa glowed in a manner similar to the way she did in the cave at Bourchul. Her hands were lined with white light. The tortured faces of the ghouls were visible in the shroud of darkness. She stepped closer to the wall and the ghouls dove her way. The ghouls tried to bite at her but got burned and fizzled, turning into a smoky combustion.

When she stepped through the darkness, more ghouls parted, cowering from her path.

Kadsa walked into the palace, intent on finding the witch. The fire in the well of Khansu's dungeon had died. There was no sign of Sion or Queen Oluchi. She wasted no time in the room and exited through the underground walkway. She paused when a pictograph on the wall of the hero spearing the heart of the darkness distracted her. This was what she didn't do but had to.

24

REIGN

The palace's interior looked like a tornado passed through it. This wasn't what she expected. Ghoulish vines like the ones in Asamando strangled furniture.

Cracks ran in the walls.

When she stepped too close to the vines, they lashed out at her and then quickly snapped back into place, slivering away. She walked past the guest room and stopped. A vine crushed her bag. Kadsa knelt beside it and made herself into a tangible entity again, making sure to keep the aura around her. Reaching for the blade in her pocket, she sawed the vine off. It cried out, retreating from the bag and the room.

The ghouls pulled away when she approached the entrance but before she could step a foot inside, the door swung shut. She banged and pushed against it to break it down. This room had to be the witch's power center. It reeked of strange herbs and pungent odors. She backed away and ran forward, crashing into the door with her shoulders. She cried out, rubbing her shoulders. Definitely the last time she'd pretend to be a brawn. In action movies, stunts like this were easier. When the pain subsided, she pushed against the door again—no budge. Loud and discordant crying burst out around her, grabbing her attention.

Kadsa drifted toward the source of the sound, tracing it to the front courtyard. She paused at the doorway, masking herself behind one of the colonnades. From where she stood, some festival was in full occurrence. Dancers swayed their bodies lifelessly. The longer she watched them, the clearer it became that something was amiss. Everything was amiss. The dancing was too slow, the drumming too fast and the singing too sad and one note.

She spotted the witch sitting on the high stone throne centered in the main courtyard. Sion stood guard by her side. His presence caused her stomach to drop. Sion would never voluntarily serve the witch. No, he was too honorable and loyal.

Queen Oluchi entered the scene when the witch shifted. She looked regally rigid, as if made of wax. Prince Sahu brought a calabash dish to the witch. He bowed and sat at the witch's feet. This scene wasn't right. Did the witch spellbind them?

She backed away, shaking her head, knowing she had to do something. But what? Backtracking, she bumped into and bounced off something large and firm.

Bokor.

Alarmed by his grim look, she staggered backward, ready to dash away. Something made her stand her ground. Something was odd about Bokor. He was scarier looking than she remembered. Never mind the smell emanating from his body, but his eyes were dead. The irises and corneas were all black. Blood soaked his robes, dripping and spotting the floor at his feet.

Kadsa's eyes drifted to the wound in his chest, the source of the thick dark blood, and froze with frightening revelation. He was dead. Her heartbeat kicked up and her stomach churned. He was not just dead, which explained the rigidity, he was a zombie. The creatures flying above and dashing about were ghouls.

Disgusting.

Bokor skipped past her as if she wasn't there, moving toward the platform. She watched him stand by the witch's side. The witch intended to rule a kingdom of ghouls and zombies, she thought. She gasped, taking a second notice of Oluchi, Sahu, and Sion.

They were all dead.

She backed away horrified, tripping and stumbling over a large thick vine; it burned her flesh and she jumped from it. The vine wiggled. Her eyes followed it outward to the platform in which Akwanshi sat.

The witch glanced back. Kadsa raced behind a tree, not certain if the witch had spotted her or not. The witch must have felt it when she touched the vine. What did this mean? Kadsa reached for her knife and studied the large, coiled vine, around thirty inches thick in diameter and ran throughout the palace, leading into the sitting room, which emanated a drowsy energy.

Anger and opportunity bubbled inside her. Kadsa attacked the vine, chopping and stabbing it. She intended to sever and disconnect it. She chopped harder. It bled black fluid, fluttered, and slivered away. She chopped until it pulled apart. The longer half of it wiggled and glided back to the dining room, breaking down the door. The remaining half of it—the part connecting to the witch, flapped until it could no longer. Black dust smoked out of the dead vine. Sickness swirled in her stomach. What was this nasty thing?

A shuffle caught her attention.

Her entire body jerked with the sight of the tall, lean witch standing at the entrance of the veranda. Akwanshi resembled a tower more than a woman. She wore clothes of vines and wild weeds. Her ears were like fig leaves, and they pointed in opposing directions. Her eyes, black like the deepest night, glared at Kadsa with enough intensity to kill her. Vines stuck out from her skin. Thorns and figs intertwined with her hair. Around her neck, a single piece of metallic breastplate stretched from her collarbone to her chin, elongating her neck in a way that was not natural.

Nothing about this woman was natural.

Kadsa's eyes lifted to the center of the breastplate, where a crystal-like object shimmered with black fluid.

"You came here to kill me," Akwanshi said and chuckled.

Her voice confused Kadsa. It sounded like many different voices, speaking with polyphonic pitches.

"This palace is not yours," Kadsa told her. "Take your zombies and leave."

"Is that a threat?" asked the witch, slithering closer. "You should know not to threaten those above you." The witch shouted the last words of her sentence, and her voice came at Kadsa like a harsh wind.

"You've lost this war. You don't want to lose anything else."

The witch did something that resembled laughing.

"You think I can be killed by a mortal girl—a false *Star*," she spat with disdain. "I am a goddess. I am the living embodiment of darkness, the most powerful of forces. I am the alpha and the omega, as they would say in your world. I am immortal."

"You're a forest witch," Kadsa yelled. "You don't know anything about my world. You're just a crazy woman with too much time on your hands."

Akwanshi stepped closer to her, and Kadsa gritted her teeth when she felt a warm energy; the same sensation emanated from the sitting room and now off this woman. It had a nauseating effect, twisting and stirring her stomach. She must be using magic.

"I know plenty about your world, Abnr's Gift." She hissed the last two words. "I know that right now, chaos is overcoming your world. It's everywhere and it is everything. There are hurricanes, tornados, heat waves, tsunamis, ice storms, and random and violent outbursts of murder. They've been happening all over. That is the range of my power. You cannot stop this reign. The best I can do for you is make you a servant in the Temple of the Dark Goddess."

"I will never serve you. Never. I hate you." Kadsa leaped at the witch, but Akwanshi sidestepped her.

"Why do you hate me?" the witch asked coolly.

Kadsa swallowed the lump in her throat. Did she expect her to answer?

"I didn't bring you here, child. If anything, I'd love to help you get home."

"I don't need your help with anything," Kadsa spat. "You're surrounded by light."

"Am I?" asked the witch dryly, daring her, as if she wasn't aware of the arrival of day in the kingdom, growing in strength by the second.

The warmth of the sun had been heating the vines buried underneath shallow ground. The vines had been crying, threatening to retreat, but Akwanshi held them close with her magical strength and they had been draining her energy.

"I prepared for you, little girl, and because I am a woman of my words, I will help you to get home." She snapped her fingers. A large vine tumbled away from the wall, plopped against the floor, and crawled toward her.

Kadsa's stomach churned at the disgusting sight of this living vine. It reminded her of snakes. The vine wiggled and contracted, and then opened like a cocoon, spitting something out, wrapped in phlegm.

"I believe this man belongs to you," Akwanshi spoke, bitterness palpable in her tone.

The cocooned mucous thinned, revealing more of the man's features.

Kadsa's mouth gaped. "Grandpa Edoje," she yelled, rushing toward her grandfather on instinct, but stopping herself mid-track when she noticed the vines stirring, as if ready to attack.

"How? Why?"

"Your grandfather cheated me," said the sorceress spitefully, taking pleasure in the horrified look on Kadsa's face.

"What are you talking about? You kidnapped him." "Actually, he came here on his own. All the same, he was a wanted man."

"What are you talking about?" Kadsa shouted, noticing that the mucous thinned enough to reveal his stiff, scrawny face.

"Oh, you don't know?" crooned Akwanshi. "Your grandfather didn't tell you?"

Kadsa steeled herself to shut out the witch's words. "Tell you what, *child*," Akwanshi started. "You give over his Majesty, Khansu, to me, and you can have your grandfather and go home. I will spare you both. I will forgive him and send you back myself. Just give me the young man. Where is he hiding?"

"I don't know where Khansu is. And if you're so powerful, you should know where he is."

Akwanshi hissed. "Then you'll never get your traitor of a grandfather. I guess blood doesn't matter to you, after all. Or does it?"

"What did you do to him?"

"He doesn't have a soul," Akwanshi said coolly. Fury overtook Kadsa and she launched at the woman.

Akwanshi knocked her away with a phantom blow that felt like a punch in the chest.

Kadsa crawled to her feet in time to watch Akwanshi open her mouth. Three phantoms lashed out and stormed her, battering her on the ground and drawing blood, before re-entering the witch's mouth.

Akwanshi pulled Kadsa forward with a thin, smoky tendril of magic that cocooned her in suspended air. The witch mumbled an incantation and Kadsa stiffened, while the smoky tendrils tightened around her, restricting her body from even kicking.

Akwanshi snapped the necklace from Kadsa's throat and tossed it to the ground.

"Where is the prince? His soul belongs to me." "Did you tell him that? He disagrees."

"He cannot hide from me," Akwanshi proclaimed and sniffed the air.

"If you're so powerful, why can't you find him?" "When the night is settled, I will find him—the divine king, and whatever influence you have over him will be vanquished."

"You won't live to see nightfall." Kadsa groaned and pushed with all her might against the tendrils that held her suspended above ground.

"You will acknowledge Nenet as the eternal one and only deity." Akwanshi's words were a command.

"I'm not religious, but being here, I have to say that Abnr seems better than anything you touch," Kadsa said, all snarky, struggling against stiffness.

Akwanshi hissed. "Now I will have to determine what kind of death is fitting for you, the great joke of the gods. Now I know. I will drain your blood, because it has a good taste to it, like candy." The witch licked her lips.

Kadsa was disgusted. This witch had tasted her blood.

"I will drink it and I want the *people* to watch," she mused. "It will be an example to them, a final judgment cast on their dead deity." She walked away, disappearing into the sitting room with the broken-down doors.

Kadsa cast her eyes on her grandfather, lying free of the mucous but still unconscious. She had so many questions. He didn't look all right.

Kadsa, a fragile voice uttered her name. At first, it made no sense, like a whisper in the wind, but then she heard it again. That voice. Her grandfather. How was he...? She trailed off. No!

Yes, he confirmed. *I am talking to you through your mind.* She didn't say anything.

Listen to me Kadsa. I don't have much time. She poisoned me to take my soul. So, listen.

She stayed quiet.

I was meaning to tell you. I didn't think you would leave me without a trace. I didn't prepare you for this place. I am sorry.

Kadsa closed her eyes, as her journey played itself out in her head—everything from day one—the hike to Tibesti plateaus, the dark forest, the Jakuba and The Divide at Faro.

You said this place was home. I'm sorry I doubted you. Kadsa, nothing you've done has disappointed me.

Kadsa steeled her emotions hearing him say this.

"Our people are from here. I am from here. I was born here. This is my home. My real name is Edoje, from the tribe of Abasi, the founders of the city of Iunu, in Mehronur. Not long ago by the time of this world, I was a young priest-in-training living in Mehronur.

"Akwanshi contacted me to help her find the doorway to the world you call your own. I agreed ... not because I trusted her and not because I wanted to help her, but because I wanted to save our kingdom, our home. If I could go outside, I could find help. So, I took the task. I found the doorway and figured out how to open it. The crystal, it was my key to controlling the

doorway. I brought it with me. Later, I met your grandmother among the Teda people. We settled in Kenya due to the conflict in Chad. I spent the next forty years trying to find an answer to unlocking the enchantment of my dying world."

"You knew the magnetic rock was there."

Grandpa Edoje struggled to answer. "I studied it. When I found the rock, I realized then it was the same rock that had brought me to earth. It was the prophesied "star." Something went wrong. The constellation changed on me. I couldn't get back, couldn't re-open the doorway. I studied that rock, unable to figure out how to unlock it."

"It's the tower of Abnr. The rock's designed to energize things. It spreads light in the kingdom. The Dark Enchantment has lifted."

"That's good." Grandpa Edoje sighed. "I left this world before the Dark Enchantment fell, but I knew it would come.

The texts in the Great Library speak of a period of darkness." He took in a painful breath. "I am sorry again, Kadsa, that I couldn't help you. Time moves so fast in your world, and quickly. I was an old man. The son I thought would inherit the godtalker's gift did not. Then you came and I knew you were the answer. The prophetic gift manifested in my vision. Kadsa, you are a stranger to this land but still a daughter of my blood." Grandpa Edoje paused. "You were the real key that opened the doorway. The magic I found in this world. It was you."

"Are you dying?"

"Yes," he admitted. "It doesn't matter. You are important, not me. Blood connects you to this world. You just have to accept it. You must not let the sorceress gain access to the prince. She speaks of him, of his soul, believing it can grant her true immortality. I believe the gods sent you for a reason. When you were first in Kenya, and I had asked you to look into *the crystal, you said you had seen a boy there, sleeping under a tree. It was him. I know it. Him ... and you ... together. You can stop her and save this world."* Grandpa Edoje fell silent.

Kadsa squeezed her eyes shut; emotions welled up inside of her. Her body suddenly felt weightless, and when she opened her eyes, she'd burned through the black tendrils and had fallen to the floor. She wasted no time reaching for her crystal on the ground and jumping to her feet with the large knife. She ran to her grandfather, touching him. His eyes opened, but they dimmed, no longer did she see the twinkle.

"Stop that woman, Kadsa. Save the home of your ancestors. This place is part of you," he spoke weakly.

She nodded.

Grandpa Edoje coughed. "Go now." Kadsa stood.

"And, Kadsa, I'm sorry again."

"It's okay. I understand." Kadsa shut out the pain of his last words and moved toward the central room where Akwanshi was busy healing her wounded power source with chants. Akwanshi murmured to the plant as if it was a living child, hushing and caressing it as it steamed.

It was the creepiest thing ever.

The room itself was nothing but vines atop vines and bushes and some dark liquid in a pot. Akwanshi sensed Kadsa's presence at the broken-down door and spun around, tossing a smoky black bolt at her. Kadsa threw up her light shield and the dark smoke ball bounced off it and deflected back to the witch like a boomerang. It hit her hard, and she staggered but pulled herself together. Akwanshi stormed forward, flinging dark smoke balls at her that ricocheted.

The dark bolts kept bouncing back to the witch, forcing her to dodge them each time, but she kept firing more at Kadsa, until they did the job of pushing Kadsa away from the doorway. Kadsa fell and glided across the floor hard, tired from putting up a resistance. Her nose bled. She was using too much energy to defend herself, and she couldn't replenish it. She got to her feet as fast as she could.

"Your light source is weak." Akwanshi descended on her with speed and agility, having all but destroyed the shield. "Now I'll drain you like I promised; you and your worthless god will be gone for good. So will your grandfather the traitor." Her eyes darted to Grandpa Edoje's stiff body. "You will become a servant in death, like all the others."

Kadsa gripped the knife tightly in defiance while the witch ranted. She was uncertain if the witch knew she held the weapon, or if she was simply too arrogant to care.

"You're a foolish little girl," said the witch. "How dare you challenge me—a god? It's a death wish, you most obnoxious child who hurt my babies."

"You are a forest witch," spat Kadsa, shutting her up. She too could rant about how this woman ruined her life and her grandfather's. Why should she listen to this woman, who clearly had too much time to waste? Talk about arrogance.

The witch's eyes flooded with free-flowing rage. Akwanshi lifted her hand, and pushed a thick, smoky ball toward Kadsa, knocking her hard against the wall. Before she could lift herself up, Akwanshi reeled her forward using the smoke tentacles projecting from her pendant.

Akwanshi's palm opened to deliver the phantom twist that would kill Kadsa. Kadsa's survival instincts kicked in before the black tendrils tightened around her. She screamed and pushed herself forward with the knife she never wanted to use. It happened quickly, surprising her and the witch.

The witch's eyes widened, as did Kadsa's when she spotted the knife sticking out of the witch's heart. The tension in Akwanshi's body eased. Her arms fell flaccid. She struggled to remove the knife but it was in too deep. Akwanshi's eyes widened—not with rage, but with surprise.

The witch took in a deep and desperate breath and gagged, and gasped, and gasped. Thick black fluid disgorged from her mouth and Kadsa slipped from the tendrils, collapsing to the floor. Akwanshi wouldn't give up, and continued trying to pull out the knife. Wasn't making much effort. Her breathing grew shallow and quick, desperate. One last gasp and she thudded against the floor.

Kadsa shut her eyes and took a deep breath. The heart of the darkness was dead.

A cacophony of cries exploded in the palace. Chaos broke out. The ghouls sounded lost, confused and in pain. Vines flapped with violence. Dissonant cries. Erratic and aimless, flapping about. Kadsa stayed on the floor for safety. Beside her, the witch's body convulsed.

Horrified and fearing the witch was resurrecting herself, Kadsa raced toward her body, throwing herself down on the floor again, when ghoul after ghoul began to stream out of Akwanshi's corpse. Kadsa lost count of the number of spirits that left the woman's body. At the very least, a thousand flew from Akwanshi's corpse.

Akwanshi had made herself powerful by conjuring and eating souls. When the souls leaked out, her body looked real, something close to normal. The only trace of a witch was the green, grayish color that stained her face and her skin. She was a slim, bony woman, lying serenely on the floor.

Kadsa crawled toward Grandpa Edoje. He had stopped breathing. His body was stiff.

The vines and weeds pulled away from the walls, retreating into the sitting room where Akwanshi had established her dark power source. The Dark Enchantment vanished in a tornado that tore down and carried away everything in its path. Nothing escaped the vortex—not the crying ghouls, the vines or the witch's body. It sucked everything into the room the sorceress had designated as her chamber.

Kadsa tried holding on to Grandpa Edoje's body, but the counter force pulling it was too strong. She had to let go, saving herself from the tornado by grabbing onto a colonnade and securing herself behind it.

When the storm died down, it left the palace bare. Kadsa jumped to her feet and walked toward the center room to see what remained. No signs of Grandpa Edoje's body or any furniture remained, except for the sorceress's brewing pot. The large pot crackled, and before she reached it, exploded into black dust.

Cracks remained in the walls, as the sole sign of Akwanshi's damage. Other than those, Paraa Hutat, the living sun place, was normal again.

Kadsa moved toward the voices on the balcony. Sion helped Queen Oluchi to her feet. It appeared she might have fainted or had fallen. Prince Sahu rushed into his mother's arms. They were not dead after all. The crowd in the courtyard swelled. It looked like a normal day. Yet, they didn't look certain the threat was over.

The Jakuba hovering outside entered the kingdom. They weren't Jakuba anymore, but people. People were modest, so the former Jakuba scrambled to find clothing, and to hide themselves. The transformation was complete. Kadsa could only breathe.

"Ka-Kadsa," said Prince Sahu, pointing as she approached him, his mother, and Sion.

Sion burst into unexpected laughter when he spotted her.

"I finally made you laugh." Kadsa greeted him. He definitely looked alive, more alive than she'd ever seen him. And what a good smile he had. Sahu hugged her at the waist.

"Queen Oluchi," Kadsa called, body aching, hunger and tiredness engulfing her body.

"You have saved us all," said a grateful Queen Oluchi. "It wasn't easy, but she's gone for good. I think." "You are bruised." The queen touched her forehead. "I'll survive." She wiped a smudge of blood from her nose. "I am drained of energy, but I'll recover fine."

Loud excitement rose up among the courtyard crowd as more people arrived. People greeted family they had not seen since the

Dark Enchantment. Now laughter echoed around them while they touched and admired the changes in each other.

Someone would have to address the crowd. Even though the darkness no longer existed, and the Jakuba were human again, there was still confusion about whether it was over. The best person to do that was—the crowd nearest the raised platform parted when someone entered their mix—Khansu. The crowd grumbled in confusion and curiosity when he climbed the steps to the platform.

"Khansu," she called, meeting him halfway. "You saved the kingdom. I believed you would." "You helped me. I didn't do this alone."

He watched her with warmth in his eyes, and then his brows furrowed. "You are hurt."

"I'm fine," she said. "What's a little soreness? Come here."

"Queen Oluchi." Kadsa faced the demure queen and Sion. "This is your stepson—Khansu."

Queen Oluchi, Sion and Prince Sahu studied Khansu with dull expressions. They'd never met him before, and they didn't know what his presence meant.

"Khansu is the king of Marut, according to King Remu." Kadsa continued. "Khansu, this is Queen Oluchi, wife of your late father."

Queen Oluchi's expression furled with worry and discomfort. "Divine King." She bowed with all the grace in the world

"And this is Master Sion, son of Seth Oranyan, first-ranked royal guard of his majesty, King Remu of Marut." "Divine King, I am at your service," said Sion, bowing.

"This is my son, Sahu, prince of Marut." Queen Oluchi introduced.

From his mother's side, Sahu watched Khansu with a little curiosity and nothing else.

"Queen-wife, brave warrior, and young prince." Khansu bowed. "I am happy to meet you all. I have heard many good things about you. And your father." He faced Sion. "He is brave. I have fought with him in battle."

"Seth," said Kadsa suddenly. "Where is he? Did he survive the battle?"

"I most certainly did," said the familiar voice.

A limping, older man ambled away from the crowd toward them.

"Seth." Kadsa rushed to his side. "Oh my god, you're here."

"I always thought I'd see you again."

"Sure, you did." She grabbed the arm of the fifty- something year old man with salt and pepper hair. Seeing him as a human male was strange. She had never considered how he might look as a human, but his features were just about right—hardened but dignified.

Sion stepped forward. Seth Oranyan's face twisted with all sorts of emotions. The two men stared at each other, unsure of how to greet one another.

"My boy," Seth declared, fighting to control the sentiments threatening to overwhelm him. "My boy," he repeated, raising his voice. "You've become a man. It's been too long." His voice trembled. The older man pulled Seth into his arms.

"My boy," he cried.

Sion's smile was controlled and taut.

"Father," Sion said, "I never thought I'd see you again."

Seth nodded with understanding. "We should thank Kadsa for re-uniting us."

They both glanced toward Kadsa, but she said nothing, allowing them their privacy.

"Your mother?"

"She died some time ago."

Seth's face saddened. "I am sorry."

"After the darkness consumed you, she became heartbroken. I raised myself after that. I sought to become a great warrior, like my father."

"I am proud of you." He patted him on the back. "I am very proud. Not a day went by in that forest that I didn't think of you— and your mother." He examined him at arm's length. "My boy." He embraced him again. The two laughed. "Let us start over, can we?"

Sion nodded. "We can do that."

"For what it's worth," Kadsa said when silence fell between them. "I can see the resemblance."

"Kadsa." Seth watched her. "I owe you many thanks. You are indeed Abnr's Gift."

"I didn't do this alone. Everyone here helped me." "We helped you because we believed in you," said

Khansu, staring at her in a way unlike she had ever seen. "We believed in you and we believed in Marut—that it would rise again." He paused. "As my father's son and heir," his expression peppered a little with worry. "If I become king, I intend to honor

Kadsa Abasi." Khansu faced the small crowd. "All of you who bravely fought for Marut and defended it against the darkness—all of you who believed will be honored."

The crowd cheered, though some still looked confused by Khansu's presence.

"Morning has arrived. We can rest. But come tomorrow, we celebrate. We celebrate the rebirth of Marut, land of the gods. We celebrate Abnr, and my father. We celebrate life again!"

Khansu turned away from the cheering crowd. He looked ready to walk away, but then he glanced to Queen Oluchi whose shoulders slumped.

"Queen Oluchi. You don't seem happy."

"Oh, forgive me, my king." Queen Oluchi curtsied. "I was just thinking."

"Thinking about what my reign must mean. What your role as my late father's wife will be?"

She pressed her lips together, keeping her hands clasped.

"I know your fears," he admitted, "but don't worry. There is a place for you in this kingdom and this palace. I cannot rule alone. I do not know much about rulership. I can learn much from you. I heard from your people that you are a resilient queen and I believe it is true. I should benefit with an advisor. In addition, I will look out for my brother. I consider you family and ask that you'll consider me family, also."

"Thank you for your kind words, King," she said nodding. "I am no longer a queen, but a lady. As such, I will serve accordingly. Also, I am happy to accept you as family."

Khansu nodded with understanding.

She smiled with shyness. "I am sorry, my king, for everything—Bokor, the king. I did not know what they had done to you. I did not think—"

"It's alright. It is in the past. The age of darkness has passed. There's no more to say about it. It's a new time, a new age, a new beginning for us all."

Kadsa pressed her lips into a smile while listening to this. They were family.

Prince Sahu left his mother's side, ran to Khansu, and threw his arms around his waist. Everyone laughed. Kadsa and the royals returned to the palace and settled into restoring normalcy. Khansu disappeared with the king's advisors—those who survived. Queen Oluchi took charge of organizing and reassigning kitchen and domestic staff, and Sion took off with his father to help rebuild the royal guards. Kadsa took her well-needed rest—mostly sleep.

25

FESTIVAL

By the next day, Kadsa was gathering all the dresses she'd gotten from Queen Oluchi. She had worn only a few. Queen Oluchi didn't ask for their return, and she considered stuffing one in her bag and taking it back home with her. The queen probably wouldn't miss it.

A soft knock on her door took away her attention. Kadsa dropped the dress, walked to the door and opened it to find a smiling Sion.

"You're smiling now, eh?"

"Yes." He nodded. He still had the same seriousness about him, but she liked that he was now smiling.

"And how is your father?"

"Resting. It's been a very long journey back. He has battle wounds that must heal."

"Yeah, absolutely. We're all tired and bruised." Kadsa's rib cage jabbed with pain every so often, especially if she stretched herself too much, and her back hurt.

"So, what is going on? What can I help you with?" "I came to ask something personal of you." "Okay," she said. "Go right ahead."

"I would like for you to be my wife."

She stared at him in shock, trying to figure out if he was serious. He was Sion. He was always serious.

"Wow. From smiling to marrying." She chuckled. "This is fast."

"We have known each other for some time. You are so different from all the women I have known. My father speaks highly of you, and your adventures in the forest." "Yeah." She considered what to say next. "Marriage is a complicated thing." He looked confused.

"Sion, I can't marry you." She squirmed. "I'm not even eighteen. That's too young—in my world, anyway. Don't get me wrong. I think you're very attractive and everything." She winced when she spoke these words. "But I can't. I have to get home."

Sion's confusion turned to disappointment. "Are you certain?" She nodded.

Sion waited awhile, and then he asked, "Can we dance at the celebration?"

"I can do that—yes, even if I can't dance. Most definitely."

"Thank you," he said. "I'll see you later, then."

"Alright," he said. "Have a good afternoon." "You, too."

When Kadsa finished packing, she went into the kitchen to grab something to eat. Akwanshi's nightmare takeover had disrupted everything in Hutat, including the routine of serving food three times a day. Half the staff was missing. Some of the residents had raided the farmlands. Incidentally, the witch's takeover of the palace meant many people had stayed clear of it, which meant it still had food. Kadsa was starving. The "star" had eaten up her energy.

Kadsa wolfed down a chunky piece of freshly baked bread with churned butter spread. She was looking for more food when she heard Queen Oluchi asking a cook for the whereabouts of King Khansu.

Khansu had left the former queen in charge of managing the affairs of the palace, including the festival tonight. She had been working with the High Priest of Mehronur and the vizier to get the affair together.

Queen Oluchi spotted her and became excited. "Kadsa, have you seen his majesty?"

"Not since yesterday," she admitted. Kadsa had slept most of the day, except for when she had to get up for food. "Is there anything I can do?"

Queen Oluchi studied her list. "No, I am afraid. I need to speak to the king about some of these arrangements. He is difficult to find."

"I'll let him know if I see him."

"Thank you." Queen Oluchi turned her attention to the cook, again.

Kadsa left to search for Khansu, she already had a good idea of where he could be.

"I knew you'd find me," said Khansu when she entered the fortress he once called home.

"How?"

"You found me in the beginning. You freed me from my curse. You know me." Khansu stood beside the pit, staring into it for some undecipherable reason.

"Your stepmother is looking for you. She may want to talk to you about the celebration."

He grinned. "That sounds very strange, doesn't it?" "How is it strange?"

"The very fact that we're having a festival with me as the grand master," he said. "Every year, since I was six and ten, I have snuck into the Jua festival. I watched the king read the First Words of Ndakr, and I listened with pride and felt sadness. Never had I imagined I'd have such honor, such reverence put upon me. Even after the Isaan priestess had given me the prophetic message, it never made sense to me. Four days ago, I was the most feared being in the light kingdom, and one day ago, I was on the verge of serving the witch for all eternity." He grinned, agitated. "Today, they've decided to welcome me as their king."

"Things change," she replied. "This is how it was supposed to be." She moved closer to him. "You are the king. You carry the burden of your ancestors."

Kadsa pondered this point a little bit before dismissing it. She sounded too much like her grandfather with this talk of ancestors, even if it was true.

"I'm barely twenty years old. I am not ready to be king."

"Khansu, this is your birthright. There's no one else. You believe in destiny." She sounded like her grandpa lecturing her. "Besides, it's going to be fun."

Silence fell between them.

"Do you know what the rest of the Reveal says?"

She shook her head, worried about this reveal, a prophecy.

"When light is restored, the hero unites with the king. Do you know what that means?"

She shook her head again.

"You must marry me," he told her. "It's then that we can fully restore the soul of Abnr and complete the circling, and prepare Marut for its immortal king."

"This is my second proposal in a day." It was strange how she never had a boyfriend, and now, two very good-looking men proposed to her in one day. "Khansu, I can't marry you."

"A king must have a wife. It is the natural way. I feel it is right."

"Do you?"

"Yes, I do," he said after a second of doubt.

"Well, I can't marry you. Not now, anyway." Regret weighed her down. "I must go home, back to my world." "Why are you determined to go back to your land?"

She detected sadness in his tone but she shut it out. "I miss my family."

"My mother was a stranger in this land," he said. "She came from the land of the seafarers to the east, Nahrin. She embraced this place as her home. Your circumstance is not unlike hers. Besides, you are a gift from Abnr. You belong here."

"You'll find your queen. I know it. And you'll love her. You'll see. But it can't be me."

Khansu studied her, ready to protest. "Trust me on this."

Khansu said nothing for a short time. He was trying to read her thoughts. Then he gave up.

"Aren't you going to get ready for the festival, the crowning of the king?"

"It will be a small ceremony. The council has been somewhat reluctant to have a formal affair. It will take a while for everything to get back to proper order. Until then, I'll merely be a temporary ruler. It's not a real crowning. The council and the rulers of Marut will not change your father's own decision," she assured him. "He made you his rightful successor. They'll have to respect that. The divine right of kings, remember?"

Khansu's brows knitted at the center of his forehead, and his gaze dropped to the floor.

"I'm right," she assured him. "You'll be fine." Khansu looked to the broken well.

"I have to go get ready for tonight," she said and began to walk away.

"Kadsa," he called after her. She halted.

"The fire has returned to the pit."

She glanced to the pit and chuckled. "This place is a little matchbox."

Khansu's face lit up with a shy smile and it froze her. She had not seen a genuine smile from him until this moment. She thought of Sion's smile from earlier and it made her happy, but also made her ponder the difference between it and Khansu's.

Khansu's smile quickened to life a desire inside her that made her feel awkward. Kadsa wrestled with the desire to rush into his arms and kiss him. She had never felt this before.

"Is something wrong?"

"No, nothing. I must get back to Queen—the former Queen—to get ready. Excuse me." She hurried away from him.

26

PHOENIX

Paraa Hutat included, at the very least, seven courtyards, the main four of which were public, each facing a cardinal direction, while the lesser three were private and reserved for members of the royal family. Kadsa was happy to explore each alongside Queen Oluchi as she tried to find a location for the festival. In the end, they settled on the courtyard facing east of the palace of Hutat, designated for religious ceremonies. It had the most beautiful garden and a small temple that smelled of myrrh and spicy herbs.

Marut was much more than the temple city of Hutat, Kadsa realized, and pondered how much more the kingdom had to offer and spent much time wishing to stay longer. She didn't allow the thought to settle, because no sooner, Khansu arrived to escort her to the festival.

Khansu looked handsome, having ditched the drab brown robe for a royal blue caftan with gold hemlines and intricately carved breastplate. He wore a small gold diadem with encrusted gemstones. Kadsa smiled through her racing heart, taking his hand and letting him lead her to the festival.

Dancers gyrated and thrusted in ways that reminded her of Samba dancers. The vibrant sound of drums echoed throughout the courtyard, and the singing and laughter continued deep into the night.

People came from all over Marut. Kadsa suspected many of them were already living in Mehronur, despite them stating they were from such and such place.

Khansu sat in the highchair on a raised platform designated for the royals, adjusting his diadem. Kadsa's emotions were a mixture of yearning and pride.

The High Priest of Mehronur had the honor of crowning the new king in a private ceremony. The diadem had gemstones representing the five districts of Marut. The proper crown was much heavier than this one. King Remu had worn it once. The five-ringed crown had a sword emblem encrusted in the front, along with the five gemstones, which ran down the body of the sword emblem.

Each time Khansu leaned forward, the crown flashed with brilliance and exposed cryptic symbols under the sunlight, and later, the moonlight. They called it the two crowns, in honor of Abnr and Nkzum, the overlapping celestials that hovered above the land.

The surviving councilors and viziers had agreed a lavish ceremony would not be appropriate at the given time. Kadsa had considered Khansu's worry, that the council indeed planned to strip him of his birthright, but she forced the thought out of her head.

Khansu was the king in name and birthright. The people of Marut believed all their kings were mortal manifestations of Abnr, believed to be the divine father of Ndakr, their first king. They wouldn't dishonor their *divine king* unless he dishonored them. The record books showed few kings not honored. Chief among them was Aren, a victim of Akwanshi's.

Around here, kings were the base stone that kept everything in order. Without him, the foundation would fall apart, as it nearly did after King Remu died. Khansu paced, and remained a little jittery throughout the day, though she comforted him. The people of Marut were grateful they had a king, even if he was a stranger to them. During the coronation, Jorba Xar, a high-ranked council member, bestowed Khansu with King Remu's armor. He signed the Divinity of Kings scroll, and the Council declared him the official ruler. Kadsa was a little disturbed that he inked his signature in blood, but this was tradition. These people had their ways.

Grandpa Edoje believed these people were also *her* people. She tried not to think too much about this point, because Mehronur still wasn't home, and she wouldn't get distracted into thinking of it as such.

Khansu's first act as king was to honor Seth Oranyan, leader of the district of Elon, resurrected. He declared Sion chief among guards, who got new emblems to match the new king, as was tradition. Khansu chose the emblem of Bennu, or the Phoenix, a decision made to honor Bennu for his role in his resurrection, but also for the rebirth of the kingdom after the darkness.

And so Khansu became the Phoenix King.

Kadsa noted all of this with fascination and regret. She would not see the Phoenix King rule. Each time she peeked at Khansu, she struggled to keep from getting too upset, forcing herself to accept that she would not stand by his side personally.

Khansu named the former Queen Oluchi, Royal Lady of the palace of Hutat. When it was Kadsa's turn to face him, she pressed her lips into a polite smile. He bowed before her, and she fought against looking him in his eyes as he named her to the *Order of the Ladies of Abnr*. She accepted the title Divine-Lady of the Temple of Abnr. *This felt so wrong.* Yet she smiled, bowing to thank him.

Khansu himself received gifts of food, fine fabrics, and jewelry. The festival lasted deep into the night, during which Kadsa danced with Sion as she had promised. She danced with the king also. Though both had proposed marriage early in the day, other women distracted them during the festival.

The king had a long list of young women forming lines to dance with him. A hint of jealousy bubbled inside but she didn't entertain it too much; she was leaving him anyway.

Kadsa distracted herself with the fascinating events surrounding Sion and the former Queen Oluchi. More interestingly, she noticed that even as Sion danced with her, his eyes wandered to the young, former queen, Oluchi, who looked lonely. She stole graceful yet awkward glances at them, trying her best to remain inconspicuous.

Oluchi and Sion had spent a good portion of time together in the past few days, so it made sense that they'd grow close. But, Kadsa noticed that their glances hinted at more than a survival bond. Something more lurked deep in their eyes.

Kadsa cupped Sion's chin and turned his face to hers while they danced.

"You should dance with Queen Oluchi now," she told him. "I think she deserves it."

Sion's dark eyes beamed with understanding, and because he wasn't the type to argue or deny the truth, he nodded and released her from his arms, confirming that she was right. She watched him amble toward where Queen Oluchi stood in the courtyard. The former queen smiled demurely at the sight of the handsome and brave warrior.

Kadsa became a swooning schoolgirl when Queen Oluchi placed her hand in Sion's. The dance was brief, cut short by their respect for formality and honor—they could not give people any gossip. After all, the former queen was in mourning for her husband, King Remu, evidenced by her loose hair and black clothing.

By the end of the festival, Queen Oluchi and Sion were still enamored with one another, stealing frequent glances.

Kadsa was crushed she was forgotten. She pressed her lips into a smile, nurturing the practicality of her situation—she'd have no guilt about leaving. Khansu's dance card was so full he barely had time to sit. Somehow, Kadsa knew he didn't mind. For a boy who spent his years isolated in a cold and dark fortress, and his nights wandering aimlessly through his kingdom, any interaction sufficed him.

27

VOYAGER

Kadsa spent her last night in Marut studying the stars.

The sky looked close to any night sky on Earth, but the stars hung very low. Darkness didn't completely hide the close-circling suns, whose outlines still showed them intertwined. The celestial bodies had moved to the center of the kingdom, rather than cluster above Mehronur.

Kadsa had to remember this about Marut, remember that it was special and the stars looked touchable. It surprised her that she had gotten so used to such an alien land. And, of course, her grandfather's words played in her mind—it was the home of her ancestors. Her grandfather's people came from Iunu. Yes, it was home, but even better, it was real.

Earlier in the day, she had gone to the Great Library to read up on the myths and legends of the kingdom. The people believed their gods once walked on Marut. These gods, sjeru, would one day walk on Marut again. If they made it beautiful enough, the sjeru would be pleased and come back to visit them, and one god in particular, Abnr, would become their true king.

Khansu alluded to this when he'd mentioned the circling to her in the fortress. The Maruti believed the first man came to life in this very land. Marut was the land of the ancestor-gods, the birthplace of humankind. Kadsa surprised herself by how she accepted all this. Marut was a land cloaked in a celestial magic of mysterious origins. This land, untouched by industrialism, pollution and technology, was paradise. Her thoughts strayed into sadness. If she left, she wondered, would she be able to come back? She'd miss Marut when she wasn't in it anymore.

Kadsa rode from the palace early in the morning. "You're my true friend," Khansu whispered to her when she hugged him. "I cannot see you leave. It hurts."

She walked away from him, daring not to look back and see his face in all its sadness and beauty.

Royal guards flanked her side all the way to the gates of Mehronur.

Sion Oranyan stood near the edge of the city. The wall had been partly torn down to create an entrance.

Kadsa climbed off the abada and approached Sion Oranyan, who stood with Queen Oluchi and a small group of servants.

"I wondered why you didn't come say goodbye before," she told him.

"We wanted to surprise you," Sion said.

"It's sad to see you leave," said the former Queen before she took her hands. "Do come back to visit, won't you?"

The former queen had never been this intimate before. It was as if a large burden lifted from her shoulders. Now that she was no longer queen, she had let her hair down. Shy Sahu stood by his mother's side. The boy-prince had remained indifferent during most of the past days' events.

"Can I come back?" Kadsa inquired. The question had nagged her for some time.

"You can, if you can find your way back to the gateway." Seth stepped forward, seemingly out of nowhere.

"I'd like to come back. This is not a place you forget." "Please do come back."

"Thank you for everything, again. I would never have survived the forest without you."

"No." He shook his head. "Thank you, Kadsa. You helped us live again. Thank you."

She rubbed the head of the boy-prince who squeezed her arm. "Here." She handed him the flashlight. "It's something to remember me by. You can fiddle with it."

The boy eyed it, and she showed him how to turn it on and off. Afterward, Kadsa and Sion walked by the side of the buzoa through the meadow. Flowers grew over the valley again.

"You should ask her to marry you," Kadsa told Sion when they were out of earshot.

"Of whom do you speak?" he asked, playing dumb. "You know who—a certain former queen named

Oluchi."

He stared at her dumbfounded and she laughed. "I know you *fancy* her."

He pressed his lips into a smile.

"Also, you should smile more. It looks good on you." "I have reasons to smile— if it doesn't soften me too much."

A large shadow moved across the low sky, catching everyone's attention.

"Bennu," Kadsa called.

The bird landed in front of them.

"I was wondering where you went two days ago."

"I got tired, so I went back to my slumber," he admitted. "I prefer to sleep in the morning, after all."

"This is Sion Oranyan," she said. "He's the general of the royal army. He's my friend."

"Good to meet you," Bennu said.

Sion nodded, keeping a wary distance from the bird. "Sion," she called, "Bennu can carry me to the gate."

He nodded with understanding, taking the reins of the abada.

"Good luck, Sion, and remember what I said. Marry her."

He smiled, tugged on the abada's reins, and backed away toward Mehronur's gate, where the others stood.

"Get on." The bird stooped at her feet.

Loud trampling noise brought Kadsa's attention back to the broken-down walls. King Khansu dismounted the abada and ran toward her; his royal guards ran within proximity of him.

"I have something to show you." Khansu faced Bennu, "If I may?"

"Of course," replied the bird.

"Take us to Aja's Gardens in Faro, please."

Khansu guided her to sit on the bird's back. He uttered something to his guards, stalling them, before he mounted. Bennu galloped through the meadow, lifting off and forcing her to hold her breath until he was steady in the sky.

The aerial view of the kingdom was spectacular. Everything had risen. In Abzul, the waterfalls and the wide, free-flowing river caught her attention. It coiled around the district, its tributaries breaking off in different directions.

In Faro, the most impressive sight was Aja's Gardens, flourishing and colorful, rising toward the sky. The series of four gardens sat on platforms atop each other. Priestesses marched to the top of the highest garden with baskets of reed.

"Stunning, just like I described." Bennu landed on the highest level of the temple, to the surprise of the two young priestesses who were watering the flowers. They bowed to them, revealing their headbands made of ostrich feathers.

When Khansu dismounted, the young women hurried away. Kadsa rushed to the wall and leaned over it. It must have been sixty feet to the bottom. She rushed toward the flowers, touching them. The myrrh, sage, and rose bushes mingled orderly with all sorts of other plants she couldn't name.

"I want to give you a flower to remember me by." Khansu stood by her side. He strolled toward the garden and ran his fingers over the freshly sprung roses. With his index finger, he tapped a single-stem red rose on a thorny branch and handed it to her.

"You will think of me, won't you?"

"Yes," she agreed, nodding. *This is heavy. Can he hear her racing heart?* "Yes, I'll think of you."

She tucked the rose with care into a side pocket of her bag, making sure it couldn't fall out or get crushed.

"You can still stay," he told her when she gave him her attention again.

"I know, but I can't. I have to go home."

"Kadsa," he said somewhat hesitantly. "Promise me that if you ever return to Marut, you will marry me."

Kadsa's eyes widened, and her heart stopped. She wasn't even an adult. Marriage was nowhere soon. His brown eyes were pleading and fretful.

"Yes, I will marry you if I come back to Marut."

What am I saying? She should tell him marriage didn't work that way in her culture. Her heart sank. What if she could not return to Marut? Was her reply dishonest? She compelled the thought out of her head when he smiled. *That smile.* A wallop resonated in her heart. She felt dizzy and grabbed hold of the rail.

"All right. I will let you go."

"Will you follow me to the doorway?" she asked. "This will be my last stop. I cannot go farther. I'm afraid I cannot watch you leave."

"I understand." She nodded; the emotions were barely at bay. They eyed each other awkwardly, before Kadsa walked backward to reach Bennu near the wall.

"Bye." She waved to Khansu.

Khansu clasped his hands behind him rather than wave back.

She mounted Bennu's back and they were off again. King Khansu remained standing at the same spot. He became a speck on the landscape. When she couldn't see him anymore, tears fell from her eyes.

"Hush my dear, hush," Bennu said comfortingly.

Kadsa yelped when Bennu flew near a waterfall that drenched her.

Bennu laughed.

"You did that on purpose." "I very much did."

"Okay, fine, I'm done crying."

Bennu landed in a back village in Abzul and Kadsa clumsily climbed off his back.

"This is it," he declared.

"This is it." She exhaled, and then saddened. She was going home. She was excited. Yet she didn't want to leave. But she had to leave. She had a mother to return to—that was what she'd always wanted. Khansu! *Don't think about him.*

Kadsa studied the high, freestanding crystalline monument formed from the magnetic rock. It had turned murky. "I guess I can't magically wish my way home like Dorothy."

"You put the key in place. Open it."

"You know my grandfather gave me this rock." "Did he?"

"Yes," she said nodding. "He forced it into my hand. He was from this world. He carved the key from this very rock that forms the basis of this tower."

"Then he taught you to use it."

She shook her head and walked to the gray magnetic rock, from which the tower had magically grown. "Nah, I'm Abnr's Gift. I get to figure everything out by myself."

She knelt beside the rock, setting her crystal into its chipped indentation.

"Hey," she called, standing. "Will I lose my ability to understand your language?"

"I doubt it, but we'll see."

A crack of thunder echoed through the sky as the murky rock ignited. She feared it might be the Mpundulu. The creepy bird didn't show up—just cosmic happening. The tower steamed when hit by lightning. She and Bennu ducked for cover when the rock energized. A second crack of lightning echoed in the sky.

"What about the crystal?"

"Take it with you. It's yours, isn't it?"

Kadsa yanked the crystal from the tower's base. The misted crystalline tower sucked her inside of its white light. In that instant, the earth trembled. Kadsa forced the silver chain around her neck, squeezing it for dear life.

Time and space shattered; the forest moved in circles. From her squinted eyes, she saw Bennu rushing off to his cave. She stayed low while the tower did its teleporting magic.

28

HOMECOMING

Kadsa didn't open her eyes until the shakes stopped. The forest looked normal, though she couldn't say how exactly. This wasn't where she had been. Could she trust herself to identify the forest as it was before Marut? The high peak glistened some feet away. She cut through trees, twisting and dodging branches until she reached the area. Golden sunlight streaked between sand-colored cliffs.

Kadsa couldn't say for certain where she was. The cliffs might or might not be Bourchul or the Tibesti Plateaus. Even her memory of the cave was somewhat vague. Tibesti felt very long ago. Nothing that stirred to life in her brain felt real. The images wilted and faded, becoming almost detached. She took a deep breath and willed herself to focus. That's what she had to do. A few more steps took her from the tree-covered forest to the cliffs, at whose base stood fig trees.

She halted mid-stride, jolted by the wayward thought of not wanting to go home, but then she swallowed and walked on, shaking her head to throw off sudden jadedness. Still, the thought nagged—what was there for her, now that Grandpa was gone?

But she reminded herself, her mother was still in this world, and that had been her focus all along, to reunite with her mother.

Sparsely strewn boulders covered the ground. A deep, large gash zigzagged up the cliff's surface toward the glint of light. The gash was wide enough for a human or animal to fit through, even together. The high cliffs stood out in the area of canopied forest.

Kadsa marched toward the gash. The cliffs were fortresses that locked the narrow pathway. The only way out was upward. She exhaled and gripped the crystal.

"Take me to the top," she muttered into it, closing her eyes. It felt like nothing was happening and she opened her eyes. She was standing in the same spot.

"Come on, we made it this far," she said, squeezing the crystal in her hand. It still wasn't working. Nothing for her was ever simple. She would have to climb to reach the top. *Just return to Marut and Khansu.* No, she wouldn't go there. She needed to get home—to see her mom.

The cliffs had rugged natural pegs and ledges, and reminded her of Mehronur's high wall. These natural towers were higher, standing over three hundred feet.

Kadsa fastened the straps of her knapsack, buckled it around her waist, and then retied her shoelaces. She reached for the nearest peg, making sure her grip was firm before starting the climb.

The pegs were firm, and every so often, there were cavities in which to place a foot. She was careful not to panic, and muttered the phrase, "Don't look down" under her breath to keep her focused.

Small pebbles slid from the rock's surface. Dust made it impossible to keep her eyes open.

When she was some thirty feet from the top, she glimpsed a peculiar *thing* sticking out from the rock. It was impossible to say for sure what it was. It soon revealed itself as a tree branch. What in the world, she thought, but didn't dwell on why a tree grew sideways out of the rock's surface.

Moving on, she pushed herself until she stood on rocky terrain, surrounded by scattered trees. When she looked down, she caught her breath. She had climbed from a barely visible narrow vertical slit in the cliffs. No way could anyone know another world existed down there, and no one could have found her.

Small pebbles and dried weeds covered the massive rock plateau. A long time ago, a river or lake might have filled it. *Marut was gone.* Moving on. Looking around, she questioned if she was in the right place. Only thick trees existed around the plateau. She really didn't want to climb anymore. Her arms were tired and strained. She had little choice and soon hooked her feet into the side of the cliff. The climb wasn't long this time around. More trees covered the surface. A thinly strewn forest. Familiarity blended into the cool breeze whipping her face. Images from her past rumbled to life in her head.

Tibesti plateaus.

Kadsa ran through the thin bushes, stopping abruptly when she ran into three men and a woman engaged in deep conversation. Tourists. The expressions of the people ranged from curiosity to confusion. Though her mind raced with questions, she didn't have the energy to get them out.

"May we help you?" asked the woman when she didn't speak.

Kadsa admired their new-world clothing. She chuckled, her expression muddling with heavy emotions.

"My name is Kadsa ... I mean, Kadsa Abasi." She ambled closer. "I'm a...." she trailed off and looked around. She was spacing out. Confusion.

"Is this Tibesti?"

Red rocks everywhere. It had to be, but she wanted to be sure.

The men spoke in French. Kadsa waited. She closed her eyes with the intention to shut out the conversation and gather her thoughts, but their words intruded on her quietness. Her brows furrowed. They were discussing where she could've come from, deep within the crevices of the rocks. It was near impossible, they argued.

"I'm Kadsa Abasi." Her mind was slow to comprehend the meaning of her own words.

The tourists fell into silent awe, and then one of the men called out to someone. "You have to come see this," he yelled in English.

A tall, dark-skinned man stepped out from the woods. Kadsa held her breath, nearly calling him Grandpa. He was much younger, and judging by his appearance, he looked like a tour guide.

"Where did you come from?"

Kadsa glanced back into the crater. What could she say about where she came from?

"Can you give me a ride to N'Djamena?" she asked, limbs heavy, strained. Her throat was scratched up and dry, and she swayed woozily. "Please help me?"

Her stomach rumbled.

"I know who you are," he said. "You're the missing girl—Skylar Abasi."

"Missing?"

"There was a woman here looking for her daughter," said the tour guide.

"I am Kadsa…Skylar. That's me." Her heart raced. Her mother truly came. She swallowed, face twisting when she remembered her grandfather's fate, if any of it was real. Hunger chewed up her stomach and it grumbled.

"I need to eat. Are you guys returning any time soon?"

The tourists took quick looks round.

"We were on our way back," said one of the men. "Good." Her stomach growled, again. She dizzied.

Her legs gave way, and a shriek of panic broke out around her.

She woke to the tourists grumbling and the car bumping along. She deciphered, quickly enough, that the female tourist was cuddling her, and they were in a vehicle.

"Wait 'til everyone hears this."

"But how did she survive?" asked a man. "It doesn't make any sense that she was down there the whole time."

She fumbled in the woman's arms. "She's awake."

Kadsa prodded herself up, while the woman babied her. "We're almost there, sweetheart."

The tourists gave her water, after which, about half an hour later, they drove her to a local clinic.

Kadsa was a little confused when she spotted the calendar. Rarely did she or her grandpa focus on the time of day, week, year, but she had always been aware of the calendar. According to this one, she had been gone for nearly half a year. From July, when she'd gone in search of Grandpa, to now January.

The clinic fed and then checked her a second time. Left alone, Kadsa's brain mulled over all the things the doctor had said. The memory of Marut flooded her mind. She held her breath, confused and self-conscious about the very vivid experience. For a second, she considered if it was all real, but the thought made her sulk in shame. It was real. She had been missing for months. Where had she been if she hadn't gone there?

"Is your father or mother with you?" asked the doctor.

What would she tell everyone about Grandpa Edoje? She couldn't tell them the truth about what happened to him. She'd give anything to see Grandpa Edoje. Who else could she speak to about all this? All this time, her grandfather knew of a secret world and told no one.

"I have to call my mother," she said, the statement rushed out with urgency. "I have to tell her I am okay."

The doctor's hard face mellowed out with sadness. "You can use my phone."

———

Nearly a week later, Kadsa was on a plane to Toronto.

After she'd gone in search of Grandpa, Lorraine had contacted the consulate. No one had been able to find her. The consulate had convinced Lorraine she was a fraud, but her mother wouldn't have it and came down to look for her. She had put out notices, fresh notices that covered the consulate.

Lorraine had sounded livid at first, demanding to know if she was for real. Eventually, she came around, after Kadsa repeatedly apologized. The test she'd done prior to Marut was a match, of course, and the consulate people explained this, along with the story of her mother hopping on a plane to come to Chad herself.

Kadsa apologized for disappointing her. Lorraine wanted to know if Grandpa Edoje had something to do with her sudden disappearance, again. Though she defended him, her mother didn't seem convinced.

When Kadsa informed her that Grandpa Edoje had died, she responded, "Good."

Kadsa did not argue.

The airlines offered her a free flight package as a publicity stunt. They gave her a ton of free goodies, including a free two-way ticket to use when she pleased. She'd never been on a plane before, but after seeing the world from Bennu's back, which was infinitely cooler, she wasn't so impressed with this.

Lorraine recognized Kadsa before Kadsa spotted her, screeching out "Skylar!" from half-way across the tarmac. The woman dashed forward, her salt and pepper dreadlocks bouncing on her shoulders.

Kadsa burst into tears.

Lorraine scooped her into her arms, practically lifting her off her feet.

"Mom?" she asked, though the word was alien coming from her mouth. She had been practicing what to call her.

One day, after meeting the family she'd longed for her whole life, Kadsa couldn't sleep, even though she laid on the single bed Lorraine said had always been hers. She didn't remember ever sleeping here. She struggled to remember if she'd ever slept in a real bed. Lorraine had decorated the room with mostly photos and stuffed animals. Everything looked alien to her.

Kadsa tossed and turned, closing her eyes for a short moment before a thought popped into her head and pushed her eyes open. She faced the glass container on the night table.

Khansu!

The rose floated as if it was in zero gravity. Sparkly dust glittered off its crimson-red petals. Beside it, a soft white light glowed from the crystal.

She had to return to Marut. But not now.

Someday, though.

Time needed to pass. Things needed to cool down. She'd get to know her mom, and then she'd go back. Home was where the heart was, and her heart was in Marut.

The light in the crystal intensified, illuminating the room.

Kadsa's slept only with the thought of Marut in her heart.

ABOUT THE AUTHOR

K. M. McKenzie writes stories about other worlds, reluctant women, and the noumena of existence. She has been published in *CosmicHorror.net*, Toronto Fringe's Next Stage Audio series, *Polar Borealis, Scare Street, Shoreline of Infinity*, and *Strange Economics*. When not dreaming up worlds of imagination, she's struggling with her kitchen witch skills. She also self-publishes contemporary stories (pseudonym Kebra McKenzie). She is Caribbean-Canadian, and lives just outside the city of Toronto.